HANNIBAL'S CHILDREN

JOHN MADDOX ROBERTS

2003
50TH
ANNIVERSARY

ACE BOOKS, NEW YORK

HANNIBAL'S CHILDREN

An Ace Book / published by arrangement with
the author

PRINTING HISTORY
Ace hardcover edition / May 2002
Ace mass-market edition / April 2003

For information address: The Berkley Publishing Group,
a division of Penguin Putnam Inc.,
375 Hudson Street, New York, New York 10014.

ISBN: 0-441-01038-5

ACE®
Ace Books are published by The Berkley Publishing Group,
a division of Penguin Putnam Inc.,
375 Hudson Street, New York, New York 10014.
ACE and the "A" design
are trademarks belonging to Penguin Putnam Inc.

PRINTED IN THE UNITED STATES OF AMERICA

10 9 8 7 6 5 4 3 2 1

PROLOGUE

A T THE BEGINNING OF THE THIRD CENTURY B.C. the western Mediterranean was dominated by Carthage, the greatest city-state of North Africa. The Carthaginians were a maritime people, trading throughout the Mediterranean and into the Atlantic beyond the straits of Gibraltar. They sailed northward as far as Britain and may have sent expeditions around the southern tip of Africa. The might of their navy was legendary.

The Carthaginians were descendants of the Phoenicians, and their language was Semitic: related to Arabic, Assyrian, Hebrew and others of that once-numerous language group. Their religion was polytheistic, its principal deities being Baal-Hammon (often miscalled Moloch) and the goddess Tanit. Many of their gods demanded human sacrifice and the Carthaginians were not sparing in their offerings. In extreme circumstances, they sacrificed even their own children, and the noblest families took great pride in delivering their children to the flames of Baal-Hammon.

Following the death of Alexander the Great, Carthage resisted the spread of Greek colonies and influence in the area it regarded as its own. It founded colonies in Spain to counter the power of the Greek colonies already there (Cartagena was originally Cartago Nova: New Carthage). When it established a military presence on the island of Sicily, Carthage came into conflict with a new, upstart power that had established hegemony over the Italian peninsula: Rome.

The Romans were an agrarian people with a republican form of government. In character, they were as unlike the Carthaginians as possible. Where the Carthaginians were seafarers and were content with controlling coastal cities, the Romans were reluctant sailors and had a passion for land above all things. They seized as much of it as they could and never let it go. The Carthaginians preferred to use mercenary troops in their land wars, using citizens to man the navy and to protect Carthage, which was always in danger from an uprising by its subject North African possessions.

For Romans, military service was every citizen's duty, and the surest way to advancement was through distinguished service in the legions. The Romans approached war in a manner like no other people. They thought little of individual heroics, preferring subordination of even the noblest men to the machinelike teamwork of the legion. They saw war as a task, not a glorious adventure, and they went about it in a methodical manner. They understood that wars were won as often by the pickaxe and spade as by the sword.

When they were beaten, they held an inquiry to determine what had been done wrong and then corrected the error. Even when they were victorious, they assessed what had worked and what had not, and made corrections. Romans seldom made the same mistake twice. Perhaps most amazingly, unlike any other people of the time, the Romans were not demoralized by defeat. If their army was destroyed, they raised another army, and then another if necessary.

They did not blame defeat on the anger of the gods or the superiority of the enemy. Men made mistakes, and mistakes could be corrected. They knew that the ultimate weapon was the discipline and cohesion of the legion.

The Romans called the Carthaginians *Puni*. It was their pronunciation of the Greek word *Poeni*: Phoenician. Hence the wars that followed were called the Punic Wars. There were three Punic Wars. The second of them was among the most decisive in human history.

The first war with Carthage ended with Roman victory. Rome beat Carthage on land and in the usual methodical fashion learned to sail and actually beat them at sea. Rome gained the island of Sicily with its rich cities and fertile land. Then for several years Carthage was occupied by a revolt of its mercenaries and subject cities, a war so savage that it appalled even the Romans, Greeks and other Mediterranean nations, accustomed though they were to almost continuous warfare. The Romans were distracted by an incursion of Gauls in northern Italy.

Eventually warfare resumed between Rome and Carthage, and the second war was very different from the first. This time, the commander of the main Carthaginian army was Hannibal, and the Romans were to learn at bitter cost that he was one of history's handful of truly great generals. In one battle after another he smashed the Roman legions, and he did it with armies that were inferior both in numbers and quality. He won by sheer generalship and it was something the Romans could not match.

At Trebia, Lake Trasimene and, most devastatingly of all, at Cannae, Hannibal crushed his enemies. Cannae stands to this day as possibly the most perfectly planned and executed battle in all of history. Devastated, Rome scraped together another army.

History tells us that Rome appointed Quintus Fabius as Dictator, and Fabius refused to fight Hannibal in open battle, that instead he harassed his rear and his lines of communication, gradually wearing him down, never giving him a chance to employ his fabled generalship. This tactic earned him the surname Cunctator: the Delayer. Hannibal looked for allies and sought an alliance with the young King Philip V of Macedon, who had inherited the formidably professional army of that nation. Philip promised aid but never showed up in Italy.

In time, Publius Cornelius Scipio, a soldier of qualities comparable with Hannibal's, took the war to Spain and cut Hannibal off from his land route to Carthage. Then Scipio went to Africa and Hannibal was forced to leave Italy in order to protect the homeland. At Zama, Hannibal met with defeat for the first time and Scipio earned the surname Africanus. Rome was saved.

There was a third war, and this time Carthage had no Hannibal. The Romans conquered Carthage and destroyed it with a thoroughness that passed into proverb.

This is the history we know. The Second Punic War was one of the rare occasions in history where, had it turned out differently, everything afterward would have been utterly different and the Western world would have been dominated by a people as different from us as the Aztecs.

In *Hannibal's Children*, things turned out differently.

CHAPTER ONE

ROME, 215 B.C.

BEHIND THEM WERE THE SEVEN HILLS AND THE SAcred city of Quirinus. Before them lay the plain, and upon the plain the army of Carthage stood in unprecedented power. For the first time their general had numerical superiority. He had not needed greater numbers at Lake Trasimene, nor at Cannae. On those fields he had ambushed, surrounded and crushed two Roman armies larger than his own, feats of generalship worthy of a war god.

Upon a wooden tower erected behind the huge host stood two men clad in glittering iron and bronze. One of them, Philip of Macedon, had provided the numbers. His phalanx held the center of the line, the sixteen-foot pikes standing like a dense forest in the morning sun. The Romans had no fear of Philip or his pikes, however great their numbers.

The rest of the army was divided in two parts and held the flanks: check-trousered Gauls with lime-washed hair and blue patterns painted on their bodies, gripping long, slashing swords; black Nubians covered with ocher and chalk, holding short spears and long shields of zebra hide; squat Spaniards with their hair in plaits who fought with little round bucklers and down-curving falcatas that could take a man's leg off with a single swipe. There were Cretan archers and slingers from the Balearacs and light horsemen from Galatia. Libyans in white tunics rode bareback with quivers of javelins slung across their shoulders. There were Ligurians and Spartan mercenaries and men from half the nations of the world standing under arms, ready to take the seven hills for Carthage.

The Romans did not fear this polyglot mass of humanity, however colorful and fierce. They reserved their fear solely for the other man on the tower: the Carthaginian Shofet, son of Hamilcar Barca, the general so brilliant he could smash armies larger than his own, repeatedly, the leader so gifted that mobs of savages who at any other times would have been happy to cut one another's throats, under his command acted in concert with superb discipline, with never a hint of misbehavior or mutiny, however terrible the hardships of campaigning or the casualties of battle.

The Romans feared Hannibal.

"Where are the elephants?" a velite asked. He was young, no more than sixteen. The fearsome losses of the war had forced the Senate to accept younger and younger men into the legions. The velite wore a snarling wolf's mask cover on his skullcap helmet. A small, round shield was his only other defense. A short sword was slung over his shoulder and he held a pair of javelins. He and his fellow velites were skirmishers. In battle, they rushed forward and cast their javelins, then fell back through the gaps in their own lines. Sometimes the velites weren't swift enough and they were caught between the shields of the opposing armies. Then they were slaughtered. The boy knew this.

"We killed them all," said the hastatus behind him. He was a grizzled old veteran, called back to the standards to make up the losses at Cannae. He was a front-ranker in the heavy infantry, wealthy enough to afford a fine coat of Gallic mail. His bronze helmet sported scarlet side-feathers, its forepeak embossed with a rudimentary face. Between its cheek plates his own face was weathered and seamed with scars. He had a bronze greave on his left leg and his oval, four-foot shield was as thick as a man's palm, built of layered wood and faced with hide, rimmed and bossed with bronze. The heavy javelin in his right hand was three times the weight of the boy's weapons. He could cast it through a shield and the man behind it. The short sword at his waist was the most efficient battle implement ever devised.

The boy knew that, one day, he would take his place in the ranks of the heavy infantry, if he lived. The man behind him and the thousands of others like him were the legions of Rome, the toughest, most expert, hardest-fighting military force the world had ever seen. They were seldom defeated, never outfought, but occasionally outgeneraled. The man across the field from them could do it every time.

"Here they come," somebody said. At first the boy thought the enemy was advancing, but he saw no movement in the formidable ranks. Then he saw the delegation riding from the war headquarters outside the Capena gate of Rome. In their lead was the Dictator Fabius, elected by the Senate to supreme command in the national emergency. Behind him were the military tribunes. The boy recognized Publius Cornelius Scipio, no more than three years older than himself, incredibly young for his high rank, but a survivor of Cannae and the man credited with holding the remnant of the army together when others counseled abject surrender.

Next to Scipio rode Appius Claudius, another Cannae veteran. Behind them was Lucius Caecilius Metellus, a voice for caution whom some suspected of cowardice. White sashes girded their muscle-embossed cuirasses and the patricians among them wore red boots with ivory crescents fastened at the ankles. Their faces were unanimously grim.

"Where are they going?" the boy asked.

"Going to have a few words with old Hannibal, I expect," said the hastatus. "Much good it'll do them."

The little band of officers rode toward the enemy lines and they scanned the forces arrayed before them with the reflexive calculation of military men; looking for weaknesses, assessing the strength of the enemy. Were they well fed? Did they show fear? Were their weapons ill kept? Did they look downcast or discontent? The officers saw nothing to encourage them. It was as fine an army as they had seen, despite its bizarre aspect. The men were fit, sleek and competent. Above all, they displayed an almost sublime confidence. Led by Hannibal, they could not lose.

"I will kill him," said young Scipio. "Just let me get close. I will draw my sword and cut him down before his men can save him. You know I can do it. We will all die, but Rome will be saved. This rabble won't fight without Hannibal leading them."

"Who do you think you are, Scipio?" said Metellus. "Mucius Scaevola? Do you think this is the time of legend, when enemy kings were careless? We'll be relieved of our arms before we're in javelin-throwing distance."

"I can kill him bare-handed," Scipio insisted.

"Let's have none of that," said the Dictator. "We ride to a parley and that is what we shall do—talk." To meet this emergency the Senate had bestowed absolute imperium on Fabius. He had the power to command armies, negotiate peace in the name of Rome, execute citizens without trial; in fact, all the power once enjoyed by kings. But only for six months. At the end of that time he had to lay down his office, exchange the purple toga for white, dismiss his lictors and retire to private life. He could never be called to account for his actions as Dictator. He could make all his decisions as seemed best to him, with no fear of reprisal afterward. If he felt the terrible weight of history upon his shoulders, he did not show it, riding erect as any young cavalry trooper, sublimely confident, arrogant as only a Roman patrician could be.

After the defeat at Cannae, Fabius had urged that the Romans not engage Hannibal in open battle. Instead, he devised delaying tactics: raids against supply lines, attacks on small garrisons, feints and countermarches, all to wear down the formidable Carthaginian's forces, drain his resources and destroy his morale through frustration. Unable to bring the Romans onto the field for a decisive battle and unable through lack of numbers to assault Rome directly, Hannibal had stewed in impotence, as Fabius had planned. Then, once more, he had done the unexpected.

Hannibal's next victory was one of diplomacy. He had forged an alliance with Philip of Macedon, the notoriously unreliable adventurer-king who had more than once promised the Carthaginian support, then found excuses to keep his massive army at home. This time, Hannibal's persuasion had been effective. The Macedonian king had sent an immense phalanx of superbly-drilled pikemen, descendants of the men Alexander had led from Greece to India, conquering everything in their path. They were tough men of the mountains and plains, given a miniature spear as soon as they were old enough to stand, to be replaced by larger weapons as they grew until, at military age, they handled the sixteen-foot sarissa as easily as a man wields a fishing pole.

"I was expecting to see the Sacred Band, but it looks like they stayed home," said Appius Claudius. It was a joke among the Romans that the Sacred Band, an elite force of highborn young Carthaginians, never showed up for battle. In fact, the only Carthaginians in the army opposite them

were Hannibal and a handful of his highest officers. The rest
of the force was entirely mercenary. The Carthaginians were
seafarers and sent troops abroad only as sailors, keeping their
large land force close to home to guard against uprisings of
their oppressed subjects. It was a system of warfare incomprehensible to the Romans, for whom hand-to-hand combat
against a foreign foe was the very basis of citizenship.

As they neared the enemy line, a man rode out to meet
them. His helmet and armor were Macedonian, but Scipio
knew him to be a Spartan mercenary captain named Aga-
medes.

"There's that arrogant bastard again," said Claudius. "The
same one who demanded our surrender after Trasimene. He's
looking cheerful this morning."

"He has a right to be smug," Fabius said quietly. "They
have us in a nutcracker and they know it."

The Spartan rode up to them. "Greetings, Romans. The
general is prepared to accept your surrender now."

"Your general will sacrifice to our ancestors in the temple
of Jupiter before he gets a Roman surrender," Fabius said.
"We've come to talk with him, not with you, hireling."

The Spartan's grin turned to a scowl. "You are high-
handed for a pack of beaten farmers. You should never have
thought that Italian peasants could ever amount to anything. The gods don't like that sort of presumption." They
ignored him. "Very well, you can negotiate terms. You'll
find the general is a generous man. First, though, you must
surrender your arms."

When they reached the base of the tower, a pair of Cretans
wearing twisted headbands relieved them of their swords
and daggers. With harness creaking they ascended the broad
wooden stair that served instead of a ladder, coming at last
to the wide platform some forty feet above the plain.

"I've been admiring your army, Dictator," said the man
who leaned on the railing at the front of the platform. He

spoke in Greek, the one language common to all of the men present. "It is impressive, but not as fine as the Roman armies I defeated at Trebia and Lake Trasimene and Cannae. I do not see so many well-salted soldiers this time. I do see a great many boys."

"It is good for men to learn war at a young age," Fabius answered.

"But their first lesson should not be the last. That is a great waste." The Shofet was a handsome man of medium height, clean-shaven in the Hellenistic fashion that was followed even in Carthage of late. A broad patch covered his left eye. He suffered from a chronic ophthalmic complaint and rarely had any use of that eye.

"That army before us," said a very young man who carried himself regally, "is no more than a morning's work for my men. Is there any reason why we should be haggling with these people?" The king of Macedonia was only twenty-four years old, but his kinsman Alexander had set the fashion for youthful conquerors.

"You are rash, my friend," Hannibal said. "The Romans may have found wisdom, and wisdom should always be honored. What says the Senate? Will you seek terms?"

"The Dictator overrules the Senate," said Scipio. "He speaks for Rome in his own right."

"Ah, I forgot," Hannibal said ruefully. "Those stories I hear about his Master of Horse—what is his name? Minucius? Yes, Minucius. I hear that Minucius is a firebrand and would have battle immediately."

"The Master of Horse carries out the Dictator's orders," Scipio said. "That is the law." It was the law, but in truth Minucius defied the Dictator and acted as if he were an equal colleague. He had been elected to his office by popular acclaim instead of appointed by the Dictator himself. It was a violation of custom that had resulted in serious consequences.

"Does it matter?" said a man who closely resembled Hannibal, but stouter and with two good eyes. This was Hasdrubal, the Shofet's brother and second in command. Fierce old Hamilcar Barca, their father, had made both his sons swear upon the altar of Tanit to destroy Rome, the upstart city-state that had challenged and humiliated him and Carthage.

"There was a time for you to treat with me," Hannibal said. "After any of the battles, I would have been pleased to offer you the most generous terms: the destruction of your fleet, your withdrawal from Sicily and Messana, things that would have cost you little and assured your survival and the friendship of Carthage. But"—he shook his head as if in deep sorrow—"but you Romans are stubborn. You had to keep fighting when such defiance was foolish. You harassed me and would not come to battle. You suborned my allies, the cities of Italy that threw open their gates for me and in return suffered no harm whatsoever from my army. Now I am not so favorably inclined. Now I am of a mind to be harsh."

"We will not surrender," Fabius said. "Rome will not pass beneath your yoke."

"That settles it then," said young Philip. "Let's fight!"

"Don't be hasty," Hannibal said.

"What do you mean?" Philip demanded. "Either they surrender or they fight us. What other options have they?"

"There is a third course," Hannibal told him. "A very ancient one."

"What might that be?" Fabius asked.

"National exile," said Hannibal.

For a moment the Romans lost their fabled gravitas, shuffling and looking at one another in wonderment. This was totally unexpected.

"Explain," Fabius said.

"When the Great Kings of Persia were displeased with a

subject state, they could banish the whole nation to some-place in the vast interior of the Empire, where they could dwell in obscurity and cause no more distress. This is what I offer you."

"Leave Rome!" Scipio said, aghast. "Never!"

"I believe I was talking to your Dictator," Hannibal chided.

"This is unprecedented," Fabius said.

"Perhaps it is here," said Hannibal. "But I make you this offer and for the last time. Take what you can transport, pack up your household gods, and leave Italy. Go to the northeast, beyond the alps into the place you call Noricum. Do not trouble the Gauls, they are my allies now. Find for yourselves a new home in the north and never bother Carthage again. These are my terms. If you do not accept them, I will annihilate those boys and old men in arms over there"——he jabbed a finger toward the last Roman army— "and then I will exterminate all that lives in that city. I will pull down its walls and demolish its buildings and heap earth over it, and on top of the grave of Rome I will erect an altar to Tanit."

For a while the Romans were silent. Then Fabius spoke. "I must consult with the Senate and the people."

"I thought you were Dictator," said Philip. "You speak for them all."

"Nonetheless, I will consult with them."

Hannibal glanced at the angle of the sun. "You have until sunset. If you have not answered by then, get a good night's sleep, for we commence battle in the morning and every one of you shall die. The very names of your houses will be forgotten. Now leave me."

Without further words the Romans left the platform. At its base they collected their arms and their horses and they rode back toward their lines.

"This is absurd!" Scipio cried. "Surely you don't propose to lay these terms before the Senate?"

Quintus Caecilius Metellus pointed toward the Roman army. "Look at them! In four or five years, the boys will make passable legionaries. The last credible Roman army died at Cannae. These are just fodder for Hannibal's veterans and hirelings. You don't eat seed corn, Scipio."

Scipio began to draw his sword but Fabius barked, "Enough! This is not for you to decide. Keep quiet and pretend that the Romans are still a unified people. If Hannibal finds out otherwise, we are truly lost."

There was no illusion of Roman unity in the Senate that afternoon. Because of the emergency they met in the war headquarters instead of the Curia.

"The time to fight is now, this very hour!" shouted Minucius. "The men are ready for battle! Make them wait another day and they will lose their edge. Their nerves will begin to assail them."

"That is exactly why we must not fight," Fabius asserted. "What stands between Hannibal and Rome is the seed of an army. Given time, we can raise and train new legions. But if we lose one more battle, there will be no more legions, no more Rome."

He gazed around him at the sadly depleted ranks of the Senate. They provided much of the officer class of the legions. Senators served not only as generals and tribunes, but as centurions and decurions, and there was no disgrace in a man serving as a common soldier in the years before his elevation to the Senate. More than half of the senators who had sat in this august assembly at the start of the present war were now dead on the field of battle. Almost all of the older men had lost sons and grandsons.

An elderly senator stood, trembling with wrath. "We cannot give up our lands, our estates! The land belongs to our ancestors and our descendants!"

The rest murmured agreement. Fabius had known that this was the argument that would weigh the heaviest. The Senate, both its patrician and plebeian members, were the landed gentry of Rome. For them, losing land was worse than losing sons. They could prattle on as much as they liked about the importance of breeding and high birth, but without land and the wealth it brought them, they were nothing. Old patrician families had fallen into poverty, and they plummeted into the general populace like a rock dropped down a well. It was a prospect they did not want to face.

"We will lose our lands anyway," Fabius said without pity. "The Carthaginians will take them. If we migrate, we will take new lands. We have done this before. Was Rome not founded by a wandering war-band led by Romulus and Remus?"

"The Carthaginians don't take land," said Quintus Caecilius Metellus. "They exact tribute."

"I won't hear it!" Fabius shouted. "Romans do not pay tribute! Would we become like the people of Utica? Better to be exterminated first!" He was roundly cheered, with the Scipio family cheering loudest.

Gaius Regulus, the oldest senator, stood and there was silence. "What do the gods say?"

Fabius turned to the man who sat beside him, dressed in a simple toga, wearing a cap surmounted by a wooden disk. From the center of the disk a spike jutted, a few threads of wool dangling from its tip. He was the Flamen Dialis, high priest of Jupiter. Beside him stood a single lictor. He was also very old and he heaved himself to his feet with difficulty.

"The flamenae, the pontifexes and the augurs are all in agreement: The omens have never been worse for Rome. The sacred birds will not eat, and they die in unprecedented numbers. The sacrificial animals struggle to escape from the altar, and then they are found to have diseased or malformed organs. Just yesterday, the augur Aulus Perperna saw an eagle alight upon the roof of the temple of Jupiter Best and Greatest. It had captured a serpent, and as it lowered its head to devour its prey, the serpent sank its fangs into the eagle's throat. The noble bird gave a great cry and tried to fly away, but a moment later it fell dead before the altar of Capitoline Jupiter."

At this even the most ardent for war turned pale. It was one thing to fight men. But to fight against the gods themselves?

"Noble Senators," Fabius said, "I think the will of the gods is plain. I am Dictator, but a decision this momentous must be put to the vote. I will have a division of the House: Those for immediate battle, to the right. Those for migration, to the left."

There was a shuffling of sandaled feet, together with a scraping of hobnails, for many senators were in military uniform. Slowly, the bulk of the assembly drifted to the left. At first, some hesitated to show what might be interpreted as timidity, but as more gathered to the left, others followed. At last, only a half-dozen senators stood to the right, all of them members of the Cornelia Scipiones. Then the youngest of the Scipios, the hero of Cannae, spoke.

"Kinsmen, let's not defy the gods as well as the noble Senate. We will found a new Rome in the north, as Aeneas founded a new Troy in Italy." With this, he walked to the left of the chamber and the rest of the Scipios followed.

The Flamen Dialis spoke once more. "There must be one condition, or we cannot go."

ONCE AGAIN, THE ROMANS STOOD BEFORE HANNIBAL. This time, the Carthaginian met them before his command tent, with all his commanding officers and ranking allies around him. Beside the tent was a strange object: a table surmounted by a standard that consisted of a golden pole. At its base was a triangle topped with a pair of stylized arms, hands upraised. Above that was a golden disk, and above the disk a silver crescent, points upward.

"What is your decision, Dictator?" Hannibal demanded. "The sun is almost at the horizon."

"We will go," said Fabius, his face frozen. From the crowd surrounding Hannibal came many exclamations, some of satisfaction, others of disappointment.

"You are wise," said the Shofet.

"But there is one condition," the Dictator said.

"No conditions!" barked Hasdrubal. "Go or die, it is all the same to us!"

"Peace, brother," Hannibal said. "I would hear this condition."

"I have spoken with the Senate, with the priests and with the citizens assembled in arms. We are in agreement. You must swear not to lay violent hands upon the tombs of our ancestors or upon the temples of our gods. You may loot the temples of their treasures, but leave the buildings and the images of the gods unmolested. Otherwise, we must stay and die, right here, right now." Now he, too, gazed at the setting sun. "No need to wait until morning. A night battle will suit us as well. We do not need sunlight to find our way to the underworld."

There was stunned silence. To offer battle when the outcome was certain annihilation was astounding but not unheard of. To offer a night battle was appalling. At last Hannibal spoke.

"You Romans are a truly remarkable people. I will be almost sorry to see you gone." He walked to the strange structure by his tent and placed a palm against the golden triangle. "Upon the altar of Tanit I, Hannibal, Shofet of Carthage and general of all her armies, swear that neither I, the men under my command, my allies nor any Carthaginian will ever molest the tombs and temples of the Romans. In this I include their sacred groves, shrines, holy wells and their mundus to the underworld. This I enjoin upon all my descendants as well." He took his hand from the altar and faced the Romans again.

"Now go. Take what you can carry, but go. You have the turning of one moon. Tonight the great moon of Tanit is full. At the next full moon I will slay without mercy any Roman I find in Italy."

THERE WAS A FINAL ASSEMBLY IN THE TEMPLE OF CAP-itoline Jupiter: Jupiter Best and Greatest. The Senate was present, as were all the priesthoods: the flamenae and the pontifexes; the college of augurs; the Salii, known as "holy leapers"; the keepers of the ancilia, the quinqidecemviri, who kept the Sybilline Books; The Rex Sacrorum, King of Sacrifices, who stood second only to the Flamen Dialis; the Arval Brothers; the Pontifex Maximus, who ruled over all aspects of religious practice. Behind him stood the Vestal Virgins. There were other priesthoods, some of them so ancient and obscure that most Romans were scarcely aware of their existence, each dressed in its own regalia.

When all the prayers and invocations had been spoken or chanted or wailed in their archaic languages, when all the protective and apotropaic spells had been laid, the Pontifex Maximus spoke.

"I now invoke an oath upon the whole Roman people." Four priests entered the temple. They wore long-sleeved tunics and upon their heads were bulbous turbans encircled by scarlet and yellow stripes. They carried a sacrificed pig, each holding a leg as its slashed throat dripped a line of blood upon the floor of the temple. They halted before the Pontifex Maximus and one of them handed him a rod of iron.

"If we do not return to take back our sacred seven hills, may the curse of Jupiter fall upon our descendants thus!" He raised the rod and brought it down upon the carcass with terrible force. The temple filled with the sound of snapping bones. "If Rome is not liberated from Carthage, may Jupiter smite us and our children thus!" Again the rod fell and bones crunched. "If we do not raise Rome anew, more splendid and beautiful than before, may Jupiter curse and destroy all our progeny thus!" The rod fell a third time and he cast it aside to clatter on the floor, the blood that now coated it splattering the nearest bystanders.

"This I swear by all the gods, by Jupiter and Mars, by Juno and Quirinus, by Janus, god of beginnings and endings, and by . . ." Here he raised his hands in a significant gesture and all present save he, the Flamen Dialis and the Virgo Maxima, chief of the Vestals, covered their ears. Then, in a quiet voice, he pronounced the Secret Name of Rome, the most sacred and terrible oath of Roman religion, known only to the three of them. Then the carcass of the pig, bearing the dreadful oath with it, was taken from the temple to be thrown upon the sacrificial fire. The ancient terracotta statue of Jupiter, painted red except for his black beard and golden eyes, looked down upon them benignly. In later years, many of those present would claim that they saw him nod approval.

"THERE THEY GO," SAID PHILIP OF MACEDON. HE stood on the terrace of a fine villa that stood on a hill overlooking Rome's Colline Gate. A colorful procession had begun to stream through the gate, led by men who bore poles from which hung the sacred ancilia, the shields of Mars. Only one of them was the true ancile, which had fallen from the heavens centuries before. The others had been made to foil thieves. Now no one knew which was the true ancile, so all were accorded equal honor.

"It is about time," said Hannibal. The Romans had used up half their allotted month making preparations for the migration. Already, many of the outlying communities were trekking north, a vanguard of soldiers at their head. Other communities, under Roman domination in recent years, were already discarding Latin and reverting to their native Oscan, Faliscian, Marsian or other dialects, preferring Carthaginian domination to the perils of a march into the cold and unknown north.

Behind the shield-bearers came wagons bearing the holy objects of Rome: the Sybilline books, the ancient statue called Palladium, the Tables of the Law and a hundred lesser items, all of them revered. The Vestals bore a litter with a bronze tripod upon which burned the sacred fire of Vesta.

Then came the general populace, their belongings borne upon wagons and pack animals and the backs of men and women. They carried provisions and farm implements and baskets and jars of seed corn with which to sow new fields in some unknown land.

"Look at them!" Philip said. "Farmers who thought they could challenge the world. Plenty of stubbornness, but no sense of glory." Hannibal just watched and said nothing.

By late afternoon the last of them were out of the city and all the gates stood open. The people were dwindling northward on the Via Nomentana, with a rearguard of soldiers behind them. The whole procedure had been as precise as any military operation.

At Hannibal's signal the Carthaginian drums thundered and his army, cheering like madmen, poured into the city. The sack of Rome had begun.

"There go the last of the Romans," Philip said, pouring himself a cup of wine from a golden pitcher. He poured another and handed it to the Shofet. "We'll not see them again and good riddance. The world is better off without them."

Hannibal looked at the king bleakly. "Pray to all your gods that we never see them again."

CHAPTER TWO

ROMA NORICUM, 100 B.C.

THE SMOKE FROM THE BURNING OPPIDIUM WAS choking, but the fires were burning low now, the bodies frozen in postures of death, the smell of death beginning to overwhelm the smoke. The legionaries went from one body to the next, making sure that each was dead. Where there was doubt, a quick stab of the gladius removed it.

Marcus Cornelius Scipio surveyed the scene and he could take no pleasure in it. The oppidium was a small place, the last holdout of an obscure band of Celts, no match for the Roman legions sent against them.

"That's the last of them then, Commander?" said his senior centurion.

"The last," he affirmed. "Now we'll have peace for a few years." He watched the auxilia herding the women and children into a compound. The slavers who followed the legions like a cloud of vultures were already gathering, assessing the new livestock and calculating their bids.

"Peace," said the centurion. "I don't like peace. The men get soft. They lose their edge. Peace is no good for the Republic. You're young, Commander. You don't remember. Back when I was a decurion, we had five years of peace. The legions turned into worthless slaves. Praise to Jupiter those Cimbri invaded. It saved us from turning into Greeks." For Romans, the Greek traders who brought goods from the luxurious south were the epitome of all that was decadent and weak.

Marcus Scipio had to smile. "I don't think we need to fear that much peace. A year or two at most."

The centurion grunted. "Well, next year I'm Prefect of the Camp, then I retire. But I hate to think my boys are going to turn into Greeks." He spat onto a smoldering timber raising a spurt of steam.

"The Alemanni up north are planning a march south," Marcus said. "They'll be here before long, never fear." He was a very young man, no more than twenty-five, but most army commanders were young. He was dressed much like a common soldier in a mail tunic of iron links belted with a sword and dagger. His tight-fitting leather breeches reached just below the knees and on his feet he wore hobnailed caligae. Most of his gear was of Gallic make, modified to suit Roman tastes. Only the twin white plumes on his iron helmet denoted his rank.

"You can finish up here, Aufidius," he said to the centurion. Aufidius was primus pilus, "first spear." He was centurion of the first century, first cohort and the senior centurion of the legion. His greaves and side-to-side crest signified his rank.

"Go on back to the camp, Tribune. You've earned some rest."

Marcus took his cloak from his cantle and threw it across his shoulders. Like most legionary cloaks it was deep green with interlacing stripes of black woven through it. It was another Celtic item, ideal for scouting and hunting. He mounted and turned his horse's head toward the camp. It was two hours' ride southward along the Rhenus, and as he rode, he found himself already growing depressed with the prospect of peace, but not for the same reasons that troubled the centurion. In Roma Noricum, peace meant political strife. As long as there were barbarians to fight, incursions to repel, a sort of unity prevailed in the capital, although there could be plenty of rancor even in wartime. Without external hostilities to distract them, the senatorial families and their allies were at one another's throats, clawing for power and influence, trying to maneuver their patriarchs and sons into the best command positions, the important magistracies, the most prestigious priesthoods.

Always, there was the struggle between the old families and the new families. The old families were those that had made the long trek of the Exile, the families from Rome of the Seven Hills. The new families were native, Romanized by their conquerors. They had full rights of citizenship and could hold all the highest offices and all but a few of the priesthoods, but they lacked the social prestige of the old families, and this rankled. He was still brooding on this when he rode in sight of the camp.

"Camp" was a poor word for what Roman legionaries built wherever they stopped for the night. The surveyors rode ahead of the legion and found a good site, laid out its walls and streets and marked the tent sites with colored flags. When the legion reached the site, the men set down their packs and got out their entrenching tools. Still in full armor, they dug the ditch and heaped the soil on the camp side, building an earthen wall, atop which they planted the palisade poles they had been carrying all day. They posted sentries and only then went inside to pitch their tents. This was done at the end of every day's march. If they moved on in the morning, they demolished the camp so that enemies couldn't use it.

If a camp was to be occupied for a longer period, it was improved continuously. The camp Marcus surveyed below him had been in use for six months. Its earthen rampart was twenty feet high and topped with a log wall featuring wooden walks and loops for the bowmen. The trench below it was another fifteen feet deep and bristled with wooden spikes. Its streets were graveled and the road connecting it with the great River Road was being paved with cut stone.

There was no enemy present strong enough to justify such fortification, but this was the Roman custom. Besides, should the Germans continue to menace the district, it would form the basis for a permanent stone fort. Then a new town would form around the fort and thus would the empire of Roma Noricum be extended, with new peasant families dwelling here to breed more sons for the legions.

He rode in through the porta praetoria, down the main street of the camp, accepting the salutes of the men on guard. He had taken only three cohorts north with him to mop up the Celtic remnant. Two cohorts remained to guard the camp, the others scattered along the river on guard duty. He rode past the camp shrine where the standards were kept, the manipular standards topped with a bronze hand, and the silver wolf that was the standard of the legion. The standard bearers stood before the shrine with wolf skins draped over their helmets and hanging down their backs, the paws knotted upon their breasts.

He crossed the via principalis, the road that crossed the via praetoria at right angles and separated the legionary camp from the section occupied by the extraordinarii: the long-service soldiers whose special skills and duties relieved them from regular duties, the small citizen cavalry force, the medical staff, the priests and the handlers of the sacrificial animals and the scores of other supernumerary personnel required by an army. It also contained the praetorium: the commander's tent. In this case, it was Marcus's quarters. Quintus Valgus, General of the North, had divided four of his six legions among his subordinate military tribunes, and Marcus had been assigned to the Fifth Legion, the Northern Wolves. He could not have asked for better.

Gallic mercenaries quartered among the extraordinarii guarded the big tent. In battle they ran barefoot alongside the Gallic cavalry. They were greatly favored as guards by Roman commanders, not only because of their great loyalty, but also for their exotic appearance. Their bodies and faces were painted and tattooed in bizarre patterns, their lime-washed hair standing in orange spikes, their necks encircled by twisted bronze torques, their legs encased in brightly checked trousers. Two were always on duty flanking the entrance, long, slashing swords naked in their hands.

Gauls never saluted, but the men called out a greeting as their commander passed between them, employing the traditionally extravagant Gallic praise: "Hail to thee, darling Tribune, crusher of rebels, who single-handed swipes the heads from enemies by the thousand!" Marcus managed to keep a straight face as he entered the tent. Rufus, his body servant, came from the rear to help him out of his armor.

"Looks like everything went well," said the old slave. His hair, once the red that had given him his name, had gone white in the service of the Scipios. He lifted the helmet from his master's head and placed it upon its stand, carefully so that the plumes would not be bent. He turned as Marcus bent over, and grasped the lower hem of his mail shirt. With some difficulty he tugged it over his master's head like an exceptionally heavy tunic, letting it turn inside out as it rolled over its wearer's arms. When it was off, he rolled it up and stowed it in its sealskin bag.

Marcus sighed and, as always when he disarmed, felt as if he could fly. A Roman soldier was not supposed to notice the weight of his arms, but Marcus knew this to be nonsense. Even an officer's forty-odd pounds of equipment were a burden. A common legionary's sixty or more could be a man-killing load on a hard campaign. Legionaries were simply instructed to ignore it. Hardship was beneath the notice of a Roman citizen. Supposed to be, anyway.

He was just getting comfortable, caligae off, feet propped on a table, cup of warmed, watered wine in his hand, when word was relayed from the porta praetoria: "Messenger coming! Yellow plumes!" The call was relayed down the via praetoria until it reached Marcus in his tent.

"What now?" he groaned. But he was intrigued. Yellow plumes in the messenger's helmet meant dispatches from the Senate. Maybe war had broken out somewhere else. Tired as he was, it was an exciting possibility. War was a citizen's work, and war was where advancement was to be found. He already had enough campaigning time to qualify to stand for the office of quaestor, but he'd need several more campaigns before he could hope to be elected aedile, much less praetor.

Some men of good family pursued their public careers piecemeal: They put in a few years with the legions, then stood for quaestor, did a little more campaigning and stood for aedile, then more military service and a praetorship. Others entered the legions young and did all their required military service, then just took the offices in succession, assuming they could get elected and had the wealth to support the office. Marcus preferred the latter, although he hadn't yet convinced his family that it was the right way for him to proceed.

"Marcus," his father was fond of growling, "too many men spend their lives soldiering, and when they finally stand for office, they find that they have no friends, no contacts and no experience in government. So they don't get elected and they end up spending their whole lives in the legions."

"There's nothing dishonorable in that," Marcus pointed out, many times.

"Honor is a fine thing," his father had said, "but dignitas is better." He referred to the collective honors bestowed upon a public man by the Senate and People of Rome. Among these honors were the elective offices bestowed by the popular assemblies: the Centuriate Assembly, consisting of the citizenry arrayed in their military units regardless of class, which elected consuls, praetors and censors; the Plebeian Assembly, consisting only of that class, which elected the Tribunes of the People and the plebeian aediles; and the Popular Assembly, consisting of all classes arranged by tribe, which elected the curule aediles, the quaestors and the military tribunes.

"Most professional military men," Marcus had said upon most occasions, "are simply unable to support the expenses of office, unless plunder should bring them wealth. Lately, we've been fighting very poor barbarians. But I should be able to bear the expense when the time comes."

"Don't be so sure of that," his father had warned. "Without the right friends, public office can be very expensive, indeed."

The argument had never been settled and Marcus did not expect that it would be any time soon. Just now he had more immediate concerns. For instance, what did this messenger portend? Already, he could hear the approaching hoofbeats. He got up, straightened his dingy, heavily used tunic and stepped out of the tent to wait beneath the broad awning. Curious officers were already making their way toward the praetorium. The messenger was pounding up the street, making legionaries and slaves jump from his path, intensely aware of the drama of his own arrival. A few feet from the awning he drew rein smartly, causing his handsome

Gallic mount to rear on its hind legs. The instant it settled, he threw himself from the horse and presented his documents.

"Dispatches from the Senate for Tribune Marcus Cornelius Scipio!" he shouted, as if Marcus were deaf.

"Smartly done, messenger," Marcus commended. The self-importance of the messengers always annoyed him, but he was willing to allow them their little self-dramatizations, for their duty was one of the most extreme hazard and hardship. They were expected to behave as if mere terrain, weather and enemy action did not exist.

Marcus took the oilskin-wrapped parcel and stripped off its cover. Within was a document sandwiched between two wooden leaves. On the outside of the leaves were the gilded letters *SPQR*, the abbreviation for "senatus populusque romanus," the Senate and People of Rome. It was the formula that embodied the Roman state and was placed on official documents, monuments and public property.

He untied the ribbon that bound the case and opened the leaves to reveal a single piece of parchment. Egyptian papyrus was hard to come by, and this bit of parchment had been scraped and reused so many times that it was almost transparent. His eyebrows rose as he read.

"What is it?" asked Publius Rutilius, another tribune but lower ranking. Other tribunes and senior centurions came close to hear. Little formality was observed in the north while campaigning in the field, even though discipline was otherwise the strictest imaginable.

"It seems I am to return to the capital," Marcus said. "I am required to report to the noble Senate for some sort of special assignment."

"What sort of special assignment?" asked Decimus Norbanus, another tribune and a member of the most prominent of the new families. He was blond as a German and taller than the tallest members of the old families.

"It doesn't say." Marcus showed them the parchment with its laconic message. "The Senate doesn't waste much ink on lowly tribunes."

"Who's to take command?" Rutilius asked.

"Norbanus," Marcus said. "He's senior. Until the Senate sends someone out to take command, he's in charge." He saw the satisfaction oozing over Norbanus's face. He didn't like the man, but he was competent to run things for a while, since the fighting was all over. "Decimus, get your things together and move into the praetorium. I'll be out within the hour."

"So soon?" Rutilius protested. "We should throw you a party, at least. Tomorrow will be soon enough."

"The Senate sent a special messenger," Marcus pointed out. "They want me there fast." He didn't point out that, should he tarry, Norbanus would get word back to Roma about his dilatory behavior. The Norbani were the most prominent of the new families in the Senate and controlled a huge plebeian voting bloc. They were implacable rivals to the old, aristocratic families exemplified by the Scipios.

While he packed, he pondered on the message. Special assignment could mean almost anything: an embassy, a commission of inspection, a committee to try out some new weapon or military tactic or camp arrangement, even to work on the ancient, onerous problem of designing an acceptable tent, one that was strong enough to keep out the weather, and light enough to transport easily. So far, only leather seemed to work, but it was hellishly heavy and strained a legion's transport facilities.

He put it from his mind. He'd learn what it was about when he got to the capital.

"I'll just take my traveling kit," he told Rufus. "You and the other slaves come along after in the wagon." Rufus had two boys to help him keep up the praetorium.

"Why not just sell those two good-for-nothings?" Rufus said.

"You can't drive the wagon all that way by yourself. Besides, nobody here would buy them except Norbanus or one of the itinerant slavers, and they'd pay all but nothing."

Rufus shrugged. "All right. But they'll be even less use in the capital than they are here."

It was late afternoon when Marcus tightened the last strap on his packhorse's harness. The animal carried his armor and shield, for the road back was safe enough, the enemy subdued and even the bandits all but exterminated. Roman justice did not tolerate disorder once imperium was established. Roman citizens and even newly absorbed barbarians deserved to pursue their livelihoods in peace, without fear. The cross stood as a constant reminder to any of a mind to take up their old predatory ways.

Even so, when he mounted, Marcus wore his sword and dagger belted to his side. Peacetime or no peacetime, he was not going to be a fool.

His friends and fellow officers gathered to bid him goodbye and they all vowed to get together sometime, perhaps at Saturnalia or the next Cerialis races, if duties should permit. Even Norbanus gave him a hearty handshake and he congratulated Norbanus on his new command. As he rode out, the legionaries lined up along the via praetoria and cheered him, raising their spears and shaking their shields. He was a popular commander. He had led them to victory and had gotten few of them killed.

As he left the camp, he fought down a sentimental lump in his throat. Most legionaries stayed with the same legion for their whole careers, but an officer's life was full of arrivals and departures. They held both civil and military offices, and were shuttled around as the Senate saw fit. Still, this had been his first command of a legion, and he would miss serving beneath the silver wolf standard.

A misty drizzle began before he was a mile from camp, and it continued until after dark. His woolen cloak was nearly waterproof, but it was decidedly heavy by the time he stopped at a relay station for the night. They were established every twenty miles along every Roman road, manned by state-owned slaves. They provided fresh horses for messengers, and quarters for traveling officials and stabling for their animals. It was cheaper than staying at an inn and usually a good deal cleaner. In any case, there were few inns so far north.

A stable hand took his horses, and he followed the man to the stables and made sure that his animals were properly rubbed down and fed and put in stalls with clean hay. He stowed his gear in a dry corner of the hayloft, and only then did he go to the main building to eat and bed down for the night. State slaves could usually be trusted to perform their tasks properly, the whip being a fine incentive, but a man was always well advised to oversee such things personally.

The station building was made like a standard legionary barracks: a long, one-story structure with a veranda running its length along one side. At one end was the kitchen and mess area. In the middle a door gave access to the officials' quarters. At the end nearest the stables were quarters for the messengers. The slave staff slept at the kitchen end. It would house as many as a hundred men, although there were seldom more than ten to twenty there on any given night.

Marcus entered the mess area. Just inside its entrance was a wall-niche holding a tiny shrine to Mercury, the patron deity of this and all other messengers' facilities. He took a pinch of incense from the bowl and dropped it into the smoldering brazier before the statue of the god. A fragrant smoke arose as he passed into the main room. There was no bustle to serve him since this wasn't an inn. It was a government facility and he was just a tribune. A tribune could be anything from a staff errand boy to a legion commander,

depending upon how his commander wanted to use him.
Marcus had commanded a legion, but just now he was on
detached duty and a commander without his soldiers was
no commander at all.

He took a seat at one of the long tables that ran the length
of the room. About ten others were already present, some in
messenger's garb, some in military uniform, a few in civilian
clothes. A pitcher was shoved toward him and he poured a
cup of rough soldier's wine. Baskets and platters on the table
held bread, cheese, dried fruit and olives preserved in brine.
Even here, so far from the body of water they had once called
"our sea," the Romans had to have olives. They imported
few commodities from the south, but they imported great
quantities of olives and wine.

Recognizing his tribune's sash and generally weathered
and battered appearance, his new companions of the road
asked for news from the battle front and were suitably impressed when they learned that he had been recently in command of a legion, and that it was the one that had brought
hostilities to a close. In return he asked news of the capital,
but none of them had been so far south in months. All they
had to report were rumors, which were as much use as the
widely traded stories of the latest omens.

The men in civilian clothes turned out to be state freedmen, administrative specialists sent out to lay the ground-
work for organizing the new northern province, which was
to be known as Albria, so called from its principal river, the
Albris. It was the first time Marcus had heard the name, and
he had been fighting there for two years. It was the Roman
system: first conquest, then organization and limited citizenship. If there were no rebellions, the inhabitants would
have full citizenship in a generation or two. The grandsons
of the warriors he had been fighting these last two years, the
survivors among whom were sullenly beginning to accept

their lot, might win seats in the Senate. It had happened many times before.

Dinner and conversation done, he went back onto the veranda and walked wearily to the officers' quarters. It was like a room in any Roman barracks: a double line of bunks against two walls of the room, pegs above the beds for slinging armor and other gear, a stand against one wall containing pitchers and basins for washing up. The facility was too small to have a true bath, though it boasted a regulation latrine.

He picked a vacant bunk, kicked off his caligae and threw himself onto the bed. Without the worries of a whole legion on his mind, he found it amazingly easy to sleep.

The next morning he woke an hour before sunrise, as he always did, and for a moment was puzzled not to hear the bustle of a legionary camp coming to life. He rose to sit on the edge of the bunk and pulled on his caligae, drawing their laces tight to the ankles, then walked out of the room and back to the mess area. He breakfasted on a piece of tough bread, dipping it into a cup of warmed wine that was half vinegar.

He took his cloak from the rack by the fire where he had spread it the night before. It was almost dry. He wrapped himself in it against the morning chill. Fall was well advanced. When he went back outside, the eastern horizon was showing a streak of gray and a blustery wind whipped up flurries of dry leaves. He walked to the latrine, thence to the stables, where he roused a stableman with a few kicks and got his beasts saddled and packed. When he rode out, the eastern horizon was pink.

Nine days later, he sat his tired horse on a bluff above the Danubius River, overlooking the capital city of the empire, Roma Noricum.

CHAPTER THREE

THE CITY LAY ON THE NORTHERN BANK OF THE
Danubius, surrounded by hills once heavily forested but
now carpeted with cultivated fields, vineyards and orchards.
Smoke rose from the altars before the great temples of Jupiter, Juno, Venus and Mars, and the lesser temples of Mercury, Quirinus, Janus, Aesculapius and a score of others. Its
streets were narrow, lined with two- and three-story houses,
most of them still built in the traditional Mediterranean
fashion, despite its unsuitability for the climate.

Near the center of the city, on a piece of high ground
well above the river's highest flood stage, stood the Curia,
meetinghouse of the Senate. It was an austere structure, a
slab-sided rectangle relieved by a Doric façade, looking
much like the one in Rome of the Seven Hills except for its
roof, which was somewhat higher-pitched to shed the occasional heavy snow.

The Curia overlooked the Forum, a broad, generously pro-

portioned plaza that served as marketplace, meeting site for
the Plebeian Assembly and the Popular Assembly. It was
also the center of most festivals and the setting for the fu-
nerals of the most prominent men. Around its periphery
were situated altars to the personified virtues: Discipline,
Peace, Valor, Social Concord, Liberty, Piety and a score of
others. The whole city was dotted with the shrines of lesser
gods as well. These were revered by the common people,
who found the state gods too lofty and remote.

The state gods were Jupiter, Juno, Saturn, Mars, Vesta
and Venus. Other prominent gods had their own temples
and cults: Flora, Ceres, Bona Dea and many others. The
small gods had shrines, springs, wells and holy groves, both
in the city and in the countryside. There were gods for sick-
ness and for finding lost objects, gods who were patrons of
travelers, merchants, craftsmen and soldiers, gods for particular sites. There were gods for every household and for
specific parts of each household. It was difficult for a Roman
peasant to believe that a god as all-powerful as Jupiter took
much interest in his problem with corn rust. But there was
a special god, Robigo, who could be invoked to protect the
crops from that scourge. All he asked was the sacrifice of a
red dog at his annual festival, the Robigalia.

Marcus rode down the bluff and onto the river plain. Soon
he passed the great temple of Mars situated by ancient tradition in a field outside the city. He had no temples or
shrines within the walls. The broad field to its north was
the Campus Martius, drill field for the legions and meeting
place of the Centuriate Assembly. It was devoted solely to
military purposes and it was dotted with armories for training weapons and armor, sheds for drilling in inclement
weather, obstacle courses, even a full-sized replica of an oppidium wall and ditch for storming practice. Every able-
bodied Roman male between the ages of sixteen and fifty
was a soldier and was never allowed to forget the fact. Most

long-service legionaries were drawn from the peasant class, but the artisans and small merchants of the city had to be ready to take up arms when the cornicen sounded the call to the standards.

On most days he would have seen at least a few units on the field training. Boys began training in centuries at the age of fourteen and there were almost always youth classes drilling on the field. This time he saw none. He wondered whether an augur had seen an omen and declared the day a holiday.

He rode into town through the Via Borealis gate. He was tempted to go immediately home and see his family, but it was only mid-morning, so he thought it best to report to the Curia. The streets were thinly populated and he attracted little attention. Returning soldiers were among the more common sights in the streets of Roma Noricum.

Most of the shops he passed were closed and shuttered. The whitewashed walls were covered with scrawled graffiti and professionally lettered announcements. The former were mostly good wishes or execrations hurled at friends, enemies and political figures. One of the latter announced an upcoming gladiatorial contest. One Publius Castricius was putting on a show of twenty pairs in honor of his late father, the former praetor Sergius Castricius. Marcus didn't know father or son, but he hoped he would be in Rome for the fights. It had been a long time since he'd seen a good munera.

Abruptly, the narrow street widened into the broad expanse of the Forum and Marcus felt that he had truly come home. The wide plaza was on low ground, dominated by the surrounding temples, the Curia and Archive, all of them situated on high ground. The Forum was packed with citizens, shouting and arguing, which was what usually happened when a large number of citizens got together, unless they were hearing a speech or attending a sacrifice. They presented a colorful display, for while some retained the traditional white toga, many more favored the striped and checked cloth produced by the Gauls.

On the speaker's platform below the Curia, several orators were haranguing the crowd at once. Marcus suspected that they were Tribunes of the People. Those politicians were the most frequent rabble-rousers and troublemakers. He wondered what shift of policy had set them off this time, not that it mattered lately. It took only a short span of peace to bring all the old resentments out into the open and boiling.

He left his horses in the Curia's stable and made his way back into the Forum and up the stairs of the Senate house. A lone lictor stood in the doorway, shouldering his fasces—a bundle of rods tied around an axe, symbol of praetorian and consular authority. Marcus held up his senatorial dispatch and the man stepped aside for him to enter.

Within, the uproar was even louder than that in the Forum, if only because of the great crowding. The Curia had been one of the first buildings erected when the exiles founded Roma Noricum. It had been built to house a Senate of no more than three hundred members. In little more than a century, the citizen population had more than tripled, both because the old families were making up for their losses by raising many children, and because of the influx of new families. The highest ranking of the latter, families such as the Norbani, were the descendants of the noble local families that had supported the Romans in their conquest of the Danubius basin and its surrounding territories. In return for this invaluable service they had been awarded full citizenship and the greatest of them had been elevated to Senatorial distinction.

Marcus saw an old friend seated in the rear of the chamber, sneaking occasional sips from a silver flask. He stepped to the man's side. "Still the most energetic senator in Noricum, I see."

Aulus Flaccus looked up and beamed. "Marcus Scipio! Good to see you back. Here, sit by me."

Marcus sat. "It would never occur to you to stand and greet me."

"Why? It's as easily done sitting. Have a sip. You'll need it if you're going to endure the Senate for more than a few minutes." Aulus Flaccus was short, pudgy and saturnine, the very opposite of the Roman ideal. He was slow and lazy, or made a show of it. He and Marcus had been friends from childhood.

Marcus took a drink. It was imported Illyrian of the finest quality. Flaccus only drank the best. "What's the argument about?"

"The usual." Flaccus referred to the perennial dispute between the old families and the new. The new families wanted to expand the empire north, east and west, conquering the fierce but primitive tribesmen of those dark, forested lands. The old families were determined to march south and retake Italy, to reestablish the capital at Rome of the Seven Hills and be once again the preeminent power of the Mediterranean.

"It's been going on all my life, and my father's," Marcus said. "What makes this different?"

Flaccus took another swig, earning scowls from more traditionally minded senators. He gestured with the flask toward the side of the chamber where the priestly colleges sat dressed in their sacerdotal robes and insignia. "They've been taking the omens. For months, the gods have been sending signs that it is time to go south and take Italy back."

Marcus felt his scalp prickle. Retake Italy! It had been the dream of the Scipios for five generations. And it was the will of the gods. For more than a hundred years, they had scanned the skies, watched for lightning, listened for thunder, observed the way the birds fed and took note of every abnormal birth, both human and animal. Each time, the signs had been unfavorable, or at best ambiguous. There had been times when hopes had been raised by some prodigy, some extraordinary phenomenon, some wondrous dream sent to a consul or a flamen. Each time, the omens had proven to be false.

Something truly unusual must have happened to raise such an uproar. "Is it certain?"

Flaccus shrugged. "It depends on how much trust you put in omens. Since Quinctilis people have been seeing things. Every time the sacred geese feed, they start at the northern end of the line of grain and eat their way south. If it's lined east to west, they won't eat at all. Thunder always seems to come from the right. Wolves, boars, foxes, eagles, bears, horses, rams, serpents, lions and scorpions keep doing unusual things. Doubtless if we had hippogriffs, dragons, capricorns, sphinxes and chimeras they would be doing likewise." These creatures, natural and fanciful, were the totem beasts of the fourteen legions.

"Ten days ago," he went on, looking uncommonly sober, "on the ides of November, a flight of fourteen eagles flew low over the city. They circled the temple of Jupiter Best and Greatest all morning, then flew south until they were out of sight."

"Could this be true?" Marcus said. He had never heard of such a prodigy. It was as if Jupiter himself had spoken from his throne inside the temple.

"The whole city saw it," Flaccus said. "I saw it myself."

Marcus was glad that he was sitting, because he was not sure his knees would have supported him. "That's it, then," he said. "We're going."

"Not if they have anything to say about it." Flaccus gestured once more, this time toward a large crowd of senators grouped in the middle of the chamber. They wore tunics with the broad purple stripe of the senator, and those holding higher magistracies wore togas with a broad purple hem, but in every case the garment, tunic or toga, was of Gallic cloth, striped, checked and interwoven with lines of brilliant color. A few men, daringly, even sported long hair and flowing mustaches. This was an affectation Marcus had never seen before in the Curia. It portended an even deeper split than usual.

"What is wrong with them? Can't they recognize the will of the gods when they see it?"

"They aren't as fond of omens as the old families," Flaccus said. "Or rather, they fancy different omens than we do. And different gods." It was no surprise. The new families were careful to perform all the rites demanded by the state gods, but in their homes they kept shrines to the gods of their ancestors.

"Who's the ringleader?" Marcus wanted to know.

"Old Norbanus."

"What happened to Tubero?"

"Died last month. Norbanus took over the leadership of the opposition. If this keeps up, we'll all be chucking rings into sacred pools and be stuck here in the frozen north forever." He didn't look terribly distressed at the prospect. Flaccus had served a quaestorship and had done his military service sitting in a general's tent making himself an invaluable secretary. This had earned him a purple stripe and a seat in the Senate. He had done nothing else in the years since. He was a bottomless well of senatorial gossip.

"What is the sticking point this time?"

"Whether the decision should come from the Senate or the Popular Assemblies. You can guess the rest."

Indeed he could. The old families dominated the Senate; the new families controlled the largest voting bloc in the Assemblies. "But war has always been the prerogative of the Senate."

"War isn't the immediate question," Flaccus said. "A mission to Carthage is under discussion."

"Foreign relations and diplomacy are also senatorial privileges."

"What we are discussing here"—Flaccus made eloquent gestures indicative of uncertainty—"is neither war nor diplomacy. It is an ostensible mission of trade and exploration, but actually a spying expedition, to get the lay of the land, find out how powerful Carthage is these days, who their allies are, if any, that sort of thing."

Marcus nodded. "It makes sense. Marching against an unknown enemy would be folly."

"Exactly. But the nature of the mission is ambiguous enough that it is unclear who should have authority. If it's for war, the Senate is in control. If it's for trade, the equites demand authority."

"Of course it's for war!" Marcus said. "All espionage is military in nature."

Flaccus patted him on the shoulder. "Marcus, you're such a political infant. Even within the Senate, it's hard enough to get a majority for this war. The Assemblies are against it. But everyone likes the idea of a mission to find out what is happening down south these days. All we ever hear is what the Greek traders choose to tell us, and who can trust a Greek? The merchant community would like very much to open up trade routes to the south."

The merchants of Roma Noricum were almost all members of the equites, the class of wealthy plebeians. Their name meant "horsemen" and dated from the days when the highest property assessment meant assignment to the cavalry when the legions were called up. Soldiers served at their own expense. An equites had to provide his own horse and see to its maintenance. In recent generations, as cavalry duties were levied mainly on the Gallic allies, it had become purely a measure of wealth. Equites were frequently far wealthier than the senatorial class, and had therefore a larger clientage with consequent power in the Popular Assemblies.

In many ways, they were the most powerful class in Roma Noricum.

Marcus nodded, accepting it. "Surely a compromise can be reached."

"That's what is going on now," Flaccus affirmed. "The compromise is just taking longer to reach, with more attendant noise."

"Who looks likely to prevail?" Flaccus would know if anyone would.

"The old families, because of their prestige and because of their attachment to the old empire. They'll name the leader. The new families will get the choice of subordinate commander and make sure that he has almost equal authority."

"Of course." Marcus sighed. Divided power was the ancient bane of the Romans, and the new families had nothing to do with the institution. In the dim, semilegendary days of Tarquinius Superbus and Junius Brutus, the Romans had expelled their Etruscan kings and founded the Republic. Swearing never again to allow a single man to have supreme power, they had divided the highest offices among a number of office-holders: the Pontifex Maximus to rule on religious matters, the Princeps Senatus to set the order of debate in the Senate, a number of assemblies to pass laws and, most importantly, two men to hold imperium, the ancient power of kings to raise and lead armies and to pass judgment on capital cases. Each could overrule his colleague and while it had for centuries prevented the rise of a king among the Romans, it had also lost them many battles and bogged down much legislation in acrimony and stubborn obstructionism. Roman politicians who craved high office were chronically jealous of all others with the same ambition.

The founders of the Republic had foreseen this problem and had provided for it. In cases of extreme national danger, the Senate was empowered to raise a Dictator. At a vote of the Senate, the consuls would appoint a Dictator from among the senators. The Dictator had total imperium and could take any measures he thought necessary to meet the emergency. His power was limited to six months, after which he had to retire to private life. Unlike any other magistrate, a Dictator could never be called to account for his actions in office.

"Is there going to be a vote?" Marcus asked.

"Either that or we'll all starve to death here in the Curia. And I'm out of wine." Flaccus held the flask to his ear and shook it, as if to confirm the bad news.

A white-haired man caught Marcus's eye and beckoned him. Marcus got to his feet and crossed the chamber. The man who had summoned him was Publius Gabinius, the Princeps Senatus. He was a white-haired man dressed in a snowy toga. He sat on the lowest bench, hands folded on a walking stick, chin resting atop hands. In years past he had been the conqueror of the Helvetii and the Bituriges. He was the leader of the old families faction.

"Welcome back, Marcus. I presume you own a toga."

Marcus looked down at his travel-stained military attire. "The summons was urgent. I thought it best to report to the Senate immediately, rather than go home to bathe and dress."

"Most dutiful," Gabinius said dryly. "Actually, it may be for the best."

"The best for what?" Marcus wanted to know.

"You shall see." Gabinius rose and tapped his cane on the floor. In the hubbub few noticed, but the senior consul did. He was Titus Scaeva, a new family patriarch. In most years one consul was old family, the other new.

"The Senate recognizes Publius Gabinius," he said in a voice that could be heard above the general noise.

Gabinius stepped forward into the orchestralike speaking area of the Curia. The rest of the senators gradually ceased speaking and retired to their seats. The Princeps turned to face the house.

"Conscript fathers of Rome," he began, "we waste here a great deal of time and energy in fruitless debate. The fact is, we are going to send an expedition south. It is a thing we have desired for more than a hundred years, and now the gods themselves bid us be about the work. All that truly remains to be decided is the leadership, personnel and organization of the expedition. I hereby nominate as leader young Marcus Cornelius Scipio." He gestured grandly toward Marcus. "He is a hero of the northern army, just this hour returned to Roma Noricum from a decisive victory over the Galli." There was immediate applause, hearty from some quarters, tepid from others.

The House looked him over and Marcus realized what Gabinius had meant. In his hard-used, travel-stained military garb he made a stronger impression than the noblest senator in civilian garb. He looked every inch the serious, hard-fighting military man.

"Not only is he a victorious legionary commander," Gabinius went on, "but he is a descendant of one of the noblest of the old families. His great-grandfather was Publius Cornelius Scipio, who saved his father's life at Lake Trasimene and led the Roman remnant to safety after Cannae." Here the senators made gestures to ward off ill fortune, as all Romans did whenever those accursed defeats were mentioned. "It was his great-grandfather who conducted the great march of exile, who founded this city and set about the conquest of Gaul and Germania, a conquest his descendants have expanded in every generation since. Who can deny that young Marcus Scipio is the perfect choice for leadership of this expedition?"

"I can!" shouted a check-clad senator, leaping to his feet. It was Titus Norbanus, leader of the opposition.

"I do not recall recognizing you, Norbanus," the consul said. "Sit down and wait your turn."

"My son Titus should lead," Norbanus said before he resumed his seat.

"There is no reason," Gabinius said calmly, "why young Norbanus should not have the second position of leadership."

Marcus tried not to wince. A long history of enmity lay between him and Titus Norbanus. They were in the same age group, had trained together for years and had always been bitter rivals. He was the very last man Marcus would have wanted as subordinate commander. But that, of course, was precisely why Gabinius had made the suggestion.

"I agree," said the consul. "Let's have a vote on this proposal. Marcus Cornelius Scipio as leader of the expedition, Titus Lucerius Norbanus as his second in command. Yes or no?" There was shouting and vituperation, but the proposal was carried by a slender margin. "That's taken care of, then," said the consul. "Pontifex Maximus, see that the proper sacrifices are performed and the auguries taken to determine the gods' approval in this matter. In the meantime, I name the ten ranking senators after Gabinius as the committee to name the rest of the members of the expedition. Have the list before me by noon tomorrow. This session is adjourned." The six lictors that stood behind him thumped the butts of their fasces on the floor and the meeting broke up.

Marcus blinked. Scaeva certainly had a forceful way of getting business done. He could only approve. While a new family man, Scaeva had always been a voice for moderation and good sense. It didn't hurt that he had won the civic crown at the age of sixteen during the siege of Mogantum. He rose from his curule chair and came to take Marcus by the hand.

"Good to see you back in the capital, Marcus. We've been hearing wonderful things about your work up north. Command of the Northern Wolves at your age! I envy you."

"You are too kind, Consul. And while I am flattered that the Princeps Senatus has proposed me for the leadership of this momentous expedition, I am not so sure that I want the command."

"Eh?" said Gabinius. "What's this? Refuse the command? It'll make you the most famous man in the Empire!"

"Not with Norbanus as my subordinate. He'll be suborning my other officers from the moment we depart. I'll have to watch my back every day and night."

The consul frowned. "What of that? Doesn't every commander have that problem? Did you think one of your close friends would be named as your second? Like it or not, this is the way things get done."

"Exactly," Gabinius said. "You ought to be able to handle the likes of Titus Norbanus. He's just a forum politician, a rich man's son with a smooth tongue. He hasn't a single military victory to his name."

And that, Marcus knew, was exactly what would make Norbanus dangerous. His politician's skills would make him persuasive to other members of the expedition. His jealousy of Marcus's military reputation would do the rest.

"I'll confer with the family," he told them.

"Your family?" Gabinius snorted. "When did the Cornelia Scipiones ever pass up a chance for honor? They'll think you're insane for consulting with them."

"Nevertheless, I will speak with them. And should I accept, I shall want authority to veto any man the committee tries to foist on me."

Gabinius smiled thinly. "That is entirely too reasonable to be acceptable."

"I think something can be worked out," said the consul.

"And I don't doubt it will be complicated," said Gabinius. "But this must be done. Are we agreed on that?" The other two nodded.

"I think you should take Aulus Flaccus," Scaeva said in a conspiratorial tone.

"Flaccus?" Marcus responded. "Can he even ride a horse? He's the most inert man in the Senate!"

"All the more reason for him to get off his fat rear and do some work for us," said the consul. "And he is your friend. You can trust him. I'll persuade the committee to place his name in the pool."

"I admit," said Gabinius, "the thought of Flaccus doing anything active sends the mind reeling. But he's shrewd and something of a scholar. He has read a great deal of history. He is observant and will make a good spy. Besides, he can help you write your reports to the Senate. Your own prose style tends to the soporific, Marcus."

"I'm a soldier, not a philosopher."

"The head of this mission," Scaeva said, "had better be both a soldier and a philosopher."

THE DOMUS OF THE SCIPIO FAMILY SPRAWLED OVER A low hill to the east of the city. Early in the conquest, it had been decided that Roma Noricum would not be walled. The legions would be its protection. It was thought that a walled city would breed an unhealthy mentality. It would be an admission that an enemy could get that close. As a result, it had none of the crowding and clutter that had blighted Rome of the Seven Hills. The streets were broad and straight and there was plenty of space between houses and those who could afford it built spacious villas on the surrounding hills. These were always built within sight of the city. Men of important families had to be able to see the signal flags and fires that would summon them to the standards in time of war.

Marcus rode through the beautifully tended fields, the orchards and vineyards that surrounded the villa. After five generations, these vines were at last producing an acceptable vintage. The cattle were fat and sleek; the sheep grew fine, dense coats. From being a crowd of landless refugees, the Romans had risen to the eminence of a wealthy, powerful nation.

There were those, Marcus reflected, who took this as a sign that they had no need to return to the south, no need to retake Italy and the Mediterranean littoral, of which they had once been lords. But Marcus knew better. Here they were landlocked, with no access to the great markets of the world save through Greek middlemen. This was unacceptable.

And there was another, deeper cause for discontent: Every Roman knew that, somewhere to the south, the Carthaginians were laughing at them. Or, worse, had forgotten them. This was not to be tolerated. Roman honor forbade it.

His return had, apparently, been reported to the family. The household slaves and freedmen were lined up before the main house and a mob of his relatives stood at the top of the stairs, waving and yelling. A slave took his reins as he dismounted and climbed the steps, accepting the embraces of young brothers and sisters and cousins. Romans ran to large families. When he got loose of the younger crowd, Marcus embraced his mother, Caecilia. She was a daughter of Metellus Suebicus and had the spear-straight bearing bred into women of her class from infancy. She was in her early forties, her hair still glossy black, her face only faintly lined.

"The hero returns," she said, smiling, accepting his kiss on her cheek.

"Hero? We've lowered the standard for heroism if what I've been doing up north qualifies." He looked around. "Where is Father?"

"Still in the east," she told him. "Still commanding the Ninth and Eleventh. They're building a chain of forts against Dacian incursions. He calls it garrison duty and says he's bored to death. He says the Senate extended his command for another year because nobody else wants the job."

"That sounds like Father. Is the old man here?"

"Waiting for you by the pool. He's too proud to come out and greet a mere grandson, so go in and tell him everything that's happened before he gnaws his nails off. I'll see to your welcome-home dinner. We'll get properly reacquainted tonight."

Marcus passed inside the house and tossed a bit of incense into the brazier that burned on the altar of the family gods. From the cabinets that lined the atrium there gazed down the wax death masks of his ancestors going back to the day of Numa Pompilius. They had been carefully packed and carried all the long way from Rome of the Seven Hills. Noble families would lose their treasuries before they lost their ancestral masks.

Publius Cornelius Scipio, grandson of the hero of Cannae, sat impatiently by the catch basin in the center of the house. Although he shared the same name with his father and grandfather, he was known to everyone as Scipio Cyclops. There was so much repetition in Latin names that most men went by nicknames. The old man had lost an eye in his first campaign against the Suebi and any physical peculiarity was fair game to the crude Roman sense of humor.

"Welcome home, Grandson," the old man said, extending a hand.

Marcus clasped the hard old hand warmly. "Respects and greeting, Grandfather."

"I hear you have done the family and Rome great honor in the north. You are your father's son, and my grandson." Spoken simply, it was the equivalent of a lavish speech of praise for the fierce old man.

"I would never have returned without honor," Marcus said. "But I must admit that it wasn't much of a campaign."

"What of that?" said the old man. "I lost my eye in a

stupid little skirmish. Death is the same in a small fight as in a great battle. Honor is in looking death in the face and doing your duty. You have done yours and Rome is the better for it. Now, sit here by me and tell me all about it."

Marcus took a chair and a slave brought in a pitcher of watered wine and refreshments. In the austere Scipio household these were simple: bread and sliced fruits and cheeses. The greatest concession to luxury was a dish of imported olives.

"I'll give you the whole story, Grandfather, but first I would like to know why you weren't at the Senate meeting this morning. I was summoned by the Senate and I reported to the Curia first thing."

"Ah!" Cyclops made a disgusted, impatient gesture with his hand. "I stopped attending a month ago. There is no productive work going on there, just endless bickering between old families and new, as if we weren't all Romans."

Marcus told him what had transpired at the meeting and Cyclops struck the table with his fist, rattling the platters.

"By the Styx! At last something meaningful happened and I missed it! But this is wonderful, Grandson. There could not have been a better choice to lead the expedition. I'll be named to the committee, of course. I may have to recuse myself since my grandson is to lead it, but—"

"Actually, Grandfather, I am not sure that I should accept this commission."

"What!" The old man's frown was terrible. "I cannot believe that a Scipio would turn down the most important command offered by the State in a hundred years! Explain yourself, Grandson!"

Marcus, veteran commander of legionaries that he was, quailed beneath the old man's displeasure. "Grandfather, you know that I am a soldier, like all men of our family back to the beginning of the Republic. But I am no more than that. This command calls for a diplomat, a scholar, a

man of business. I am none of those. I can handle the role
of military analyst, better than any other man of Rome, if I
may say so. I'll render the Senate an analysis of every stone
in the walls of Carthage, if I should get that far. Let the
Senate assign me that position and I'll fulfill it with honor.
But not the leadership."

The old man softened. "I understand your reservations,
Grandson. But this is an opportunity you must not pass up.
You must rise to the office, Marcus! You may surprise yourself. Besides, in those areas where you lack confidence, find
subordinates who are expert, just as you did in the legions.
Am I not right? Didn't you indebt yourself to the commanders of other legions to get the finest primus pilus you
could? Did you not pass a few bribes to get the best supply
man to be found?"

Marcus smiled wryly, remembering. "I did. He was a
freedman named Numerius. He knew supply regulations
that hadn't been written yet. He found winter boots for my
legion that were better than anything available from the
regular sources, and he got them well under the footwear
budget."

Cyclops spread his hands. "You see?"

Marcus told him about the short conference after the Senate meeting.

The old man nodded. "Scaeva and Gabinius are good men,
wise counselors. You should listen to them. They saw exactly
what I have just advised you about. Flaccus is the scholar
you want. So what if he is a wretched soldier? What you see
as your weaknesses are tasks for subordinates anyway. Assign
them their jobs, review their reports and post them to the
Senate. That is a commander's duty, and it is the command
position that counts. Accept it, Marcus!"

No family conference was required, it seemed. If Cyclops
said Marcus was to accept the Senate's commission, then the
matter was settled. He was going to Italy.

CHAPTER FOUR

THE EXPEDITION SET OUT IN A DRIZZLING RAIN. IT was not a military expedition, so there was no fanfare, no music, no crowds of young girls to shower them with flower petals. As they made their way through the city, people watched them with curiosity, occasionally shouting good wishes, but generally the mood was quiet. It was not a glorious occasion, yet all felt that something of great consequence was at hand.

Marcus turned in his saddle to look back along the line of men following him. There were forty members in the official party, mostly young, all of them from good families. Many were friends. A few were avowed enemies of his family. As to the rest, he would learn about them soon enough. Besides the official party, there were a score of slaves to tend the animals, set up camp and perform all the other tedious duties of such an expedition. There was no escort of soldiers. This was, ostensibly, a trade and diplomatic mission. The men of the official party were all soldiers, anyway.

The trek south toward the mountains would be through territory long held by the Romans, peaceful and free of brigands. Each man wore a sword belted to his side, but the other arms and military gear were carried by pack animals.

"Is this a good omen?" Flaccus asked, riding up beside Marcus.

"Omen? The augurs took them this morning and everything was favorable."

"I mean this rain. Surely, if Jupiter looked favorably upon this expedition, he would give us a warm, sunny morning to start it."

Marcus grinned. "But as Jupiter Pluvium he is the god of rain. This may be his blessing."

"I see we can look forward to many stimulating discussions of religion." Flaccus drew the hood of his cloak over his head as the rain intensified. He had been appalled at being named to the expedition, but his family's pride would not allow him to back out. Since he was clearly the best man for the role of recorder and historian, he insisted on an extra pack animal to carry his writing gear, portable desk, inks, parchments and so forth. Then he had loaded the beast with extra comforts for the road.

The lands they rode through for the first few days were peaceful, fertile and intensively cultivated. The Romans were a race of farmers, and wherever they went, they instituted the sort of agriculture that had made Italy abound in produce and population, the sort of population that had allowed Rome to raise new legions after every disastrous defeat inflicted by Hannibal. They were determined never to be weakened by insufficient manpower.

These lands had been among the earliest conquered during the migration from Italy; a migration that had been spearheaded by a military invasion, for good land always has occupants, and the fine, fertile river valleys beyond the Alps had been no exception. A mixture of Celtic and Germanic tribes had stood in their way, and they had been crushed, for all they had was numbers and valor. These things were as nothing in the face of Roman organization and discipline. Above all, the natives raised no leader like Hannibal.

The wisest of the natives had allied themselves with the newcomers and assisted in the conquests. It was their descendants who now had seats in the Senate. The land through which the party rode, once the site of bloody battles, was divided into spacious farms and many of these were dominated by splendid villas. Families that had been peasants in Italy were now equites, while people of native descent were small farmers and tenants. Slaves captured in war did much of the field labor.

In the evenings they stopped at the inns that were spaced every ten miles along the fine roads. The roads themselves were splendidly made of cut stone, straight as a chalkline no matter what the terrain. If a gorge was in the way, it was bridged. If a hill intervened, it was cloven as if with an axe, and the road passed through. Only the great mountains forced the Roman roads to climb or bend.

At the inns and on the road Marcus got to know the men of his company. Some of them he had known for years, others he knew by reputation, and still others were total strangers. Quintus Brutus came from a very ancient patrician family, as ancient as the Scipios. Although still a young man, he was already a member of the college of augurs and he acted as the expedition's priest and omen-taker. Lucius Ahenobarbus was not a member of the patrician family of that name, but a descendant of their freedmen. These Ahenobarbi were merchants and contractors, and understood business in a way the land-based old aristocracy did not. Marcus would depend upon him for financial advice and analysis.

Most problematic of all, though, was Titus Norbanus. He was a tall, handsome man with a fine martial bearing although he had no great reputation as a soldier. He had a splendid voice and a rhetorician's way with words, and would be invaluable as envoy and negotiator. He was invariably polite and affable when he and Marcus spoke, apparently quite content with his secondary position. Marcus did not believe any of it for a moment. They were rivals from childhood and the rivalry had often been bitter. Norbanus acted as if this was boyish foolishness long behind them. Marcus did not believe that, either.

He could not explain why he disliked and distrusted Norbanus so. It was just that he was Titus Norbanus, and he could not be trusted.

Marcus was brooding upon this, seated at an inn fire on the evening of the ninth day since their departure, when Norbanus stopped by him.

"Come along, schoolboy," said Titus. "It's time for our lesson."

Marcus set aside his cup and rose. "I thought I'd outgrown this years ago."

"No such luck," Norbanus said, clapping him on the shoulder in a show of joviality that, to Marcus, rang utterly false. They went to a corner of the great room where an imposingly fat man stood with the rest of the party seated around him. Marcus and Norbanus took their places and waited in silence, just as they had when they were schoolboys, before donning the toga of manhood.

The fat man was Metrobius, a freedman and Roma Noricum's best teacher of Greek. Every well-born Roman boy learned Greek, for it was the language of the civilized world, but few of them used it after their school years. It was the task of Metrobius to sharpen their rusty language skills. Nobody in Roma Noricum knew the Punic language, but it was certain that, in any land that touched the Mediterranean Sea, there would be people who spoke Greek. The Greek merchants who traded in Roma Noricum boasted that Greek was still the language of all educated people, and of all who traded or traveled, though the days of Greek power were long eclipsed.

It was the order of the Senate that, every day of the journey, Metrobius was to conduct a class in Greek grammar. He drilled them like boys because it was the only way he knew to teach. They obeyed him like dutiful pupils from long-drilled habit.

Metrobius pointed at an unfortunate man who looked less than attentive. "Give me the opening lines of the Iliad."

The man stood and shuffled. He was clearly more comfortable with his sword than with any book. "Ah, let me see—'Sing, o muse, of an angry man, of the wrath of Achilles, son of—' "

"Not that wretched Latin translation!" Metrobius yelled. "I want the original Attic Greek!"

"Oh. Well, ah—" He did not reach the end of the first stanza.

"Stop!" The fat man covered his ears. "The most famous poem in the world and you made six mistakes in grammar, syntax, pronunciation and case in fewer than ten words! Where did you learn Greek? In a Druid temple?"

"No," said the man. "You taught me."

Marcus laughed with the others and was immediately punished. The fat finger pointed at him. "You! The second ode of Pindar, if you please."

Marcus stood and cleared his throat. He was fairly confident here because he had an excellent memory, although he would have preferred to recite a speech of Demosthenes. There was no help for it, though. Traditionally, language teachers taught by use of Greek poetry. Rhetoricians made their students recite speeches by rote. He launched into the lengthy ode and Metrobius nodded, finally stopping him halfway through.

"You seem to know the poem well enough, but your pronunciation is absolutely wretched. Sit down. Now, you." He pointed at Flaccus. "I suppose you are not unacquainted with the roll of the ships from the second book of the Iliad?"

"I believe I recall a bit of it," Flaccus replied.

"Then, if you please, let us hear a 'bit' of it."

Flaccus stood and adjusted his traveling cloak, managing to arrange it in the traditional drape used by orators for the most dignified effect. Then he launched into the famously difficult passage detailing the leadership of the Greek expedition, the list of towns and nobles and how many ships were contributed by each of them:

"I will name the captains of the fleet and the numbers of their ships.

"The Boeotians were led by Peneleos and Leitos, Arcesilaos and Prothoenor and Clonios. These came from hilly Hyria and rocky Aulis, from Schoinos and Scolos, Eteonos, from Thespeia, Griaia and wide-reaching Mycalessos, from the districts round Harma, Eilesion, and Erythrai, from Eleon, Hylae and Peteon, Ocalea and the well-built fortress of Medeon, from Copai and Eutresis and Thisbe with its multitudes of doves, from Coroneia and grassy Haliartos, from Plataia and Glisas, from the strongly-walled fortress of Hypothebai and from sacred Onchestos, that glorious grove of Poseidon, from Arne, adorned with clusters of grapes and from Midea, from divine Nisa and the coastal town of Anthedon, from these came fifty ships and in each ship a hundred and twenty young warriors of Boeotia.

"There were those who dwelt in Aspledon and Minyan Orchemenos, led by Ascalaphos and Ialmenos, son of Ares. Their mother was Astyoche, a maiden of high rank; their father was mighty Ares, who lay with her in secret. She bore her sons in her upper chamber in the house of Actor Azeides. They brought thirty ships to the sandy beach at Troy.

"The Phocians were there . . ." And on and on it went, the names of heroes, the roster of followers and ships, town after town, not omitting the virtues of the leaders and even the relative merits of the horses. The rolling, almost musical accents of Attic Greek were a joy to hear.

"Excellent!" Metrobius commended when Flaccus came to the end of the book. "Memorization flawless, pronunciation impeccable, diction all but perfect. This is how Greek must be spoken."

"Some of us were studying Greek while the rest of us were soldiering," someone said, raising a laugh.

"I have a suggestion," said Titus Norbanus.

"Let's hear it," Marcus said.

Norbanus stood. He did not arrange his cloak but he had the bearing of an orator without need of accessories. "It is clear that, except for Flaccus, we are all wretchedly out of practice with our Greek. From now until we reach our destination, I propose that we speak only in Greek, even in casual conversation. Anyone caught speaking Latin gets fined. By the time we have to deal with the Carthaginians, we should all be comfortable with the language."

There was a great deal of grumbling, but Marcus spoke over the noise. "That's an excellent idea. A sesterce fine for anyone who speaks Latin from here on, to be paid into the general travel fund."

"Why, Marcus," Flaccus said in Greek, "you just gave that order in Latin." Amid general hilarity, Marcus took a big copper coin from his pouch and tossed it to Ahenobarbus, who acted as treasurer for the expedition.

Twenty days later they were in Italy. The alps lay behind them. The pass through the eastern end of the range was not the highest or most rugged, but the weather had been wretched and they were no longer on Roman roads. The slow passage had one beneficial effect: They were all now more or less comfortable speaking Greek. Even the slaves, who had never studied the language, were able to understand the simpler nouns and verbs barked at them. Metrobius and Flaccus had been merciless in their criticism and correction, and now the least apt among the party could at least make himself understood.

On the afternoon that they rode out onto the broad plain at the foot of the mountains, Marcus called a halt and ordered them all to dismount. When all were gathered around him he spoke.

"At last, after more than a hundred years, we Romans stand upon the sacred soil of our ancestral land." He looked around until he found a small boulder, lifted it and carried it to the spot where he had dismounted. He set the stone firmly in place and straightened. "On this spot we will erect an altar to Jupiter Best and Greatest. I want every man to pitch in."

Now he scanned the gently sloping plain before them. Here and there were stone huts surrounded by low walls and pens. It was fine high pasture and there were many flocks within view. He pointed to the nearest hut. "Quintus Brutus, go over there and buy the best ram you can find. We will make a sacrifice here before the sun goes down."

Brutus went off on his errand and the men, noble and common, free and slave, set about gathering stones and piling them at their dismounting spot. They were experienced at military engineering and masonry, so it was not a haphazard heap of stone, but a stable, roughly rectangular altar that rose upon the plain.

"Build it high, men!" called Titus Norbanus. "Someday, a great monument will stand on this spot. When we are dead, men will say, 'This is where the reconquest of Italy began.'" The men cheered his words.

Marcus cheered with the rest, but he was not entirely pleased. Ever since his proposal about speaking Greek, Norbanus had been taking more and more upon himself, insinuating his own policies into action. Marcus resented it, but there was little action he could take. Norbanus never failed to defer to him and his suggestions almost always were good ones.

The altar was almost chest-high when Brutus returned with a fine white ram. "For this service," Marcus announced, "we will dispense with Greek and speak in the language of Jupiter and Quirinus. Brutus, be so good as to take the omens."

Brutus went to his pack mule and removed his striped toga and his lituus, the crook-topped staff of his vocation. Draping his toga with muttered prayers in archaic Latin, he walked to a high spot near the altar and with the tip of his staff marked out a circle. Standing within the circle he faced north and waited. All kept silence while the augur performed his craft. Far to the east, a dark cloud had formed and lightning flashed. Seconds later, a dull muffled thunder reached them.

"Thunder on the right!" Brutus announced. "Jupiter approves!"

"Jupiter, greatest of the gods," Marcus called, "we are here in your sacred land to fulfill the vows made to you by our ancestors. We ask you to look with favor upon our undertaking. We will rebuild your temples, reconsecrate your sacred groves, and reinstitute all your services and festivals. This is our pledge." With this he raised the last skin of their carefully hoarded wine and poured it out upon the altar. Norbanus handed him a sack of meal and he poured its contents likewise upon the stone. Then two sacerdotal slaves came forward. One handed Marcus the curved sacrificial knife. Then the man grasped the ram while the other held a bronze bowl beneath it. Marcus drew a fold of his cloak over his head and the watchers did likewise.

The animal scarcely moved as Marcus, with a quick swipe of the keen blade, cut its throat. The slave with the bowl caught the blood that gushed from its severed jugular. When the flow ceased, Marcus raised the bowl high. "Thus do we seal our pledge, and consecrate ourselves to our holy mission." He poured the blood onto the altar.

With great efficiency the slaves butchered the animal while fires were built. When all the meat was cut into small morsels, it was set on spits and cooked over the coals. Then all sat upon the ground and ate the tough, gamy meat until it was gone. A fire was built upon the altar and the hide, bones and offal were ceremoniously thrown upon it and all was consumed. When all these rites were concluded, the men began to speak again, in Greek.

"So, Brutus," Marcus said, "what language did the shepherd speak?"

"It sounded like some form of Latin, but so corrupted I could understand perhaps one word in ten. But he understood a few words of Greek and sign language accomplished the rest. Any peasant understands your meaning when you hold up a silver coin and point at a sheep."

"What was his attitude? Did he seem astonished? Frightened?"

"He gaped, seemed afraid at first, but only for a moment. He pointed toward the mountains and I think he asked if we came from that direction. I indicated we had and he shook his head, as if he never heard of such a thing."

"They probably haven't in a long time, around here," said Flaccus, who was taking notes.

"Was he armed?" Marcus asked.

"He had a sword belted on, and came out of his hut with a spear. Once he was satisfied we weren't a threat, he left the spear propped against his hut."

"Maybe bandits in the area, then," Marcus observed.

"Or he could be part of a local militia," Norbanus said. "Roman peasants always kept their arms handy in case of a call-up. It was the law."

"We'll learn soon," Marcus said. "I think we have little

to worry about from bandits." The rest chuckled at the thought.

That night Marcus lay back and stared up at the sky. The slaves had erected his tent, but he preferred to sleep outside in good weather, with only his cloak for a cover and his saddle as a pillow. His spear was stuck in the ground by its butt-spike, his shield leaning against it. His sword lay beside his right hand. The sky above him and the ground beneath were much the same as he had experienced on hundreds of other nights, but now there was a difference: This was the sky of Italy. He lay upon the soil of Italy, the soil in which reposed the bones and ashes of his ancestors going back a thousand years.

He was startled when a shooting star streaked across the sky. Was it an omen? It had crossed from north to south. Was that significant? He chided himself for being so eager. Every celestial oddity did not mean an omen. A man on night-guard might see a few falling stars on any clear night. There weren't enough momentous events to account for them all. Most, he thought, were probably just pieces of stars that broke off and fell to earth.

They resumed their trek south before first light. As daylight brightened, they saw a land of small farms, decent if not exactly prosperous. They saw no military camps, no forts, no garrisons. This, they knew, had once been a northern frontier area of the old Republic. The natural barrier of the mountains precluded a heavy legionary presence, but there had been raids by the mountain tribes and pirate incursions from the sea, so there had always been small forts and roving patrols. Now, it seemed, there were none.

"If Carthage is still in charge here," Norbanus noted on that first morning, "then she isn't very interested in defending her conquests." This seemed perverse to the Roman mind.

"If so," Marcus said, "then it is something valuable to know."

By late afternoon they came to a small, fast-flowing river. "If my maps and texts are correct," Flaccus said, "this is the Plavis River. We are in the old district of Gallia Transpadana."

"Then, before long," Marcus said, "we should strike the coastal road."

"If it's still there," said Norbanus. He rode along on a splendid horse, finer by far than Marcus Scipio could afford.

"It will be there," said Flaccus, "unless the Carthaginians took it on themselves to physically root out every trace of Italian civilization. It takes more than a trifling century or so to obliterate a decent road."

They reached the road by evening and dismounted to examine it. It had once been lightly paved or graveled, but soil, grass and weeds had made encroachments. Still, it was usable, and far better than the dirt paths they had followed in the mountains.

"This is nothing like a Roman road," Norbanus said.

"Actually," Flaccus said, "we learned road building from the Etruscans."

Marcus smiled. "Doubtless we practice the art better than they did. This is a good sign. If the old coast road is still in such shape, the others should be as well. We'll be able to reach the Seven Hills on halfway decent roads the whole way."

Flaccus scratched his chin. "Actually, I think a little side trip is in order. One farther south."

The rest looked at Marcus expectantly. "Well," he said, "it will take us a bit out of our way, but why not? This is a reconnaissance, not a race."

They remounted and continued to ride south, taking a narrow dirt road that took them southward along what was now a coastal plain. The ground to each side grew marshy and settlement thinned. They pitched camp upon the first high, relatively dry land they encountered. The air held a new, unfamiliar smell. It was something alien to them, yet it was familiar, as if it stirred a memory bequeathed by their ancestors.

The next morning, as the sun rose, they looked upon a seemingly limitless expanse of water. Rivers and lakes they had seen in plenty, but never anything like this. The sight and sound of the waves breaking upon the rocky beach was something new to them yet, like the smell, it seemed somehow familiar as well.

"So this is the 'wine-dark sea' of which Homer sang!" said Metrobius, sounding like a man in the grip of ecstasy. "It was upon these waters that Agamemnon's fleet sailed to the beach at Troy. It was upon these waters that Ulysses sailed, lost, for ten years."

"This is the Adriatic," Flaccus said, unrolling one of his maps. "It is the branch of Our Sea that lies between Italy and Illyricum. Farther south lie the Ionian and the Sea proper."

"This is just a branch?" said Pedanius, the horse-doctor. "It looks like all the water in the world!"

"Yet even Our Sea is just a part of the world's waters. Beyond the Pillars of Hercules is Oceanus, which is believed to be limitless." Flaccus, as usual, sounded deeply satisfied with his scholarship.

"All right," Marcus said when he had looked his fill, "we've seen the sea. We'll see a great deal of water before this mission is done. Let's get back to the road."

The road took them westward, then south. The first town of any size they encountered was Patavium, where the coastal road met the southwest-leading Bononia Road. As they approached the walled town, an armed militia rode out to meet them. They wore oddments of armor and rode upon scrubby horses. Clearly, the once-prosperous town had fallen upon hard times. They drew rein just out of javelin-cast and their leader rode a few paces forward. He wore an excellent bronze cuirass and helmet and was clearly some sort of local dignitary.

"I am Cassius Porcina, captain of the civil guard of Patavium." He looked them over with curiosity bordering on wonder. "Who might you be?" He spoke a heavily accented but understandable dialect of Latin.

"We are Romans," Marcus said.

The man blinked. "Romans? The Romans disappeared in my grandfather's day."

"We come from Roma Noricum," Marcus explained. "We are on a mission of trade and diplomacy for our homeland."

"Oh, Noricum. I've heard of that place. So that's where the Roman refugees settled? I thought there were nothing but bearded, skin-clad savages up there beyond the mountains."

"There are still a few of those," Marcus affirmed. "Mostly, though, we are civilized. We've been cut off from the south for a long time and we want to reestablish relations. Just now, we are riding to Rome to sacrifice at our temples and restore the tombs of our ancestors, which must have fallen into disrepair by this time."

Cassius nodded. "Very pious and I wish you well." He looked them over again, appraisingly. "I am rather surprised that you've made it so far unmolested. There is a great deal of banditry around here. A group as well-found as yours, riding practically unarmed, must be a great temptation."

"We shall have to be vigilant," Marcus said.

The captain shrugged. "Well, you look peaceful enough. You may enter the city. Perhaps you can interest the merchant council in some trade agreements. The gods know we don't get much foreign commerce here."

Marcus rode alongside the captain as they turned toward the city gate. "Is this still Carthaginian territory?" he asked.

Cassius laughed. "Carthaginian? Oh, certainly they claim us. They send collectors each year to take our tribute, never doubt it. But no Carthaginian face has been seen in this district since Hannibal pulled his army out in my grandfather's time." Apparently his grandfather's time encompassed all of history prior to recent memory.

The town had a few fine buildings, most of them growing shabby except for the homes of the most important men and a few of the temples. That evening they were entertained by the merchant's council to a modest dinner. These men, at least, had done some traveling and possessed useful information.

"Carthaginians?" said a wool trader. "You'll find factors for their trading companies in most coastal cities, the ones with decent ports. But they maintain garrisons only in the most important ports. In Italy that means Brundisium, Tarentum and Messana. Tarentum is their Italian capital and has the largest garrison. It is the residence of the governor of Italy, one Hanno, a royal cousin like all the governors."

"How do they dominate all of Italy with so little military presence?" Norbanus asked.

"They have large forces quartered in Sicily. Lilybaeum and Panormus are fort cities, and there are smaller forts and camps all over the island. Only Syracuse remains independent."

This statement drew immediate attention. "How did Syracuse retain its freedom when all other cities fell before the Carthaginians?" Marcus asked.

"There was a protracted siege with heavy losses on both sides. Carthage was unable to breach the walls or control the harbor, and eventually a peace was negotiated. Some credit the fantastic war machines designed by the mathematician Archimedes with saving the city. Others think Carthage was simply exhausted after so many years of war. Also, some of their African subject cities rose in revolt, and they had to deal with the problem. In later years, they seemed content to leave Syracuse alone."

"Who rules in Carthage now?" Flaccus wanted to know.

"The Barca family have ruled since Hannibal's day. He overthrew the republic and set himself up as sole king. The current Shofet—that is what they call their king—is Hamilcar the Second. I believe he is a great-grandson of Hannibal."

"And is Carthage unchallenged these days?" Marcus asked.

"In the west, I am afraid so. With the fall of Rome, there was no credible military power remaining and all was reduced to subjugation, save Syracuse. In the east, it is a different matter. The descendants of Alexander's generals still control Greece and Macedon, Syria and Egypt. They fight much among themselves, but Carthage has never been able to overcome their combined might or their military expertise. Carthage has not produced another general of Hannibal's caliber." He sat back and took a long drink of watered wine. "But it is trade you are interested in, is it not? These military matters can hardly concern you."

"That is quite true," said Ahenobarbus, smoothly taking control of the dialogue. For the next few hours he learned all he could from the merchants. Marcus was content to let him dominate the conversation. This was his realm of expertise and he would glean much valuable intelligence unwittingly delivered by the traders.

The next morning they resumed their journey southward, this time on the Bononia road. As soon as they were away from the city, Norbanus leaned over and spat on the roadside. "Tribute! These people pay tribute to an enemy that does not even bother to establish garrisons in their country to keep them in line! What has happened to Italian manhood?"

"Things have sunk to a sorry state since our ancestors

left," Marcus said. "But what do you expect? These are the descendants of the people who stayed behind, renounced their share of Roman inheritance and submitted to the yoke of Carthage. Oxen can't breed fighting bulls." He drew rein as soon as they were out of sight of the city. "I want every man to arm himself now. We must not appear too warlike. Cover your armor with your cloaks, helmets and shields to be hung from your saddles. We can expect attack at any moment from here on."

"You're pessimistic today," Flaccus grumbled.

"Word will have gone out from the city that we are on this road, with good horses and full purses and that we look like peaceful traders. There are always people happy to inform bandits of such a thing, for a share of the spoils."

They took their military gear from the pack animals and donned it. Each man had a short shirt of mail of the type worn by cavalry, and an iron helmet. The shields were of light-cavalry design, small and round. Each had a long cavalry sword as well as a short infantry gladius, a sheaf of javelins and a lance. Only fat Metrobius was spared the military preparations. He was too old, too fat and had been nothing but a scholar all his life. Remounted, they rode on.

They encountered no bandits that day, nor on the next. But on the third day, they found their way barred at the bridge across the Padus River. They had crossed a number of smaller rivers since leaving Patavium, and had been gratified to see that their bridges were still intact, if not quite up to exacting Roman standards of design and construction.

"It seems," Flaccus said, "that someone doesn't want us to cross the Padus."

"Or else wants us to pay for the privilege," Norbanus said, fingering the hilt of his longsword.

"Or," Flaccus speculated, "it could be that they just intend to kill us and take everything."

"What disappointed men they shall be," Marcus said.

"But, it should do no harm to talk with them. Maybe they'll see reason." He counted the men before them, ranged in front of the northern approach to the fine bridge. There were some eighty-five or ninety of them, half mounted, the rest afoot, all armed. There was no attempt at uniformity of clothing or equipment. All were well armed, some partially armored. "Who do you think they might be?"

"The usual rabble," Norbanus said. "Runaway slaves, ruined peasants, army deserters. Bandits are the same everywhere."

"They could be men of spirit," Marcus speculated, "men who will not pay tribute or be dominated by cowards."

"At the moment," Flaccus said, "their spirit seems misdirected. Toward ourselves, to be precise."

"I agree," Norbanus said. "Let's get rid of them."

"Talk first," Marcus said gently. "We are diplomats, after all." These words were greeted with sighs and groans, which he ignored as he rode forward. He stopped the customary distance and waited to see who the leader of this ragged band might be.

A man wearing an old-fashioned helmet and breastplate, riding barefoot, rode forward a few paces. "Greetings, Romans," he called. He was gap-toothed and scrubby bearded, but he had an air of authority, like a centurion of long service.

"So you know who we are. You have an excellent intelligence service."

The man grinned. "Intelligence service? You mean the world is full of men willing to betray strangers for a handful of coins."

"I'm following you, but your accent is strange to me. Are you Samnite?" He chose the nation at random, naming an old enemy people.

"No, they live far south of here. I'm Ligurian. I think we

should discuss the terms upon which we will allow you to continue breathing."

"By all means," Marcus said, leaning forward, listening with evident interest.

The bandit chief looked puzzled and, for the first time, uneasy. "You don't seem very frightened."

"Should we be?" Marcus said. "You seem to be splendid fellows and we're all friends here, are we not?"

"They're all mad," said one of the bandits. All of them fingered their weapons, staring greedily at the fine animals and clothing and equipment.

"This is how it will be," said the leader. "You will all dismount and strip. All of your valuables go on the ground. Then you can walk back to Patavium unmolested. We won't hold you for ransom or sell you as slaves, so long as you make no resistance."

Marcus gazed past him. Heaped at the end of the bridge was a tangle of ropes, chains and shackles. "What are those for?"

The man followed the direction of his gaze. "If you resist, we ransom or sell the survivors. It's the custom."

Marcus straightened. "This is how it is going to be. We will not give you a single animal or a single coin. You will stand aside and allow us to cross, and you will live. We're Romans, you see. We don't negotiate with bandits, pirates and the like. We crucify them." He looked at a nearby copse of trees. "Plenty of good timber for crosses here. We don't have nails, but wood pegs work as well and hurt worse." He took his helmet from his right saddle horn and fastened its chinstrap.

"Eh?" The bandit leader was nonplussed. Then he saw Marcus shrug his cloak from his shoulders, revealing his glittering iron mail as he took the round shield from his left saddle horn. Behind him the rest of the party did the same. In an instant, the trade delegation had become a cavalry troop. For a moment he was shaken, but then realized that he still had the advantage of numbers, by more than two to one. He turned to order his men forward, but Marcus did not wait.

It was always, he knew, best to seize the initiative in the face of superior numbers. He drew his sword and spurred his horse in a single motion. He did not bother to give orders to his men. They knew exactly what to do. This had been drilled into them from the day they first straddled a horse. In an instant his horse was even with that of the bandit chief. He leaned over his saddle and thrust with his arm at full extension. The bandit, expecting a cut, was caught by surprise as he raised his wooden shield, still trying to draw his sword. The point went into his throat just beneath the chin, passing through and separating the neck vertebrae. He went backward out of his saddle, dead before he hit the ground.

As Marcus was withdrawing his sword, a footman rushed up on his left and tried to seize his bridle. Marcus punched with the iron-sheathed edge of his shield, a straight thrust that crunched into the man's temple, dropping him instantly. Then the other Romans were even with him, formed into a skirmish line, their lances and swords rising, falling, thrusting like some great mechanical device. Each man engaged the enemy before him while keeping an eye on those attacking his comrades to right and left. A moment's inattention by any of the bandits and a lance would be into his side and out again before he was even aware of it. It was Roman practice in such a fight for a horseman to protect himself from the man directly before him while using his offensive weapons principally against attackers to either side. They had learned that they inflicted far more losses on an enemy this way than by heroic, one-on-one duels.

In an amazingly short time, most of the bandits were on the ground and the rest were running, some of them onto the bridge from which they jumped into the waters below, so desperate were they to escape this unprecedented killing machine. Marcus reined in but some of the younger men continued to chase the running bandits, spearing them or cutting them down as if this were a stag hunt, not a fight against men. Marcus did not call them off. He did not like bandits and it was just as well that the people in these parts learned the terror of Roman arms. It would make for less trouble later.

Titus Norbanus rode up, his sword red to the hilt, his mail splashed with blood as well. "A few seem to have gotten away," he reported.

"How many?" Marcus asked.

"Four or five, I think."

"Just as well. Let them spread the word."

"But we promised them crucifixion!" Norbanus protested.

Marcus scanned the little battlefield. "There are probably some here you can crucify."

"No, they're all dead," Norbanus said, sounding deeply disappointed.

Flaccus rode up. "I'm glad of it. Crucifixion is a lot of work."

Norbanus looked him over. "That's a clean sword you have there."

Flaccus held the weapon up as if studying it. Its polish was unmarred, its edge innocent of notches. "So it is. This means I won't have to clean it, doesn't it?"

"Since you rested during the fight," Marcus said, "you can see to disposal of the bodies."

"Of course. I'll summon the slaves. They can go round up some peasants and we'll have these poor wretches piled up and incinerated before nightfall." He sheathed his sword and rode off, calling for the servants.

Marcus dismounted and walked down to the river to wash the blood from his sword. Blood was the worst thing in the world for a sword, oddly enough. Leave it on too long and it would etch and stain the blade, ruining the fine polish. As he swept the blade back and forth in the flow, he reflected that it was going to take more than a long march and a fight with bandits to make a Roman of Flaccus.

Fifteen days later, they came within sight of the walls of Rome.

CHAPTER FIVE

They stood on the plain north of the city and gazed upon the walls built by the king Servius Tullius. On the heights within the walls they could see the great temples of Juno and Jupiter. All their lives they had been told of these places and they knew the topography of Rome and the surrounding countryside as well as they knew their own city.

"The walls!" somebody said with a sob in his voice. The great, ancient wall was reduced in places to rubble, only small sections still standing to their full height.

"What did you expect?" Titus Norbanus said. "Hannibal would never leave a strongly fortified enemy city within his domains, any more than we would. He pulled the walls down, so we will build them up again."

"That we will," Marcus affirmed. "Come on, let's go see what the Carthaginians left us."

So they rode across the river plain, along the old northern road that led them to a gap in the wall where once had stood the Colline Gate. Within, they found a dismal expanse of tumbled masonry, overgrown with bushes, weeds and even full-grown trees where once had stood the proud houses of the patricians, the tenements of the poor, the markets and plazas of the great city.

"This is the temple of Quirinus," Flaccus said. The structure stood atop a rise of ground, the Quirinal hill. Its pillars and portico were still intact, but the roof was gone.

"So much for Hannibal's oath to leave our temples and shrines intact," said Norbanus.

"A century of neglect could have done this," Flaccus told them. They rode up to the steps before the temple, dismounted and climbed to the top of the stair. From this prominence they could see a great expanse of city. The temple of Quirinus was one of the most ancient in Rome, a small, modest structure in keeping with the simplicity of their distant ancestors. Nearby stood the equally ancient temple of Salus.

"They burned the city," Marcus said. "Only that could account for such devastation."

"First loot, then burn," Norbanus said. "That's the way it is usually done."

They remounted and rode on, until they came to the valley between the Capitoline and Palatine hills. This had been the Forum, the very heart and center of Rome. Once drained by the Cloaca Maxima, the valley had reverted to its original character as a marshy glen with a small lake in its center. In the marsh, amid blowing reeds stood the small, circular temple of Vesta, where once had burned the sacred fire.

"The Vestals will weep when they see this," said Brutus.

"It will look better by the time they arrive from Noricum," Marcus assured him. "The Cloaca Maxima is down there somewhere. The drains have just clogged. A legion with its engineers will have this valley drained in a week. In another month, the mud and reeds will be cleared away, the pavement uncovered and restorations well under way. It will look like a city again, before we bring the Vestals and the sacred objects back home."

"First we will have to retake this district," Norbanus pointed out.

"First we will reconquer Italy," Marcus said. "Then, the rest of the old empire."

"And after that, the world?" Norbanus said, smiling.

"Why not?" Marcus answered. "It's there to be conquered, and we haven't been wasting our time up north. We've kept in practice."

It might have been worse, Marcus reflected. In an odd way, it was Rome's good fortune that it occupied such an indifferent site. But for its exceptional inhabitants, Rome was just a second-rate Italian city on a third-rate Italian river. Carthage was interested only in controlling coastal cities and extracting tribute from the interior. The new occupants seemed inclined only to till the soil and use it for pasturage.

Marcus turned his horse and spurred it toward the Sacred Way that wound its way up the slope of the Capitol. Once, triumphal parades had taken this route, the climax of the magnificent ceremony that reaffirmed the inevitable primacy of Roman arms. The victorious general, dressed in a purple robe, his face and hands painted red, crowned with a golden wreath, rode in his chariot with enemy kings and chiefs walking in chains behind him. For a day, the triumphator received semi-divine honors as he rode through the city after the great wagons, floats and litters heaped with loot and arms taken from the enemy. The Sacred Way ended atop the Capitoline hill, where he sacrificed at the altar of Jupiter Optimus Maximus and was feasted at a great banquet hosted by the Senate.

Now the Sacred Way was a sorry sight, its monuments toppled, the great buildings that had once bordered it tum-

bled in ruin: The tabularium that had held the state records
was rubble, the lesser temples and shrines falling into decay,
although they could detect no signs of outright vandalism.
The huge temple of Juno Moneta stood roofless, and on the
highest peak the smaller but even more ancient temple of
Jupiter Best and Greatest stood likewise open to the elements.

"When we rebuild," Marcus said, dismounting, "let's use
only stone and bronze. No more wooden roofs for Roman
temples."

Slowly, they walked inside. Even in its half-ruinous state,
this holy site filled them with awe and reverence. Here had
taken place some of the most decisive debates of the Senate,
when the Curia had been too small to hold the crowd or
when the augurs had declared that Jupiter himself wished
to participate. Here the leaders of Rome had taken their
most solemn oaths. Here generations of triumphators had
dedicated their victories to the chief god of Rome's pan-
theon.

In the center rear of the temple Jupiter still sat enthroned.
The ancient image was of terra-cotta, his skin painted red,
his hair and beard black, his robe gilded. One hand was
raised in benediction, the other resting upon the arm of his
throne. He seemed all but untouched by the intervening
years. Dust lay upon him, and leaves hammocked in the
folds of his robe, but his shell-inlaid eyes were bright.

"We will cleanse the temple," Marcus said, "and rebuild
his altar fire. Then we will sacrifice to Jupiter, and renew
the oath of our ancestors."

Silently, they set about the ritual cleansing of the temple.
Many of them were highborn men, but there was nothing
demeaning in this holy work. They fashioned brooms from
reeds growing below, and they carried up pots of water and
used their saddle blankets to scrub the floor, and they
worked on their knees to eliminate the accumulated dirt and

detritus of more than a century. Marcus used his own cloak to clean the image of Jupiter, and Flaccus used tints from his store of colored inks to fill in scratches and chips in the aged terra-cotta.

When they had done the best job they could, Brutus built a fire at the altar before the temple. Norbanus had found a suitable animal on a nearby farm: a fine white bull with no blemishes. The beast was duly sacrificed and its blood poured over the altar. Curious locals, most of them shepherds who grazed their flocks within the city itself, witnessed the solemnities. So much of it had reverted to the wild that there was abundant pasture within the walls.

"Who are these?" Marcus asked when the simple ceremony was done.

"Bruttians," Norbanus said, spitting.

"So Hannibal rewarded their treachery with the lands our ancestors vacated." Bruttium in southern Italy had sided with Carthage against Rome without a fight. "That can be set aright."

One of the shepherds climbed the steps and addressed the Romans, gesturing toward the dead animal and gesticulating. His dialect was so thick that they hardly understood a word.

"As near as I can understand," Flaccus said, "he wants to know why we aren't hauling out the animal's liver to read it."

"They must still take the haruspices here," Marcus observed. "Etruria is right across the river. The Etruscans were the great entrails-interpreters."

"They're a superstitious lot," Norbanus said. "Bruttians must be stupid enough to believe in their mummery."

That night they posted guards to keep intruders out and passed inside the temple. There, beneath the waxing moon, they reaffirmed the vow sworn by their ancestors, omitting only the Secret Name of Rome, which was known to none of them.

On the next morning they continued their ride south, fortified by their reconnection with the city of their people.

"At least we're on real Roman road," Flaccus said, admiring the beautiful cut stone of the Via Appia. This, the oldest of the Roman highways, connected Rome with Capua. It was already almost a hundred years old when the Romans left, and except for some encroachment by weeds at the curbs, it was as fine as the day it was inaugurated by Appius Claudius.

"We should be on good roads from here on," Marcus said, "all the way to Tarentum."

As they rode south, the land began to present a different appearance. The near-desolation of the north gave way to prosperous farms, for this was the matchlessly fertile Campanian plain. Huge grain fields, vineyards and orchards stretched as far as the eye could discern. Cattle in immense herds grazed the meadows and sheepfolds the size of small towns held flocks of countless woolly beasts. The Romans looked upon these things in wonderment.

"I never saw so much land under cultivation," Norbanus said, "unbroken by forest or boundary walls."

"And," said Flaccus, "you will notice that there are few towns or villages, and not even many farmsteads. These are not farms, my friends, they are plantations. Southern Italy is no longer a land of free peasant farmers. These lands are worked by slave-gangs under overseers. You see those long buildings?" He pointed to a series of such on a nearby hillside.

"I thought they were storage sheds," Marcus said.

"They are slave barracks. The men you see on horseback are the slave drivers."

"It's an efficient way to farm," Norbanus said, "but how does such a land raise soldiers?"

"Maybe it doesn't," Flaccus said. "Perhaps it isn't supposed to."

They found this thought infinitely depressing. The native Italians were their kin, even if they were not all Latins. Only the Etruscans were wholly foreign. That they should have lost their martial heritage was a terrible thing to contemplate.

"Surely," Marcus said, "a mere century is not sufficient to utterly emasculate a warlike people."

"Why not?" Norbanus answered. "We've reduced scores of races and made them pass beneath our yoke."

"But those were barbarians!" Marcus protested. "Besides, we never break them entirely. That would be a waste of good legionary material. Once they've had time to learn a civilized language and get used to our laws, we make citizens of them. That is the proper way to conquer, not this enslavement of whole nations."

"You don't have to convince me," Norbanus said.

Their journey took them through once-prosperous towns, now mostly in a sad state of decline. Without the powerful presence of Rome, Bovillae and Lanuvium had reverted to backwaters with half their former populations. Capua was still a fine city, but once it had been glorious.

Everywhere they went, they were regarded with wonder, like some new form of omen. People asked one another how a nation erased from history could reappear. Rome was as dead as Troy, yet here were true Romans in their midst. What might this prodigy portend?

The farther south they went, the more prevalent grew the Greek language, until they spent days hearing no other tongue. The many Greek settlements of southern Italy had reasserted themselves, at least culturally. All were still subjects of Carthage.

Almost a month after their arrival in Italy, they came to the gate of Tarentum.

• • •

FOR HANNO THIS DAY, LIKE ALL OTHER DAYS, BEGAN
with prayer. The musicians awakened him with a traditional
tune played on the Egyptian harp, with tambour and sistra
providing a soft, rhythmic pulse to quicken his senses and
prepare him for the day. The Libyan slave girls drew aside
the filmy curtain that protected him from night-wandering
spirits and mosquitoes, and they helped him to rise and sit
on the edge of the bed. A boy held a golden basin before
him and Hanno splashed water in his face, then poured a
cupped palmful over his head as he spoke an invocation of
the gods of water.

Another slave girl, this one a tattooed Scythian, brought
him his robe and draped it over his shoulders, easing his
arms into its fringed sleeves, while a Libyan placed his pearl-
sewn slippers on his feet. Thus prepared, Hanno heaved his
corpulent bulk erect and strode across the tiles to the shrine
of Tanit, highest of the baalim who were the chief gods of
Carthage. He raised his hands beside his face, palms outward, and intoned:

"Lady of the crescent moon, look upon thy servant with favor
Lady of pearl, grant thy servant abundance
Lady of ivory, protect holy Carthage and her Shofet
Lady of incense, intercede for us with the multitude of gods
Lady of grace, queen of beauty, tower of strength, avert from us
all evil."

With the last words he took a pinch of fine, yellow frankincense and strewed the soft crystals over the charcoal that
smoldered before the statue of the goddess. At one time,
Tanit had been depicted in abstractions: the cone and stylized arms, the crescent. Now, under Greek influence, she
was a figure of polished marble, a beautiful nude woman

crowned with a crescent moon, one hand raised in benediction.

His morning devotion done, Hanno walked out onto his terrace and sat in his deep-cushioned chair. His hairdresser oiled and arranged his dense, curly black hair with consummate skill while his breakfast was set before him: hot breads and sliced fruits, spitted quail, chilled oysters, boiled eggs wrapped in medicinal herbs, dried dates and figs, pots of honey and a dozen sauces.

While he ate, Hanno surveyed his domain. He was governor of Italy, a cousin of the Shofet, a man of great and ancient family. Italy was culturally backward, but it was a rich agricultural province. In the early days, there had been uprisings among the native populace, especially the hill people called Samnites, but these had been put down with great savagery and mass crucifixions, and Italy had been docile for many decades.

His city of Tarentum, while far short of Carthage in magnificence, was still a splendid city with many fine temples, both native and Punic. Like many cities in the south of Italy, Tarentum was founded as a Greek colony and was once the first city of Magna Graecia. It boasted a beautiful theater, a great gymnasium, a painted portico and, in the center of the agora, a wonderful statue of Zeus by Lysippus.

The Tarentines had saved their city's splendor by very wisely opening their gates to Hannibal without a fight. It meant severing their political ties with Greece, but the hand of Carthage lay more lightly on Tarentum than on most Punic possessions. Besides having the only truly secure harbor in Italy, the adjacent territory raised multitudes of sheep, and Tarentum was famous for its wool industry. Its olive orchards were the most productive in the world.

In all, Hanno reflected with some satisfaction, he could have done far worse. If this was not the most splendid outpost of the far-flung Punic empire, it was fine and comfort-

able, and he was well away from the intrigue and peril of
the Carthaginian court. Here he had only to collect revenues,
settle occasional disputes between resident Carthaginian
merchants, hold court once each month and maintain the
majesty of Carthage before the barbarians.

There was a single flaw in Hanno's satisfaction: the royal
missive he had received from the capital just a few days
previously.

Governor Hanno, it began after the usual salutations, *His
Majesty being engaged in preparations for most justified war
against impious and treacherous Egypt, you are commanded to raise
from among His Majesty's subjects in your province soldiers to the
number of two myriads. You must exert yourself to the utmost to
further His Majesty's holy mission. Begin recruitment at once. Details will follow.*

That was bald enough, Hanno thought, chewing thought-
fully. He hoped that these details would include such things
as financing this recruitment program. And what could the
Shofet be thinking? Since the conquest, it had been Carthaginian policy to keep Italy unmilitarized. The natives had
proven to be the most stubborn, warlike and intransigent they
had ever encountered. Even after the passage of generations
as virtual slaves, Hanno feared that putting weapons in their
hands might awaken ancestral memories of their warrior
heritage.

He was distracted by a stir in the city below. His terrace
overlooked the agora and he saw the morning throng divide
before a line of horsemen. Preceding them on foot was a man
in Punic uniform, the officer of the gate. Situated as it was
on a stony peninsula, Tarentum had but a single gate. At
the officer's gesture the men halted before the entrance to
the governor's palace. As they dismounted, the officer
crossed the courtyard and ascended the broad ceremonial
stair to the terrace where Hanno sat shaded by a canopy of
purple cloth. At a precise ten paces before Hanno, the officer

dropped to his knees and touched his brow to the flagstones.

"Exalted lord, a very strange delegation has arrived in the city, craving audience with your eminence. Rather than interrogate them myself, I judged that my lord would wish to question them himself."

"Rise," Hanno said. "What makes these newcomers so special?"

"Lord, they claim to be Romans."

Hanno almost choked on a date. "Romans! That cannot be!"

"Yet this is their claim, Lord."

The governor scratched in his scented beard. "I suppose it is not beyond possibility. Greek merchants have informed us that the wretched rabble so generously spared by my ancestor founded a squalid little nation somewhere in the barbarous north. This could prove to be entertaining. Yes, do send them up. Will I require an interpreter? I believe the Romans spoke Latin, which is related to the Oscan spoken by some of the natives here."

"They speak passable Greek, Lord."

"Indeed? That is intriguing. Perhaps they are Greek imposters, mountebanks expecting hospitality and presents by claiming to be ambassadors from a distant land."

"I think not, Lord," said the officer.

As Hanno watched the men ascend the great stairway he, too, knew that they were not Greeks. He had never seen men who carried themselves with such self-assurance. Their bearing was erect and soldierly and they wore robes gracefully draped over one arm, giving each man the poise of an orator. Even the slaves who held the horses below bore themselves regally among the idlers of the agora.

The officer of the gate walked beside them, cutting a poor figure as he explained palace protocol to the visitors. When they reached the terrace, they advanced closer to the governor than was customary.

"Stop!" the officer cried. "On your faces!"

They ignored him entirely. One, apparently their leader, stepped two paces forward and inclined his head slightly. "Have I the honor of addressing His Excellency, the Governor of Italy?"

Hanno waved a hand to silence the sputtering officer. "You have. I am Hanno Barca, cousin in the second degree of His Majesty, Hamilcar. I fear you did not understand my officer's instructions."

"We understood them quite clearly," said the leader. "Roman citizens do not prostrate themselves. Nor do we kneel or bow." The officer of the gate went pale. Hanno's slaves were so shocked that the fan-bearers halted their metronomic motions.

Hanno all but gaped, then he erupted in convulsive laughter. "You must be Romans! Our historians avow that the Romans were the most arrogant race we ever encountered."

"It is not arrogance," the leader said. "It is a quality we are schooled in called gravitas. We do not tolerate foolishness or obsequiousness in men of public service."

For a few moments Hanno toyed with the idea of having them all crucified over the main gate of the city. It was his usual course with insolent foreigners and rebellious subjects. But, it was yet early in the day for executions, and he was in an excellent mood. Besides, something about these bizarre northerners tickled his sharp political instincts, and he had learned to trust those instincts. In Carthaginian court politics, one always walked a tightrope above sharp swords, and he had yet to lose his balance. He felt that they might be of use to him and decided to sound them out. Plenty of time to kill them later, should they prove disappointing.

He mused over one little problem: the slaves and the guard captain who had witnessed this breach of decorum. It wouldn't do to have anyone see this act go unpunished. If he decided not to kill the Romans, he would have the witnesses done away with instead: a simple, satisfactory solution.

"Gravitas, eh? It is a good word. Now, you must sit down and tell me all about your country and your mission."

"In the name of the Roman republic, I thank you," said the leader. "I am Marcus Cornelius Scipio, empowered by the republic to negotiate trade agreements and to open diplomatic relations with Carthage."

"Trade agreements? We are always eager to open new markets. As for diplomatic relations, those you must discuss at court, where I am certain His Majesty will give you a most sympathetic hearing. But first, you must be my guests."

"I thank you. Allow me to introduce my party." One by one, he introduced them. Their names sounded so similar that Hanno was certain he would never remember most of them. No matter. He would remember the two or three most prominent and the rest would be "my Roman friend."

While these formalities were observed, household slaves quietly and efficiently brought folding chairs onto the terrace. These were not mere camp chairs, but elegant furniture crafted from rare woods inlaid with ivory, their seats made of brilliant carpeting that was visible only briefly as still more slaves covered them with rare animal pelts. A small table was set beside each chair, covered with spotless linen and loaded with wine and delicacies.

"Your hospitality on short notice is more than splendid, Excellency," Scipio said, taking his seat. The others sat in order of precedence, even Flaccus showing himself as punctilious as the rest, in the presence of barbarians.

Hanno waved a hand dismissively. "Just what we keep handy for when unexpected guests drop in. Tonight I shall entertain you at a proper dinner and tomorrow we shall have a banquet, with all the best people of the city attending."

"That is short notice for all the important people to drop their plans." This from another man. What was his name? Norbanus, that was it. Hanno did not miss the flicker of annoyance that crossed the face of the one called Scipio. Norbanus had spoken out of turn.

"Everyone will be more than happy to meet such fascinating newcomers," Hanno assured them. Not, he reflected, that their wishes were of any account when he desired their presence. "In the meantime, quarters will be prepared for you here in the Residence. It will be my great pleasure to provide for all your needs and desires."

"This is most generous," Scipio said. "You will find that our wants are minimal."

"Indeed?" Hanno said. "But then, you are a martial people. Most commendable. Our own soldiers, officers and men, while on campaign practice the virtues of austerity as well. But what need is there to be frugal in the midst of abundance?"

"It is our belief that luxury and soft living weaken a man, Excellency," Scipio said. "Even when we are away from the legions, we avoid those practices that might unfit us for service."

"Most wise, I am sure," Hanno said, nodding, making a mental note to see which of these Romans actually lived up to this ideal. But he was intrigued by that word: legions. Had the Romans maintained their vaunted military organization and discipline? It was so superior that the Carthaginians had imitated it in many regards. He began to detect a possible answer to his recruitment dilemma, should conditions prove favorable.

"I must confess," Hanno admitted, "that my knowledge of lands north of the alps is sketchy. We Carthaginians are sea-traders and send few expeditions inland. We have only the reports of Greek traders for information about the remote north, and they prefer to guard their trade secrets closely. It was my impression that your ancestors who dwelled formerly on this peninsula had founded a small nation beyond the mountains. Am I to take it that your New Rome is a rather prominent city-state?"

"We call it Noricum, or Roma Noricum," Scipio answered. "And, yes, we have prospered up there. Noricum is the militarily dominant state of the region, as well as the most prosperous commercially and in all categories of agriculture."

"How good to hear," Hanno murmured, certain that the man was holding back a great deal, which was only the path of wisdom. "And how comes it about that you have decided to return to Italy after all these years? You do understand that the banishment of your people has never been repealed?"

"That is understood. In truth, for generations all the omens proclaimed that our gods wished us to stay north of the mountains. However, of late, certain signs have indicated a change in divine attitude and the Senate has decided to investigate the possibility of a Roman-Punic friendship. After all, many years have passed, times have changed, new persons occupy the thrones of nations—there is no reason why the enmity of our ancestors should separate us forever."

"I am certain that the Shofet will accept your suit in exactly that light," Hanno assured them. "I shall be most happy to have a ship fitted out to bear you to the capital, so that you can present your credentials to His Majesty personally."

"This goes beyond generosity and hospitality," Marcus said, exulting inwardly. A chance to see Carthage itself? He had never dared hope for such luck.

"It is nothing. I want only good relations between our nations."

That afternoon, given freedom of the city, the Romans explored Tarentum. They were fascinated to see the workings of a genuine port. In the presence of barbarians they maintained the unflappable Roman demeanor, but this required an effort when their urge was to goggle and stare.

Tarentum was unlike anything they had seen before. Capua had given them some preparation, but it was a pale imitation. Here the streets were covered with bright awnings and fountains bubbled at every street corner. The temples were adorned with colorful marble and every open space featured splendid sculpture and painted porticoes. Huge sections of stony ground had been hewn away and filled with soil from the mainland and planted with splendid gardens. The agora was lined with shops offering luxury goods from all over the world: bolts of purple cloth, spices, incense, papyrus, gold and gems, fine art works, pearls, furniture of the rarest woods, exquisite perfumes, books copied from the library at Alexandria; the variety seemed endless.

"Now I understand," said Titus Norbanus, "what a crude frontier fort Noricum is."

"It's what I've been saying all along," said Flaccus, stroking the magnificent leather case of a scroll, just a single volume of a fifty-scroll set of the works of Homer complete with commentary, the entire collection resting in a case of pearl-inlaid ebony.

"I've seen ten perfume shops," Marcus told them, "and not a single armory."

"All to the good," Norbanus responded, lifting a massive golden platter wrought with a scene of satyrs pursuing voluptuous nymphs. "We've traveled the length of Italy and have seen not a single fort or military camp. Give me five legions and I'll occupy the whole peninsula in a single summer."

"That part is easily done," Marcus said. "But what would we have to hold it against? We must learn about Carthaginian military strength. For all we know they can have a vast army here within days. We've heard that Sicily is heavily garrisoned, and it isn't far."

"Let's have a look at the harbor," Norbanus suggested.

"Good idea," Marcus concurred.

They took the broad avenue that led from the agora to the waterfront, and there they stood, all but stupefied with amazement. The tip of the peninsula was the entrance to the fine harbor and even as they arrived, a two-masted grain ship was in the process of rounding its point. It was the largest object they had ever seen afloat, but it was one among many wonders.

"Look!" Norbanus said, face aglow, pointing toward a long, low shape that seemed to be walking across the harbor. It was a war galley under oars, the first they had seen. The long oars moved with a precision that was wonderful to see. Its bronze ram cut the water, sending up a spray of foam. Crouched above the ram, its toes in the foam, was the effigy of a squat, ugly, crouching god or demon. Lining the bulwarks above the rowers were rows of overlapping shields painted with a triangle-and-crescent device. The marines who stood on the deck wore glittering armor. They had seen many drawings of these vessels, but beholding the real thing was a thrilling experience.

"Carthaginian military might at last," Marcus said.

"If paint and gilding win battles," Flaccus said, "we're defeated already." The rest chuckled, assessing the power of the ship with eyes that missed nothing. They traced its path and saw that it was heading toward a low building situated near the mouth of the harbor. Beneath its castellated ramparts were twenty-five openings at the waterline. As they watched, the galley entered one of the openings and disappeared.

"So that's the naval dock," Marcus said. "They have docking for twenty-five such galleys."

"Maybe for more," Flaccus remarked. "Each could be deep enough to hold more than one."

"Let's go have a closer look," Marcus said. As they strolled toward the naval facility, one of the party pointed to a pair of islands just beyond the entrance.

"Forts out there," he said. The islands were heavily fortified and they could just discern the angular forms of catapults atop the walls.

"This place could be hard to crack," Norbanus said. "Just a narrow isthmus connecting it to the mainland, with a strong gate, the approaches by sea well guarded. There may be a harbor chain like the one at—where was it, Flaccus?"

"Rhodes," said the scholar. "If there is one, it should be easy to find. They require large anchor points and heavy machinery to lift and lower."

"Find out," Marcus said. "You can poke around without looking like a spy."

Along the waterfront they heard for the first time many people speaking in the guttural Punic tongue. To their ears, accustomed to Latin and Greek, it was an ugly language. Wandering among the waterfront stalls and taverns, they saw Punic soldiers and sailors. Immediately they noted that the soldiers all conversed in Greek, the sailors in Punic.

"They still rely on mercenaries," Norbanus said with contempt. "Only the navy men are native Carthaginians."

"Some of the soldiers seem to be using the Laconian dialect," Flaccus noted.

"Spartans?" Marcus said. "If so, they've fallen far, to be hired lackeys for Carthage."

"Spartans were hiring themselves out as mercenaries long before our ancestors left Italy," Flaccus said.

Marcus beckoned to Metrobius and the fat teacher came to him. "Metrobius, you know Greek better than any of us. I want you to circulate here, talk with the soldiers, find out where they come from and anything else that might be of use to us."

"You'll have my report this evening, Commander." He walked off and was soon lost in the crowd.

They came to the naval dock and found it to be fortified with its own wall on the landward side, heavily gated and manned by soldiers who wore armor of bronze scales and conical helmets. At their approach, one of the guards called something and a tall man emerged from the interior. He wore a Greek-style cuirass of silvered bronze, its shoulder rings supporting an extravagant purple cape. He was bareheaded, his hair dressed in long, oiled ringlets, his beard square-cut. His complexion was dark, his eyes black, flanking a great beak of a nose that divided his face like the prow of a warship. They did not need to be told from what nation this man hailed. The writings and tales of their great-grandfathers had described this physiognomy in detail: highborn Carthaginian.

"Greetings, sir," Marcus said. "We are a delegation from Rome, and we were just admiring your admirable naval base."

"I know who you are. I've heard the rumors." His Greek was fluent, but so guttural that he sounded as if he were gargling some of the words.

"Might we come inside and tour your facility?" Marcus asked.

"That is forbidden."

"But your governor gave us freedom of the city," Norbanus said.

"It may be his city, but this is my naval base, and it is forbidden for any foreigner not in the service of His Majesty to set foot within any Carthaginian military base."

"You must hold to your duty, of course," Marcus said. "We intended no disrespect."

The man unbent fractionally. "I am Egabal, Commodore

of the Tarentine Gulf and of the Adriatic fleet."

Marcus made the introductions and Egabal looked them over. "I suppose, living in the far north, you've never seen a civilized naval base?"

"Until a few days ago none of us had even looked upon a sea."

"Well, then, there's no harm in your seeing the outside. That much is open to everyone." He strode to the water's edge and leaned on the balustrade, his scarred brown hands making an odd contrast with the polished white marble. He raised one of them and pointed at the great façade of the dock, which curved away from them with its row of gaping tunnels.

"There you see the ship sheds. Inside are all the facilities necessary for fitting out the ships, arming and victualling them. Inside, each of those is long enough to hold three ships at once. If a middling large fleet must abide here, twice that many can be accommodated."

"How is that possible?" Flaccus asked him. "We saw a ship go in a short time ago. There seems to be little leeway on each side. If they are only long enough for three, how do you crowd in three more?"

"Easily. First, three ships go in, prow to stern. They are unloaded and dismasted, then they are hoisted to the ceiling with rope and tackle. Then three more are rowed in to dock beneath them."

"Whole ships hung from the ceiling?" Marcus said, trying to visualize such a thing.

"It is how warships are always stored for the winter. Even the Greeks do it, and they were never the sailors we are."

So, Marcus thought, 150 ships constituted a middling sized fleet, unless this man was lying or exaggerating. "It is a magnificent establishment."

Egabal shrugged. "It's not much compared to the great naval harbor of Carthage, but it's impressive to barbarian eyes." The Romans remained stone-faced, merely filing the small insult away as one more offense for which Carthage must one day be made to pay.

That evening, after a sumptuous dinner at the palace, they heard Metrobius's report.

"Many of the soldiers are Greeks, almost all of the marines. I encountered a number of Argives, a few Athenians and men from the islands and the cities of Magna Graecia, but no Spartans. I learned that all the training officers and drill instructors are Spartan professionals, so the Laconian dialect is the language of the whole army, even among the non-Greeks. The army also includes a great many Spaniards and men of Libya, Numidia and Mauretania, along with Balearics, Sicilians, Corsicans, Sardinians and men from all the islands of the western sea."

"But no Carthaginian ground troops?" Marcus asked.

"They never leave their homeland and are kept in reserve against uprisings by the natives and foreign threats to Carthage herself. The elite of the army is the Sacred Band, which is made up of highborn young Carthaginians."

Norbanus snorted. "Elite! A pack of privileged boys who have never campaigned in foreign lands are the elite of this army?"

"They're probably just the best-dressed," Flaccus said. "Shiny gear and bright plumes always seem to give men a high opinion of themselves. Did you see the purple cloak Egabal wore? Back home only a triumphing general gets to wear such a thing. Here, a navy functionary rates one."

"I am preparing a report for the Senate," Marcus said. "I will include all we've seen and learned, but I have a feeling that the true revelations lie ahead."

"Carthage," Norbanus said, dreamily. "We are going to see the heart of enemy territory with our own eyes! Even our ancestors never had that chance."

"Actually," Flaccus said, "while it sounds like a most in-

teresting trip, I will be more than happy to forego it in order
to stay here in Tarentum and be your liaison—"

"You're going with us, Flaccus," Marcus said. "You're just
afraid to go out on the open sea."

"It's unnatural to go floating about on water like that,"
Flaccus protested. "Neptune did not give us scales and fins."

"You are going with us, Flaccus."

"Very well, Commander," Flaccus sighed.

That same evening, in another part of the palace, Hanno
drafted two letters. The first he dictated to a scribe.

"Begin with all the usual salutations to His Majesty," he
told the old man who sat at his feet cross-legged, a writing
table on his lap, pens and pots of ink on the floor beside
him. The man scribbled industriously.

"Majesty," Hanno began, "this day your city of Tarentum
was visited by a most unexpected apparition—a delegation
of Romans! I assure Your Majesty that your servant has not
taken leave of his wits. It seems that the rumors of a state
in the north founded by the Roman exiles are true. Not only
that, but these latter-day Romans have prospered beyond
expectation. They have retained some of their martial organization and I believe that Your Majesty may find them
to be of some use in your most justified and holy war against
the decadent Ptolemies of Egypt. To this end, I shall within
a few days place these Romans on a trusty ship and dispatch
them to the capital where they may afford you some amusement as well as provide a martial resource. I remain etcetera
etcetera. Close with the usual formulas and make up a copy
fit for royal eyes."

Then he dismissed the scribe and began another letter,
this one written with his own hand.

Most esteemed and worshipful Princess Zarabel, he began. *You
are about to be visited by a delegation of Romans. It seems that
these people are far from expunged from history as we have long
imagined. The far north is a savage place, and for these to have*

*founded a state in that wilderness and made it prosper must mean
that they have lost none of their political and military skills. The
bearing of these men is dignified to an extent that you must see to
appreciate. Impoverished and downtrodden states do not produce such
men.*

*Their leader is one Scipio, a name we know from history. His
second in command is named Norbanus, and I detect both envy and
ambition in this man. He is resentful of his inferior position. Such
rivalry we know to be the bane of republics, and useful for us. For
many years the world of the Middle Sea has lain in uneasy balance,
with the Barcas, the Ptolemies and the Seleucids contending for
dominance but each unable to seize it. These crude but martial
foreigners are a new factor and they could tip the balance in favor
of one or the other of the royal contenders. The one who makes best
use of them may have a decisive advantage.*

*Perhaps we have been mistaken in our concentration upon the
Middle Sea, acting as if the rest of the world did not exist. I shall
act forthwith to dispatch agents to the north, beyond the alps, and
get an accurate report concerning this Roma Noricum. It is clear
that the Greek merchants who trade to the north have been con-
cealing much from us. I will interrogate such of these persons as I
can find with utmost rigor.*

*You, Lady of the Moon, Light of Tanit, are an unparalleled
judge of men. I know that, once you have had an opportunity to
assess them, you will read their hearts as you read the stars and
the sacred waters of Tanit. This, I feel certain, is an opportunity
that must be seized with the utmost resolution.*

*I remain your most loyal servant, Princess Zarabel, shadow of
Our Lady upon Earth.*

He finished the letter with a few more flourishes, rolled
the parchment and placed it in a bronze tube. This he capped
and sealed with melted lead, pressing a special seal into the
soft metal. At his call a man entered the room and prostrated
himself. The newcomer was a man of middle years, dressed
in a short tunic and a pointed blue cap. His skin was burned

dark and his face was seamed like old leather.

"You are to deliver this to the Princess Zarabel at once. Take my fastest cutter and leave tonight. Her reward and mine will be, as always, most generous."

The man stretched out a hand and took the tube, then he knocked his brow upon the floor. "I am your servant, Lord. None is more swift, none more loyal. The king's men will never know that I am in Carthage, they will never know that I have left."

"See that it is so. Go now." When the man had left, Hanno called for wine. He needed it. This had been a most momentous day, perhaps one of those rare days that influenced all that followed, and he gave thanks to the goddess and the other Baalim that these men had appeared at Tarentum, and not at one of the other port towns. This circumstance allowed him to give the princess some forewarning. In the murderous intriguing of the Carthaginian court, such preparation could mean the difference between ascendancy and failure, between life and death.

His own position was now most precarious. Should the recipient of the first letter learn of the existence of the second, more detailed and perceptive letter, the order for Hanno's death would arrive on the next ship from Carthage. Like many other Punic nobles, Hanno kept a selection of poisons handy against just such an eventuality. Of course, the king's officers were highly skilled at dissembling, displaying the utmost friendliness and goodwill to mask their intentions.

Life, Hanno reflected, was a chancy thing at all levels. If one aimed for the most exalted goals, the cross always waited at the heights.

CHAPTER SIX

THE SEA WAS AN ALIEN WORLD. THE ROMANS HAD ample experience of great rivers and lakes, but this was something beyond their imaginings. The seeming limitlessness of the water, its rolling swells, its strange, salty, fecund smell, all unsettled them and made it difficult to maintain their Roman gravitas. To keep up their spirits, Metrobius recited from the Odyssey, with its thrilling seagoing passages, trying to reassure them that sailing upon the sea was a natural part of the nobleman's heritage. All this unfolded to the great amusement of the sailors, who took the usual seaman's delight at the distress of landlubbers forced to take to the great waters.

Before setting out, Marcus had made a generous sacrifice to Neptune, petitioning him for a safe and favorable voyage. This god was almost forgotten by the Romans, who had been landlocked for several generations, but their augur knew enough of the ceremony to carry it off. Tarentum had no native temple of Neptune, but its temple of Poseidon

was a splendid one, and the Romans had long since acknowledged the equivalency of the Greek Olympians and the native Italian deities. They had been awed by the fabulous
image of the blue-haired god standing in his scallop-shell
chariot drawn by hippogriffs, his trident held aloft to pro-
claim his mastery over all the regions touched by his waters.

The ship was a Carthaginian war galley much like the
one they had seen in the harbor at Tarentum. It was not one
of the great three-banked triremes, but a single-banked vessel designed for coastal patrolling and pirate hunting. Beneath the image of the grotesque god, its small ram, shaped
like a boar's head, was more a gesture of defiance than a
serious weapon. Its real armament was a battery of ballistas
and catapults ranged along the bulwarks above the rowing
benches, and the weapons of the marines.

Despite their dread of the waves and their queasy stom-
achs, the Romans were fascinated by these weapons and
spent many hours examining them. The skipper, a Greek
professional named Ilas, was not reluctant to demonstrate
the machines to his strange passengers.

"This here," he said in the now-familiar Laconian Greek,
"is your man-killer." He slapped a hand on one of the swivel-
mounted weapons. It looked like a crossbow, but the bow,
instead of being a single piece of wood, was made of a pair
of straight limbs mounted in a frame equipped with thick,
twisted ropes. The limbs were thrust through the ropes,
which provided the power of the weapon.

At Ilas's barked order, three marines sprang to the machine. Two of them worked cranks to tighten the ropes
while another opened a chest and removed a short, thick
javelin. Its point was shod with a heavy iron point, its tapered tail equipped with three vanes made of thin, hard
leather trimmed in the shape of an arrow's feathers.

The ropes were tightened in moments amid an odd,
rhythmic clicking of ratchets. The two marines then seized

a pair of cranks at the back of the machine and drew back
the ropelike bowstring, seizing it at full draw with a clawed
device. The third marine laid the javelin in a trough before
the string and stood by.

"Go ahead," Ilas said to Marcus. "Just pull back on that
lever."

Marcus seized the ornate bronze bar that protruded vertically from the clawed string holder. It seemed to vibrate
under his touch and he could hear a faint creaking from the
twisted ropes. Even at rest, he could feel the harnessed power
of the machine. It was something new and fascinating to
him.

He pulled back on the lever and the Romans jerked in-
voluntarily at the loud report of the released arms slamming
into the padded posts that restrained them. The javelin shot
from the machine with unimaginable force, almost invisible
as it sped away in a low arc, spinning as it flew, dwindling
to a black dot in moments, finally disappearing from view.
If it raised a splash when it hit the water, it was too distant
for them to see.

The Romans were awed, but Norbanus said, "That's a lot
of noise and trouble to kill a single man."

Ilas grinned. "I've seen a single ballista bolt go through
three men. That happens when they're crowded together, the
way they usually are on a ship's deck. Or," he added, "when
they're in a tight battle formation on land. Besides, it works
on a man's mind, knowing that his shield and armor are no
protection at all. It's like standing stark naked beneath an
arrow storm. It can break an enemy's spirit before the armies
or ships ever close to sword range."

"A machine like this," Marcus said, "has the power of
many men."

"Still," Norbanus said, "it's better to have many men."

"Carthage has men by the myriad," Ilas told them, "and

many, many machines like this. Come, I'll show you how a catapult works."

This was another machine powered by twisted ropes, with a vertically working arm terminating in a basket of wrought iron bars. As the marines worked a windlass to crank back the arm, Marcus mused upon the sensation he had felt in shooting the ballista, a sensation he could not have explained to the others. Holding the release lever, pulling it back, letting the javelin fly with such tremendous violence, had filled him with a sense of power such as he had never felt before. He could imagine how much greater the sensation must be operating the machine against a live enemy.

When the arm was fully drawn back, it lay almost horizontal and a marine dropped a missile into the basket.

"The catapult launches at a higher trajectory," Ilas explained. "That means you can hurl heavy stones onto your enemy's deck, or over his walls. And you aren't limited to stones for ammunition. You can also use incendiaries like these." The missile in the basket appeared to be a spherical wad of tarry tow. A marine touched a small torch to it and red flames began to crawl over its surface, the dense smoke releasing a pungent smell.

"She's ready now," Ilas said. "Who wants to do the honors this time?"

The other Romans seemed reluctant, regarding the machine with some distaste. Marcus stepped forward again. The release mechanism was operated this time by a cord. He took it from the marine's hand and pulled back. This time they were prepared for the noise, but they were astonished by the display. As it flew through the air, the modestly flaming ball of pitch and tow blossomed into a spectacular fireball. It arched high, then plummeted to the water below, disappearing in an instant, leaving behind only a trail of smoke. A few moments later the sound of the splash and hiss came to them across a hundred paces of water.

"The pitch doesn't just burn," Ilas informed them. "It sticks. If one hits your deck or mast or bulwark, your only hope is to scrape it away with an iron shovel and toss it overboard."

"What's the advantage?" Norbanus asked. "Don't your enemies have these weapons?"

"Some of them do," Ilas said. "But we use them better. That's why these marines step so lively. They drill on the war machines every day of their lives."

The Romans nodded understanding. They understood the value of drill and discipline.

The ship carried a complement of twenty marines, and these were conventionally equipped. To Roman eyes, their armor was strangely old-fashioned, like that of warriors depicted on old Greek vases or painted on porticoes. Each wore a rigid bronze cuirass and a horsehair-crested helmet. Their round shields were also made of bronze and were much smaller than those used by the legions. They wore neither greaves nor footwear. Their arms were short spears, curved swords and bows. Each marine was an archer.

In the evenings, the Romans gathered on the foredeck and discussed what they had learned and what should go into the report to the Senate. Conversing only in Latin, they could speak their minds without fear of being overheard by eavesdroppers.

"We've learned one invaluable lesson," said Flaccus on the evening after the war machine demonstration. "When Rome builds a fleet, every ship is to be equipped with plenty of iron shovels. Can you imagine being on one of these things when it catches fire? First they build them out of kindling, then they soak them in pitch so that they'll burn even better." He gave an exaggerated shiver at the concept.

They had been discussing the concept of building a Roman fleet since the start of the voyage. Greatly as they disliked the idea of seafaring, they understood that, to defeat

Carthage, Rome would have to become a sea power. It was a daunting prospect, but their ancestors had accomplished it.

The story had it that, at the outset of the first war with Carthage, a Carthaginian galley had washed ashore in a storm. The Senate had sent a commission to study it, and many copies were built. Rowing benches were built on shore to train rowers, and then the new crews practiced maneuvering in sheltered harbors. When they were confident enough, they had taken to the open sea.

The Romans were inexperienced with the sort of sea maneuvering at which the Carthaginians and their Greek hirelings excelled, so they did not even try to compete in this arena. Instead, they invented a new boarding device called the "crow." This was a heavy boarding plank hinged to a turntable on the deck, held almost upright by a crane. When a Roman ship closed with an enemy, the plank was swung over the other ship and dropped. The beak of the crow was a stout bronze spike that sank into the enemy's deck, effectively nailing the ships together. Then the Romans crossed on the plank to engage the enemy in the sort of close-quarters combat at which Romans were peerless. Rome won the naval war by turning sea battles into land battles.

"But what about rowers?" someone asked. "Slaves are useless for combat, and you can't very well ask citizens to do such work."

"That's where the native Italians will get back into our good graces," Marcus said. "They can serve as rowers, with the status of allies and auxilia. When the war is over, they can be rewarded with provisional citizenship, with full citizenship contingent on their good behavior."

"A good plan," Norbanus admitted, "but first you'll have to teach them to be brave."

Their voyage hugged the coast of southern Italy, taking them past Heraclea, Thurii, Croton and others. At nightfall, they put into the nearest port or anchored just offshore. Only during wartime, Ilas told them, did Carthaginian ships risk sailing at night. They crossed the narrow channel between Italy and Sicily and they sailed along the coast of that island, past Acium and Catana until they reached the great city of Syracuse. There the Romans admired the formidable fortifications of the storied city.

"This is where the glory of Athens died," Flaccus sighed. Metrobius nodded sadly and between them they tried to point out all the crucial sites of that famous siege.

"Greeks," Norbanus snorted. "What do you expect when you use amateur leadership? What was Nikias, a cobbler?"

"He was what most of our own leaders are," Flaccus said. "He was a rich man."

They sailed along the coast of the island until they reached the western tip. In the harbor at Lilybaeum, Ilas conferred with some other skippers about sailing conditions. He returned to the ship smiling. "This is where we make the hop across to Africa," he informed them.

"What sort of hop?" Flaccus asked. Something about the sound of the word seemed ominous.

"Up to now we've hugged the coastline and put in every night. From here, we take to the open sea."

"You mean we'll be out of sight of land?" Flaccus all but squeaked.

"Just for a few hours," Ilas assured them. "This is the shortest hop to the African coast in the whole sea. To get there by coastal sailing would mean going up the Italian coast to Liguria, then westward past southern Gaul to Iberia all the way to the Pillars of Herakles, then back east along the Mauretanian and Numidian coasts all the way to Carthage. Take another month or two that way, depending on the weather."

"It's your ship," Marcus said. "When do we depart?"

"At first light tomorrow."

The next morning, just as the eastern horizon began to turn pale, the ship turned its bow to the southwest and the rowers smote the water, raising a spray as the vessel surged forward. By the time the sun was fully up, Sicily was a dark line low on the northeast horizon. Flaccus stared at it longingly.

"Stop looking at that island like a lover at his mistress," Marcus chided. "These foreigners will think we're cowards."

"It's not that I have any fondness for Sicily," Flaccus said. "It's just that I'm afraid that it could be the last dry land I ever see."

Soon they were on open water with no land in sight. Now the Romans discovered a new misery. As the ship climbed the low swells, then dipped into the troughs, its motion became like that of a very slow horse bucking. The Romans took to the rails, helpless with nausea. The sailors were much amused.

About noon a favorable wind sprang up and the rowers shipped oars. The yard was raised up the mast and the sail unfurled. It was a rectangle of heavy Egyptian linen, decorated with the triangle-and-disc of Tanit. It bellied out with the breeze and the ship surged forward. As it did, the vessel began to heel over alarmingly.

"We're capsizing!" Flaccus shouted.

"Where did you learn that word?" Norbanus demanded.

"I think it's in the Odyssey."

"Is this usual?" Marcus asked, gripping a rail to keep his balance.

"Is what usual?" Ilas stood upright, his legs flexing with the motion of the ship.

"Leaning over like this."

"This is nothing. When you look straight up and see nothing but water, that's leaning over."

Flaccus groaned.

By late afternoon Africa was a dark line on the horizon ahead of them.

That night they dropped anchor off Cape Eshmun, the place where the African coast made its closest approach to the European mainland. In the sheltered coastal waters their illness abated, but sleep came late to them, and it was fitful. Welcome as land seemed to them, this was not the familiar land of Noricum, nor their ancestral Italy. This was Africa, the land of their enemy, the heart of the Carthaginian Empire.

At dawn their journey resumed along the northern coast of the cape. Coastal shipping was heavy, with many merchant ships of all sizes cruising the shallow waters. Ilas pointed out Greek and Egyptian vessels, Phoenician, Arabian and Rhodian ships, explaining the subtle differences that distinguished each. He told them that the ugly, squat god who crouched above the ram of every Punic warship was Patechus, the god of terror. The Romans took note of everything.

Every hundred stades along the coast there stood a watchtower, fifty feet high, equipped with tall flagpoles and signaling mirrors and bronze baskets for igniting alarm fires. Upon the inland plain they saw many villages as well as more substantial towns. To support such a population they knew that the land must be of astonishing fertility. The terrain was low, but all the highest points and the headlands featured fine temples to various gods, both Punic and Greek. Compared to backward, pastoral Italy it was another world.

All around them fishing boats harvested the abundance of the sea. There were craft with nets spread on broad, winglike frames that looked as if they were about to take flight, and heavy boats that dragged bag-shaped nets along the bottom to stir up the creatures that fed there, and boats in teams that stretched floating nets between them. There were boats hauling up traps for crabs and others from which divers went down to pry shellfish from the rocks below.

"So many people for whom the sea is a way of life," Marcus mused. "It's hard to believe."

"Not all of them are naval sailors and merchantmen and fishermen," Flaccus said. "Our captain has mentioned pirates."

"What about them?" Marcus asked the skipper. "Who are these pirates?"

"Sea-banditry has a long tradition," Ilas told them. "You all know the poems of Homer. Even the heroes thought nothing of dropping in on some unsuspecting village, killing all the men, carrying off the women and children, putting the place to the sack and the torch, then sailing off on their merry way. Well, there are still a lot of people living in the age of heroes. They hide up creeks or behind islands, mostly. When a promising merchantman comes along, they run out and loot it. If there are passengers of any value, they're enslaved or held for ransom."

"And Carthage tolerates this?" Norbanus wanted to know.

"Why not? Rome did." Ilas grinned, then shook his head. "In truth, there's no practicable way to patrol the whole sea, because nobody owns it. When the Carthaginian fleet makes the west too hot for them, they just move east and work in Egyptian or Seleucid waters for a while."

"Where do they come from?" Marcus asked.

"The Ligurian coast is an old pirate haven. Cilicia is another. For some, it's their ancestral calling. Others are sailors who've fallen on hard times, or are pressed into a pirate crew. Some just take it up for the fun and adventure and profit."

"Are these ships solitary?" Marcus wanted to know.

"Sometimes. But, more often, there'll be five or six ships together. That's enough to raid a good-sized village. Sometimes they'll get together in big fleets with scores of vessels, and terrorize a whole province for months, until a real navy comes along to break them up."

"'That,'" Marcus said, "is a messy and disorganized situation. It should not be tolerated by a nation that calls itself a sea power."

Ilas nodded sagely. "So it is. You must be sure to tell the Shofet that personally, when you see him."

When they came in sight of Carthage, they did not notice it at first, because they took it to be a part of the landscape. It did not occur to them that anything so immense could be the work of human hands.

The ship rounded a low headland and sailed into a broad expanse of water, which Ilas informed them was the Gulf of Carthage. They looked along the curving shore to its western extremity, which featured a set of oddly regular white cliffs. The vessel cut across the bay, the rowers working tirelessly, until the cliffs loomed large ahead of them and they saw the symmetrical, rectangular cuts, the tops of high buildings far behind them.

Someone gasped. "Those are walls!"

"I was wondering when you'd notice," Ilas said. "Don't feel alone. Only people who've seen Alexandria or Antioch can believe their eyes the first time they set them on Carthage."

Marcus found that his mouth had gone dry. "How high are they?"

"More than two hundred cubits. They're not just walls, they're a whole fortress system. The garrison, armories, beasts and all are housed inside those walls. They're so broad on top that the young bloods of the city race their chariots there, four abreast."

It seemed hard to believe, but there stood the walls and none of the Romans felt inclined to accuse the skipper of exaggeration.

The ship sped for the walls as if it intended to ram them. Its heading took them toward the southern end of the walls,

where a dark arch awaited. As they neared, they could see
that it was a tunnel. The stone surrounding the tunnel entrance was ornately carved, depicting leaves and vines and
flowers with strange, stylized beasts and birds among the
foliage. The arch was surmounted by the image of a deity.
The upper body was that of a woman, but from the waist
down her body was that of a fish, terminating in a broad,
upraised tail. In one hand she held a cornucopia, in the other
a sword.

"Is, ah, is the tunnel wide enough to admit this ship
safely?" Flaccus asked.

"See for yourself," said Ilas, pointing. Two Carthaginian
ships, three-bankers far larger than their vessel, were emerg-
ing from the tunnel, side by side. There was room for another ship or two to either side of them. The sheer size of
the wall had deceived their sense of scale.

They passed beneath the fish-goddess into the dark tunnel, craning their necks to see overhead. Just within the
entrance there was a slot in the ceiling, from which protruded a line of pointed bars.

"Some sort of dropping-gate up there," Norbanus said.
"They want to be able to close this tunnel off if the city is
attacked."

"Who is it they're worried about?" Flaccus wondered.

They came out into daylight again, this time into a perfectly circular harbor, larger than most lakes they had seen,
its periphery consisting entirely of naval docks like the one
they had seen in Tarentum. They tried to count the openings
but were quickly lost. There was an artificial island in the
center of the harbor, likewise perfectly circular. Upon it
stood a huge building, its architecture a combination of
Greek and elements totally unfamiliar to them. All around
it grew stately poplars and cedars, and there were a number
of ships moored to its wharfs, including an ornate naval
cutter.

"Is this a temple to one of the gods of Carthage?" Marcus asked.

"That's the house of the harbormaster," Ilas told them.

"Somebody lives in that?" Flaccus said.

"It's far from the greatest mansion in Carthage," Ilas said. "But this is a very important man, a member of the royal family."

"I could get used to living like that," Norbanus said. Marcus shot him a look. His tone had not been sarcastic.

"You might not like some of the consequences of the job. He's in charge of the naval fleets of Carthage. You see that scaffold?" He pointed to a high platform towering before the great house. A gaunt wooden framework jutted from its top, like an unfinished house. "If there is a naval defeat or disaster, that's where he's crucified, along with the admirals."

"That's what I call incentive," Flaccus said.

Marcus turned to the others and spoke in Latin. "I want a count of those docks before we leave this city. I want a look inside them, too."

CHAPTER SEVEN

ZARABEL WAS CARRIED UP THE STEPS OF THE GREAT
temple of tanit in a golden litter carried by sixteen eunuchs of matched size and color. The high priest, also a eunuch, stood at the top of the stair to greet her. His head was
shaven, his pudgy body wrapped from armpits to ankles in
a gown of the finest Egyptian gauze. He clasped his hands
before his breast and bowed deeply as her litter was set down
upon the broad porch of polished purple marble. Slave girls
drew aside the curtain of golden chain links and the princess
stepped from her conveyance. Her tiny feet were bare, their
soles stained with henna, golden rings encircling each, the
rings connected by fine golden chains to bands of the same
metal encircling her ankles. She wore leggings made of seed
pearls strung into a wide-meshed net that hugged her legs
and complemented the whiteness of her flesh. The gown she
wore was black, its weave so sheer that it looked like smoke.

"Welcome, Moon of Tanit, daughter of Hasdrubal," the

priest fluted. "Welcome to your house, the house of the goddess."

The woman placed her palms together, fingertips touching her chin, and bowed. "Holy Echaz, guardian of the veil, I greet you in the name of the goddess."

This ritual accomplished, she straightened and surveyed the scene from the great porch of the temple. The city of Carthage stretched an incredible distance in all directions. Upon its highest point frowned the Byrsa, the great citadel that contained the Shofet's palace, now more than double the size it had been in the great Hannibal's day. Atop its walls stood the great observatory founded by her grandfather, Hannibal II. Its huge instruments of bronze and crystal gleamed above the parapets like the crown of a god.

Throughout the city, smoke ascended from countless sacrificial fires. The gods had granted Carthage preeminence in the west, but the gods were frighteningly mutable, and their favor had to be bought with constant sacrifice. Fruit and grain, wine and oil and incense, the blood of countless animals went onto their altar fires. The greatest gods demanded human sacrifice. In ordinary times, these human immolations were supplied by the subject peoples, levied like a tax at so many men, women or children per thousand of population.

In the truly terrible times, when famine, pestilence or war threatened the very existence of the Carthage and her empire, the children of citizens went into the fires that burned in the belly of Baal-Hammon, the god sometimes called Moloch. Even the highest nobles were not spared, and demonstrated their devotion to the gods by casting their infants and young children into the fires with their own hands. The gods of Carthage had always been satisfied with these holocausts, and had withdrawn their wrath when their hunger was appeased, and had blessed the city and its empire with matchless power and magnificence.

In every district of the city she could see the colossal images of the gods towering above the rooftops of the houses. Each district and suburb had its own god and these bronze colossi were mounted on huge carriages, so that they could be towed through the streets to meet with one another at the great festivals. They were beautiful or grotesque, animal-headed, horned, fanged, majestic, bestial. They reflected every power for good or evil in the cosmos.

She was a young woman, pale-skinned and black-haired like all the royal family of Carthage. They were the descendants of Hannibal and since his day had married only within the extended Barca family. Her hair was tightly curled and tumbled over her shoulders like black foam. Hazel eyes outlined in kohl dominated her triangular face. Beneath each eye were tattooed three lines of descending dots, the ceremonial tears shed for Adonais. Her mouth was wide, the lips stained deep purple.

She was the high priestess of Tanit, only goddess of the trinity whose other members were Eshmun and Moloch. She ruled this temple and its eunuch priesthood. She was the only surviving sister of the Shofet, Hamilcar II, and between the royal siblings lay a violent hatred.

"Has the incense been delivered?" she asked.

"It has been arriving since midnight, my lady. Do you wish to inspect?"

"Of course."

They passed within the temple, its interior laid out in the Greek style, with a long nave illuminated by a clerestory. Its walls were painted with scenes from the tale of Adonais, who was once the Phrygian Attis, but who over the centuries had entered the cult of Tanit. The paintings depicted his birth from a tree, his youthful infatuation with the chaste goddess, his despairing self-castration and, finally, his death and dismemberment at the tusks of the great boar.

There was no image of the goddess, not even the usual abstract symbols of her ancient cult. Instead, this temple held in its sanctuary the holiest object of Punic religion: the veil of Tanit. Only the eunuch priests could look upon it. Even Zarabel had never seen the veil.

A flight of steps descended to the uppermost of the temple's cellars. Zarabel inhaled rapturously, for this was the storeroom of the aromatics used in the ceremonies and sacrifices of the goddess: myrrh, nard, cardamom, calamus, attar of roses and a hundred other barks, gums, resins, essences and perfumes. Overwhelming all was the scent of the noblest of them, frankincense.

It was this precious substance that an endless chain of slaves carried in hundredweight bags, casting them upon a growing pile while a priest seated at a small desk marked each bag on his tally sheet. The slaves emerged from a tunnel that connected the temple to its dock beside the commercial waterfront. The temple maintained its own fleet of vessels to transport tribute from all the lands of the Empire, as well as to bring in the necessary materials for the service of Tanit.

Of these exotic substances, none was more precious than frankincense. The shrubs that were its source grew in only a few restricted areas of Ethiopia and Arabia Felix, their location closely guarded for centuries by fierce tribes. Every temple of every god in the world demanded frankincense and the greater the god, the more was needed.

"The amount seems extravagant," Echaz commented.

"The Greek Herodotus wrote that at the great feast of Bel in Babylon, one thousand talents of frankincense were burned at his altar. Does Tanit deserve less?" Zarabel took a short curved dagger from her sash and slit open one of the bags. Thrusting a fine-boned hand within, she withdrew a handful of the crystals. The yellow crystals sifted between her fingers, falling in golden strands as she raised the substance to her nostrils. Eyes, nose and fingers told her that it was the finest quality, as ordered. Any man who tried to sell her less held his life cheap.

"Where is the white Ethiopian incense?" she demanded.

"Over there, Princess," piped the accountant. He pointed his stylus toward a neat stack of small wooden chests. The Ethiopian merchants, conscious of the higher value of their product, shipped it only in chests made of the finest cedar from Lebanon. The chests themselves were more valuable than most cargoes. She ordered one opened and a slave brought an iron prybar. Very carefully, so as not to damage the valuable wood, he loosened the boards of one, raising the bronze nails until he could pull them free with his powerful fingers.

Zarabel raised the lid and lifted out some of the translucent white crystals. These would burn more fragrantly, leaving less ash residue, than the yellow sort. They would be cast upon the fires at the opening of the ceremony, and at the most crucial moments of the rites, and at the final invocation.

Following the last porter in the slave-chain came a man dressed in a blue tunic, traditional garb of the Carthaginian merchant marine. He wore boots with pointed upturned toes and there was a long curved dagger thrust beneath his sash. When he saw the princess he swept the high-crowned cap from his head and bowed deeply.

"Light of Tanit, I rejoice in your presence. I live for your service. I kiss your shadow."

"Captain Mahabal," she said, inclining her head slightly. "I see that your voyage was successful."

"Six months ago I sailed from Carthage with six ships and a cargo of goods. I returned with six ships laden with frankincense. It was a successful voyage."

"Well done," she acknowledged.

He bowed even more deeply. "My lady does me too much

honor." He straightened. "I heard a strange rumor as I was overseeing the unloading, my princess."

"What sort of rumor?" she asked. It was not idle conversation. All her servants had instructions to keep her informed concerning events in the empire. She received no intelligence from her brother.

"A warship arrived today from the base at Tarentum. On board were some very strange foreigners. They claim to be a delegation of Romans, come to present their credentials to the Shofet!"

"Romans?" she murmured, releasing the handful of white incense. "How curious."

"Curious?" said Echaz. "I would have said impossible! The Romans are an extinct people."

"They seem to think they are not," Zarabel said. Without another word she strode back to the stairway. When she climbed back into her litter she told the lead bearer, "Take me to the Shofet's palace."

HAMILCAR II, SHOFET OF CARTHAGE, WAS A TALL, wiry man with hair and beard dressed in the Greek fashion. Though he was of the purest Carthaginian blood, like so many kings of the Middle Sea he affected Greek fashions in everything from dress to coinage. For centuries Carthage had struggled with the Greeks for commercial and political domination over the western sea, but in so doing she fell under the Hellenizing influence of her traditional enemy. The priesthood and traditionalists fumed that the Baalim were coming to resemble the Olympians, that the young men were exercising naked in the palaestra, that the poems of Homer were more popular than the ancient tales of the Punic gods and heroes and monster-slayers. All to no avail. Like other peoples of the Middle Sea, the Carthaginians were growing besotted with the vital, invigorating culture of Greece.

It was a good thing for Carthage, Hamilcar mused, that for all their wonderful multiplicity of talents, the Greeks lacked the most important of them. They were political imbeciles, unable to unite for any length of time against a common enemy, unable to form lasting governments. The Greeks treated political life as if it were a contest in the Olympics, with each man, each faction, each city and city-state, each empire contending with all the others for pre-eminence. No sooner would they defeat a foreign enemy than they fell to war among themselves, wiping out all their gains and bleeding themselves white.

Even the empire of Alexander had not put an end to it, although the Macedonians were certainly more militarily talented than their Greek cousins. The successors of Alexander had not been able to hold the empire together and had fallen out among themselves like the Greeks, but at least they had split into a number of sizable, powerful nations and empires ruled by Macedonian-descended dynasties, all of them troublesome to Carthage.

Hamilcar had called a morning meeting of his military counsel to discuss his plans for one of those dynasties, the Ptolemies of Egypt. For centuries Ptolemaic Egypt had lain between Carthage and the Seleucid dynasty that ruled Persia and Asia Minor. The first Ptolemies, descendants of Alexander's general of that name, had been capable rulers, but the line had grown weak and decadent. Now Egypt, incomparably rich and fruitful, presented a tempting target for conquest. The question remained: Who would do the conquering?

The Seleucids of Persia had fought a long series of wars to dispossess the Antigonids of Asia Minor, and now they controlled a vast territory from the Hellespont to the Red Sea, from the Middle Sea to the borders of India: all of the old Persian Empire except for Egypt. The current king, Seleucus V, was now casting covetous eyes upon the kingdom of the Nile. He was being hard-pressed by Parthian invaders from the east, but the spoils of Egypt would give his faltering empire new vigor.

"How stand our preparations?" Hamilcar asked his senior general, Mastanabal. The Shofet sat at his ease on the great throne, made of solid gold and draped with the skins of rare albino lions. His advisors sat before him in two rows facing one another; an even score of the most distinguished men of Carthage.

"Ten myriads are now encamped at Utica and Sicca, undergoing the final stages of training and drill, my Shofet," Mastanabal said. He was a traditionalist who eschewed all foreign influences. His hair and beard were long in the ancient Carthaginian fashion, and when not in military uniform he wore the elaborate robes and jewelry of his station.

"Ten myriads will not be sufficient," Hamilcar said. "Enough to take Egypt, certainly, but not enough to hold it should Antiochus strike. We need more."

"I spoke of the regular troops who will fight as infantry, of course," Mastanabal said. "We have seven wings of Spanish and Gallic cavalry and pledges of up to twenty thousand irregular Libyan cavalry. With our war elephants, our fleet and with the Sacred Band in reserve, we should have more than sufficient forces for the campaign and the conquest."

"We need more," Hamilcar insisted. "I've ordered troops raised in Italy and I am in negotiations with Lysimachus of Macedonia to supply us with phalanxes of pikemen."

"My Shofet," said Hirham, an elderly nobleman, "surely Seleucus is in identical negotiations with Lysimachus as well. You cannot take the field depending upon such aid. Only when the soldiers are here and securely under your command can you count on Macedonian support."

"Of course, of course," Hamilcar said impatiently. "But I must have more troops."

While he listened to his admiral drone on about ships, oarsmen, marines and supplies, he let his mind wander.

He was a king. The ancient title, Shofet, meant "judge," but the shofets of Carthage had been kings in all but name since the first Hannibal. But his empire was built on commerce and the military reputation of Carthage had been in decline for some time. A king who had no reputation as a warrior was an object of contempt. Rivals would feel free to encroach upon his holdings. His great navy was of no avail against the desert tribes to the south and west. Sea power would not deter Antiochus from marching his massive army into Egypt.

A preemptive invasion of Egypt would put a halt to the ambitions of Seleucus and would give pause to the growing menace of Parthia. It would establish Hamilcar II as the greatest king of the known world. Above all, he wanted to be compared favorably with his ancestor Hannibal the Great.

While they were deliberating, a naval messenger arrived and laid a bronze message tube by the Shofet's right hand. Silently, the man withdrew. After a few minutes of pondering, Hamilcar picked up the tube, noted the design on the seal and idly broke it. He withdrew the papyrus and read with growing amusement and puzzlement. When they heard him chuckling, the council turned to see what caused their Shofet such mirth.

"Romans!" he said at last. "Our governor Hanno has sent a delegation of Romans to call on us! What next? Assyrians? Hittites?"

"Can this be?" said Hirham.

"It seems they've been living among the blond-haired barbarians of the north and have founded a state up there in the wilderness. I thought they must have all perished, but it appears that they still live, if these aren't imposters."

"Why would anyone bother to impersonate Romans?" Mastanabal said.

"We shall see," Hamilcar told them. "Hanno says they may afford me some amusement, and if anyone knows about amusement, it's Hanno." The others chuckled dutifully. Tarentum was the sort of place the Barca family sent relatives who were considered unfit for important military commands or governorships.

"Refresh us, Lord Hirham," the Shofet said. "You are an historian. We all know the name, but I confess I know little else about the Romans except that they were our stubborn enemies. What sort of people were these Romans?" Hirham was a tiresome old pedant, but his knowledge of Carthaginian history was comprehensive and he fancied himself the Punic Herodotus, having written many long and boring books on the subject.

"At the time of our first war with them," Hirham said, "they were the lords of most of Italy. They were actually little more than a confederation of tribes that spoke a language called Latin. They had recently established ascendancy over the Samnite people, who spoke a related but differing language. Prior to that time we had numerous treaties with the Romans, involving trade relations, forbidding them our shores south of the Fair Cape, specifying that, should a Roman ship strike our shores due to war or weather, it could carry away no more than was required for repairs or sacrifice to the gods. Likewise, they were not to—"

"Yes, yes," the Shofet broke in, "very erudite. But what sort of people were they?"

"I know they gave us a hard fight," Mastanabal said.

"Decidedly," Hirham concurred. "They were a martial people in a most—unusual way."

This was more like it. "How so?" Hamilcar asked.

"They were not an ever-victorious people like ourselves. They did not cultivate an image of invincibility like the old

Spartans. They could scarcely have done so, considering how many times they were defeated in their early history."

"Then where did their martial renown come from?"

"The Romans had a certain—ah—persistence in prosecuting a war. Unlike other people, they were never demoralized by defeat. Instead, they analyzed what they had done wrong and corrected the error. They did not blame their defeat on the gods or on impiety or on performing some ritual incorrectly. They found out what the mistake was, and they never made that mistake again."

"Most unusual," Hamilcar said, nodding.

"And they learned from their enemies. At first, they were armed like the Greek hoplites with spear and round shield. They found that the long oval shield used by their Samnite foes was better and they made it standard throughout their legions. When they first fought our Spanish troops, they were very impressed with the Spanish short sword and adopted it. Likewise, they adopted the Gallic mail shirt and so forth. Unlike the Greeks they created very little for themselves, but they readily adopted all the best things from their neighbors and even from their enemies.

"They gained great renown from their war with King Pyrrhus of Epirus. He was the greatest general of his day, with the finest army in the world. He defeated the Romans in a number of battles, but at such cost to himself that he was obliged to retire from Italy. After he was gone, the Roman Senate sent a commission to study the excellent fortified camps he had built in southern Italy. The Senate ordered that henceforth all Roman camps were to be constructed on that plan."

"What sort of nation wins by losing?" Mastanabal asked.

"This, perhaps, was the greatest strength of Rome," Hirham said. "The Romans did not believe in myths of invincibility, such as that enjoyed by the Spartans before Leuctra. Defeat, even a catastrophic one, was never more than a temporary setback. If their army was destroyed, they raised another army and made sure that it did not fall prey to the mistake that destroyed the last one. Nor did multiple defeats deter them. Even the great Hannibal, after all his victories, feared that the Romans migh raise one last, formidable army to face him."

"Impressive," said Hamilcar. "What sort of soldiers were they?"

"The legions were made up of property-owning citizens, mostly small farmers, bearing standardized arms and equipment. The better-off men were heavy infantry, the poorer sort light-armed skirmishers. They had few cavalry and those were inferior. Their greatest military strength lay in their discipline. They scorned individual heroics and stressed great cohesion and instant obedience to orders. Your ancestor Hannibal the Great was very impressed by their fine order and discipline."

"And their government?" Hamilcar asked.

"A republic not dissimilar to our own of that time. The duties of government fell upon the wealthiest men, who served at their own expense. Where we had the Hundred, they had a body called the Senate, which was composed of men who had held elective office. At the top, where we in those days had two Shofets, they had two officials called Consuls, each of whom could overrule the other. They did not want too much power concentrated in the hands of one man. The period of office was a single year for all officials, and elections were held annually."

"That sounds cumbersome," Hamilcar remarked.

"So it was," Hirham agreed. "The great families competed vigorously for office and honors, and they subverted each other at every turn. This division of power was probably their greatest weakness. Your ancestor took advantage of it on more than one occasion."

"Yes, I remember," Hamilcar said. "These consuls commanded the army on alternate days, did they not? And did Hannibal not choose to fight the battle of Cannae on a day when he knew the less capable man would be in command?"

Hirham nodded. "No general was ever more wily than Hannibal."

"Well, then," said Hamilcar in high good humor, "so much for the old Romans. Shall we see what their degenerate descendants are like?"

"Begging my Shofet's favor," said Mastanabal. "I have a war to prepare for. May I be excused this 'amusement'?"

"You may not," Hamilcar snapped. "Hanno thinks they may have some military potential for us. He is no Hannibal, but no Barca is an utter fool. You will remain and give me your assessment of these people."

The general touched his breast and bowed. "Of course. I crave my Shofet's pardon."

"Granted." He gestured toward the chamberlain who stood by the door. "Admit these Romans."

The Romans entered the great hall, stone-faced as always when on official business before foreigners. The pose, usually so natural to them, was difficult to maintain on this occasion. Their trek from the naval harbor to the great palace of the Byrsa had been a dreamlike and humbling walk among wonders.

Once past the stunning naval facility they found themselves in a great plaza where it seemed that half the world traded or lounged. They had thought Tarentum to be marvelous, but this great market was itself as large as Tarentum. In its center towered a colossus of bronze, a god fifty feet high with the body of a man, the head, talons and wings of an eagle. It stood upon a four-wheeled bronze base, its lower half smudged with soot and the whole idol reeking of the rendered fat of sacrifices.

The buildings surrounding the vast, open space were immense, some of them temples, others devoted to government service, yet others with no use the Romans could guess. They were magnificent, constructed of colorful marble, bronze-roofed and glittering with precious metals, but there was a disturbing diversity of architectural styles. A typical temple would have a façade sporting Greek columns in the Ionic style, Babylonian construction for its walls and its roof in the shape of an Egyptian pyramid. Everywhere, they saw this jumble of architectural styles, as if the Carthaginians had no style of their own and plundered the world for designs they could use.

The people thronging the plaza were even more diverse and polyglot than the buildings. There were Libyan tribesmen with knotted hair dressed in flowing robes and soot-black Nubians wearing leopard skins, well-groomed Greeks beside towering, austere Ethiopians, Egyptians in black wigs and white kilts bargaining with Jewish merchants who wore striped coats and pointed caps. To their astonishment, the Romans recognized check-trousered Gauls with spiky, lime-washed hair and sweeping mustaches who conversed with tattooed Scythians in Greek. Thracian mercenaries with their hair tied in topknots policed the market, although their only weapons were long hardwood staffs. There were many, many others whose origin could only be guessed at.

As they pressed farther into the city, they encountered a greater density of the native Carthaginian population. They were for the most part a slender people, swarthy of complexion with strongly marked features, their hair and the beards of the men almost uniformly dark. Here, too, many affected Greek fashions, both men and women. The wealthy, of whom the city seemed to have astonishing numbers, were carried about in ornate litters and many of them were obese.

At one point their progress was delayed while a religious procession passed by. Disheveled, bare-breasted women whirled, swinging their snaky hair wildly, beating on tambourines. Men trilled loudly on shrill double pipes while others carried strange objects and images: a basket of pine-cones, an elephant tusk yellow with age, painted all over with mysterious symbols, an enormously fat dog. What deity was being honored, invoked or placated they could not guess. Last of all came a group of naked children whirling earthenware censers at the end of long cords, filling the air with fragrant smoke. When they were gone the Romans proceeded amid a sweet-smelling haze.

Teams of slaves kept the well-paved streets swept and cleaned. The buildings sparkled and in general the standard of cleanliness was higher than the Romans had seen since leaving Noricum. Only the images of the gods, it seemed, were never cleaned. They remained caked with soot, blood and rancid fat. This seemed a startling omission, but they were accustomed to the vagaries of ritual law, of which they themselves had no few.

As they climbed the hill toward the Byrsa, the public and commercial buildings thinned out and gave way to luxurious residences. These multistory mansions, veritable palaces, were almost uniformly of a traditional Punic design, set amid lush gardens, high-walled to keep out intruders, their featureless sides painted red, their roofs of bronze or colorful tile. Fountains jetted high in the gardens, splashing into broad pools. Children played on the grounds watched closely by nurses while the women of the households lounged about in various states of undress.

"I was under the impression," Flaccus commented, "that these eastern people kept their women locked away somewhere and never let them out unless they were covered in layers of clothing."

"It would seem," Marcus said, "that they lost that habit here in Africa. I've never seen such immodest dress."

"It looks as if the higher they are placed, the less they wear," Flaccus said. "The market women were decently covered. The women up here wear little more than jewels. Look, there's one wearing nothing at all except jewelry."

"Don't stare," Marcus chided. "People will think we're undignified."

Near the crest of the hill, beneath the walls of the Byrsa, they paused and surveyed the immense city, its spectacular temples, the immense, oppressive images of the gods, the mind-numbing scale of its walls.

"How can we take back Italy," Norbanus said, "if these people don't want to give it up?"

"There is more to power than mere display," Marcus said, trying to sound unimpressed. "Since we left the harbor, we haven't seen a single armed man."

"That may be a ritual law," Flaccus said, "like Rome used to have."

"You don't build something like this and keep it without plenty of military force," Norbanus pressed on.

"That's what we are here to learn about," Marcus answered. "Let's proceed."

The documents furnished them by Hanno got them past the guard posts of the Byrsa. Here for the first time they met with soldiers: men dressed in ornate armor bearing weapons that looked more ornamental than useful.

The first gate admitted them to a grand courtyard between the fortified wall and the palace. The gate itself was double-leaved, thirty feet high and covered with reliefs describing the exploits of Melkarth, a god-hero who, as nearly as they could decipher the images, was a sort of Punic Hercules. The courtyard formed a sloping garden with many beautiful paths ascending to the palace. Everywhere stood beautiful Greek sculpture, Egyptian sphinxes and obelisks, Assyrian winged lions, exotic trees native to the farthest reaches of the Middle Sea, the Euxine and the Red Sea. Tame deer and peacocks ambled placidly among the plantings while monkeys frolicked among the trees.

"What sort of place is this?" Marcus asked. "What do they use it for?"

"I don't think they use it for anything," Flaccus said. "A garden like this is just to be . . ."—he searched for the right word—"to be enjoyed. The Greeks had groves like this, where people came just to walk and converse and relax."

"Greeks," somebody snorted. "That explains a lot."

To reach the palace they climbed a stair so broad, so high, and so awkwardly proportioned that it had to be a setting for the palace above rather than a practical access. It seemed intended to give the impression that giants, not ordinary mortals, dwelled within the sacred precincts.

At the top of the arduous stair was an open porch the size of a small forum. The few persons upon it were rendered tiny by the scale of the place. They were all splendidly dressed men who had the look of highborn Carthaginians. They looked upon the newcomers with curiosity. The Romans strode across the polished marble pavement as if this were something they did every day.

It seemed to take an incredible amount of time to cross the plaza. They were not accustomed to man-made structures of such size. The monumental door of the palace was flanked by colossi of a seated man. On the red façade were a pair of dragons facing the doorway, executed in relief, their wings and scales and talons executed in multicolored tile, each fabulous beast thirty feet high, striding stiffly on legs that did not bend.

The guards who stood at each side of the doorway were of a scale with the rest. They were the tallest men any of them had ever seen, a pair of seven-foot giants, one white, one black. They wore billowy knee-length trousers and twisted head-cloths that covered the lower part of their faces. Their arms were crossed before their bare chests, resting atop the pommels of swords as tall as an ordinary man.

"Are these for use or are they just for show?" Flaccus muttered.

"Let's walk past them and find out," Marcus said.

When they were within ten paces, the giants moved, crossing their two-handed swords to block the doorway. It was a move they executed like a dance, as if it were more symbolic than warlike. Moments later a man dressed in the most ornate armor they had yet seen emerged from an opening just within the doorway. The swords uncrossed to let him pass, then recrossed behind him.

"Who are you and what is your business?" he demanded in Greek.

"We are a delegation from Roma Noricum," Marcus said. "We have come to meet with your Shofet. By now he has received a letter from Governor Hanno of Tarentum informing him of our arrival. We bear credentials from our government for his examination."

"Yes, the messenger has arrived. You may come inside to await the Shofet's pleasure." At his signal the swords were raised and they passed within.

"Roman officials should not await anyone's pleasure," Norbanus said.

"These barbarians will learn that soon enough," Marcus answered. "Until then, we will abide by their customs." The anteroom they entered was larger than most temples, its walls decorated with engaged pilasters carved in the form of Titans holding up the ceiling with their brawny arms. At the base of each pilaster was a bronze brazier full of flaming hardwood, rendering the interior smoky.

"These people have a fondness for great size," Flaccus noted.

"Unlike the true Greeks," sniffed Metrobius, "the successors of Alexander sought to magnify themselves through grandiose public works: the Colossus at Rhodes, the tomb of King Mausolus at Halicarnassus, the temple of Ephesian

Diana and so forth. They set the style for such tasteless gigantism. It seems the Carthaginians have fallen into this pointless exhibitionism."

"It isn't pointless," Marcus said. "It leaves no doubt in anyone's mind how rich and powerful they are. The point is to make resistance seem absurd."

"There was nothing pointless about those walls we passed through to get into the city," said Norbanus. "Those were fortifications as practical as any we've ever seen, just ten times bigger."

While they conversed in Latin another pair of sword-wielding guards strode through the room to relieve the two at the door. This time they were a pair of matched Ethiopians. As the first pair marched by them in lockstep, Flaccus eyed them.

"That pale one is a Gaul, I'd swear it. Chatti from the look of him."

"He must have been a slave," Marcus commented. "No tattoos, no mark of the torc on his neck. The Shofet must have agents scouring the world to buy seven-footers to man that door."

They were interrupted when the glittering guard captain returned. "It seems you are to enjoy a signal honor. The Shofet deigns to receive you now."

"Well, let's not keep the great man waiting," Marcus said. "Let's go show him what real men look like." The rest followed him, chuckling a little before resuming their stone faces.

CHAPTER EIGHT

T HEY PROCEEDED BETWEEN THE LINES OF COURT-
iers toward the man who sat enthroned on a high dais.
While not seeming to, the Romans assessed the men they
were passing. Some were fat and scented and had the look
of plutocrats. Others were gray-bearded, recognizable as
counselors in any setting. Yet others were more ominous:
hard, scar-faced men whose rich clothing could not disguise
the fact that they were soldiers of long service.

The man on the throne was another pseudo-Greek, handsome and fit but without the marks of hard campaigning on
him. Behind his throne were ranged a line of guards. To
Marcus they looked like some sort of Celt, but of a breed he
did not recognize. Most had dark hair dressed in triple plaits
and they wore richly worked armbands and belts around
their brief white tunics. Each carried a small iron-bossed
wooden shield and a vicious, down-curving, slashing sword
called a falcata. They wore no armor at all. From these and
other signs Marcus guessed that they were Spanish Celts.

Such men had served Carthage for generations.

Ten paces before the throne they stopped and Marcus inclined his head. "In the name of the Senate and people of Rome I greet you, Shofet of Carthage." A pair of guards strode forward, grasped his arms and tried to force him to his knees and looked disconcerted when they were unable to do so. "Tell these men to take their hands off me or face war with Rome."

With a laugh, the Shofet signaled for the men to desist. "They must be Romans in truth! The stories of their high-handedness were not exaggerated." His courtiers looked scandalized but none of them spoke. Hamilcar leaned forward. "Listen to me, Romans. My ancestor cursed your breed and I would only be doing my duty by my gods if I should choose to burn you alive on the altar of Baal-Hammon." He sat back, lounging against the white lion skin. "But that was generations ago, and times change. It pleases me to accept your suit. Show me your credentials."

He signaled for servants to bring chairs. The Romans did not change expression at these mercurial alterations of mood. They understood showmanship and knew how to respond to it. When folding chairs were brought, they sat, arranging their togas in the approved manner while Hamilcar read the documents Marcus presented. They were written on parchment bound within wooden covers. Each left-hand page was written in Latin with the facing page giving a translation in Greek. At the bottom was appended the leaden seal of the Senate.

"It is a bit old-fashioned," Hamilcar pronounced, "but everything seems to be in order." He handed the documents to a gray counselor, who proceeded to examine them closely. Hamilcar's Greek was impeccable, but there was something a bit irregular to his phrasing and vocabulary. Marcus guessed that the language, as used at court, had changed since the time of the Roman emigration. The merchants who sometimes came to Noricum spoke the simplified dialect used for trade.

"We have dealt with few republics," Hamilcar said. "They used to be common around the Middle Sea. Now they are a rarity. Nonetheless, we do not insist upon dealing with a fellow monarch. I am, after all, no more than spokesman for the Hundred, the true ruling body of Carthage."

His courtiers nodded solemnly, retaining their impassive demeanor in the face of this outrageous assertion. Hannibal had ruthlessly purged the ruling classes of Carthage. The Hundred, once a plutocracy of wealthy men holding office through property assessment, was now no more than an advisory council on matters concerning trade. All real power lay with the descendants of Hannibal.

"Our Senate," Marcus said, "desires to reopen trade with the lands of the Middle Sea."

"A laudable goal. And you have come to the right place to begin your mission. Carthage is preeminent on the Middle Sea in all matters involving the sea lanes, both for commercial and for military purposes."

While these preliminaries were carried out, the principals were under close observation. From a passage behind the throne, Princess Zarabel watched the proceedings through an aperture in an elaborate carving. The palace had many such passages and observation points, all of them unknown to her brother the Shofet. Zarabel knew them all intimately. This knowledge was passed down through the high priestesshood of Tanit. The high priestess was always a woman of the Barca family.

She had hurried her bearers through the streets from the great temple to the palace. If anyone had wondered at her abrupt return, they had kept silent about it. From the access in her own chambers she had reached this spy-hole just before the Romans entered. Now she made a study of the delegation, and her assessment was far shrewder than her brother's. He had the blindness of one who considered himself to be all-powerful. She, on the other hand, was revered by multitudes, but in the halls of power she was regarded with suspicion and barely veiled disdain. To keep her position, even to stay alive, she had to be able to read men and use them accordingly.

Like Hanno, she was struck by the kingly bearing of these men. She deduced that this was not a sign of innate superiority, but rather of long schooling in posture and deportment. The old Romans had been enamored of the Greek rhetorical arts, which emphasized stance and gesture as much as speech. This imperious stride and posture must be a development of those arts. Even knowing such a thing, it was still an impressive display.

The leader's arrogant refusal to prostrate himself was likewise impressive, if suicidal. For a moment she bit her lip, afraid that her brother would do something characteristically foolish in the family tradition, and order them all killed. Happily, he seemed more amused than offended. This was probably because he regarded these men as foreign bumpkins who simply knew no better. In this, she knew, he was seriously underestimating them.

The leader's ability to stand unshaken while two strong Spaniards tried to force him down was likewise impressive. Either these men had knees that would not bend, or they were just tough as old boots. She suspected the latter.

The leader, whose name, she learned, was Scipio, was a most impressive figure. He was a young man, but he showed the marks of long experience of warfare, and his overall presence gave the impression of a much older man. His straight, craggy features and coarse, close-cropped dark hair resembled those she had seen on old Roman portrait busts. She looked for the other man Hanno had mentioned in his letter.

She saw him at once. He was another man of distinguished appearance and she could read, by many tiny signs of face and body, that he chafed at his secondary position. This was an ambitious, jealous man. His hair and complexion were fairer than the leader's and she noticed that a number of these men were fairer than Italian natives should be. Either the Roman refugees had taken native wives or concubines, or else local families had risen to prominence. Either explanation was likely, considering what she knew of the old Romans. She was widely read in history, far more so than her brother.

It was interesting to hear their speech. Their pronunciation was a bit strange, and the grammar and syntax were those of a previous age, Greek rhetoric as it was spoken in the age of Demosthenes. The Romans had continued to study texts centuries old, and were unaware of the new speech and literature of Rhodes, Pergamum and the Greek cities of Asia. Somehow, it reinforced the forthrightness of their manner.

Satisfied with her first assessment, she returned to her chambers and called for her body slaves. The hairdresser, cosmetician, custodian of the jewels and mistress of the wardrobe appeared at once. Zarabel gave them her instructions and they set to work preparing her for her next task of the day, which was a delicate one. She needed to make a maximum impact on the visiting Romans, upstaging her brother without angering him so severely that he would order her execution. He had done this more than once. Thus far, he had always relented before the headsman bloodied his sword, but someday he might go through with it.

The hairdresser threaded gem-studded golden rings through her hair while the cosmetician powdered her milky flesh with gold dust. She opened a small box and with ivory tweezers lifted out discs of gold pounded so thin that light shone through them. She applied one to each of the princess's nipples. The warmth of her flesh made them cling like paint.

The wardrobe mistress wrapped a long, narrow band of black silk around her hips, passed it between her legs and knotted it intricately so that it was secure while appearing ready to fall off at any moment. Its long tasseled ends fell before and behind to her ankles.

The eunuch who managed her jewelry inserted a huge ruby in her navel. From childhood her navel had been stretched by ever-larger stones until it would now hold a jewel two inches in diameter. He placed heavy serpent cuffs, bracelets and armlets from her wrists to her shoulders. Last of all, he draped a huge Egyptian collar around her neck. It was intricately made of beads of gold, carnelian, lapis lazuli and pearls. It covered her shoulders and the upper surface of her breasts nearly to the nipples.

"My princess," murmured the cosmetician, "are you certain that this is proper? You are now prepared for seduction, not diplomacy."

Zarabel studied her reflection in the polished silver mirror held by two Nubian slaves. "It is precisely what I need. I must seduce an entire diplomatic mission."

Preceded by guards and trailed by her attendants, Zarabel walked out into a main corridor and proceeded to the throne room. As she passed, soldiers and courtiers bowed deeply while slaves threw themselves onto their faces as if they were trying to blend with the floor. On her right hand and on her left stone titans held up the ceiling, fifty feet overhead. Light streamed in through tiny panes of a hundred colors set in a clerestory. Behind her she could hear a low murmur and she could easily guess its content: Where could the princess be going dressed in such a fashion?

At the door to the throne room she paused. With an effort of will she calmed her heart and put on her hieratical demeanor. Like the Romans, she understood the importance of bravura. She had attired herself like the most expensive whore in the empire. In bearing she would be what she was:

a royal princess and the holiest priestess of the Punic race. At her nod, the guards opened the door and she strode within.

The first thing the Romans noticed was the expression on Hamilcar's face: a near-comical mixture of surprise and distress. They turned to see what had thus stunned the imperturbable Shofet. Then it was their turn to look dumbfounded. Even Roman gravitas was not sufficient to maintain their stone faces.

The woman who strode so superbly into the throne room was not tall, but she had the presence of a colossus. Her slow, measured steps, her erect bearing and the strange posture of her arms: spread to her sides, forearms inclined downward, palms facing forward, were so imposing that they did not notice at first that she was nearly naked. That impression, however, was not slow in coming.

She passed through them without looking left or right, until she halted a few paces before the Shofet. Then she brought her arms up and around gracefully to cross before her bosom and bowed, keeping her legs straight, bending from the hips until her hair brushed the floor. Then she straightened.

"I greet the avatar of Baal-Hammon on Earth, the most exalted Shofet of Carthage." Her voice was low and melodious. The Romans could not understand the Punic words save for the name of the god and "Shofet."

"And I greet the princess Zarabel, priestess of Tanit," Hamilcar responded, having regained his composure. He went on in Greek. "Representatives of Noricum, I present my sister, the princess Zarabel. As you have seen, she is a mistress of the imposing entrance." It did not escape Marcus that the Shofet had said "Noricum," not "Rome."

"In the name of the Senate and the people of Rome," he said, standing and inclining his head toward the unearthly vision, "we greet the Princess Zarabel Barca of Carthage.

Rome reveres all the gods and their sacerdotes."

She turned to face him, her delicate feet seeming scarcely to touch the floor. "The gods of Carthage love the strong," she said enigmatically. "Tanit greets you."

"You may take your place, Sister," Hamilcar said. "Although you are scarcely dressed for the occasion. We are discussing trade relations with these honored envoys."

She looked the Romans over as if evaluating them for the first time. "Trade? I would rather say we should discuss military relations with these martial gentlemen."

"All in good time, Sister," Hamilcar said through gritted teeth. Her use of "we" enraged him, but he would not upbraid her before strangers.

Zarabel took her seat on the second throne. It was a pace behind and a step lower than the Shofet's. It was made of silver and covered with black leopard skins, a lesser beast than the albino lion. At least, she reflected, it was better than sitting on the bare metal. Gooseflesh was hardly regal.

For a while they discussed the possibilities of opening trade relations between north and south, of wine and oil, wool and blond-haired slaves. In time the Shofet grew tired of these things, which were better handled by the Hundred and the trade guilds. He decided it was time to broach the subject that truly interested him.

"In the past," Hamilcar said, "you were renowned for the valor of your legions. Do you still follow the martial practices of your ancestors?"

"The legions still march," Marcus told him. "The order of battle has changed in certain details since the emigration, but the legion remains the basis for our military organization."

"And you have a number of these legions?"

"Sufficient to guard our frontiers and extend our empire as necessary."

The Shofet smiled thinly. It seemed these rustics wanted

to aggrandize their primitive state with the dignity of empire. If so, a little flattery cost nothing. "I see. It occurs to me that we might address the subject of military relations. You may have heard that even now I am making preparations for war. The unprovoked aggression of Egypt has grown intolerable. I am certain that your legions have maintained their ancestral standards of training and discipline."

"You are correct in that," said Marcus.

"Then it seems to me that a few of these legions might be a splendid addition to the forces I have already assembled. We have a standard contract for soldiers and I think you will find it more than generous." He saw the Romans stiffen.

"Roman soldiers are not mercenaries," Marcus said.

"I would hardly suggest that they are," said Hamilcar smoothly. "But a contract is a simple and effective means of laying out the terms of service."

"We know little of contracts, Your Majesty," Marcus said. "We do understand treaties. If you know your history, you know that Rome has always been most meticulous in observing the terms of military alliances. We have never failed an ally in time of need."

"Your reputation in these matters is common knowledge," Hamilcar said, making a mental note to ask Lord Hirham whether the Romans had in fact been reliable allies.

"If you wish," Marcus said, "I can negotiate a treaty of military alliance with Carthage. This, of course, must be submitted to the Senate for ratification."

Hamilcar did not fail to notice the way the eyes of the other Romans shot toward their leader. The one named Norbanus almost sneered. Clearly, Scipio was exceeding his authority. That did not bother him at all. An excuse to repudiate a treaty was always a useful weapon to hold in reserve.

"Perhaps," Zarabel said, "these gentlemen would like a

tour of the walls of Carthage. I think they should find the inspection illuminating."

"An excellent idea," the Shofet said. "Men of martial heritage should not miss such an opportunity."

"Then I shall be their guide," Zarabel said, rising. "It has been too long since the people have seen me."

"I would never deny my subjects such a sight," Hamilcar said. Then, to the Romans: "We will continue our talks this evening. A house will be assigned for your use, one of the finest in the city. Tomorrow there will be a formal banquet in your honor."

"Your Majesty is most generous," Marcus said. "On behalf of the Senate and people of Rome, I thank you. I believe this presages a splendid future for relations between Rome and Carthage."

When the Romans and his sister were gone, Hamilcar beckoned to Lord Hirham. "Were the old Romans such desirable allies?"

"Decidedly," the old counselor said. "They became so expert in the arts of war and were so punctilious in observing the stipulations of their military alliances, that many nations sought treaties with them. They then commonly trumped up a war with their neighbors, knowing that having Rome on their side assured victory. There was, of course, an undesirable concomitant to such an alliance."

"And what was that?"

"Once the Romans were on their allies' soil in military force, they often stayed."

Hamilcar smiled. "Conquest through alliance, eh? Very clever. We have been known to play that game ourselves. Well, these people are not politically sophisticated. They appear to be even more unsophisticated than their barbarous ancestors, in fact. You saw how they gawked at my shameless sister."

Why did she dare to provoke him in such a fashion? Even

as the thought struck him, he knew the answer. Theirs was a power struggle as ancient as Carthage itself. It was a contest between the secular authority of the Shofets and the religious authority of the priests. As he sought to make Baal-Hammon the symbol of the Shofet himself, she exalted the orgiastic cult of Tanit. As he identified Baal-Hammon with the Greek Zeus, she emphasized the traditional nature of Punic religion. She refused to wear a decent Greek peplos, preferring a barbarous display of flesh and jewelry. He was the new, Hellenistic world, she the embodiment of dark, mystical Carthage. And she overlooked no opportunity to advance her power to the detriment of his own.

Sometimes, he thought, it seems a pity that it is forbidden to crucify members of the royal family. The headsman is far too merciful.

Outside the palace, the Roman delegation stood waiting for the litters that would bear them down to the city walls.

"This is not necessary," Marcus protested. "Romans of military age get about on their own feet within a city. Litters are for the elderly."

"But a princess of Carthage cannot allow her feet to touch profane ground," she answered. "And she cannot have her honored guests trailing her on foot like so many servants."

"It seems we are compelled to comply," said Flaccus. She studied the man. He was not as stiff-backed and martial as the others. The one called Norbanus was eyeing her with apparent impassivity but she could feel the lust in his eyes. The leader, the one named Scipio, was better at masking his feelings.

The litters that arrived moments later were designed for displaying their passengers. They had canopies to protect riders from the burning sun of Africa, but there were no curtains. The riders sat in high chairs draped with animal skins, and incense burned in brass pots at the corners of the vehicles. Each litter carried six passengers and was borne by sixteen brawny slaves matched for height and color.

Zarabel stepped onto the lead litter, a conveyance even more luxurious than the rest, carried by sooty Nubians of imposing stature. Her chair was higher than the others, covered with the skin of what appeared to be a white bear. She patted the chair next to her and Marcus took it. Flaccus, Norbanus and two of the others joined them. When all were aboard, the litters were hoisted and carried down the great ceremonial stairway of the palace. Marcus marveled at the skill with which the bearers kept their burdens level while smoothly negotiating the difficult stairs.

Once through the palace gates and in the city proper, the cortege proceeded at a brisk pace along the broad, straight streets. At sight of the royal litter, the crowds thronging the thoroughfares reacted variously. Slaves threw themselves prostrate, ordinary citizens knelt and touched their foreheads to the pavement. Those who looked like nobles or priests bowed stiffly and deeply from the waist. As they passed, the people rose and sang Zarabel's praises, calling the blessings of all the Baalim upon her. The Romans could not understand the words, but the intent was plain.

"This is what she really wants us to see," Flaccus commented in Latin. "Not the walls, but how the people praise her."

"Probably," Marcus answered. "But what I want to see are those walls. Now stick to Greek. It's impolite to use a language the princess cannot understand."

The city was large and splendid, but they were already glutted with the sight of imposing buildings of eclectic architecture. They were well satisfied that Carthage was wealthy and powerful beyond measure. They were more interested in its military preparedness.

When the walls came into view, they did not at first understand what they were seeing. From the sea, the walls had presented a sheer cliff. What they saw before them was more like a mountain cut into titanic steps. It sloped upward and away like the seats of a stadium built for gods. It took them a while to understand that the tiny dots moving along the steps were men and animals. Zarabel glanced sidelong at the Romans. Their frozen faces spoke volumes.

The bearers carried them to a ramp that sloped up the bottommost step. They ascended easily to the first level, where the ramp doubled back and ascended to the next. Each step was wide enough for a column of men to march four abreast. They did not have to estimate, because everywhere they looked, they saw soldiers drilling in exactly this fashion.

"Where are these men quartered when they are not on duty on the wall?" Marcus asked.

"They are quartered right here," the princess answered. "Their barracks are inside the wall itself."

"Inside the wall?" Norbanus marveled. "You mean you've quarried their lodgings in the stone itself?"

"This wall, which my ancestor Hannibal built to replace the old one, was built to accommodate all its defenders: barracks, armories, commissary, everything. There are provisions sufficient to withstand a siege of many years and an abundance of missiles for the engines atop the wall. There are stables—"

"Stables?" Norbanus interrupted. "Here?"

She smiled. "Well, you will see for yourselves."

They came to the fourth level. This one was five or six times as broad as the others. The princess spoke to the bearers and they turned northward along this level. It was studded with broad wooden doors giving access into the interior of the wall. Amid a clatter of hooves, a band of cavalry rode toward them. At sight of the royal conveyance their officer halted his men and all dismounted and knelt as the cortege passed. These men wore no armor, only white tunics. Their hair was knotted into many short braids and each man carried across his back a quiver of javelins.

"These are Libyan irregular cavalry," Zarabel told them. "We have multitudes of them."

The Romans had small regard for cavalry, which they considered useful for little except scouting, skirmishing and chasing down a fleeing enemy after the battle. The walls were another matter. The Romans were past masters of great engineering feats, but the scale of these walls was staggering. The thought of the amount of labor and resources demanded by the project numbed the mind.

Zarabel called a halt before a row of wooden doors and pointed to an inscription carved above them in archaic Phoenician. "This is stable number 47." At her signal the doors were opened and they were carried inside. Instantly, the atmosphere was redolent of horses. Stalls stretched far into the interior and they were carried past huge bins full of hay and grain. Slaves wearing white loincloths carried out baskets of manure while others curried and groomed the multitude of horses. To their astonishment, they came to a long stone ditch that carried a stream of fresh water.

"Where do you get fresh water so near the sea?" Marcus asked.

"The great aqueduct carries fresh water in abundance from the inland mountains," she answered. Marcus made a mental note to inspect this aqueduct.

"And this stable is one of forty-seven?" Norbanus asked. "It's almost as big as the stable of the Great Circus at home."

"One of fifty. Each accommodates one thousand horses, constituting five myriads of cavalry. Of course, there are stables for other beasts as well."

They went back outside and proceeded up a ramp to another broad level. Here the wooden doors were far larger and the Romans wondered at this. Then one of the doors opened and an immense beast ambled out, larger than any animal they had ever seen—gray, huge-eared, with a long nose like a great serpent and fierce white tusks banded with iron and decorated with gilding. The Romans gasped and stared.

"Easy there," Marcus chided. "King Pyrrhus had elephants and our men had no trouble dealing with them." Despite his words Marcus was shaken. It was like seeing creatures from an ancient myth.

"But what marvelous beasts!" Flaccus said. "How many do you have?"

"There are usually twenty in each stable," Zarabel said, as animal after animal followed the first, a man straddling the neck of each, controlling his huge mount with a goad. "As you can see, the number fluctuates." The Romans laughed nervously as a miniature copy of the great animals, no larger than a newborn calf, came out, walking close to its mother's side. To the Roman's great astonishment the elephants were arranged in a line facing them and, at a rider's call, knelt on their forelegs, trunks raised in a salute. Zarabel nodded graciously. "Finely done," she commended.

They were shown accommodations for camels, another exotic beast, commonplace mules and oxen, even great stone barns for sacrificial animals, of which the Carthaginian gods needed great numbers as well as variety. They saw antelopes, apes and ibexes, peacocks and flamingoes, zebras, even crocodiles, all of them destined to bleed and burn on the altars of the Baalim.

After the menagerie, they were finally carried to the top of the wall. It was, as they had been told, wide enough for chariots to race four abreast. As on the lower levels men drilled and the Romans examined them closely. There were men of many nations: Gauls and Iberians, Africans of many types, men armed with bows, spearmen, slingers from the Balearic Islands, Greek mercenaries from a score of cities and islands, Sicilian levies with large shields and short swords, desert men in flowing robes with swords shaped like sickles, men armed with axes and men armed with clubs. It seemed incredible to the Romans that anyone could coordinate such an army. But people who could build such fortifications were probably up to the task.

"May I ask, princess," Marcus said, "where the Carthaginian troops might be?"

"They are quartered elsewhere. Here on the wall the only men of Carthage are the commanding officers. Now I think you would like to inspect the war engines."

"I was wondering about those," he admitted. Above the rampart at the seaward side of the wall towered many intricate devices of wood and metal, each standing upon its own platform. The stone-throwers were easy enough to recognize, but there were others more mysterious: derricklike devices from which were suspended gigantic logs bristling with spikes, hulking structures that seemed to consist of tanks and spouts, apparently for projecting liquids, even broad, parabolic discs of polished bronze mounted on swivels.

Zarabel pointed at one of the spiky logs. "These are called 'ship-killers,' for obvious reasons. They can be swung out over the walls to drop on any enemy ship that strays too near. The stone-throwers can destroy them from longer range. The fire-projectors can spray burning fluids for great distances."

"What are those?" Marcus asked, pointing at one of the great mirrors. "Are they some sort of signaling devices?"

She smiled. "Those are burning-mirrors. They concentrate the rays of the sun on enemy ships and set them afire." She enjoyed the skeptical expressions of her guests. "It is quite true. I can arrange a demonstration sometime, if you wish."

"I would like to see that very much," Marcus said. He was beginning to get a feeling for these Carthaginians, and he was certain that they had not devised these bizarre machines for themselves. "Where did such things come from?"

"They were first built by Archimedes," she said.

"Archimedes?" Flaccus said. "Do you mean the mathematician of Syracuse?"

"The same," she said. "He cost us terrible losses when we besieged Syracuse a few years after you Romans left Italy. But it takes more than machines to stop the invincible armies of Carthage. King Hiero and his son Gelon were crucified on the walls of Syracuse."

"And did Archimedes likewise end up on the cross?" Marcus asked, repelled. Romans considered crucifixion fit only for rebellious slaves, insurrectionists and the lowest of bandits. Conquered kings were decently strangled in privacy, away from the vulgar gaze.

"No, he was carried away by his students in the confusion of the sack. He ended his days at the Museum in Alexandria, I believe."

The princess saw them to their new home, a virtual palace in Megara, the most fashionable district of the city, surrounded by the mansions of the wealthiest families, many of them belonging to members of the Hundred. At the moment they were in no mood to appreciate the luxuries of the place. As soon as the princess had taken her leave, the uproar began.

Norbanus turned on Marcus, snarling. "A treaty! Where did you get the authority to negotiate a treaty with Carthage? Did the Senate name you Dictator while I was looking the other way?"

"Military alliance with Carthage!" spluttered someone. "You'll be charged with treason for this, Scipio!"

"Oh, calm yourselves," Marcus said. "I never heard such a pack of bleating old women."

"Explain your actions," Norbanus demanded.

"In the first place, you all know perfectly well that nothing I do here will be binding on the Senate. I am perfectly qualified to propose a treaty, which they can accept or repudiate or make changes to as they see fit. Whatever Hamilcar thinks, what we do here will be regarded as nothing but preliminary negotiations by the Senate. But think!" Here he gestured urgently. "We have here an opportunity to seize events and mold them!

"When we undertook this mission, we hoped at best for a reconnaissance of Italy, perhaps a chance to make a rough estimate of Carthaginian strength in the area. Today, we have toured the very walls of Carthage! We can describe them to the Senate in detail! A month ago we would have been mad to hope for such a thing! My friends, I tell you that the gods of Rome sit at our shoulders. We must grasp this opportunity they have given us or we will fail the Republic as it has never been failed before."

"But are the legions to become hired swords for Carthage?" Flaccus said.

"We have done well out of military alliances many times before," Marcus said. "What would our ancestors have given for a chance to quarter a few legions within the walls of Carthage itself?"

"It would be dishonorable to form an alliance in anticipation of such a thing," said Lucius Caesar, a very young scion of a very ancient but obscure patrician family.

Marcus smiled. "I believe the Shofet would soon give us ample excuse to turn on him. Treachery is in his blood, and in the blood of Carthage."

"That may well be true," Flaccus said. "In the time of our first war with Carthage the Hundred, with typical parsimony, tried to weasel out of paying their mercenaries in full. The result was a war that nearly destroyed Carthage and inspired many of the African subject cities to revolt. Hannibal's father was hard pressed to put down the insurrection. It was said that Africa ran short of timber, building all the crosses."

"So I think we needn't worry that Hamilcar will observe

scrupulously any treaty he agrees to. He will leave us plenty of room." Marcus turned to look out a broad window that overlooked the great city. "This day we lay the foundations for a policy that will bring Carthage to her knees."

CHAPTER NINE

"BUT THOSE WALLS!" NORBANUS SAID. "THEY ARE not like the work of men, not even of giants. They are like the work of gods!" He spoke to a group of his fellow Romans on the broad terrace of their house in Megara. They lounged at their ease while servants brought them cool drinks. Marcus Scipio was closeted with Metrobius and Ahenobarbus, going over the wording of the treaties they had been hammering out, laboriously, for days.

"Nonsense," said Flaccus, who was more at ease in these luxurious surroundings than the others. "They are just stone, and not all that well cut, if you ask me. What do you need to construct such walls?" He held up three fingers and folded them as he enumerated. "Just three things: stone, slaves and time. It's said that the Egyptians piled up stone even higher, just to bury their kings. We could have built walls like that, but Rome has never depended on walls." Most nodded and said that this was true.

"But what does this say about the people who built those

walls?" Norbanus pressed on. "Their power, their wealth, are all on a scale we have never seen before. We saw a part of the city garrison. Carthage has a whole empire to defend. Her armies must be vast."

"Hirelings," snorted a hard-faced senator named Flavius Ahala. "When have legionaries ever feared hired troops, no matter how numerous? Steel in the hands of enemies never conquered us. It's the steel in the spines of citizen soldiers that won our conquests." This was richly applauded.

"Hannibal beat us with such soldiers," Norbanus pointed out.

"But he was Hannibal," Flavius protested. In the Roman mind, the great Carthaginian general had become something more than human. He was not to be compared with ordinary mortals.

"Has anyone seen these Carthaginian soldiers?" Flaccus asked. "They are supposed to be the elite of the army, the strategic reserve. I have my doubts that they even exist."

"I agree," said Flavius. "From what I've been able to learn, no war has approached the walls of Carthage for a hundred years. If the citizen troops are not sent out to fight on the frontiers, what experience can they have? It takes more than plumes and gilded armor and maneuvers on the drill field to make soldiers."

"You are saying that to reassure yourselves," Norbanus said. "We have no navy and don't even know how to sail a ship. How are we going to challenge such an empire?"

"Let's concentrate on taking back the Seven Hills and securing Italy," Flavius said. "Time enough later to think about challenging Carthage for the rest of the world."

Norbanus nodded, satisfied. Scipio was moving far too fast for his taste. It was typically arrogant, old-family pride. As if having the name of an ancient hero was enough to make a man a natural leader in a world far different than that of the old Republic. The old families took the highest offices, commands and priesthoods as if they were their natural right.

It was as if, he thought, men whose great-grandfathers were Germanic and Gallic chieftains were somehow inferior. Yet, who were the ancestors of those patricians? By their own account, Rome was founded by a band of homeless bandits who found a few squalid villages on some hills near the Tiber, took them, stole women from a neighboring town and set themselves up as kings. What were they compared with a German lord over thousands of tribesmen who could trace his lineage back to Wodens himself?

The blood in my veins is as good as any of theirs, he thought, even if his name is Scipio. We accepted their language, we took their excellent law code and military organization, we even wear their toga. But we are still free warriors and better than any pack of jumped-up Italian farmers.

"This man Hamilcar," Flavius said. "He looks like no sort of king or general. And his sister looks more like a whore than a priestess."

"I was rather taken with her, myself," Flaccus said.

Norbanus laughed. "Flavius, your idea of a priestess is a vestal virgin. The gods of Carthage are different."

"They are obscenities!" said Brutus the augur. "These barbarians practice human sacrifice! They are no better than a pack of druids."

"How shocking," Norbanus drawled. For reasons that escaped him, old-fashioned Romans were horrified by the idea of human sacrifice, although their munera were nothing but sacrifices in which one man had a chance of living by fighting well. And he did not share their disdain for Princess Zarabel.

The woman intrigued him in a way that no other had. Roman women of his class were raised to be virtuous wives and one of them who so much as spoke her mind in public created a scandal. They took no part in political life. They were always, needless to say, decently clad.

Zarabel was a creature alien to the Romans. She spoke and acted as if on equal terms with men. She gave her brother only the most formal deference. She flaunted her body without shame. She presided over a cult that was incomprehensible to the Romans. They understood the concepts of sacrifice and cosmic power, but the Punic gods competed with one another in a way that the Roman gods did not. There was some sort of power struggle between Tanit and Baal-Hammon, and this was reflected in the rivalry of the brother and sister who were scions of the Barca family.

As near as Norbanus could understand it, Hamilcar strove to make Baal-Hammon paramount god of Carthage, as Zeus was king among the Olympians. To this end he tried to identify his god with Zeus, going so far as to portray him in new statues in the traditional poses and garb of Zeus.

Zarabel, in contrast, fought the tendency to identify Tanit with Aphrodite. She played upon the innate conservatism of the people, telling them that alien gods were undermining their ancient traditions, their unique relationship with the gods. The Carthaginians were happy to use foreign soldiers, to adopt the architecture and arts of other nations, but their gods were unique and their worship was not to be adulterated with the practices and forms of other religions.

It was a clever ploy, and Norbanus was not certain how much was her own piety, how much cold and cynical calculation. Certainly, it made sense to resist the Hellenism that had swept the whole world. After all, Carthage had struggled against Greek influence in the West for centuries. It would be senseless if, after all that, the Greeks were to conquer by peaceful means. Besides, everyone knew that Greek influence sapped the strength of a nation, made it softer and less warlike. These were things to be resisted.

But more than all that was the woman herself. She was beautiful; there could be no denying that. She was wealthy and powerful in a fashion that no Roman consul could boast. She was alluring and clearly, he thought, in need of a strong man. Just as clearly, she had bestowed more of her attention on him than on the other Romans. She was, he reflected, a woman with an unerring eye for a superior man.

ZARABEL SAT ENTHRONED IN THE GREAT TEMPLE OF Tanit. Like her brother's throne room, hers was spacious and lavish. Unlike his, it held no courtiers, no soldiers or merchant chiefs. The men, women and eunuchs who sat before her in reverent silence were the sacerdotes of the Punic gods. In the fore were the priests and priestesses of the greatest gods: Tanit, Melkarth, and Eshmun. Behind them sat the devotees of the many lesser gods. Only one deity was unrepresented: Baal-Hammon, commonly called Moloch.

There were great matters to discuss, but these procedures had to follow ancient forms. The sacerdotes of each of the gods must first report the signs and omens seen since the last gathering. No decisions could be taken until the attitude of the gods was assessed. First to speak was the high eunuch-priest of Tanit.

"Holiness," he began, "we are most distressed by the signs. For the last month the Moon, sacred heavenly emblem of Tanit, has displayed a reddish color most uncommon for this time of year. Her sacred geese have been restless and have often refused to eat. Clearly, the goddess is displeased. We have offended her in some fashion."

Next the high priest of Eshmun stood. He was a tall, heavy man with uncut hair, his eyebrows emphasized with kohl to form a pair of swooping wings that met in an inverted point between his eyes. "My princess, the earth is in turmoil. The ground shook at Siccas, many buildings fell, many were killed. We anticipate a scanty harvest and wild beasts encroach on the outlying villages. Lions have never been so numerous." These were not seen as natural occurrences. There were no natural occurrences. There was only the will and whim of the gods.

A priestess rose. She wore a green gown in the form of fish scales and on her head was a fish headdress. She represented Dagon, once a minor Canaanite sea god, now exalted in Carthage. "My goddess-on-Earth, great monsters have been sighted at sea, dragons of the deep never seen in the Middle Sea before. Something has caused them to enter the Pillars of Melkarth—"

And so it went, one consecrated personage after another reporting ominous signs: fiery dragons seen hurtling through the night skies, birds, fish, beasts behaving unnaturally, monstrous births among humans and animals, floods and droughts and earthquakes, terrible storms and disappearances of ships in fine weather. Soldiers manning a border fort saw ghostly armies parading by in bright sunlight. A pure white elephant was born in the stables at New Carthage in Spain, and white was the color of death.

"Enough," Zarabel said. "It is plain that the gods are angry. But at whom?"

"Majesty," said the high priest of Eshmun, this time employing her title as princess, "Carthage lies now at the height of her power, as established by your ancestor Hannibal the Great. We are unchallenged save by Egypt, our prosperity is great." He paused, gazed around at the many sacerdotes in their holy regalia. "But this is a passing trifle, a matter of glitter and vanity. What are these things to the immortal gods? They have raised us high, and they can plunge us downward even more swiftly. We are powerless before them, and we can purchase their favor only with loyalty, devotion and sacrifice.

"In recent years," he went on in a more forceful voice,

"we have fallen from the true religion. We have given our ancient gods the futile trappings of the Greek gods, who are nothing more than outsized humans!" There were cries of agreement and curses of execration against the alien gods. "My princess, you have resisted this valiantly and have kept the worship of Tanit pure, may she bless you forever. But I fear that your efforts have not been enough. The gods of Carthage are jealous. They will not share their glory with contemptible Greek half-gods. They require proof of our unswerving devotion, or I fear that they will destroy Carthage in their wrath."

"What proof of devotion must they have?" she demanded, knowing perfectly well. Her face was painted to resemble a mask and her silver crown bore a great crescent moon above her brow, its horns pointing upward. From throat to ankle she was draped in a black robe spangled with silver stars and moons.

"Majesty," said the high eunuch of Tanit, "the gods must have a tophet."

It was what she had expected. The tophet was the most solemn of Carthaginian rites. It was the ultimate affirmation of their devotion to the gods. When the gods had shown their disfavor through famine or plague or military catastrophe, the greatest people of Carthage, the wealthy, the noble, even the royal family, brought their children to the great square where the gigantic images of the gods were assembled. The huge bronze image of Baal-Hammon, now in his aspect as Moloch, glowed from the great fire kindled in his belly. There, amid prayer and wailing and the billowing smoke of tons of frankincense, the noble children of Carthage were cast into the flaming maw of Moloch and were consumed utterly. The sacrifice was followed by a great celebration, for thus was the favor of the gods purchased. No other people were so devoted. No others were willing to make such a sacrifice. Therefore, no others were as powerful, as favored by the gods, as were the Carthaginians.

"I agree," Zarabel said, "but we will need preparation. The people are not ready."

"The people?" cried the priest of Eshmun. "What have they to do with anything? The gods do not ask for a consensus. It is because of such foreign practices that the gods became angry in the first place."

"Nonetheless," she said firmly, "as you have pointed out, the people see their nation and race at the very pinnacle of worldly power and glory. They are not skilled in interpreting the signs, as are we, the servants of the gods. To decree a tophet now would seem to them ingratitude."

"Majesty," said the priestess of Dagon, "we must not allow this state of affairs to continue too long. We could lose the favor of the gods irrevocably."

"I think we need not fear that," Zarabel said. "The people are accustomed to the tophet in times of national disaster. One such looms near even now."

"Your brother's war with Egypt?" said the chief eunuch.

"Precisely. His victory will strengthen the Hellenizing party in Carthage. His defeat will cast them into disgrace. The people will know that he has been defeated because he has displeased the gods."

No one mentioned what was on everyone's minds: that the princess had plans for bringing this defeat about. Even in such a gathering, there were some things best left unsaid.

The priestess of Bes rose. Bes was a minor Babylonian god who, like Dagon, had found a home in Carthage. He had the form of a fat, lion-headed dwarf and was the god of jollity and good times, a protector of travelers and women in childbirth. He was not one of the great and terrible gods, but was much beloved by the populace. "Holy one," she said, "the city is abuzz with talk of the Romans. Are they just men from a remote colony, or are they, too, a sign to us from the gods?"

"They are both," Zarabel said. "Yes, they are men from the remote north, descendants of our ancient enemies. But their appearance at this time, after so many generations, cannot be happenstance. Their ancestors were banished by the greatest and most victorious general ever raised by Carthage. That they should come among us just as an unworthy descendant of that same godlike Shofet seeks to equal his ancestor's glory cannot fail to be significant. The gods have sent them here for a purpose."

She did not have to explain to them what that purpose was: It was to bring low the Shofet and his bastardized, diluted cult, and raise high the cult of Tanit and its priestess. She had her plans already made.

"AMBASSADOR SCIPIO?"

Marcus looked up from his papers to see Zarabel standing in the doorway. He stood and inclined his head respectfully. "Princess. You honor me and Rome." He noted that she had employed a form of address to which he was not fully entitled. He was empowered by the Senate to open diplomatic negotiations, but he had not been given diplomatic rank. "You honor me personally far too much, in fact."

"Oh, I think not. Whatever your Senate thinks, you are a man who seizes the moment. If you are not officially an ambassador, you are one in fact through your own deeds. Any sovereign would rather deal with such a man than with some fat time-server sent out to get him away from court."

Instantly he was on his guard. Why such flattery? Today the princess was wearing one of her less distracting outfits; a neck-to-feet gown of fabulous blue silk. It left her arms bare but they were so plated with gold that the flesh was barely visible. He was sure that the relative modesty of her attire was intended to set him at his ease, just as the outrageously immodest garb she had worn on the first day had been chosen to unsettle the Romans and put them in their place as beings of a lesser order.

"I am about to become a fat time-server myself," he told her. "If I keep attending the banquets you and your brother and the trade associations keep giving in our honor, I'll look like the master of the pearl merchants' guild."

At this she laughed. The merchant chief he had mentioned was among the fattest men in Carthage, the furthest image in the world from the hard, lean Roman. "It would take years of banqueting to do that. I've seen you and your friends exercising every morning on the public drill field. I don't think professional athletes work as hard."

She had been much impressed with the disciplined way the Romans began running on the field before first light, progressing to wrestling and then to weapons practice. From an armorer's shop in the city they had ordered practice shields and weapons and she had learned that these were of double or even triple the weight of real field equipment.

She had been astounded at the ferocity the Romans displayed even in these practice bouts, knocking the wind from one another with the lead-weighted, wooden swords, smashing shield against shield with such violence that men were sometimes thrown backward a dozen paces to land on their backs half-unconscious. They hurled heavy javelins with such force that they often split the four-inch hardwood posts that were used as targets and their aim was unerring. If these were men of the highborn officer class, she thought, what must their legionaries be like?

"I thought you might be interested in a new sort of spectacle this afternoon," she said to him.

"In this city," he said, "my poor head wearies of unending spectacle, but I am game for anything new. What is it?"

"Not something Carthaginian this time. The Egyptian fleet is coming into the harbor. Would you care to come down and see?"

"Decidedly," he said, wondering what this might portend.

As usual, she had brought along one of her huge litters, but this one had room for only two riders. They were carried from the Megara down toward the vast commercial harbor, and as they went, Marcus marveled once again at the wonderful siting of this city. Nearby Utica, another Phoenician colony, was older than Carthage, and nearby Hippo-Zarytus was also a great Punic city, but none of them had the excellent, protected harbor that graced Carthage.

In characteristic fashion, the Carthaginians had improved the natural features of their site with a great seawall and mole, all of them tied into the titanic defenses of the city. Although not as impressive an engineering project as the naval harbor, it was many times larger. Marcus had visited it a number of times, but it always presented a new and lively aspect. Its great plaza was dominated by the outlandish image of Dagon. This deity was depicted with the bearded head and upper body of a man; his lower body that of a fish. He overlooked a scene of unceasing activity and color.

The wharfs were thronged with ships of every nation bringing the world's produce to the greatest city of the west. Everything from foodstuffs to dyes, from ingots of metal to living animals was unloaded in this place. Offshore, anchored vessels waited their turn to moor and unload. Among these smaller vessels were rowed or paddled; the craft of fishermen or the small merchants who sold their wares to the bored crews waiting aboard the anchored vessels.

There were even raftlike boats equipped with cranes. These were salvage vessels, for boats frequently sank in the harbor or its approaches, either from the ravages of their voyages or from a sudden storm in the harbor, for even the finest harbor could not provide complete protection from powerful winds and waves. For this task Carthage had a guild of salvage divers; men like seals who could hold their breaths for a prodigious time. They wore ingenious masks of oiled leather provided with fine lenses of flat-ground mica or crystal.

But on this day even the fascinating sight of the divers drew no one's attention. Coming in through the great harbor entrance, between the huge twin lighthouses that cast columns of smoke high into the heavens, was a line of vessels even more colorful than the ones that sailed from Carthage. They were high prowed and square-sailed, painted in colors of hallucinatory variety and brightness. In the lead was by far the largest vessel Marcus had ever beheld in his admittedly limited experience. He found it difficult to believe that anything so huge could even float, much less move under human guidance. He remarked on this to Zarabel.

"Oh, this is not a great ship," she assured him. "The pleasure-barges of the Ptolemies are the size of towns, with two hulls and decks many stories high. Of course, they are not seagoing vessels, but river craft." She sighed. "In this no one can hope to match them, for no other people have a river as great as the Nile."

"You mean there is something the Carthaginians don't do bigger than anyone else?" he said.

She smiled. "Just this one thing." Then she admitted: "Well, there are others. We don't have a statue as huge as the one at Rhodes, and the lighthouse at Alexandria is even higher than our twin ones. I am told that there are some temples larger than any of ours. You won't see so many marvels in one place, though."

"That I can believe," he said. The line of ships following the huge one seemed endless. "What does the Egyptian fleet bring you?"

"Some of them will carry the products of the interior: black slaves, ivory, feathers of ostrich and other birds, hides of many animals, the animals themselves."

"Have you no access to the interior?" he asked.

She shook her head, making the black hair move in lazy waves over her shoulders. "No. South of here lies a great desert that no one has ever crossed. It is vast. Only Egypt has access, down the river. We send fleets out through the Pillars of Melkarth and south along the coast, but the voyage is long and very hazardous. We lose many sailors to the weather and terrible diseases. It is easier and cheaper to trade with Egypt."

"And what do the other vessels carry?" he wanted to know.

"Most of them bear grain. It is Egypt's biggest export."

"Grain? But the land around you is so fertile. Why do you need to buy imported grain?"

"We sell it. This is as far west as Egyptian ships sail. From here we carry it wherever people need to buy grain. In every year, someone is having a bad harvest. It is not as glamorous as ivory and peacocks, but it is very profitable. Hungry people will trade anything for a handful of wheat."

They watched as the colorful ships dropped anchor in the harbor. A number of the long wharfs were hastily cleared so that at least a portion of the fleet could unload. Crowds thronged the harbor, for this was a considerable spectacle even in Carthage.

Marcus took it all in, but his thoughts were on what the princess had told him, especially the part about Egyptian grain. The glittering, exotic treasures of far lands had their charms, but Romans were at heart farmers. Farmers understood the importance of staple crops. For generations they had traded with Greece for wine and oil. This was something new. From Herodotus and others he had read about the astounding fertility of the Nile valley, but this was solid proof. The river-nation actually produced so great a surplus of grain that it could export vast amounts of it. Most lands were lucky to produce enough for domestic consumption.

This, he thought, could be the key to something great.

Zarabel had them carried to the quay where the flagship of the Egyptian fleet was moored. The slaves bore the litter right up the broad gangplank and set it down on the wooden deck. The ship's officers came running and prostrated themselves on the deck.

Marcus studied the sailors, who looked little different from Greeks, although some of them were darker-skinned than most. Of course, the ruling dynasty of Egypt were Macedonian-Greek, so it stood to reason that their fleet would be manned by men of that famously seafaring land.

"Welcome, Princess!" cried one of the officers, his voice somewhat muffled as his face was pressed to the deck.

"Rise, Admiral," Zarabel said. He and the other officers got to their feet. They wore a version of the traditional Egyptian dress: stiff linen kilts, striped head-cloths and broad pectorals of colorful beads. The admiral's clothing and jewelry were of finer quality than that of the others.

"You have had a successful voyage, I take it?" she said.

"A perfect voyage, Highness. Not a ship lost, no spoilage among the cargo, not even a serious leak in the whole fleet."

"Wonderful! The gods have favored you. We have come to inspect the ship and your cargo."

"It will be my privilege."

With proprietary pride, the admiral displayed his vessel's splendid appointments: luxurious cabins for the officers, a banqueting hall for visiting dignitaries, shrines to Greek and Egyptian gods, with an especially splendid one to Serapis, the Alexandrian god who was patron of the grain fleet. A catwalk down the centerline of the ship took them above the great hold. Marcus could see that this ship was one of the vessels for carrying luxury cargoes. Everywhere he saw marble, alabaster and gold. The air was redolent of perfume, incense and fragrant wood. Baled pelts of rare animals lay everywhere, and great jars of palm wine ballasted the ship.

Zarabel paused to point toward some large but nondescript bales wrapped in linen and bound with rope. "There is one of the greatest treasures of Egypt, Marcus. It isn't colorful, but we would be lost without it."

"What might it be?" he asked.

"Papyrus. It is the only decent writing material in the world, and it is made only in Egypt, from a reed that grows in the Delta and the Nile shallows."

"In Noricum we use parchment made from lamb skins. It lasts forever and can be washed and reused, but it is costly."

The admiral opened chests of books: scrolls in leather covers each labeled by author and work.

"This is another specialty of Egypt," Zarabel explained. "The great library of the museum has the largest collection of manuscripts in the world. It employs armies of copyists and sells the copies abroad."

"A nation that exports books," Marcus said wonderingly. Then he remembered something. "Did you not say that Archimedes fled to the Museum at Alexandria after the fall of Syracuse?"

"I did. Is this significant?"

"Nothing important. It just lodged in my mind." He picked up a scroll, slipped its cover off and unrolled it. It proved to be a copy of *Prometheus the Firebringer* by Aeschylus. The censors had repeatedly forbidden the performance of Greek plays in Noricum. They were felt to be weakening. He mentioned this to the princess and this set off a lively discussion about the emasculating properties of Greek culture. He did not want her thinking about Archimedes.

That evening the Roman party met and discussed their latest discoveries about Carthage, both the city and its empire. They were compiling an impressive study to deliver to the Senate, far more than they had thought they would ever have when they left Noricum.

"Carthage is not enough," Marcus asserted when he had taken all the other reports.

"That is uncommonly enigmatic for a Cornelius Scipio," Flaccus commented. "Ordinarily, you are such a plain-spoken and forthright lot. Rather unimaginative, really. Whatever do you mean?"

"This"—he poked the growing stack of parchments with a finger—"is splendid and I am proud of all of you. But Carthage, imposing as it is, is just one power on the Middle Sea. There are others and we must know about them."

"But Carthage is our ancient enemy," said young Caesar.

"And Carthage shall be dealt with," Marcus said. "But we must not be so focused on revenge that we leave ourselves open to attack by the others."

"The Seleucids are crumbling, so I hear," Norbanus said. "The Parthians will probably crush them soon."

"And will the Parthians prove any less formidable?" Marcus said. "I am told that they are a virile, warlike people of the eastern plains. They are horse-archers of a sort we have never fought before. With the bulk of the old Persian Empire in their hands, might they not be far more formidable than the degenerate descendants of Seleucus?"

"In another generation or two, very probably," Norbanus answered in a reasonable tone. "I am sure they will provide our grandsons with some lively campaigning. But that is for the far future. Right now, Carthage is all we have to concern ourselves with."

"There is also Egypt," Marcus said.

The others laughed. "Egypt!" cried Lucius Ahenobarbus. "The Egyptians worship animals! They pickle their kings so they won't rot and then pile artificial mountains of stone over them to keep the jackals from munching on them!"

"When did the Egyptians last conquer a foreign enemy?" snorted Brutus the augur. "It was around the time that Troy fell, wasn't it?"

"A bit more recently than that, I think," said Flaccus. "But not by much. Marcus, what are you getting at?"

"Today I watched the Egyptian fleet unload in the harbor. This despite the fact that Egypt and Carthage are about to go to war, mind you. There were treasure ships, certainly, but I saw vessel after vessel unloading a single cargo. They are still unloading and will be doing so for several more days. Do you know what this cargo is?"

They looked at him as if he were demented. "Cargo?" said Norbanus. "What can the wares of a merchant fleet have to do with our work and plans?"

"Those ships were full of grain," Marcus told them. "Wheat and barley by the ton. I think it safe to assume that the Egyptians aren't starving. They ship this grain here every year. The Carthaginians middleman it to the west, all the way to Britannia. And Egypt exports it to the lands of the eastern Middle Sea and to Greece as well."

He paused while this intelligence sank in. He could see the thoughts working in their heads. "Egypt must be unbelievably rich," Flaccus said.

"It is the sort of wealth that really counts," Marcus said. "The land is incredibly fertile, the peasants are industrious and the river floods every year and leaves a fresh layer of silt on the fields. The growing season is far longer than we have in the north. In an ordinary year they get two crops. In a really good year they get three. Egypt raises so much grain that they can consume only a small part of it. Some they put up in granaries against a bad year. The rest they sell abroad. Many of the lands of the Middle Sea have come to depend on the Egyptian grain fleet."

"The nation that holds Egypt," Flaccus said, "will have a stranglehold on many other nations."

"Exactly," Marcus said.

"It is too much," Norbanus said. "We can't deal with

Carthage and Egypt both. It has to be done one at a time, and Carthage must come first."

"I agree," said Marcus.

The others looked at him in amazement. "I didn't expect to hear that from you," Norbanus said. "So what is your meaning?"

"It may surprise you to learn that not everything is solved by conquest," Marcus said, grinning. "If we have Carthage, we may be able to dictate policy to Egypt without having to station a single legion on Egyptian soil. Egypt is governed from Alexandria, and Alexandria is a Greek city. The ruling dynasty, the Ptolemies, are another pack of degenerate Macedonians. The kings marry their sisters to keep the royal bloodline pure and I'm told that such breeding practices don't work as well with men as with horses and cattle."

"What is your proposal?" Ahenobarbus asked.

"I think we may be able to cement our control of Egypt with the conquest of Carthage, but to do so we must have good, up-to-date intelligence about Egypt. I propose an embassy to the court of Alexandria."

"Nonsense!" Norbanus said, jumping to his feet. "We have to return to Noricum soon, before the mountain passes fill with snow. An embassy to Egypt would entail months of delay."

"We don't all have to go back," Marcus said. "As soon as we compile our report, a party can return with it. Ten or fifteen men should be plenty. Italy is peaceful enough. The remainder can divide into two groups: one to stay here in Carthage, the other to go on to Egypt and open talks with the court. And to gather intelligence, of course."

"Why shouldn't we all go?" young Caesar asked.

"Hostages," Norbanus answered him, disgustedly. "Do you think Hamilcar will let us all go off to Egypt without leaving some of us behind for good behavior?"

"Who can blame him?" Flaccus chuckled. "If he trusts us

not to double-deal with Egypt, he is a bigger fool than I take him for. It isn't as if we were old allies."

"So who goes?" Brutus said. "Assuming Hamilcar doesn't forbid the project entirely. He must be suspicious, considering he is planning a war with Egypt."

"I will lead the Egyptian expedition," Marcus said. "Norbanus will accompany me as second—"

"I will be more than happy to stay here as hostage," Norbanus said, grinning, "against your good behavior."

"I'm getting rather fond of Carthage myself," Flaccus said. "Why don't you just run off to Egypt and I'll stay—"

"Norbanus can stay here," Marcus said. "In fact, he will serve to reassure the Shofet that we're not plotting treachery. But you, Flaccus, are going to Egypt. I will need you."

"I don't suppose we might take a nice, leisurely land course along the coast? I hear the road is excellent."

"We go by sea," Marcus said. "It is faster. I'll see about getting us passage on one of the Egyptian ships when the fleet returns. You'll like them. They're much more luxurious than the Carthaginian warship that brought us here."

Norbanus clapped him on the shoulder. "Cheer up, Flaccus. This time you'll be puking into ivory buckets."

WHEN HE TOLD ZARABEL OF HIS PLAN, SHE SEEMED pleased. "You are nothing if not energetic. I think an embassy to Egypt is a splendid idea."

"Do you think your brother will see a conflict with his war plans?"

She laughed. "Didn't you notice that Egyptian fleet yesterday? Commerce and diplomacy go on despite war. He envisages a great war with him playing the role of Hannibal. But it will be fought by professionals and they will quit when they see that there is no advantage to going on. It will peter out and end up being settled at a conference table.

"And frankly," she went on, "my brother doesn't see you Romans as much of a threat. He will send you on with his blessings. Of course, you will probably have to leave—"

"I've already made those arrangements," he told her. "Norbanus and some of the others will remain in Carthage."

She beamed. "Excellent."

CHAPTER TEN

THE SHIP WAS NOT THE MAGNIFICENT FLAGSHIP OF
the Egyptian fleet, but neither was it one of the tubby
cargo vessels. Instead, it was one of the warship escort; a
two-banked cruiser called a bireme. It was longer and
broader than the Carthaginian ship that had brought them
from Italy, with a spacious deck and sizable cabins in the
stern. Its gracefully curved bow was armed with a bronze
ram cast in the shape of a dragon's head, the single horn
sprouting from its brow stout and sharp enough to gut an
enemy vessel. Just above the waterline its painted eyes
sought out a safe path through the waters. Its name was
Drakon.

As they voyaged along the African coast, they observed
and made notes: Every cape and headland, every dangerous-
looking outcropping of rock, every town, every fort, went
into their notebooks. Marcus had laid in a good supply of
papyrus because they were running short of parchment.

"I don't like using this stuff," Flaccus had complained.

"No help for it," Marcus answered. "But it's a good sign. We're gathering far more intelligence than we anticipated when we left Noricum."

"It isn't smooth," Flaccus protested. "First of all, it is full of fibers. Second, these reeds or whatever they may be are laid down in strips and the joins always catch the tip of my pen. It does dreadful things to my penmanship."

"Learn to use it," Marcus advised without sympathy. "It's what we have."

Hamilcar had put no obstacle in their way when Marcus broached the subject of an embassy to Egypt. He had been most diplomatic when suggesting that a few of the more prominent members of the Roman party be left behind as his "guests." He had furnished letters of introduction and assured the cooperation of all Carthaginian officials wherever their travels should take them.

Zarabel had given them letters of her own to deliver and had arranged for passage on the Egyptian warship. The fleet, she explained, would be another month finishing its unloading and reloading and refitting for the journey home, while the warship was ready to carry dispatches or passengers at any time.

They were, in short, entirely too helpful and Marcus knew that they were playing their own games. That was only to be expected. He had a few games in mind as well. He knew far better than to trust barbarians, no matter how civilized they might seem to be. Just before the ship sailed, she gave him some parting advice.

"Be sure to deliver my letter, in confidence, to Queen Selene at your earliest opportunity. She is the ruler of Egypt and will be the only person at court whose word you can trust."

"Selene? I thought the ruler of Egypt was Ptolemy XIV."

"In name only. Ptolemy Alexander Philadelphus Eupator is Selene's brother and husband. He is seven years old, so you won't be doing any serious business with him."

He mused upon this as he watched the coast drift leisurely by. As a Roman, he found the concept of hereditary monarchy rather laughable to begin with. That a great nation would acknowledge a child as its ruler was doubly absurd. Such a child-monarch, not reared by a stern father, must inevitably be the creature of his ministers. Romans had severe standards for the upbringing of youth and he doubted that any such standards were applied by the royal house of Egypt.

Between bouts of contemplating politics and monarchy, he discussed naval tactics with the skipper of the *Drakon*. Use of the ram turned out to be less obvious than it first seemed.

"You have to gauge your target vessel carefully," the man explained. He was a Cypriote named Aeson. The great island of Cyprus had for centuries been a province of Egypt. For incomprehensible dynastic reasons the ruler of Cyprus was a brother of the king of Egypt. At the moment a royal minister ruled the island, since the current king had no living brothers.

"By what standard do you gauge them?" Marcus asked.

"Size and structure, mostly. The ram is a tricky thing, and can sink your own ship as effectively as an enemy's. For instance, if you're going after a light vessel, a one-banker, you put on all speed. That's for two reasons: They're fast ships and you need speed to catch them, and if you have enough speed built up and ram them just right, you can break them in two, capsize them, run right over them. Their sides are too thin to resist the weight of a two-banker. You don't want to try that with another two-banker and certainly not against a really big ship."

"Why not?" Marcus asked. "I would think that to ram such a ship you would want all the speed at your disposal."

"No. Those ships have heavier hulls and keels. Ramming

is a terrible shock to a ship no matter if you're on the giving or receiving end. It stresses the planks and springs leaks. Worst of all, you could hole the enemy vessel and get stuck there. Then the enemy drags you under as she sinks."

"So what is the answer?"

"You have to maneuver so she can't get away, then as you're almost on her, you down oars and hit her dead slow, not much more than a walking pace. With the whole weight of your ship behind the ram, it'll smash in the side of the enemy without actually penetrating. Then you back oars and get away fast, because the men on that ship will get really anxious to board."

He spoke of other tactics, how ships could approach almost bow to bow, then swerve. If your timing was right, you could haul in your oars while the enemy ship's were still out, shearing them away like a scythe going through wheat. The flailing oar-butts inside the enemy vessel would reduce the rowers on that side to blood-soaked carcasses. An enemy thus crippled could then be destroyed at leisure.

He showed how stone-hurling engines, cleverly operated at close range, could be used to smash the enemy's steering oars. There was even a way to use oars offensively, when your vessel was higher in the water than the enemy's. When the ships drew alongside, the lower bank of oars were drawn within the hull and the upper bank raised as high as possible, then dropped. As the ships dragged past one another, the oars could sweep the enemy deck clean of men, hurling them overboard, crushing limbs and skulls.

"Yours is highly skilled work," Marcus said.

"It is that," the skipper agreed.

"The warships I have seen seem to carry few marines. Do you not favor boarding?"

The Cypriote snorted. "That is for lubbers who can't make a ship fight for them. Marines are there to operate the engines. And," he allowed, "they repel boarders when we have an enemy fond of such tactics, like pirates. Boarding is a pirate specialty because they prefer capturing ships to sinking them."

This, too, Marcus filed carefully in his memory.

Military matters were not all that concerned the Romans. Marcus explained to his companions about the peculiar situation at the court of Alexandria.

"I never thought when we set out," Flaccus said, "that we would be dealing with women, first Zarabel, now Selene. I shall have to brush up on my seductive skills."

"You will need all your arts of dissimulation if that is your idea of diplomacy," Marcus told him. He drew out his purse and searched among its contents, selecting a broad silver coin. It was an Alexandrian tetradrachm, splendidly struck, bearing a portrait on one side and an eagle on the other. He tossed it to Flaccus. "Here's what she looks like."

Flaccus studied the portrait, dismayed. The other Romans crowded around and burst into laughter. The coin showed a hatchet-faced matron, her beetling brows and wattled neck displayed in a clean-cut, merciless profile.

"I hereby appoint you official seducer of the Roman delegation," Marcus said.

"Is it possible such a hag has a seven-year-old brother?"

"They are probably half-siblings," Brutus said. "The Ptolemies have degenerated into oriental potentates. The last king probably bred the child off a fifteen-year-old granddaughter when he was an old man."

"Disgusting," said young Caesar. He came of a famously straitlaced family.

"Our mission is not to assess or judge the moral tone of the Alexandrian court," Marcus reminded them. "It is to make the best use of whatever opportunities we find there to the advantage of the Republic. I warn you not to underestimate any of the powerful people we meet there. To us they may be ludicrous buffoons, but these are the descendants of Alexander and his generals, and they have kept control of tremendous power and riches for a very long time. Even if they are not hardened warriors, they understand their own world far better than we."

"This court, these half-Greeks," Brutus said. "Are they really Egypt? The native population must be vast to make the country so productive. What of them?"

"A good question," Marcus said. "I intend to find out. We Romans have subdued native peoples far more numerous than we, but we have not truly remained a separate people. We absorb our conquests and turn the people into Romans. They breed sons for the legions and in time become full citizens.

"The Carthaginians, as you all observed, are different. Wherever they go, they remain conquerors in an alien land. Subject cities ten miles from Carthage are still natives with differing language and customs. The Alexandrians may be something like that, or they may be something else entirely."

"We would do well to remember," Flaccus pointed out, "that the Ptolemies are not truly Greek, but Macedonian. The real Greeks regarded the Macedonians as little more than barbarians. When Philip conquered Greece, he forced them to acknowledge him as a Greek and his son Alexander made it his life's work not just to conquer the world, but to spread the light of Greek culture wherever he went. When he died, his generals divided his conquests among themselves and ruled as Greek monarchs in foreign lands, but they remained Macedonians and the backbone of their armies was always Macedonian troops.

"These were not the sort of Greeks to swoon over the plays of Sophocles or chat about philosophy beneath shaded porticoes. They were tough mountain tribesmen and superb soldiers."

"Men much like our own ancestors," Marcus said. "It would be best to keep that in mind."

BY THE TIME *DRAKON* WAS SAILING ALONG THE COAST of Cyrenaica, the Romans were almost accustomed to the rolling motion of the vessel and even Flaccus was no longer pale-faced and shaky. Despite the volume of coastal traffic, the sea was immense and they often sailed or rowed for hours without seeing another vessel. This changed abruptly as they rounded a rocky cape and found two lean, predatory ships waiting for them on its far side. The instant *Drakon* came into view, the smaller ships, both single-bankers, began rowing toward her at speed.

Drakon was under sail with a favorable stern wind, headed straight for the others. Immediately, Aeson shouted for the sail to be furled, the yard lowered, the mast unstepped and the oars run out. The Romans marveled at the lively efficiency with which this complex set of orders was carried out. Sailors scrambled to the mast as rowers unshipped their oars and marines sprang to the war engines.

"Who are they?" Marcus demanded.

"Pirates!" Aeson said. "But what can they want with us? They never attack a warship unless they're cornered, and I'm not pirate hunting. Now get away and let me fight my ship."

Marcus beckoned the Roman party to him. "Arm yourselves. There is going to be a fight."

"Should we wear armor?" Flaccus asked. "If we do and fall overboard, we'll sink like bricks."

"Might as well," said Brutus. "Drowning is the least of our hazards, I believe."

"Full gear," Marcus ordered. "The Greeks don't favor boarding and deck-fighting. The pirates will want to board. Hand-to-hand fighting is our specialty, isn't it? Now get your shields. The missiles should be arriving soon."

As he spoke, the frantic activity continued all around them. The catapults and ballistas began to launch missiles with a deafening clatter, but the pirate vessels were low in the water and difficult to hit. To make matters worse, with the yard lowered but the mast still up, the ship began to wallow, making accurate fire impossible and the task of the rowers more difficult. Getting the mast down required the coordinated effort of every sailor on the ship and the job was unfinished when the first arrows began to arrive.

The Romans were mailed, helmeted and shielded in a matter of moments. Unlike other forms of armor, the Gallic mail shirt slipped on over the head like a cloth garment and could be donned in seconds. With helmets on and shields up, the Romans were invulnerable to the storm of missiles that rained on the ship: not only arrows, but lead sling pellets that could crush in an unprotected skull. The nearly naked sailors began to take heavy losses, as did the marines who worked their engines in armor but without shields.

Marcus had been impressed with Aeson's tales of sea fighting, but it was clear that the man could put little of his experience to work when caught so completely by surprise. The pirates, on the other hand, knew exactly what they were doing. Marcus knew all too well that surprise and sheer luck determined the outcome of a fight more often than strategy or tactics.

Before Aeson could get his ship properly ready to fight, the first grapples sailed across the distance separating the ships. The surviving marines ceased work on the futile machines and picked up their small shields.

"At least they're not trying to ram," Flaccus said, his face rigid between the cheek plates of his helmet.

"We could cut the grappling ropes," Caesar suggested.

"No," Marcus said. "We want them to get close."

"Why?" Flaccus asked.

"Because our swords are short!" Brutus said, raising a raucous laugh among his companions. The sailors and marines stared at them as if they had gone insane.

The pirates were attacking from the starboard side. Marcus guessed that this was because they would have to face only half of the ship's artillery this way. The pirate's deck was crowded with men, all screaming and waving their weapons. Most were armed with small shields and short curved swords or wicked-looking axes. Some wore helmets but only a few had body armor. Many were entirely naked except for their weaponry.

"What are you fools doing?" Aeson shouted.

"We're going to board them," Marcus said.

"*You* are going to board *them*? You will do no such thing! If you want to make yourselves useful, try to repel them when they start to board!"

"We don't fight that way," Marcus explained. He turned to address his followers. "We won't try to board until the ships are actually touching. Too much chance of falling between the hulls if we try to jump across, and we'll be unbalanced at best when we land on their deck. Let's have two staggered lines. At my command, the first line throw their pila, then the second. We're going to board amidships, so that's where you throw. The second the hulls touch, the first line steps across. Second line, wait until the first is firmly established, then come across. We'll clear the center of the deck, then the first line will face left, the second face right and clean the decks from the center to each end. Then we'll see about the other ship."

Aeson gaped at this demonstration of lunacy for a moment, then barked orders at his oarsmen. They leaned on their sweeps for the oar-battering maneuver he had described but the pirates were expecting it and the general chaos robbed the tactic of effectiveness. Pirates seized the oars and dragged them from the hands of the rowers or hacked through them with axes. Only a few were injured by the flailing wood.

When the ships were no more than five paces apart Marcus pointed at the mass of men crowding the rail opposite. "Your spears go between that tattooed lout with the axe and the black man with the red shield. Now throw!"

As if controlled by a single brain, the right arms of the first line rocked back, paused, then snapped forward. The Roman pilum was a heavy javelin with a thick, four-foot shaft of wood and another two feet of iron shank tipped with a small, barbed point. It was designed to nail an enemy's shield and deprive him of its protection. At this range, the terrible missiles went through the light shields of the pirates as if they were made of parchment, skewering the men behind them. So crowded was the deck that some of the spears pierced the man behind the primary target as well.

While the pirates were reeling from this unexpected onslaught, the men of the second line hurled their weapons. The result was consternation on the opposite deck and suddenly there was a gaping hole in the wall of men along the rail opposite. Two seconds later the ships crunched together and shuddered.

"Now!" Marcus shouted. The Romans already had their swords out. Marcus stepped onto *Drakon*'s rail, then made the short hop to the deck of the pirate vessel two or three feet below. The Romans had been drilled from early youth in the procedures for assaulting an enemy parapet, and this was nothing more than the familiar drill in an unfamiliar setting. The surprised pirates rallied when they realized that the line of strange warriors before them had no more than ten men in it, with ten more lined up on the rail behind them. With savage howls, they assaulted the small line of Romans.

At this point, the murderous Roman gladius began to do its work. The sword was no more than twenty inches long, but its twin edges were viciously keen, the blade as broad as a man's palm and tapered to an acute point. While the pirates assaulted the line with their all but unprotected bodies, the Romans ignored the flailing weapons and concentrated on killing. Their long shields did not overlap or even touch, but were separated by about eight inches. The swords darted through this gap in underhand thrusts, each thrust gutting a man or opening his neck to the spine. Even the merest stroke from one of the terrible blades was sufficient to open an arm or leg to the bone.

"Shove!" Marcus shouted. Each man took a step forward, thrusting out with the boss of his shield, pushing the pirates back. Then the metronomic thrusting of the swords began again, littering the deck with bodies and parts of bodies. Each thrust was delivered with incredible speed, the arm drawing back instantly within the protection of the shield, making a hit on the sword arm all but impossible.

Crowded together and unable to achieve proper distance or balance, the pirates could not strike effectively. With their bodies covered by their shields and armor, the only real target offered by a Roman was his head, and this was protected by the superbly designed Gallic helmet. Only when a weapon came straight for his face did a Roman even bother to take defensive action, and then it was only to incline his head slightly so that the enemy blade slid off the brow or cheek plate of his helmet.

With the first shoving maneuver, the second line boarded. The two end men of the second line used their shields to protect the flanks of the first line, which were growing exposed as they advanced. The lines began to lose their fine cohesion as they trod on bodies and the deck grew ever slipperier with blood. But by this time the pirates were already beginning to lose heart. This was like fighting some sort of reaping machine. Every man who got within an arm's reach was eviscerated.

The marines and sailors aboard *Drakon* began raining javelins and slingstones among the pirates not engaged by the Romans and within a few seconds the center of the pirate deck was secured. Then the Romans did their facing movement and the butchery resumed in a different direction.

Marcus engaged each enemy that came before him, his shield raised to just below eye level. He dispatched each with a short, upward jab. The years of drill and practice made this second nature, allowing him freedom to assess the situation and maintain such control as was necessary over his line. As leader, he held the right flank of the first line. It was the post of honor and it carried an extra danger: He was vulnerable to attack on his unshielded side.

A naked pirate, painted scarlet all over and armed with an axe, came screaming at him. The axe presented a problem. Brought straight down with full force it could cleave even his fine helmet. For this special peril, Marcus deviated from the usual underhand thrust, instead raising his sword overhead, the blade horizontal as he thrust with his shield and leaned in close. As the axe came whistling down, his blade sheared through both of the pirate's forearms, and arms and weapon went flying. The maimed pirate howled in horror, staggering back, waving what remained of his arms and spraying fountains of blood from his severed arteries.

Soon the pirate attack lost its brainless ferocity and the freebooters began to fall back, unable to cope with this unprecedented killing machine. Some dived overboard and began swimming for the other ship. As the pirate mob broke up, the Romans gave a savage shout and waded into them, the line widening as they began to wield their blades in short chops and slashes, foregoing the exclusive use of the point. It was time for the slaughter.

Marcus saw the man who had to be the captain, waving a sword, shouting and trying to make his men resume the fight, but the heart was gone from them. This man wore a

fine Greek helmet and a corselet of crocodile hide. Strangely
to Roman eyes, he wore heavy facial cosmetics, his lips and
cheeks rouged, his eyes outlined with kohl. Enraged, the
man came for Marcus, perhaps hoping to break the Romans
by killing their leader.

The line had opened so that Marcus fought alone, engag-
ing the enemy captain man to man. The pirate was too wily
to obligingly expose himself to the short sword for which
he had quickly gained respect. He wielded his curved blade
in short, zigzag cuts while protecting himself adroitly with
his small, round shield. Marcus advanced against him, forcing him back. The man had no choice but to retreat unless
he wanted to go shield to shield. He had only a short space
of deck in which to retreat.

When he was almost against the bow rail, the pirate chief
lunged forward, diving to the deck and rolling, trying to
amputate Marcus's leading foot. It was a clever and effective
move, but Marcus merely grounded his shield and the
curved blade clattered off its bronze rim. Marcus stabbed
downward through the man's neck, his point sinking into
the deck beneath. He jerked the blade free and the pirate
chief thrashed on the deck for the space of a few heartbeats,
his blood fountaining across the planks, then he lay still.

The Romans found themselves to be the only living creatures aboard the ship. They raised a cheer, taunting the pirates who were still floundering in the water, striving
frantically to reach the other vessel, which was already backing off, its oars churning the water to foam.

Even as they cheered, the surviving marines aboard *Drakon* finally got their incendiary missiles prepared and their
engines working. With an immense clatter, five of them
fired at once and five balls of roaring flame converged on the
second pirate vessel. The same wind that had sped *Drakon*
along the coast now spread the fire with incredible swiftness
the whole length of the ship. Men screamed and burned and

jumped into the water. The destruction was as complete as it was rapid. For the Romans, the vicious hand-to-hand battle had been no more than ordinary legionary's work, but this fire at sea was appalling.

When they reboarded *Drakon*, the sailors were already erecting the mast while the oars flailed the water. Under Aeson's frantic orders the sail was hoisted in haste.

"Aren't you going to put a crew aboard the ship we captured?" Marcus asked him.

"Ordinarily," said the skipper, "I'd do exactly that, or at least take it in tow. It would fetch a fair price at auction in Alexandria. But, if you'll notice, there's a ship afire just to windward and the flames and sparks are blowing this way. We're getting away from it as fast as possible."

"What about the survivors?" Marcus said, pointing to the men flailing in the water.

"Pirates are worth practically nothing. Only the mines and quarries buy them. We'd get a handful of drachmae for the lot. It's not worth the risk."

"I meant we could use a few for questioning."

"We're getting away from here, Ambassador," Aeson said. "They can be our offering to the sea gods."

"I quite agree, Marcus," Flaccus said. He was watching the burning ship with horror. The heat was intense even at a distance of fifty paces and the sailors were sluicing the ship with buckets of seawater as glowing cinders landed on the deck and sail. "Let's leave our captain to his work."

The Romans were already cleaning the blood from their gear. In the close confines of the deck fight they had all been liberally splashed with it, and blood was notorious for corroding fine steel. They carefully washed every trace from their metal and only then did they bother to clean their bodies and treat their wounds. The sailors and marines regarded them with wonder and Marcus had a feeling there would be no more landlubber jokes from them.

"Who is hurt?" he asked. Flaccus had a bad gash on his sword arm. Others had minor nicks and cuts, and some had trod on the dropped weapons that littered the pirate deck. Their hobnailed caligae protected their soles, but there were some cut ankles. Marcus looked at unwarlike Flaccus disgustedly. "I might have known you'd get hurt."

Flaccus shrugged. "I'm a philosopher by nature, not a soldier." His sword arm was red to the shoulder, but only a little of the blood came from his wound.

Marcus commandeered a bucket of seawater from a sailor and dipped his blade into it, carefully sponging the steel until it was bright again. He sighted along the edges but found no nicks or notches. This was another reason the Romans favored stabs to the belly or throat. They were much easier on the blade than cuts that might land on armor or metal shield rims.

They stripped off their tunics and plunged them into buckets of water to soak the blood out and as they did this, they discussed the action just past.

"What do you suppose that was all about?" said Brutus. "Those thieves weren't attacking a warship for the prospect of loot."

"They were waiting for us," Marcus said. "I would speculate that Hamilcar put them up to it. He acts the generous host but he doesn't want us dealing with Egypt. Not while he's preparing for war."

"I knew we shouldn't have trusted a Carthaginian!" Caesar said.

The older men laughed. "Who was trusting anybody?" Flaccus said.

THEY ENTERED THE GREAT HARBOR OF ALEXANDRIA from the west on a glorious morning so windless that the smoke from the great lighthouse towered straight up like an offering ascending to the gods. The lighthouse itself was at the eastern tip of the island of Pharos, but even from the western end it bulked huge, standing a full four hundred feet high, ornate with marble columns in every Greek style. It was built in four stepped-back sections, the terraces green with lush plantings that hung over the railings, bedizened with dazzling flowers.

"A lighthouse makes sense," said Brutus. "But why tart it up with all that decoration?"

"It's a matter of aesthetics, Brutus," Flaccus informed him. "You wouldn't understand."

The western harbor was called the Eunostos, the harbor of "happy return." Within, it proved to be even greater than the harbor at Carthage. As if the lighthouse were not wonder enough, the island was connected with the mainland by a causeway called the Heptastadion, because it was seven stadia in length. The causeway was raised and pierced with arches so that ships could sail beneath it to the smaller Palace Harbor on the eastern side.

Lining the shore they could see broad plazas, gigantic warehouses, statues of gods and kings, ships without number from all parts of the world. Their skipper pointed out some of the wonders of the city. The vast temple that hulked a half-mile inland in the eastern part of the city was the Serapion, temple of Serapis, patron god of Alexandria. The strange, conical hill near the center of the metropolis was the Paneum, an artificial mound planted with the flora of Thessaly and topped with a circular shrine to the goat-footed nature god. Beyond the Heptastadion lay the sprawling palace and museum complexes. The whole city was built of white stone and it shone in the morning light like a philosopher's dream of a city, not a real city where men and women lived out their lives.

They did not moor in the Eunostos but rowed beneath one of the arches pierced through the causeway into the

Palace Harbor. Here there were few commercial vessels but many warships, royal galleys and pleasure barges of stunning size and luxuriance. In the harbor was a small island with its own miniature palace, a marvel of perfect proportions.

Marcus noted that, while Alexandria lacked the architectural chaos of Carthage, its predominantly Greek design had an Egyptian overlay. While the buildings were almost exclusively Greek, some were ornamented with Egyptian hieroglyphics and the statues of gods and kings, while Greek in execution, were often arranged in traditional Egyptian poses; stiffly seated or striding, wearing items of Egyptian dress or bearing the attributes of Egyptian gods.

Drakon steered a course toward the structure that dominated the waterfront: a palace wing built on the scale favored by the Successor kings. It looked like a place where giants would live. The Ionic columns were at least fifty feet in height, the pediment they supported featuring a battle between gods and titans, the figures twice human height.

The wharf to which they made fast was adorned with marble facing, carved with stone wreaths alternating with cattle skulls, the bollards to which the ship moored carved in the shape of giant scarab beetles. To Marcus's question the skipper explained that this beetle was a creature sacred to the native Egyptians. Its habit of rolling balls of dung along the ground suggested the passage of the sun across the sky.

"They think a shit-rolling bug represents the sun god?" Brutus said with wonder. "Barbarians are a strange lot."

"It certainly lacks the majesty of Apollo's solar chariot," Flaccus agreed.

Marcus had more important things than dung beetles on his mind. Before him lay the huge and ancient land of Egypt. It lay between Carthage in the west and the Seleucid Empire and the Parthians to the east. All his political and military instincts told him that Egypt could hold the balance of power in the world. If he performed his task here properly, Egypt could deliver that world to the upstart, returning Romans.

CHAPTER ELEVEN

IT SEEMED TO THE ROMANS THAT, FOR SUCH EXOTIC newcomers, they were attracting very little attention on the Alexandrian waterfront. Here in the royal harbor the ships weren't as numerous as in the Eunostos, but they seemed to hail from as many corners of the world. Common sailors were everywhere, but there were also a great many finely dressed people embarking and disembarking. Probably, Marcus thought, they were envoys to the Alexandrian court. There were also many with the look of scholars and these he assumed were bound for the great Library and Museum.

While ships of war and passenger vessels predominated, there were cargo ships, some of them unloading luxury goods for the palace, others that seemed to be laden solely with books. *Drakon* was just one Alexandrian warship among many and the toga-clad strangers that descended its gangplank rated little more than a glance from the colorful throng ashore.

"I suppose a reception committee was too much to hope for," Flaccus said.

"How could they know we were coming?" said Marcus. "Come on, let's see about some sort of lodgings. Then we can go petition the court." He saw their downcast faces and added: "Our lavish treatment in Carthage was a fluke. We happened to arrive at the right time. Don't expect it to happen twice."

Aeson came ashore and said, "You can bunk at the naval barracks. I'll be delivering my dispatches to the palace. I think you can expect to be summoned soon after that. I don't know about your diplomatic plans, but someone is definitely going to want to hear about that fight with the pirates."

The naval barracks was adjacent to the palace dock. The Romans had not spotted it for what it was because it looked no more military than the palace itself. Aeson saw that they were assigned quarters in a wing reserved for high-ranking officers, then went to deliver his dispatches.

The rooms were comfortable but spartan, their furnishings spare. Flaccus studied the accommodations glumly. "This is a bit of a letdown."

"How soon we grow spoiled," Marcus said. "It beats staying in some flea-ridden hostelry. This will do until we establish our credentials with the court. Then we can see about getting a proper house in the city."

While they saw to the arrangement of their sparse luggage, Marcus mulled over the events of recent weeks. It disturbed him that his fellow Romans of the officer class were so quick to grow accustomed to the luxury of the south. He wondered if the famous austerity of his countrymen was bred from the mere absence of temptation. Of his immediate followers, only young Caesar and Quintus Brutus seemed to show no taste for high living. He found himself worrying that the much-anticipated return to Italy might expose his nation to a decadence unknown in the brutal north.

And there was the matter of the pirate attack. Clearly, the pirates had been put up to it. The others assumed that Hamilcar was behind it, but Marcus was not so sure. There were other powers at the Carthaginian court, and Zarabel was far from the least of them. That she had shown them such favor meant nothing. He knew that, to gain advantage over her brother, she would not hesitate to exterminate a few interloping foreigners.

And, he was all too aware, there was a more subtle motive for her to want him out of the way. With his death, Norbanus became leader of the Roman delegation, and she could manipulate Norbanus far more easily than she could a man like himself. There were traps everywhere, and he feared that Alexandria would prove to be no less perilous than Carthage.

SELENE II, QUEEN AND REGENT OF EGYPT, WAS GETting very bored with documents. She sat at her desk with Memnon, the First Eunuch, and Sylphius the Chief Scribe, performing the unglamorous but necessary paperwork of government. The desk, by the standards of the Successors, was a plain and modest item: a thin slab of polished marble laid atop gryphons carved from the same stone.

"The tax accounts from the Fayyum, Majesty," said Memnon, sliding another stack of papyrus before her. She vowed a ram to Zeus-Amon if she could just be presented with something interesting. Her vow was rewarded almost immediately.

The Keeper of the Accounts Room Door came in and thumped his staff on the floor. "Majesty, Captain Aeson awaits with dispatches from Carthage."

Selene ran the naval list through her mind and came up with the man: Aeson, captain of the *Drakon*, a bireme. "Bring the dispatches to me and dismiss the captain," she said.

"Begging Your Majesty's indulgence, Captain Aeson says that he has an extraordinary report that must be delivered personally."

"Says he so?" This, at least, seemed mildly intriguing. Either the man was presumptuous or else he had something truly interesting to report. "Send the captain in."

She watched as Aeson made his way the length of the room. He was typical of her captains: a salty, weather-beaten Greek in a faded tunic. He halted before the desk and bowed.

"Majesty, I bring dispatches from Carthage." He set the dispatch case before the scribe.

"And something more, I understand?"

"Yes, Majesty. I bring a delegation from Rome."

"Rome no longer exists," she said mildly, wondering if the man was addled.

"These are from the northern land where the old Romans were exiled. I can assure Your Majesty that the Romans still exist, and they are as formidable as ever."

This was an unlooked-for diversion. "These men are from Noricum? I've heard of the place, but never seen anyone from there except for a few slaves sent down to the Euxine markets. They really call themselves Romans?"

"That is the case, Majesty. They speak Latin, though they are passable in Greek. They wear the toga and they are fighting men such as I've never seen before. The old tales from the day of Hannibal must be true."

She leaned forward. "You've *seen* them fight?"

"I have a most amazing tale to relate."

Selene clapped her hands. "A chair for the captain, and refreshments." She addressed him. "Make yourself comfortable, Captain. Then tell me all about it."

Slaves brought the chair and a table and a platter of honeyed squab, figs, dates, cheeses and a pitcher of wine. The skipper was uncomfortable. "Majesty, I cannot sit and eat before royalty."

"Nonsense," she said, rising and circling the desk. The captain sprang to his feet. "Sit down, Captain." She gestured to a slave, who poured two cups full. Selene took one and handed the other to Aeson. The eunuch and the scribe made scandalized sounds, which she ignored. She perched herself on the desk. "Have something to eat, then tell me about these Romans."

She listened intently as Aeson delivered his tale. He described his annoyed amusement when he was ordered to deliver these primitive landlubbers to Alexandria. He said that his scorn was tempered somewhat when the Romans asked such penetrating and perceptive questions about naval matters. He described these odd men, their dress and manner, their way of speaking, their obvious pride and equally obvious discipline. Then he got to the fight.

"Two pirate vessels attacked an Alexandrian warship?"

"They didn't just attack. They were lying in wait and it was us they were waiting for. They must've had a lookout on top of the cape, because they were already churning the water white when we came into view. They were making straight for us and they weren't mistaking us for any rich merchantman, either. We never had time to properly prepare for battle. The first one was on us before we could even get the mast unstepped."

"And yet they didn't take your ship," she said. "Even after starting with such a clear advantage. We'll leave aside for the moment just why they were mad enough to assault a warship with no prospect of a rich haul. Tell me why you are alive and how your ship returned unharmed."

"Well, Majesty, this is the part you are going to find hard to believe."

"Go ahead. I've heard many marvelous stories and I'd like to hear another."

He told of the unequal battle when he thought *Drakon* was surely lost, how annoyed he was when the Romans, unbelievably, put on armor and calmly prepared to fight as if this were a land battle. Then, baldly and factually, he told how the Romans made an opening at the enemy rail with their spears, then stepped across and proceeded methodically to turn the enemy vessel into an abbatoir.

"They acted like it was a routine task, Majesty. Like this was something they did all the time. There were no heroics. The unit behaved like a machine for slaughter. When they came back aboard, it turned out the least warlike of the lot, the one named Flaccus, had taken a small wound. The rest of them seemed to think this was hilarious, like getting hurt in such a trifling fight was proof he didn't have the stuff of a real warrior in him."

"You've made my day much more interesting," she said. "I thank you. Now go and tender your report to the naval authorities and see to the replacement of your lost crew and such repairs as your ship needs. You've done well."

The captain rose, bowed and left the room. Selene turned to her scribe. "Find me whatever the library has on the Romans. There should be plenty. They were becoming a prominent nation before Hannibal expunged them."

"As Your Majesty wishes," the man said, clear from his tone that he regarded this as a matter unworthy of her attention.

Selene had her own opinion on this.

MARCUS AND SOME OF THE OTHER ROMANS WERE AT weapons drill the next morning when the summons came. They had brought their practice swords from Carthage and were going at it in full gear. Marcus glanced over the rim of his shield when he saw the man in messenger's uniform come onto the terrace. In the instant his attention wavered.

Brutus leaned into him with a shield-slam, knocked him off balance and cracked his lead-weighted wooden blade into the side of his helmet.

Marcus blinked the stars from his eyes and signaled for the messenger to approach. "The Queen-Regent Selene desires the attendance of the delegation from Noricum at this afternoon's court," the man said, handing him a document intended to pass him through the doorways of the palace to the august presence.

Marcus dismissed the man and called his following together for a briefing. Before it broke up, Caesar nudged Flaccus. "Better brush up on your seductive wiles, Flaccus. It looks like we're going to call on the old lady."

Flaccus sighed amid general hilarity. "The things one must do to serve the Republic."

Two hours later they arrived at the gate of the palace. Except for its massive scale, the imposing building maintained the pleasing, austere harmony of classical Greek architecture, eschewing the overelaboration so common to Successor aesthetics. The only Egyptian elements were two sphinxes flanking the great doorway, and these were Greek in execution if not in inspiration.

Instead of a military guard, a steward dressed in a snowy robe met them. "You would be the delegation from Noricum?"

"We are Romans," Marcus answered.

"Your pardon, gentlemen," the steward said gravely, "but Her Majesty has instructed that you be addressed as envoys of Noricum until certain diplomatic questions are answered. If you will come this way."

"She's not taking any chances," Flaccus said in Latin as they followed the man. "The Seven Hills are on Carthaginian territory now, so she's not ready to address us as Romans just yet."

"We'll just have to convince her that Rome is ours, not Carthage's," Marcus said.

The walls were decorated with the ever-popular motif of the battle of gods and giants, with the latter depicted as all manner of grotesques: men with serpents for legs, or bodies covered with eyes or with dragon tails or lion heads. The gods were depicted as idealized humans, identifiable by their attributes: Zeus with his thunderbolts, helmeted Ares and Athena, Apollo with his bow, Artemis in her hunting tunic and boots.

They came to a double door of bronze worked in a foliate design and were admitted to a spacious room they took at first to be an anteroom to the throne room proper. In this they were mistaken.

At one end of the room a young woman in a plain blue gown was deep in conversation with a number of elderly men who had the look of scholars. She glanced toward them and came forward. "You are the delegation from Noricum?" she said.

"Romans," Marcus said. "We are here to meet with your queen." He looked past her for someone more official. "We expected to be presented at court. Who are you, girl? One of the queen's attendants?" He wondered what made the jaws of the old scholars drop in unison. He looked around to see if some prodigy had occurred behind him.

"No," said the young woman. "I'm Selene."

It took a moment for the words to register. "I suppose it's a common name around here. The Selene we wish to see is—"

"Foreigner!" spluttered one of the graybeards. "You address the queen of Egypt! You speak to Selene Ptolemy the Second!"

For the first time since leaving Noricum, Marcus was utterly nonplussed. The young woman before him raised a fine-boned hand and quirked an eyebrow quizzically. He took the small hand in his much larger one, a hand that seemed to have turned numb. Flaccus stepped in and appropriated the queen's hand in his own.

"We are most charmed, Your Majesty. I am Flaccus, and I've been named official—"

Marcus trod heavily on his foot and regained her hand. "You may address me, Majesty. I am Marcus Cornelius Scipio and I am head of the Roman delegation." He stopped and took a deep breath. "I fear our rustic simplicity has played us an ill turn and I apologize. Would it be utterly oafish of me to note that Your Majesty looks very little like her coin portrait?"

At this she released a full-throated laugh and even a few of the elders managed dry chuckles. "This explains it! I fear you've been deceived by our propaganda. Since the Successors of Alexander took over his empire, it has been our custom to portray reigning queens as stern-faced old matrons on the coinage. It's thought that people won't take a young queen seriously."

"I see. That does explain it." Gods! he thought. I must sound like an utter bumpkin!

She laced an arm through his. "Come along and walk with me, Marcus Cornelius Scipio. While we walk, you can introduce me to your friends."

She conducted him out of the room onto a terrace, thence to a staircase that descended to a splendid garden. This, for a court proceeding, seemed amazingly informal to Marcus. He introduced the other Romans and she greeted each courteously, putting everyone at their ease until she had them all conversing as casually as if they were home among friends. It was, Marcus thought, an amazing performance.

"These are myrrh trees from Ethiopia," she explained, showing them some shrublike growths with aromatic leaves. They already knew that the garden contained flora from all over the Ptolemaic dominion.

"I always wondered where that stuff came from," Brutus said.

"Merchants trade it so far north?" she asked. To Marcus's amazement, she wanted to know details of commerce: prices, middlemen's percentages and other unqueenly things. It was hard to imagine anything more different from Carthaginian royalty. It did not make him drop his guard. This might be a pose. She might be playing them for fools. At least she didn't try to put them off balance by appearing nearly naked, as Zarabel had.

"Your Majesty is well versed in the details of trade," Marcus noted.

"Queens usually are," she said. "Kings love war and conquest. Queens know that real wealth and prosperity come through profitable trade."

"Few nations are so favored by the gods as Egypt," Flaccus noted. "You have a great deal to trade with."

"That is true," she agreed. "But peaceful trade is more than just wealth. It is vision. A predecessor of mine, one Queen Hatshepsut, reigned over Egypt as pharaoh in her own right some fourteen hundred years ago. The glory of her reign was a huge trade expedition she sent along the coasts of Arabia and Ethiopia. The ancestors of these myrrh trees may have come to Egypt on that voyage. The details of it are carved on the walls of her temple. She expanded Egypt's knowledge of the world and bettered the condition of the whole nation. She was succeeded by Thutmose the Third, another warrior-king. He killed a great many foreigners but he did nothing to enrich his kingdom."

Marcus disliked hearing conquest spoken of thus dismissively, but he knew that certain allowances had to be made for a reigning queen, especially one as rich as this one. "Truly, Your Majesty, a nation of prominence and power will have neither without both military strength and a profitable balance of trade."

"Well spoken. You people are not as rustic as you would have us believe."

"We lack your level of sophistication. This does not mean we are stupid. Perhaps we overemphasize military virtue to the detriment of foreign trade, but it is our backwardness in the latter that we hope to correct with this mission. You, on the other hand, would be well advised to reevaluate the importance of your military." He could almost hear the eyes rolling behind him. Once again, he was overstepping his authority.

She blinked, seeming astonished for the first time. "Your nation's reputation for blunt speech is not exaggerated, I see. What do you mean?"

"You must be aware that Hamilcar of Carthage is preparing for war against you. He makes no secret of it."

"Certainly. It is far from the first time Carthage has sought to take advantage of us. There will be some fighting on the Libyan border. There will be some naval forays. He will probably make an attempt to take Cyprus. We have met these threats before."

"I saw something of the scale of his preparations. I believe you should take this threat more seriously."

"Why?"

"Because Hamilcar wishes to hire Roman legions for his war. If he does that, you can kiss your kingdom—"

"Scipio!" Brutus barked. "The Senate has not—"

Marcus whirled to face him. "The Senate has bestowed upon me power of negotiation. Do not interfere." Brutus held his glare for a moment, but Roman discipline prevailed. Brutus lowered his eyes and stepped back.

Selene chose to ignore the little byplay. "I know your reputation. At least, I've read of the reputation of your ancestors. I think it would take more than the addition of a few of your legions to turn Hamilcar into his ancestor." She studied his expression for a moment. "You mean it! You really think that you are that good."

"I would not question the quality of Your Majesty's army and navy," Marcus said. "But when was their last war?"

"Four years ago Antiochus of Syria invaded the Sinai and I had to repel him."

"And this war required what part of your military forces?"

"I sent six myriads, but in the event only a third of the force was used. There was a battle near Gaza and Antiochus withdrew."

"I see. Majesty, about how often are your men required to fight?"

She looked mystified but amused. "I would say that there is fighting in two or three out of each ten years. What is your point?"

"It is this. The legions of Roma Noricum have been engaged in active campaigning every year since we left Italy. That was one hundred sixteen years ago. For all those years, at least half the legions of Rome have been committed to active campaigning in any given year. Rarely does any legion go for two years without heavy fighting."

"I see. But you have been fighting barbarians."

"They are hard-fighting warriors and they are not as undisciplined as you might think. I have seen something of the armies of Carthage. They are well equipped and finely drilled, but few of them are what Romans would consider veterans."

"And what is the Roman definition of a veteran?" she asked.

"We rate a man as a veteran if he has ten campaigns behind him. Not ten fights: ten campaigns. A legion is considered inexperienced and unreliable if no more than half its men are veterans."

"You have high military standards."

"So we have. We learned a great deal from Hannibal. We

believe that military preparedness is the highest of priorities and we vowed never again to go to war with hastily raised armies of conscripts. No man can seek public office unless he has those same ten campaigns behind him. A praetor—a senior magistrate—is also a qualified general. We are soldiers from birth: farmers, shopkeepers, artisans and the wealthiest equites and patricians."

She nodded. "Captain Aeson reported to me about your fight with the pirates. He was most impressed."

"It wasn't much of a fight," Marcus said.

"That was what so impressed him. I believe you when you tell me you are a nation of born soldiers."

"Not born," he corrected. "Made. Soldiering is something that must be learned early and in a hard school. Your own ancestors, Philip and Alexander's Macedonians, understood this."

"We shall talk about this further," she said. "But let me show you the royal menagerie. We have some of the world's fiercest animals in our collection."

The queen assigned them accommodations in the huge palace complex and when they went to their new quarters that evening, the rest of the Roman party took Marcus to task for his actions that day.

"Wasn't proposing a military alliance with Carthage enough?" Brutus said. "Now you want to do the same with Egypt?"

"And why are you dealing with this woman?" Caesar asked.

"It's that coin portrait," Marcus said.

"Your sense eludes me," Brutus said.

"She said that reigning queens are so depicted on the coins. She does not consider her unripe husband the king and herself the queen-consort. She is the real ruler of Egypt."

"There is likely to be a faction at this court that does not share that opinion," Brutus pointed out.

"Undoubtedly. Would you rather deal with this very clever and sane woman, or with a boy who is almost certainly controlled by courtiers and counselors? I understand that these positions are usually filled by eunuchs at the Alexandrian court."

"Just what is this southern enthusiasm for de-balled men?" Caesar wanted to know.

"Kings get nervous when they have too many real men around them," Flaccus told him. "They fear revolts and worry about the paternity of their sons."

"For the next few days," Marcus told them, "we will be organizing our mission here. We will also do what everyone who visits Alexandria does: We will go sight-seeing. You all know the drill. Fortifications, naval installations, road approaches. Flaccus, I want you to climb to the top of that lighthouse and draw a map of the whole city."

"All the way to the top?" Flaccus said, aghast. "I'll never make it!"

"Hire a litter to carry you," Brutus advised.

"It's a sad day," said Marcus, "when a Roman official can't manage a few thousand steps on his own feet."

"It's a few thousand steps *straight up*!" Flaccus said.

"Do it."

"What will you be doing?" Brutus wanted to know.

"I've decided to take up the pursuit of culture," Marcus said.

"Culture?" said young Caesar with wonder in his voice.

"Exactly. I am going to pay a visit to the Museum."

CHAPTER TWELVE

THE COURT OFFICIAL IN CHARGE OF FOREIGN EM-
bassies wanted to provide guides, litters, personal servants and every comfort and convenience. It was Alexandrian
practice to treat envoys lavishly. Marcus politely declined
all offers. He wanted neither guides nor spies.

The Museum proved to be a large complex of buildings
adjacent to the palace. For the most part, they differed from
the palace in being proportioned to a more human scale.
Even the temple of the Muses from which the complex took
its name was an exquisitely modest building. The largest
edifice was the great Library, which housed countless
thousands of volumes, together with facilities for making
copies of the books stored there.

The rest consisted of lecture halls, porticoes, courtyards,
dormitories and dining halls. Here scholars from all over the
Greek world came to study and to teach. Here they could
live at the king's expense with no obligation to perform any
work for the court.

In the entrance hall a learned-looking slave addressed the assembled visitors, informing them that Ptolemy I Soter, "the Savior," founder of the Alexandrian dynasty, had founded the Museum and Library. He pointed to the long list of librarians engraved on the marble wall, beginning with Demetrios of Phaleron and followed by the Librarians of almost two centuries.

Their first great task, he informed the public, was to produce an authoritative text of the poems of Homer. Over the centuries the many texts of these poems, drawn from far older oral sources, had grown corrupt. The scholars of the Library collected every version and ruthlessly purged them of anachronisms, words that had not existed in Homer's day, verses obviously composed by later pretenders. After many years of toil, they produced the purified version now current throughout the world.

Marcus found this interesting, but literary matters did not just now intrigue him. Wandering at large, he came to a wing surrounding a long courtyard in which stood strange devices of stone and metal, marked in some arcane system, clearly instruments of some sort but he could not guess their purpose. He accosted a Museum slave and asked what they might be.

"These are the instruments of the astronomers," the man told him. "By sighting along some of them at night, and observing the shadows cast by others during the day, they divine the nature of the heavens."

"Where do the mathematicians have their quarters?" Marcus asked.

The man led him to another courtyard almost identical to the last, except that instead of strange instruments, this one featured several marble-bordered expanses of gleaming white sand, lovingly smoothed and surrounded by benches. Upon the sand the lecturers drew figures with long wands, explaining the wonders of geometry to their students. The slave introduced him to the master of the mathematicians' wing, one Bacchylides of Samos.

"A Roman?" said the scholar, quirking a sardonic eyebrow. "I heard a rumor that some Romans had arrived. I cannot speak for the mathematicians, but you are going to be in great demand by the historians of the Library."

"Just now my interest is in mathematics," Marcus told him.

"How may I be of service?"

"I learned recently that Archimedes, the mathematician of Syracuse, spent his last years here in the Museum."

"Indeed he did. He was a strange and controversial man, but distinguished in his way. He was a great student of mechanics, which is not a field much pursued here."

"Why not?"

"You are blunt, I see. The fact is, most philosophers follow the precepts of Plato, who taught that philosophers corrupt the purity of their thoughts with manipulation of mere matter. Archimedes had a weakness for building machines, which for most of us partakes too much of the ignoble work of a laborer. If you were to ask most of the philosophers here what was the greatest achievement of Archimedes, they would say that it was his discovery of the relation between the surface and volume of a sphere and its circumscribing cylinder."

" 'Most,' but not all?"

"Perceptive as well as laconic. Yes, there is still an Archimedean school here that thinks we place too much value on Platonic detachment. They revere the works of Archimedes and continue his researches into mechanics."

"I would very much like to visit this school," Marcus said.

"Then, if you will accompany me, I shall take you there."

The Archimedeans occupied a wing of their own, partly to segregate them from the more respectable philosophers, partly because they needed space for their experiments. The courtyard was cluttered with a mass of wheels, screws, levers, ropes and pulleys such as Marcus had never seen before. One thing was plain: This was a place where men *did* things. For the first time among the foreigners of the south, he felt that he might be among kindred spirits. Romans appreciated art, literature and philosophy after a fashion, but they truly loved engineering.

"Chilo," Bacchylides called, "you have a visitor."

The man who came to greet Marcus wore a dingy tunic, powdered with sawdust. His beard was ill trimmed and he was brushing dust from his hands. "If it's about the machinery for the new harbor chain, tell the First Eunuch that we will have the design perfected in about ten days and we'll send the drawings to—" he looked Marcus over. "You're no court official. What brings a barbarian to the School of Archimedes?"

"Not precisely a barbarian," Bacchylides explained. "This gentleman is a Roman. He is an ambassador from the Republic of Noricum."

Chilo grinned. "Really? It's not quite like Odysseus coming back from the dead for a visit, but it's close. The old Romans were people who appreciated good engineering. Let me see—I think roads, tunnels, bridges and aqueducts were their specialties."

Marcus grinned back. "We're still good at them."

"At last! Somebody who doesn't think abstract thought is the highest of virtues."

"I think I can leave you here in the capable hands of Chilo. Good day, Ambassador." He walked off stiffly and quickly.

Chilo grinned after him. "Can't get away from the defilement of work fast enough, can he?" He turned and clapped Marcus on the shoulder. "Come on, Ambassador. Let me show you my school."

The men busy assembling and testing the machines didn't look like any group of scholars Marcus had ever seen.

They were mostly young and incredibly busy working the devices, many of which clearly were miniatures of far larger machines. They laughed raucously when one performed as desired and cursed luridly whenever one failed. Chilo explained that some of the machines were water lifters, pumps, dredgers and other practical devices required by Egypt; a land of canals and mud. Others were more fanciful, including a boat to travel beneath the water and a flying machine. Neither of these, Marcus was not surprised to learn, had yet been made to work.

Slaves entered the courtyard bearing trays of food and pitchers of wine. Work stilled for the moment. And men sat on benches or on their machines to eat. Marcus joined Chilo on a bench.

"We have a fine dining hall," Chilo said, "but we seldom use it at midday. We prefer to stay close to our work while the light holds. Plenty of time for relaxing after dark."

"You are men dedicated to your discipline," Marcus noted.

" 'Discipline'," Chilo said. "I like that. It sounds much better than 'craft' or 'work.' Not so degrading. It sounds like a soldierly virtue."

"It is. Has to be, if you would rather stay out here with your machines than go inside and eat."

"We love it," Chilo said fondly. "And here at the Museum is the best place for it. Anyplace else in the world, some city or tyrant might employ us to design an aqueduct or a pump or a superior catapult, but at the Museum we can do pure research."

"What does that mean?" Marcus wanted to know.

"In pure research, we strive to discover fundamental principles, to learn how the world works. We are unencumbered by the need to accomplish a specific task."

"Yet you seem to do a good deal of work for king and court."

"Well, yes. After all, we are the men who can accomplish things, and the king has many projects. It is a small price to pay for the freedom and resources we enjoy here."

"What do you do for him besides the earth and water—moving projects?"

"You already know about the harbor chain. Unfortunately, we are often called upon to provide novel devices for the royal pleasure-barges, or spectacular effects for the lavish parties the court puts on. It is a trivial waste of time and resources."

"What about Queen Selene? Does she make use of your services?"

"Oh, yes. And at least her projects are useful. She rarely demands anything frivolous. She has us working on a new crane to more quickly load and unload ships in the harbor. A great deal of time is wasted while they wait for an unloading dock."

"Are you asked to design many new war machines?" Marcus asked.

"Rarely. The Egyptians are complacent in military matters. The ruling Macedonians think warfare reached its height with Alexander the Great and there is no sense in trying to improve upon his tactics and drill. The machines used on their ships have changed little in two hundred years, and since they rarely indulge in city sieges, we're not often called upon to design heavy artillery."

"That seems a waste of a fine resource," Marcus said.

"True. It wasn't always so. Demetrios the Besieger, son of Antigonus One-Eye, built wonderful and very imaginative machines just the generation after Alexander. They rarely worked, but he had the right idea. Let the machines do the work and take most of the damage and save your men for the decisive thrust."

"An excellent concept," Marcus commended. "But, do

you really think you can build a machine that can fly like a bird, or a boat that can travel under water?"

Chilo took a drink of watered wine and pondered his answer. "I'll tell you one of the basic answers to such a question. The fact is, nobody can think of any convincing reason why we can't."

Marcus set down a honeyed roll. "Could you expand upon that?"

"It's like this: Most people will tell you that these things can't be done because they have never been done. We do not accept such reasoning. Long ago, somebody paddled out on the water astride a log *for the first time*. Somebody piled stone upon stone to build a house *for the first time*. Because these things had never been done before did not mean they could not be done, merely that no one had ever tried before. Others will give you philosophical or religious reasons why things cannot be done. We do not accept them. Here we believe in experimentation and proven results."

"Another excellent principle," Marcus said. "But do you not fear attracting the anger of the gods when you attempt these fabulous things?"

"To believe that the immortal gods can be jealous of mortal men is to hold a very low opinion of the gods. Here most of us respect the gods. But we do not believe that they are Homer's Olympians, fighting and bickering and seducing each other's wives. If we poor, limited mortal men can be philosophers, then the gods must be philosophers beyond our imagining. If we here can build clever machines of stone and metal and wood, what is that to gods who invented this world and the whole cosmos surrounding us? No, my friend, we fear men, not the anger of the gods."

"I want to hear all about you," Marcus said. "And about your master, Archimedes."

It had been his lifelong experience that men needed little prodding to speak of their fields of expertise, their lonely manias, especially if they seldom had someone to listen. So it was with these men. First Chilo, then one after another of the others spoke of their projects, their dreams, and of the man who had founded their school. He was not sure that he could believe everything they said about the man.

Still, these were men who thought they might someday fly.

A FEW DAYS LATER MARCUS AND THE REST OF THE Roman party had an opportunity to see one of the more lavish indulgences of the royal court. The young king was to receive them, and the event would be aboard one of the royal barges of which Chilo had spoken.

They had learned that Alexandria was built upon a narrow spit of land between two bodies of water. To the north lay the broad waters of the Middle Sea. To the south was Lake Mareotis. A channel linked the Eunostos Harbor with the lake, and yet another channel connected the eastern tip of the lake with the westernmost mouth of the Nile. Thus the seagoing vessels could pass from the harbor to the river without sailing westward and navigating the hazardous, multiple mouths of the Nile with their ever-changing sandbars and baffling false channels. Likewise, the rich river traffic of Egypt found its outlet at Alexandria.

The city itself was laid out in a grid with wide, perfectly straight streets. The eastern part of the city was the district of the huge Jewish population. To the west was the Rakhotis, or native quarter. In the center was the Greek section and here were to be found the greatest buildings, temples, shrines and formal gardens of the city. Alexandria was uniformly beautiful and harmonious, which Carthage, for all its magnificence, was not.

At least there was harmony in its symmetry and proportions. There was little harmony among the inhabitants. Disputes among the numerous ethnic groups were frequent and full-scale riots were no rarity. Alexandrian mobs had been known to depose kings who displeased them too greatly.

They had also learned something of the Ptolemaic dynasty. Founded by Alexander's general, Ptolemy Soter, the early kings had been intelligent, liberal rulers of great capability. They had turned the ancient, backward, weak land of Egypt into a great power, installing a royal bureaucracy of great efficiency, breaking the power of the ancient priesthoods and deposing the feudal landholders.

Three or four generations into the dynasty, the quality of royal competency declined alarmingly. The kings had adopted the quaint Pharaonic custom of marrying their sisters to keep the royal bloodline pure. Many attributed the decadence of the dynasty to this practice. Weakness of mind and outright insanity began to crop up with some frequency. Some kings were merely eccentric, others truly monstrous, such as the brutish Ptolemy Psychon, so named for his great obesity. He had murdered most of his own family, and this was among the mildest of his atrocities.

Oddly, the women of the family seemed to have retained the virtues of the early kings and, when they had an opportunity to rule in their own right, usually proved to be exemplary monarchs.

They came to the royal wharf on the lake side of the city and, once again, were forced in spite of themselves to gape.

"That thing *moves?*" Flaccus gasped.

Had it been a temple, it would have been of but middling size. But it was not a temple. It was a boat, but such a boat as they had never dreamed of. Half as long as a stadium, its superstructure was a palace three stories high, with tall pillars and a pitched roof, pillars and roof alike gilded, with carved frieze and pediment bright with paint, and between the pillars instead of walls there hung curtains of costly fabric or chain mesh of silver and gold. This incredible structure was situated atop twin hulls, each greater than the largest warship they had yet seen.

"Well," Marcus said, "it floats. I'll believe it moves when I see it."

So stunning was the barge that they scarcely noticed the crowd of people aboard it, colorful and striking though they were. There were hordes of seminude dancing girls, giants and dwarfs, transvestites of both sexes, apparent hermaphrodites, women wreathed in ivy vines like maenads, men in leopard skins, persons in the regalia of native Egyptian priests, foaming priestesses in transports of prophetic ecstasy, boys swinging smoking censers on long chains, towering black guardsmen with zebra-hide shields and carrying spears with blades as long and keen as swords. And these were only the ones that first caught the eye.

"So this is the royal court," Flaccus said. "Looks to be a lively place."

"Keep your faces straight," Marcus instructed them. "Act only politely impressed, and try not to laugh."

A man dressed in an odd combination of Greek and Egyptian court robes came down the gangplank to greet them. His face was heavily painted and he wore a square-cut black wig dusted with gold powder. He clasped his hands before his breast and bowed deeply.

"Welcome, envoys of Roma Noricum," he trilled. "I am Dion, Second Eunuch to the court of King Ptolemy. His Majesty is most anxious to meet you."

"Took his time about satisfying his anxiety," muttered Caesar.

"We are most eager to open negotiations with your king," Marcus said.

"Then, if you would be so good as to follow me, gentlemen."

The eunuch led them up the ramp and boys fell in beside them, swinging censers to cover them with fragrant smoke.

Barely nubile girls draped them with wreaths and slaves dipped bundles of withies into golden bowls of rose water and sprinkled them with the mild perfume. Dark young women wearing golden belts and nothing else unrolled a scarlet carpet before their feet as flower petals sifted down from the ceiling.

They entered the great interior hall of the vessel and found that its ceiling was a full three stories up, the upper two floors forming balustraded galleries. Massed at the railings were more of the bizarre inhabitants of the Ptolemaic court, but the Romans would not crane their necks to gawk at them. Ahead, at the end of the long room, sat enthroned the King of Egypt, Ptolemy Alexander Philadelphus Eupator, fourteenth monarch of his line by the official count, although pretenders and doubtful or de-legitimized heirs had been plentiful.

The boy sat rigidly, encased in court robes of stiff linen embroidered with gold thread, magnificent jewelry, wearing the simple diadem of Hellenistic royalty, holding crossed before him the crook and flail of the pharaohs. Young as he was, his expression was neither childlike nor truly adult, but rather a sort of reserved wariness, as if he had seen little in his short life to inspire him with confidence.

"Your Majesty," said the Second Eunuch, "I present the envoys from Roma Noricum."

"We are pleased to receive men of such distinction," the boy intoned, as if the formula were some prayer that he chanted without thought.

A man who stood at the king's right hand came forward. "I am Eutychus, the First Eunuch. I will accept your credentials and present them to His Majesty."

At Marcus's signal Caesar came forward with their documents and placed their documents into the soft hands of the eunuch. He was careful to avoid touching the half-man's flesh. Eutychus showed the documents to the king but the gesture was symbolic. The king barely glanced at them.

"These presents merit our closest study and I am certain that we shall find all in proper order," said young Ptolemy. "In the interim, please accept my humble hospitality." This he said with more enthusiasm.

At a gesture of his flail, a horde of slaves appeared, the first wave of them bearing furniture: chairs and couches, cushions and drapery. Many carried legs and struts and lengths of wood, and with amazing speed they assembled long tables down the length of the great room. A higher table was set before the throne, at right angles to the lower boards. The Romans barely had time to marvel at the splendid, exotic wood, inlaid with ivory and mother-of-pearl, before it was covered with cloths no less valuable.

With equal efficiency, staff-bearing stewards conducted the Roman party to their places at the high table. The couches were covered with cushions stuffed with rare herbs and no sooner had their feet left the floor than they were relieved of their sandals. Simultaneously, basins were held beneath their hands and water poured over them from pitchers of finely wrought gold. Food appeared as if by the working of some subtle god.

Where, Marcus wondered, was all this food coming from? They had seen no smoke rising from the barge, so there was no kitchen aboard, at least none equal to this prodigy of cookery. Lines of slaves filed in, each bearing a tray or bowl of some delicacy, even more elaborate than the viands they had enjoyed in Carthage. The slaves seemed to be organized in regiments distinct as to nation and costume: Blacks with sooty skin dressed in leopard-skin kilts and feathered headbands carried the fruits. Fish came in carried by Greeks dressed in white chitons. Brawny, pale-skinned northerners wearing fanciful fur loincloths, their arms and necks encircled by rings of bronze brought in meats. They worked in teams of four, bearing gigantic platters upon which rested entire roasted animals, some of them quite unknown to the Romans.

If their soldiers were as well trained and disciplined as their slaves, Marcus thought, these people would rule the world. Even as he thought this, a team of sleek, near-naked men rushed in, waving long, curved, swordlike knives. Behind them were girls in wispy tunics with double flutes in their mouths, the instruments bound by ribbons tied behind their heads. In time with the rhythmic music of the flutes, the men carved the roasts, their movements as graceful as those of dancers, reducing the smoking carcasses to steaks and slices and tiny chunks with incredible speed and skill.

"It's stifling in here," Ptolemy complained, sounding for the first time like the boy he was. A steward clapped his hands and the curtains between the columns rose silently to reveal an expanse of water stretching in all directions. The Romans stuffed food into their mouths to keep from gasping. The immense barge had set out upon the water and they had not noticed. At the stern, Marcus saw another barge connected by a broad gangway. It was from this barge that the slaves were carrying the provisions for the banquet. Even as he watched, the gangway rose and the barge backed away. Behind it were others, doubtless bearing the other necessities required by the Alexandrian court while roughing it on the water.

"How is this vessel propelled?" Marcus asked. "I hear no oars working."

Eutychus smiled indulgently. "First, enjoy and refresh yourselves with a little food and wine. Later, you shall have a tour of this pleasure-barge."

"Is there more than one?" Flaccus wanted to know.

"There are a score or so," said the eunuch. "This one is specially designed for banqueting. Others are for sight-seeing or sport or for the king's personal use."

"We thought all you Romans were dead," Ptolemy said,

picking sullenly at a dish of eels in some sort of dark sauce.

"Quite a few of us are still alive," Marcus said. "The mainland Greeks we trade with could have told you, but I suppose they had their reasons for keeping our existence to themselves."

"Trade secrets," the boy said, as if the subject of commerce bored him beyond bearing. "We heard that you fought some pirates on your voyage here," he said, brightening. "Was it exciting?"

"Combat is always exhilarating," Marcus told him. "But it wasn't a desperate fight." He saw the two principal eunuchs eyeing him with calculation.

"I've never seen a real fight," Ptolemy admitted. "Boxers and wrestlers can't be much like real battle."

"Sharp steel and the intent to kill put a different complexion on matters," Marcus said. "Real fighting must be taken seriously."

"I wish I could see a real fight," the boy said. "But a king is never allowed to get close to a battle."

Things must have changed since Alexander and the first Ptolemy, Marcus thought, filing this information away for future use.

"Don't despair," Flaccus put in, having swallowed enough wine to talk too much. "One of us may die here and the rest can stage a munus. Then you may see some real fighting."

"What is a munus?" Ptolemy asked.

Marcus shot Flaccus an annoyed look. "It is a ceremony we hold at the funeral games of a great man. Specially trained men fight to the death. The losers accompany the shade of the dead man on his journey." He heard one of the eunuchs mutter, "Barbarous!"

For the first time the boy seemed intrigued. "Who are these men?"

"For the most part they are slaves or men condemned to death. By fighting well a number of times they may win their freedom and pardon. Sometimes free men volunteer because they love fighting or like the excellent conditions in the training schools. The food is the best, the quarters are better than soldiers enjoy, they have first-rate medical attention."

"Well," the boy said, "perhaps one of you *will* die!" Clearly, he was looking forward to the prospect and considering arranging it personally.

"I should point out," Brutus said, "that none of us are distinguished enough to rate a munus."

"Oh," Ptolemy said, disappointed.

For a while they amused themselves watching the court attack the banquet. Plainly, they had nothing resembling the Roman sense of decorum. Like famished beasts, they bolted handfuls of meat, sloshed it down with huge goblets of unwatered wine and talked constantly while they were doing it. They pawed the slaves and each other without regard to age or gender.

"We could conquer these swine with a cohort of auxilia," Caesar said in Latin.

"Don't mistake the court for the army," Marcus said. "And speak in Greek. We can compare notes later. Just because they have no manners is no reason why we should imitate them."

When the rest of the court were rolling on the couches, stuffed to repletion, the Romans took up the offer of a tour of the remarkable vessel. Stepping onto an outer deck, they could see the oars working in a mysterious silence. The loudest sound was the faint splash as the broad ends dipped into the water and were pulled back, then raised to dip again. Banks of oars worked on both sides of each hull, supplying adequate power to move the immense barge through the water of the lake.

"What makes them so noiseless?" Caesar asked.

"I will show you," said Dion, the Second Eunuch. He led

them to a broad stairway that led below, into the portside hull. Within, it proved to be much broader than the hull of a warship, flat-bottomed and ballasted with meticulously cut stone polished to a high luster. To each side were three levels of benches, as on a trireme. At the lowest bench, pulling the shortest oar, sat a single man. On the next bench up two men drew a longer oar and on the highest bench three men toiled. The oarsmen worked naked, their benches heavily padded with sheepskin.

At once, the Romans saw why the oars worked so silently. Instead of common wooden oarholes, the oars passed through holes encircled with pads of stuffed leather. The men themselves were heavily muscled and they sweated mightily at their exertions. At intervals along the stone flooring burned braziers of incense, that the passengers above might not be offended by the odor of perspiring rower.

Here there was no *hortator* to keep time for the rowers with the rhythm of drum or flute. Instead, a small man conducted them silently with movements of his arms and hands.

"How can they coordinate?" Marcus wanted to know. "Between the two hulls, I mean. Without a drum to time them, surely one side must row a little faster than the other and send this thing in circles."

The eunuch pointed to a small port beside the timekeeper. "Through there he can see the pace-oar of the other hull. With gestures he speeds or slows his rowers. A slight discrepancy is inevitable, but the steersmen above can easily compensate. This is not a warship, after all, just a barge for leisurely outings on the lake and the river."

"Can it go all the way to the river?" Brutus asked.

"Oh, certainly. At the eastern end of the lake we will enter the canal to the Delta and thence proceed upriver."

"We are going to the Nile?" Marcus said, astonished. "We did not come prepared for such a voyage!"

Dion waved a hand airily. "Oh, we took the liberty of bringing your belongings aboard, not that you will need them. Everything a civilized human being needs is to be found aboard the king's pleasure-barge."

Seeing that any sort of protest would be pointless, the Romans went on with the tour. "What do you want to bet they didn't bring our weapons aboard," Flaccus said from the side of his mouth.

"Who needs weapons with this lot?" said Caesar.

"Shut up," Marcus said. "Greek only, remember?" Despite his apparent impassivity, he was alarmed by this development. Surely even a court as lax and decadent as this one would not spirit off a foreign embassy without prior notification. Or would they?

CHAPTER THIRTEEN

ZARABEL WATCHED THE ROMANS IN THE COURT-
yard below. They were arguing over something. She
could not understand Latin, but the subject was of little
import. She could read the language of posture and gesture
as well as anyone. Better than most, for to survive in the
cutthroat environment of the Carthaginian court required
an almost preternatural sensitivity to such wordless signals.

What she saw below confirmed what she already knew to
be true: With Marcus Scipio gone, the Roman party left
behind deferred to Titus Norbanus. They argued, they dis-
puted, but in the end it was his word that carried weight.
When he spoke, the others straightened and listened without interruption. No other member of the party received
such respect.

As had become her custom these recent days, she studied
him closely. She liked what she saw. It was still difficult for
her to accept men with such fair hair and skin, with eyes so
blue, as civilized people. Yet, a few of these Romans were

as pale as Gauls or Germans. She suspected that this meant an admixture of northern ancestry, for none of the historical sources she had consulted spoke of the Romans as being a fair-skinned people. It seemed not to lessen them in the eyes of their more conventionally tinted fellows. Of course, these Romans were but marginally civilized at best.

Norbanus was of the fairer sort. He was a large man, ruddy of face and yellow of hair, with regular, square features set in the harsh expression that seemed to be habitual with Romans. He had the soldierly bearing and hard, athletic build of the others as well, but none of these things gave her particular pleasure. What Zarabel found to her liking was the weakness she could discern beneath his Stoic mask.

When Norbanus looked at her, she felt the lust beneath his disdain. Of course, they all pretended contempt or indifference, but Norbanus was less adept at hiding his true feelings. Indeed, of all the Roman party only the amiable, now-departed Flaccus had not bothered to put up a hypocritical front in her presence, allowing his sensual tastes to be seen by all, whether the subject was women, food, wine or leisure.

But there was more in Norbanus to be exploited than this commonplace appetite. When he looked upon the treasures of Carthage his eyes lighted with greed. At banquets, he imitated the others in foregoing the exotic delicacies and rare wines, contenting himself with simple fare. But when he was entertained by the grandees of Carthage away from the other Romans, he indulged himself shamelessly. Her spies had reported this with great diligence.

She had taken him to see some felons executed upon the great walls, and his pleasure in the great cruelty of the tortures and crucifixions spoke volumes of his true tastes.

This, she knew, was a man she could bend to her will, manipulate into any form she desired. He was just the sort of man Zarabel favored above all others.

"Gylon," she said quietly. Her personal eunuch appeared by her side as quietly.

"Mistress?" He was probably still in his teens, although it could be difficult to tell, with eunuchs.

"Go and invite the Roman Norbanus to dine with me. Wait until he is separated from his companions."

The eunuch bowed. "As you wish, Mistress."

She watched as Gylon entered the courtyard, busying himself for a while with imaginary tasks, until the Roman dispute ended and the men wandered off. As Norbanus was about to leave, the eunuch stepped to his side and spoke a few words. She saw Norbanus look up toward her balcony, and then around to see if any of the other Romans were near. At last he looked back up and nodded. Zarabel smiled and nodded in return. Some men were so easy.

She made careful preparations. She owned some of the subtlest scents in the world, but subtlety would be wasted on such a man. She chose a simple infusion of rose and civet, known to make men susceptible to feminine charms. Her gown was cut to display her flesh abundantly. Just as important was her jewelry: heavy necklaces, armlets and bracelets, a belt of heavy golden plaques to display both the narrowness of her waist and the greatness of her wealth. Her jewels were large and colorful, the better to catch the Roman's eye.

She had spent much time of late studying. She had committed to memory all that was known of the Romans, but she had made certain to research other, similar peoples. Although the Romans were in some ways unique, in others they were much like other conquering, imperial peoples: the Assyrians, the Persians and, most of all, the Greeks.

She had paid especial attention to the Spartans, a nation as relentlessly military as the Romans, although without the Romans' matchless political skills. The Spartans had prized strength and hardihood, the ability to live frugally while

practicing unending military drill. They had despised
wealth and luxury and had even made their money from
common iron. The men lived on the coarsest, scantiest food
imaginable and affected to glory in their simplicity.

But the weakness had been there. In Sparta, among their
peers, they successfully maintained their vaunted simplicity
and rigor of life. All that changed when they conquered
foreigners and lived among them. The Spartans, so incor-
ruptible at home, proved to be eminently susceptible to
bribery when among lesser peoples. They had been able
to resist wealth and luxury because they were not exposed
to these things. The moment they had access to gold, fine
food and wine, comfortable houses and furniture, the de-
lights of beautiful, sweet-smelling women, their austerity
disappeared and they indulged shamelessly in these things
they had despised.

Zarabel suspected that the Romans would share this
weakness, and Norbanus most of all. She was counting on
it.

TITUS NORBANUS WAS IN HIS ELEMENT. WITH SCIPIO
out of the way, he could run the mission to his own satisfaction. He was sick of the patrician's smug superiority, his
easy assumption of authority, as if breeding were all a man
needed to excel at an important task. As if Italian breeding
were superior to German or Gallic.

Norbanus considered himself to be a Roman, albeit a Roman of Northern ancestry. He was as good as any other,
including Caesars who could trace their ancestry to the goddess Venus. Certainly as good as the Cornelia Scipiones, a
family noted for producing military heroes and little else.

He gloried in his physical endowments: his great height,
conferred by generations of Germanic chieftains, a taller people than any from Italy; his golden coloration, his brilliant

blue eyes, his wavy golden hair, cut short in the Roman fashion but forming a dense cap on his large, square-featured head.

He prized his great strength. Titus Norbanus had always excelled in athletic competition and martial exercises. The Romans had adopted the obstacle course first used by the Gallic warrior class. Even as a boy, Norbanus could run through the woods at full speed, picking thorns out of his feet without breaking his run, leap over branches as high as his head, swim a broad river without coming to the surface. He could ride two horses at once and he was the best wrestler in Noricum. He could lift twice his own weight from the ground and was renowned for his skill with sword and spear. In martial exercise he had no peer, with the possible exception of Marcus Scipio.

That exception ate at him as he prepared to visit the princess. She, at least, discerned clearly who was the better man. The plebs and common ruck of Noricum might revere the name of Scipio, but royalty perceived kingliness when it was before them.

He knew that he and Zarabel were a match. She had steel in her that her brother lacked. The Shofet was a vainglorious fool who could be manipulated by his counselors. She was a true descendant of her ancestor, old Hannibal. Already, Norbanus was forming, dimly, a plan of union. Why fight Carthage to reconquer Italy and the old empire, when an alliance could combine their might? Not just the limited military treaty Scipio had suggested, with the legions acting as virtual mercenaries, but a true alliance. An alliance, perhaps to be followed by a merger.

He knew that the traditional Romans would be horrified at the suggestion, but the New Families like his own would be far more reasonable. They lacked the visceral hatred of Carthage nursed by the Old Families. He had no use for such irrationality. The doings of a hundred years ago had no meaning to him. Today, and the opportunities of today, were what mattered.

In Zarabel he saw an opportunity such as came to a man only once in a lifetime, if that. He intended to take every advantage of that opportunity.

ROMA NORICUM

The uproar in the Curia surpassed anything seen there since the day of its founding. The second batch of reports had been read to the Senate and the acrimony had not let up for a moment since. Families old and new drew up their battle lines and shouted across them with red-faced rancor and men shifted from one side of the room to the other as alliances changed.

Even while the screaming debate roared on, the serious business of the Senate continued unabated. In one corner of the room a team of draftsmen under the supervision of two senators were busy drawing up a huge map of the Carthaginian Empire as described in the reports. On a great strip of canvas they used different colors of ink to indicate fortified cities, garrisons, naval harbors and all other salient features. In another area a team of architects built a detailed scale model of Carthage using the espionage expedition's meticulous notes as a guide. From time to time, a senator would cease yelling and walk over to study the map and the model. Even in this extremity of conflict, they could not suppress their fascination with these military preparations.

Gabinius, the Princeps Senatus, tired of the debate and came to observe the walls of Carthage as they rose in replica on the senate floor. The elder Titus Norbanus, leader of the New Families, came to stand by him. "Are such mammoth walls truly possible?" Norbanus wondered aloud.

"They are quite feasible," said the head architect. "If you have the engineering skills you can build as large as you can afford. So long as the foundations are deep and sound, stone will go as high as you can stack it. From what our people have described, there is little complicated engineering involved here, just great wealth and a lot of time for building. Herodotus says that the great pyramids of Egypt each took about twenty years to erect. These walls, with their stadium-seat design, could have been erected in less time than that. Carthage has an endless supply of slaves and subject people, and there is no shortage of stone. I am more impressed by the naval harbor. It is a masterpiece of efficient design."

"Young Scipio speaks much of the war engines," Gabinius said, running his gaze along the wall's broad crest. "If they're as formidable as he says, it could make a seaward approach completely unfeasible."

Another senator came to stand by the Princeps. He was Marcus Brutus, father of the augur on the expedition. "Scipio is too impressed with toys and novelties. The walls are barrier enough. Carthage is a naval power, well prepared for naval war. It is pointless to attack your enemy's greatest strength. It is his weakness we want to know about, and exploit."

"Very wise," old Norbanus agreed. "Of course, Carthage's true weakness is that it employs foreign troops to do its fighting. It gives us the opportunity to get legions into Carthage without having to invade at all."

"That is true," Brutus admitted, "but the thought of an alliance with Carthage is detestable!"

"Besides," said Gabinius, "having legions on soil controlled by Carthage is not the same thing as having them within the gates of the city itself. You're familiar with the reports by now. Virtually everything outside those walls is foreign territory to them. That great heap of stone is what constitutes Carthage."

"It is almost as good," Norbanus countered. He had not just heard the official reports. He had been receiving secret letters from his son. "With our legions as part of Hamilcar's army, we will learn everything about how they make war, about the quality of their troops. Our commanders will become personally acquainted with the highest Carthaginian officers and learn all of their qualities. A war is half won when you know these things."

Brutus and Gabinius agreed that this was so, and they were instantly suspicious. Why was Norbanus suddenly enthusiastic about this prospect? As leader of the New Families, he should have been the most strenuous opponent of a war against Carthage. The two of them waited until he was called away by others of his party and discussed the new development.

"What is that man up to?" Brutus said. "Six months ago, he was the loudest voice for pushing our borders to the North Sea and eastward to the Urals and west beyond the Seine. The south has never interested him or his kind."

"He's greedy," Gabinius said. "The reports speak of fabulous wealth to be had. Whatever those other lands have to offer, there is little wealth but a lot of hard fighting."

"It has to be more. We should never have allowed his son on the expedition, far less as second in command, and the latest report has him in charge at Carthage while young Scipio vacations in Egypt!"

"Marcus Scipio went to Egypt for good reason. He was sent to gather intelligence and he's getting all he can."

"We didn't commission him to be the biggest traveler since Herodotus! A reconnaissance of Italy was what we specified. A quick look at Carthage was all to the better. But he is trying to shape Roman policy for years to come!"

"Policy we can always repudiate," Gabinius said. "And he knows it. In the meantime, forget about war with Carthage. We need the support of the Norbani if we are going to retake Italy, so let's not concern ourselves about his motives just yet. The elections are coming up. I suspect that his election as Consul will be the price for his support. Whom shall we put up as candidate from the Old Families?"

"It will have to be Decimus Scipio, Cyclops's son."

Gabinius grinned. "The fathers of the two expedition leaders as Consuls? Each able to overrule the other? I like it. What about the Tribunes? Norbanus will try to have them ram legislation through the Assemblies to take the command away from young Scipio and give it to his son."

"We'll have to get together enough plebeian families beholden to us to elect a few Tribunes of our own," Brutus said. "It's going to cost."

"The prize will be worth the price," Gabinius said, making a mental note to write that down among his collection of aphorisms.

By late afternoon the hubbub died down. Fatigue was setting in. From outside the Curia could be heard the roar of the crowd assembled in the forum. The Tribunes of the People had been haranguing them all day and from time to time senators had gone out to the speaker's platform to add their own opinions.

This day the presiding Consul was Aulus Catulus, an Old Family patriarch. When he stood, his lictors pounded the floor with the handles of their fasces and the noise died down. The senators resumed their seats and waited.

"Senators, decisions must be made," Catulus began. "This bickering must stop. It is time for a formal debate. Publius Gabinius Helveticus, as Princeps Senatus it is your right to speak first." Catulus resumed his seat in the curule chair.

"Conscript Fathers," Gabinius said, "these unprecedented reports from our expedition of reconnaissance make a number of things abundantly clear: First, Italy is for all practical purposes ungarrisoned. It is ours for the taking, from the alps to the Seven Hills all the way to the Strait of Messina. Second: Carthage is incredibly wealthy. Third: Powerful as she is, Carthage has a number of weaknesses, foremost among them her dependence on hired foreigners as soldiers. Fourth: Hamilcar is in preparation for a war with Egypt and would like an alliance with Rome." Many senators, mostly Old Family, jumped to their feet and yelled their opposition. They quieted when the Consul threatened to have his lictors throw them out.

Gabinius resumed. "These things we know to be true from the first-hand reports of our officers. They have learned secondhand that the once great empire of the Seleucids is crumbling under heavy pressure from the Parthians. The Seleucid monarch also contemplates an invasion of Egypt, to restore his fortunes with that nation's legendary wealth. We have Marcus Scipio's report informing us just how wealthy that nation is." This was greeted with murmurs of appreciation. The gold and jewels of Carthage were a fantasy to them, but the rich soil of Egypt was the very essence of reality.

"Here is my proposal: We make a temporary alliance with Hamilcar." The word "temporary" forestalled the most vehement of the protestors. "We send him, say, four legions with attached auxilia for his campaign against Egypt. We must allow him to think that this constitutes the bulk of our available manpower, leaving us only a skeleton force to guard our frontiers."

"And use the other ten to reconquer Italy!" shouted an aged Caesar, one of the most fanatic of the back-to-the-Seven-Hills movement. There were shouts of agreement.

Gabinius smiled. "Not quite. We will need *some* troops to man the borders, but auxilia and veterans called back to the standards to handle that. The barbarians are not terribly threatening at the moment. No, what I propose is an expansion of our forces. I propose that we raise ten more legions."

There was stunned silence. Twenty-four legions beneath

the standards at once! It was an army unheard of in all of Roman history. "Impossible!" shouted some.

"Not at all. For a hundred years and more our empire has expanded and prospered. Lands once wild and tribal are now under heavy cultivation, and our farmers raise many sons. We have long regarded this as a manpower reserve against times of crisis, but why not put the bulk of them under arms at once? All freeborn Romans should be soldiers, is that not so? Let them get some experience, then. We face great wars of conquest in the future. Italy must not be merely retaken, it must be defended. The only way to defeat Carthage is to go to Africa and destroy the city itself. And after that there will be other foes, and they will not be disorganized tribesmen with courage and little else. There will be civilized armies to defeat. Our fourteen legions will not be enough."

A stern-faced senator rose and received permission to speak. "Where will we find arms and equipment for all these men? And money to pay for it all?"

"We have plenty of iron and skilled workmen," Gabinius said. "The treasury is full. Besides," he said, smiling, "ten new legions means ten new legionary commanders. Surely we have men who are brave, public-spirited and rich who would jump at the chance to win fame and glory, and who would be happy to part with some of their wealth to see that their men have fine arms and armor and warm cloaks and good boots."

This raised a chuckle, even from the opposition. The tendency of rich men to vie for command positions and to ingratiate themselves with their legionaries through such tactics had grown notorious.

"Gentlemen," Gabinius went on, "the reconquest of Italy must be our priority now, and that reconquest will necessitate eventual war with Carthage. We have no choice. Listen!" He paused dramatically, with a sweeping gesture toward the doorway of the Curia. From without came the rumble of the crowd. "Do you hear that? That is the voice of the Roman people. *They* demand this of us. Is it because all of them want to return to the land of their ancestors? Not at all. The majority of them are not of Italian ancestry. No, they want this because the immortal gods themselves demand it! For all these months, the omens have continued favorable. If we hesitate, if we fail in this task, the anger of the gods will fall upon us, and what will you tell those people then?"

At this, all fell to speaking in low voices among themselves. Some believed in the veracity of omens, some did not. But all understood the power of omens among the populace. Nothing of importance was done without consulting them. Interpretation of omens was an important function of state officers. Omens and politics were inextricable.

One by one, in order of their ranking in the Senate, the most prestigious senators rose, each to have his say in the matter. As might have been expected, the Old Family senators were unanimously in favor of the march on Italy, although they were less than enthusiastic about the proposed military alliance with Carthage. The New Family patriarchs put up far less protest against the project than they might have a few months before, and they had very little objection to the alliance, especially if it was to be followed by a war of conquest. Already, the prospect of the vast wealth that would inevitably fall into their hands was working on them. The clincher was the speech by the elder Titus Norbanus.

"My honored colleagues," he began, "there is much to be said both for and against this proposal by Publius Gabinius. But, as he has pointed out, any objections must go against the manifest approval of the immortal gods. They make it plain that this project must take place, and it presents Rome with an unprecedented opportunity to rise to the majesty intended by the gods—to be not just the greatest power in this part of the world, but to dominate the *entire* world. It is our destiny! We have the men and we have the wealth to carry out this conquest. We owe it to our posterity to seize this moment that they, our sons and grandsons, may live as lords of the world!"

There was frantic cheering at these words. Relayed by heralds to the crowd waiting without, the roar grew deafening. Gabinius, Brutus and many others smiled cynically. This seeming reversal of position on the part of the leader of the opposition left much unsaid: Those ten new legions would be raised almost entirely from the population of New Families. The Old Families no longer constituted a majority even in the fourteen traditional legions. This would greatly raise the power and prestige of his following.

And Norbanus's own son would be elevated to greatness. Right now he was the ranking man on the spot in Carthage itself while Scipio was gallivanting off in Egypt. Clearly, old Norbanus wanted to maneuver his son into the major command position in the wars to come. But that was a difficulty to be dealt with later. They had to have his support if they were to retake the Seven Hills.

By nightfall it was decided. The military reoccupation of Italy was to proceed. The ten new legions would be raised. A small deputation of distinguished senators would travel to Carthage to make arrangements for a military treaty with Carthage. All understood that the arrangement was to be strictly temporary.

Roman aims and policy were about to take a radical change in direction.

CHAPTER FOURTEEN

T HE PYRAMIDS TURNED OUT TO BE AS MIND-
numbingly huge as the early travelers and historians had
reported. The Roman party found themselves duly impressed, but at least these immense heaps of stone were not
alarming. The walls of Carthage had been alarming. The
tour had taken them far upriver to see the equally stupen-
dous temple complexes near the old capital, Thebes. On the
journey upriver they had passed the pyramids by moonlight
and had remained aboard.

The majestic river itself had been a revelation. They had
fancied that the Rhenus and Danuvius were the broadest
rivers in the world, but the Nile could have swallowed the
flow of both northern rivers without rising appreciably in
its banks. Ministers of the king had explained to them about
the river's annual flood, depositing the rich silt that made
Egypt so wealthy in crops, and the art of surveying that
made it possible to reestablish the boundaries of land after
each flood. This was the sort of activity the Romans could

appreciate. Surveying was something they understood.

All along the river, they saw water-raising machinery such as Marcus had seen in the Museum. With hydraulic screws and buckets moving on endless chains and in rotating wheels, water was raised from the river and dumped into channels that would bear it to the fields. All of Egypt was irrigated, because rain was a great rarity.

Yet, despite the sophisticated machinery, most farmers made do with the most primitive of machines: a long, cranelike shaft with a bucket or skin bag for water on one end, a huge ball of mud on the other as a counterweight. The farmers hauled the bucket down to the river and filled it, then let the counterweight raise the now-full bucket to be pulled in and emptied into an irrigation channel, then the process began again. The peasants performed this labor for hour upon hour, watering their fields one bucketful at a time.

"Machinery is fine," Flaccus remarked, "but it is expensive. Manpower is cheap, and Egypt seems to have no end of manpower."

Indeed, they had never seen a land as densely populated as Egypt. The whole nation was really just a narrow strip of green land bordering the river. No more than a mile from the river's banks, the cultivated land ended and the desert began with startling abruptness. Within that narrow strip of green land lived millions of Egyptians, all but a handful of them members of the peasant class whose toil produced the nation's astounding wealth.

"The river is their life," Brutus said one day, "but that desert is their security. They've never had to face anything worse than raids by desert tribes. Egypt doesn't share borders with any nation possessing a real army. In the northeast, they have the Sinai as a buffer zone between Egypt and the Seleucids. In the northwest, Libya amounts to nothing and separates them from Carthage."

Scipio nodded. "It's how they can maintain so dense a population. The land is never ravaged by war and they don't need to use the young men as soldiers. They can spend their whole lives doing nothing but farm."

"What a strange place," Caesar said. "It doesn't seem natural." He waved an arm toward the shoreline, where life was pursued as it had been without change for thousands of years. "It seems too . . ." He tapered off.

"I believe the word you are looking for is 'serene,'" Flaccus said. "Serenity is alien to us."

"That's it," Caesar agreed. "This whole country is like an old man sitting under his arbor, watching his grapes grow."

"So what is to keep Hamilcar from conquering this place?" Brutus wanted to know. "We know that he has an immense army and is planning to make it even stronger. With our legions thanks to you, Marcus." He waited for Scipio to rise to the jibe, but the leader simply listened attentively. "The Libyans won't stop him. He's probably already made arrangements with them. They may have formed an alliance. The Libyans will want a part of the spoils if they're to loot Egypt."

"He can cut off Alexandria with his navy," Caesar concurred, "and bring up his army to take the city."

"In the first place," Marcus told them, "he can't cut off Alexandria by sea. As we've already seen, the city has direct access to the Nile. The Delta has hundreds of river channels and even Hamilcar's navy can't block all those mouths. More importantly, it gives Alexandria access to the interior, which can keep the city supplied forever."

"Nonetheless," Brutus said, "the fact remains that Hamilcar doesn't have to take all of Egypt, as he might have in the days of the pharaohs. If he takes Alexandria, the rest of the country falls into his hands."

"That would require an immense siege," Marcus pointed out.

"Well, what do you think he's preparing for?" Brutus cried, exasperated. "He isn't amassing that army to take a few border forts and skirmish with some desert tribesmen! If a siege is what is required, that is what he'll do. Carthage took Syracuse by siege, so they know how it's done. We've all gone over the defenses. Alexandria isn't protected the way Carthage is."

"The walls of Carthage are a great redundancy," Flaccus said. "They are designed to overawe more than to protect. Building stables and barracks into the walls is very clever, but what military purpose does it serve? The defenses of Alexandria are more than adequate. The place was designed by Alexander and his generals, and they were men who knew more than a little about siegecraft."

"Flaccus is right," Marcus said. "Besides the supplies and the walls, the Archimedean School has designed wonderful fighting machines."

"You and those machines!" Caesar spat. "They are toys!"

"Toys?" Scipio said. "You saw them demonstrated at sea. Did they seem like toys then?"

"That was different," Caesar maintained. "A ship is a sort of machine. When machine fights machine, they have their uses. But we turned that pirate vessel into a slaughterhouse with a handful of legionaries."

"That's right!" Brutus said. "The ultimate weapon is the Roman legionary. A few legions would take Alexandria in a day."

"But I thought you objected to using our legions for the purpose, Brutus," Scipio said.

"Don't try to trick me! I am saying that good foot soldiers won't be stopped by big, noisy contraptions good for nothing but scaring the horses. Hamilcar's army may not be legion quality, but they can't all be bad. They are probably up to this task."

"Perhaps, Marcus," Flaccus said placatingly, "it might be

time for you to tell us just what you *do* intend. If mystifying us all is your intention, you've succeeded. I may say without bragging that I understand the Senate better than any man here. The Senate loves success, even when it is accomplished by less than traditional means. But the Senate at its most whimsical will never countenance using our legions on *both* sides of a foreign war. Not at the same time, anyway. Is that your intention? For us to back one side, then switch to the other?"

"You are close," Scipio said. "First, let me say this: In large part, I agree that Alexandria will not hold against a determined Carthaginian siege. That is not because of the inadequacy of the defenses, but rather because of the quality of the leadership. The king is a boy, surrounded by corrupt buffoons. The nation is generally well run because of Selene. The royal council is content to let her run the place most of the time because it relieves them of the labor. But they and the army will not follow her in war because she is a woman. Instead, they'll dress the boy in military clothes and try to defend Alexandria themselves. They fancy the blood of their warrior ancestors is sufficient to give them proficiency in the military arts."

The others chuckled. "The girl would make a better soldier than any of them, I'll grant you," Brutus said. "But what are you trying to tell us in your oblique way?"

"We can't afford to let Alexandria fall," Scipio told them.

"Why?" Caesar wanted to know. "What is Alexandria to us? Or Antioch or Babylon, for that matter?"

"Egypt is Carthage's enemy and rival, as Rome was once. Let Hamilcar have an easy victory and he will fancy himself invincible, in the usual manner of triumphant kings. He will also have the wealth of Egypt to add to that of Carthage. I don't intend to help Egypt defeat Carthage. I want Hamilcar to get bogged down into a long, costly war here."

Flaccus was first to see the light. "If the fighting is too

much for his troops, he'll want more of our legions."

"Exactly," Scipio said.

Young Caesar was not far behind. "Our legions will use Italy as a staging area! Hamilcar will be too preoccupied here to notice that we've reoccupied one of his less important provinces!"

"We'll have Italy back without a voice of protest being raised in Carthage," said Flaccus.

"It hardly seems honorable," Brutus protested. "And our legions will suffer, being sent here to take part in a futile war."

"When is war ever easy on the legions?" Scipio said. "Their purpose is to make Rome strong, safe and great. The enemy involved needn't be the army directly before them. If there is any dishonor involved, let it be upon me. Anyway, Roman commanders are nothing if not resourceful. They'll figure out ways to let Hamilcar's mercenaries absorb the bulk of the casualties."

"You haven't explained one thing," Caesar said. "How do you propose to keep Hamilcar from taking the city?"

"Oh, that's simple. I will assist the king here in conducting the defense."

They gawked at him, then Flaccus spoke.

"And I thought Titus Norbanus was a cold-blooded bastard."

CARTHAGE

The war council was conducted formally. Hamilcar wore military uniform, as did all the council who were not of advanced years. On some, the effect was fairly ludicrous. The exception was the Roman delegation. It was now swelled by a number of prominent men, most of them senators, who had been dispatched from Noricum to handle the details of the new "Alliance."

Now that their mission was overtly military, they all wore military garb, in which they looked much more comfortable than they had in their togas. There was little agreement among their equipment, for uniformity was not imposed upon the officer class. Some favored the old-fashioned cuirass of hammered bronze, sculpted to follow the muscles of the torso, others favored the more practical shirt of Gallic mail, sometimes with added defenses of iron plate. The helmets they cradled beneath their arms were of various Greek, Italic or Gallic designs or combinations of two or all three, some plain, others crested or plumed. Whatever their taste in armament, all of them looked eminently competent.

This impression was not lost upon Hamilcar. He felt that he was getting a better bargain than he had expected if the quality of Roman soldiery was uniformly high. They might just bear watching, though. He nodded to Norbanus, and the Roman commander stepped forward with easy elegance.

Norbanus was one who favored the Attic bronze cuirass, and his was decorated with embossed figures of gods and goddesses silver-gilt to contrast with the warmly gleaming bronze. His parade helmet was copied from the famous lion-mask helmet of Alexander the Great. He looked no less deadly for all the finery, though.

"Your Majesty," he began, "the noble Senate has agreed to send you four of our legions to aid in your conquest of Egypt. They sail from Tarentum within the month, if the weather cooperates."

"I shall sacrifice for happy winds," Hamilcar said. "But, four legions? How many men is that?"

"A legion comprises about six thousand men, all citizens," Norbanus explained. "But when we say 'legion,' we mean a full legion plus the same number of attached auxilia. These are mostly men from recently conquered territories who earn their citizenship by service in the auxilia. There are many Gauls and Germans among them, but they are all loyal soldiers of Rome. Thus, four legions mean about forty-eight thousand fighting men, plus their attached noncombatants: medical staff, surveyors, smiths, carpenters, tentmakers and so forth. These latter are mostly state-owned slaves."

"I see," Hamilcar said, a bit skeptical that the Romans could get so many men under arms at such comparatively short notice, much less be ready to embark them. "And how do the legionaries and the auxilia differ, other than the matter of citizenship?"

"Lentulus Niger will explain," Norbanus said. "He is acting as quartermaster for this expeditionary force." He stepped back and another man stepped forward. Niger was a stocky man with unkempt black hair and wearing a short beard, a rarity among the close-barbered Romans, and a sign that he was in mourning. He wore a plain tunic of Gallic iron mail and carried a severely plain iron helmet; pot-shaped with broad cheek guards and a trailing plume of black horsehair.

"Citizens in the legions are all heavy infantry, armed with heavy and light javelins, short sword and dagger. All wear helmet, cuirass of Gallic mail, and bear the scutum, the long shield. None wear leg armor save centurions, who are permitted greaves as a sign of their rank.

"Auxilia comprise the other arms, although some of them are heavy infantry as well. They are the cavalry, the light infantry, skirmishers and the missile troops: archers, slingers, javelin men and so forth. All of the light-armed troops are armed with sword and light shield for close combat. Auxilia are organized only as cohorts, never as legions. The cohort consists of five hundred men organized into five centuries of one hundred, each commanded by a centurion.

"Since the Cornelian reorganization of some sixty years ago, each legion is accompanied by twelve cohorts of auxilia, although this can be varied at need. The usual mix is four cohorts of heavy infantry, two of archers, two of skirmishers including the javelin men, three of cavalry and one of slingers."

"You Romans do not make great use of cavalry?" one of the Carthaginian generals queried.

"They are not terribly useful in the terrain of Gaul or Germania. Here in Africa, we may wish to increase our cavalry forces and reduce some of the others. Experience will determine that."

"This is all most impressively organized," Hamilcar said. "Are your supply services as efficient? I do not want your legions extorting the necessities from my cities on the march. I also have an agreement with Libya not to loot as we pass through. Of course, once we are in Egyptian territory, your men may lift as much as they can carry."

"Attached to each commander's staff are commissariat officers," Niger told him. "There is also a paymaster, the quaestor, who is a serving magistrate, answerable directly to the Senate. We prefer not to depend upon forage and local supply. Your cities need not worry."

"How—how businesslike," Hamilcar said, raising a chuckle from his council. He was hard put to know what to make of these Romans. They seemed to approach warfare as they would an engineering project. This caused another question to occur to him. "As to siege works, earthworks and so forth, labor may be levied upon certain towns, but not others, slave gangs may be rounded up in Egyptian territory, but this must be cleared through my own commanders, who may have their own uses for them. Is this understood?"

"Every Roman soldier, of whatever category, carries pickaxe and spade," Niger said. "We neither need nor want great mobs of slaves interfering with our army. We will accomplish all the necessary engineering works ourselves."

The Carthaginians were dumbfounded. Soldiers who did the work of slaves! Men who laid down the sword and picked up the spade! What sort of warriors were these?

Norbanus and the other Romans knew exactly what these men were thinking and they smiled inside. These barbarians would learn soon enough what they were dealing with. Romans had won as many wars with the pickaxe as with the sword.

Zarabel was, as usual, watching the proceedings from her hiding place. It galled her to have to do this, but to demand attendance at a council of war would strain her brother's always-chancy tolerance. Of course, she could get a full report afterward from Norbanus or other sources, but that would inevitably lack the nuance of a firsthand look at the proceedings. This was most informative.

The new Romans were up to her expectations. Scipio and his party had not been some sort of aberration. She had already entertained them and spoken to them. They were as businesslike, direct and unsophisticated as the others. Yet, unlike her brother and his ministers, she did not mistake this for simplicity, far less for stupidity. What these men lacked in polish they more than made up for in native intelligence and clarity of purpose. They were here on a mission and she was not at all satisfied that it was that of a simple military alliance. She sensed an agenda here.

She already knew of the Romans' near-religious zeal to take back their Seven Hills and the rest of Italy. She also knew that not all the Romans were fanatical in this aim. She knew further that certain of them, including Marcus Scipio and Norbanus, were playing games of their own. Perilous as this was, she welcomed it. These Romans represented her chance to topple her brother and to put herself and the cult of Tanit in their rightful position.

Besides, since the Romans showed up, life had been exciting and stimulating. She was no longer bored.

ROMA NORICUM

"What is the problem?" Decimus Cornelius Scipio, the new
Consul, presided this day over yet another of the unending
meetings that devoured all his time now that the epochal
retaking of Italy was under way. Next to him, in the seat of
Junior Consul, sat his colleague Titus Norbanus the Elder.
This meeting concerned purely military matters, so it was
staffed by the Senate. In token of the state's status of total
war, they had exchanged the white toga of peace for the red
sagum of war.

"We've run out of totem beasts," the soldier said. He was
a legionary staff officer, but he was also a priest of Bellona,
the goddess who oversaw all military matters. "For many
generations," he pointed out, "we used only the sacred animals as standards for the legions. The eagle has pride of
place and has always been the standard of the First Legion.
The wolf, Minotaur, horse and boar were used for legions
Two through Five. In the Cornelian reorganization, when
so many more legions were called for, we added the serpent,
the dragon, the bear, the hippogriff, the chimera, the gor-
gon, the lion, the elephant and the raven. Now we are raising
ten more legions. We need ten more standards and we must
either add ridiculous creatures or duplicate some of them,
either of which would be pernicious."

The consuls and the rest pondered. This was not a trivial
problem. Soldiers held their standards sacred, as deities em-
bodying the living spirit of the legion. The standard was
carried by the bravest of the brave and to lose it was un-
speakable shame. This had not occurred in many generations.

"We can't have lizards and mice as standards," Norbanus
said, "and we already use the most formidable creatures of
legend except perhaps for Pegasus and Cerberus. What's to
be done?"

Publius Gabinius stood and was recognized as Princeps Senatus. "As a matter of fact, I have been giving this problem consideration for some time and I think I've reached an acceptable solution."

"I am sure we'd all be glad to hear it," said Consul Scipio.

"As was just said, the eagle has always had pride of place, as the sacred bird of Jupiter. Likewise, many of the most potent omens sent to tell us of the gods' will in the matter of the reconquest came through the agency of eagles. I propose that, as part of the military reorganization now taking place, we make the eagle the standard for *all* the legions of Rome. The other totem creatures may be retained as standards for the lesser formations within the legions, and for the cohorts of auxilia."

"This is radical!" protested an old senator.

"No less radical than this project upon which we have embarked," Gabinius answered.

The debate that ensued lasted through much of the day, but in the end it was agreed upon. Henceforth, all the legions would follow the eagle.

SENATOR GAIUS LICINIUS RUFUS, OVERSEER OF ARMAMENTS, toured the workshops of Gaul, where much of the ironwork for the legions was carried out. In the armor factories of the province he had been well pleased with the construction of the new mail shirts. For the sake of simplicity they had been standardized in three patterns: knee-length with shoulder doublings in the Greek or Gallic styles for the heavy infantry; mid-thigh length without shoulder doublings for light infantry; waist length with Gallic-style shoulder doublings for cavalry. The Gallic craftsmen were superb and meticulous. No Roman soldier would die because his armor was of shoddy quality.

Helmets were another matter. "This is dreadful!" Rufus

said, turning the new helmet over in his hands. It was of a new pattern: Made entirely of iron, it was little more than a crude pot, descending a little below the ears in back, with a broad, flat neck guard, with cutouts for the ears and wide cheek guards cut back to clear the eyes and mouth. It had the crudest of finishes and entirely lacked the graceful rolled and roped edges of the traditional bronze helmets. It had no provision for crest or plumes and its only concession to decoration was a pair of crudely embossed eyebrows on the forehead.

"It's not pretty, I'll grant you that," said the master armorer. "But it's better protection than the old bronze pots. Ask any soldier whether he'd rather have a helmet that looks good on parade or one that'll keep a sword out of his skull and neck in battle."

"The lowest auxilia have better helmets than this!" Rufus protested. "The legions will rebel!"

"No they won't," said the armorer. "Fact is, if you want to raise ten entire new legions plus support troops and do it fast, you have to sacrifice some quality. It was decided to go for practicality instead of beauty. This helmet is stronger and better designed than the old ones and it doesn't require as much skilled labor. Look, later on, when things have settled down and the soldiers have a little money in their purses, they can tart these up as much as they like: add plumes and crests, solder enameled bosses on them, put bronze piping around the edges, cover them with gold leaf, whatever. In the meantime, they can fight in them."

"But Roman soldiers never went into battle looking *ugly*!" Rufus protested.

A month later he was in the valley of the Rhenus, looking over the new swords. Cut off from the wonderful iron deposits of Spain, the Romans had established their sword works here, where the tough local iron was excellent for swords and the heavy forests provided abundant charcoal for forging.

He walked down a long table, picking up and hefting some of the new weapons. As with the helmets, these swords had been simplified for mass production. The pommels were simple balls of hardwood, the grips of bone variously stepped, grooved or checkered for a firm grip. The blades were the sort the Romans favored: no more than twenty inches long, pointed and double-edged, but here some changes had been made. These looked like shortened versions of the cavalry longsword. Instead of the graceful curved edges that produced the traditional wasp waist, their edges were perfectly straight and parallel. Instead of the usual long, tapering point, these were short and acutely angled.

He had to admit that they balanced just as well in the hand as the old style. In fact, they felt somewhat better. A little experimenting on animal carcasses in a butcher's stall satisfied him that the odd-looking point penetrated just as efficiently as the old style and, as the swordmaker pointed out, it was stronger and less likely to bend against shield or armor. Rufus sighed. It was hard to turn loose of traditional things, but concessions would have to be made if they were to take back the Seven Hills. He pronounced himself and the Senate satisfied.

THE CONSULS INSPECTED THE NEW LEGIONS AT A grand review on the Field of Mars. The older, established legions were already encamped at the foot of the mountains except for the four destined for Carthage and the war with Egypt. Those had already crossed into Italy.

"We are being watched," Consul Norbanus said.

"Naturally," said Consul Scipio. "Romans seldom get a spectacle like this."

"I mean we are being watched by those Greek merchants."

Quintus Scipio turned around. They stood atop the great reviewing platform from which the consuls and other magistrates traditionally inspected the massed legions. He saw the little knot of Greeks watching from the fringes of the crowd, their expressions intent and calculating.

"Yes. Well, they aren't very effective spies. Everyone knows them for inveterate liars. Do you think Hamilcar or anybody else would believe them were they to report what they see here?"

"Safer to kill them," said his father, Scipio Cyclops. As one who had held all the highest offices, he rated a place on the stand.

"Safer, perhaps, but would it be wise?" the younger Scipio remarked.

"What do you mean?" Norbanus wanted to know.

"If the merchants fail to return home, suspicions may be roused. They do not act entirely as individuals. They belong to syndicates. Inquiries will be made."

"There is that to consider," his father admitted.

"They're Greeks and they're merchants," Norbanus said. "Let's just bribe them."

"With what?" Quintus Scipio asked. "We've bankrupted the treasury preparing for this war."

Norbanus chuckled. "How innocent you are. A one-time cash payment is not how you bribe these people. They would just go to Hamilcar and demand a bigger bribe to tell what they know. He would be more likely to believe them if he has to pay for the information. No, the way to bribe them is with something that will continue paying them in the future. We are going to reestablish Rome in Italy. That will mean a whole new market for them. Promise them long-term contracts, monopolies and so forth. It's what they value."

"Excellent idea," Quintus Scipio said. "You can take care of the matter since it's your idea." He knew that part of each contract would stick to the fingers of his colleague, but that was only to be expected.

Three new legions stood on the Field of Mars, fully equipped. The rest would be ready in the next few months. These were mainly new recruits, with a leavening of veterans drawn from the established legions. All of the centurions and decurions were veterans, naturally. The raising of ten new legions had brought about an unprecedented rash of promotions. Men who mere months previously could not have expected to wear decurion's plumes for another ten years now gloried in the crest, vinestock and greaves of a centurion.

The military tribunes and senior staff were drawn from the senatorial class, and some of these glittered with bronze finery, colorful plumes and weapons decorated with precious metals. Others were as unadorned as the commonest legionary. There had been special elections to appoint the junior officers, special meetings of the Senate to approve the commanders and legati. As always where the Senate was concerned, there was maneuvering and shifting of alliances and voting blocs. The men lucky enough to hold high rank during the reconquest could look forward to glittering political careers. They would be the favorites at future elections; their names would appear on monuments. Prominent senators indebted themselves for years to come in order to secure these commissions for their sons.

The priests of Bellona went forward dressed in their ritual regalia to pronounce the blessing of the goddess upon the legions. The soldier's oath had been taken at the formation of the new legions, but the necessary ceremonies remained to be accomplished.

Because of the unprecedented military situation there had been an extraordinary election of censors, an election that ordinarily would not have taken place for another three years. The legions had to be purified, and only censors could perform this ceremony, the lustrum.

The two distinguished senators, both of whom had held all the highest offices, came forward and pronounced the prayers in a language so ancient as to be unintelligible. Then commenced the suovetaurilia: the great sacrifice to Mars. The three victims were brought forward: a spotless white bull, an enormous ram and an equally huge boar. All had been scrubbed and their horns and tusks gilded. Drugged to keep them quiet, bound and draped with garlands of flowers, they were raised on ornate litters and carried by temple slaves in solemn procession amid clouds of incense smoke from censers swung on long chains by white-clad boys.

Three times the beasts were carried around the assembled legions. The procession halted at the great altar of Mars and the creatures were unbound and led before the altar where the Flamen Martialis waited, wearing his white coif surmounted by the wooden disk and spike. He drew his curved sacrificial knife and cut the throat of each animal. Slaves caught the gushing blood in golden bowls and poured it over the altar. Then the priests of Mars roared out the ritual laugh three times and all was silent while the augurs scanned the skies for omens. In time a flock of raven was observed alighting in a tree on the south end of the field and the Flamen Martialis pronounced the god satisfied.

The Senior Consul, his red sagum draped in the manner of a commander delivering the adlocutio, now spoke.

"Soldiers of Rome! You have taken your oath and you have been purified. Now you go forth to accomplish the greatest task ever entrusted to the legions. Yes, what you are about to do will be remembered as greater than the war with Hannibal, for this time we shall prevail! Greater than the wars against the Gauls and the Germans that brought us our empire of Noricum, for this time we do not fight a campaign here and there against this tribe or that league, and we do not fight primitive warriors.

"Soldiers! You are about to begin the reconquest of our sacred homeland! You will meet, fight and destroy utterly the greatest empire in the world! You will humble Hannibal's children and make them pass beneath the Roman yoke! This generation, with you leading the way, will accomplish the sacred act of vengeance vouchsafed to us by our ancestors.

"Generations to come will calculate the year from this date, when Rome raised the most powerful army in history to take back the sacred Seven Hills!" He raised his arm in salute and the assembled soldiers roared out their battle cry, pounding the butts of their pila against their shields as the priests of Mars known as the Salii, the "holy leapers," performed their vaulting dance around the altar of the god. They wore ancient helmets and they carried the twelve sacred shields called ancilia, one of which had in ages past fallen from the heavens. As they danced, they performed the act forbidden at any time save one such as this: They beat the shields with their staves to call upon Mars for aid in the coming war.

At last there was silence. The priests of Saturn entered the field, bearing the standards of the legions: the images of the sacred beasts for the lesser formations and the new golden eagles for the legions themselves. These were given to picked men who wore pelts of bear or wolf or lion draped over their helmets and shoulders. The senior of these bore a new title: aquilifer, "eagle-bearer." His would be the greatest responsibility of all the six thousand soldiers of the legion: It was his duty to walk forth alone if the legion faltered. He was to die before allowing the sacred emblem to fall into enemy hands.

When all else was done, the priests called fetiales came forth and walked to the little enclosure of land dedicated to Bellona and designated as enemy territory. One of the priests carried the ancient bronze spear of Romulus. At the boundary the senior priest pointed to the enclosure with his wand. "Behold Carthage!" he shouted. A younger priest stepped forward and solemnly cast the ancient spear into the enemy soil where it stood, quivering.

The Senate of Rome chanted as one man: "Go! Take back the Seven Hills!"

The assembled legions roared their assent.

The reconquest of Italy had begun.

CHAPTER FIFTEEN

THE BOAT LOOKED LIKE NOTHING MARCUS HAD ever seen before. If pressed to describe the thing, he might have said that it was like two boats fastened together, with the upper one hull-up, so that the whole thing was shaped like an enormous wooden spindle. Oars protruded from ingenious oarlocks, waterproofed with tarred leather sleeves. A pair of steering paddles protruded from its rear like the legs and feet of a goose. In the upper bow was a small window of thick glass. It rested on a launching slip like the egg of some vast bird. A small crowd of curiosity-seekers stood around waiting to see what might happen.

Marcus stood with Chilo, the head of the Archimedean School of the Museum. Selene sat near them in her elevated royal litter. Since this was not an official function she was dressed informally, in a plain, white gown with a gold-embroidered border. The gown was Greek but her hair was covered with an Egyptian-style coif, the first article of native garb Marcus had seen her wear.

"Do you believe this thing can really travel beneath the water?" Flaccus asked, looking queasy. He was the only member of the Roman party besides Marcus who had come to view the launching. The others deemed it a waste of time.

"Of course," Chilo said. "We wouldn't risk men's lives in it if we did not. The design has worked well when we built miniatures."

"I can make toy soldiers do things that living soldiers cannot," Flaccus said. "It is not natural for men to travel beneath the water."

"You think it's unnatural to travel *on* the water," Marcus said.

"The boat is watertight," Chilo asserted. "It will hold enough air to last the men inside for an hour or more. What we seek to find out today is how well we can make it move beneath the water, whether we can control its speed and direction sufficiently."

"I think it is most exciting," Selene said. "These men will be doing something no one has ever done before." No other member of the court was present. The pleasure-loving rulers of Egypt found nothing very interesting in the experiments of the Archimedeans. They had expressed only the mildest interest when Chilo had pointed out that his vessel would be useful in salvage operations.

"How can oars work under water?" Marcus asked. "If they can't be lifted free of the water, I would think that the pulling stroke would move the boat forward, then the return stroke would move it an equal distance back."

"The oarsmen are skillful," Chilo said. "You notice that the paddle ends are broad but very thin? Likewise, the shafts are of a flattened oval cross-section rather than truly round. After each pull stroke, they will twist the oars to a perfectly horizontal position and thus will cut through the water with very little resistance on the return stroke."

"We shall see," Marcus said.

A man's head appeared through the open hatch atop the hull. "All is ready," he reported.

"Good luck, Tyrophanes!" Selene cried.

"Then launch!" Chilo called. Slaves wielding sledgehammers knocked the chocks free and the bizarre boat slid down the greased skids to enter the water with a restrained splash. It settled so deeply that Marcus feared that it would sink, but as it lost way it floated with about a foot of its upper surface still above water. With a wave and a grin, the captain of the vessel disappeared inside, pulling the hatch shut behind him. The bronze wheel protruding from the hatch turned as it was tightened from within against its oiled leather gasket.

"Now what?" Flaccus asked.

"Tyrophanes will open the valves in the hull to fill the water skins inside. These will provide enough weight to cause the boat to sink entirely beneath the water."

"How do they come back up?" Flaccus said, his face a little pale.

"There are screw-presses to expel the water once more and then the boat will rise," Chilo explained.

"Something about that just doesn't sound right," Flaccus protested.

"The principles of buoyancy were articulated by Archimedes himself," Chilo told him. "It is all quite elementary." But his own face was somewhat pale and grim, belying his confident words.

"There it goes!" Selene said.

While they watched, the boat subsided slowly beneath the surface of the lake. Some in the little crowd cried out, then there was only a low muttering. All stared out at the calm, unruffled waters of the lake, saying very little. This silence held for perhaps fifteen minutes.

"Well, that's that, then," Flaccus said finally. "The poor buggers have all drowned."

"There!" Selene shouted, jumping to her feet in her excitement. She was pointing to the east and everyone looked in that direction. Perhaps three hundred yards away the boat had surfaced. The hatch flew open and Tyrophanes leaped out and clasped his hands overhead like an Olympic victor. The crowd cheered as if they were at a chariot race.

"You see?" Chilo said. "I told you!" But sweat streamed from his brow and he looked as if he hadn't breathed the whole time the vessel was beneath the water.

The boat returned to the slip, running on the surface this time. Tyrophanes and the brave scholars who had taken the ride with him were cheered and congratulated. Even the slave rowers received applause.

"All right, it works," Flaccus said with poor grace. "Now how do you propose to sink an enemy ship with it?"

"That will take some work," Chilo said, beaming. "This is merely an experimental vessel, not a warship. That would have to be much larger. A ram would be the most efficient weapon."

"Ramming makes even a galley spring leaks," Marcus pointed out.

"We've been thinking more along the lines of a great iron saw on top of the vessel," Chilo said, "to rip the enemy ship open."

Marcus turned to Selene. "See if you can get the shipyards to build a diving warship to Chilo's design," Marcus said.

"I think I can do it," she said. "I have my resources."

"Excellent," Marcus said. "Now, Chilo, how about one of those flying machines you've been telling me about?"

Flaccus rolled his eyes and groaned but no one paid him any attention. Marcus, Chilo and Selene had their heads together in earnest discussion.

·   ·   ·

MARCUS SCIPIO SPENT EVERY HOUR HE COULD SPARE at the Museum, in the newly expanded facilities of the Archimedean School. He had prevailed upon Selene to divert all the funds she could to advance the school's research into new weapons for use in the upcoming war with Carthage. She exerted herself splendidly for the best of reasons: Marcus assured her that, when the time came and Carthage was destroyed, Rome would make her true Queen of Egypt. Life was a high-stakes gamble in the Ptolemaic family and she deemed the prize worth the risk.

He no longer had to explain things or justify his actions to the rest of the Roman delegation because all had left save Flaccus. They were eager to take part in the upcoming wars and had no taste for pseudo-diplomatic service in Egypt. Pleading that they had done all the useful reconnaissance they were going to do, they had taken their leave, some for Carthage, others for Italy. They wanted in on the reconquest they knew was to come and considered Marcus Scipio and Flaccus utter fools for plodding along at this civilian work.

Marcus was certain that his work here was far more important to the future of Rome than any service he could perform as a commander of legions. He knew himself to be a fine soldier, but the legions were full of fine soldiers. Here, he could alter the course of history for all time to come.

As for Flaccus, he cared nothing at all for glory, but he liked the easy life and luxury of Egypt very much indeed. "I don't care if I never see Noricum again," he told Marcus. "As for Italy, it won't be a fit place to live in for a good many years to come. So if you like, I'll stay here and write up your dispatches for you. Just don't expect me to go back with you when you leave."

An endless stream of designs poured from the school, some of them logical, some clearly impractical, all of them intriguing. The improved catapults and ship-killers were the most prosaic. The chemical weapons were as dangerous to the experimenter as to any enemy. Chilo did not like them anyway as they did not involve his beloved principles of Archimedes.

"Mere apothecary work," he sniffed when a young man named Chares demonstrated an astonishing new explosive. Marcus was not so contemptuous. Quietly, he told Chares to continue his researches.

Work proceeded on the submersible vessel. Tyrophanes reported that the maiden voyage had not proceeded as perfectly as it had appeared to observers. When the ballast skins were filled, the vessel had descended as predicted and there was no serious leakage. The oars had worked well as propulsion. Other things had not gone so well. Controlling depth had been a problem. The plan had been to cruise at no more than a few feet beneath the surface, but more than once the vessel dived and struck the mud of the lake's bottom. Direction had been a difficulty as well. Visibility through the small port had been no more than a few feet in the murky water and steering had turned to guesswork. It had transpired that men working oars used up the air far faster than men at rest. Foul air had forced Tyrophanes to surface when he did and he then found that he was nowhere near where he had thought himself to be.

The scholars were already at work on these problems. Marcus admired their near-Roman ability to define problems and seek solutions. Most foreigners simply didn't think that way.

The man responsible for designing the oars thought he had a solution for the depth control problem: If vertical steering oars could make a ship move right or left, might horizontal steering oars not move it up or down? Chilo set him to designing such oars.

A young man from Cyprus who loved to experiment with mirrors and lenses said he could design a device that would allow the steersman to see above the water while the vessel was submerged. Marcus thought this sounded like magic, but Chilo told the boy to proceed with his experiments. This was a problem that would have to be solved if the submersible vessel was to be of any use.

"I'm not satisfied with the oars," Chilo said one day when they broke for lunch. "They work, but not well enough."

"What else is there?" Marcus asked. "Under water you don't have wind to move you, so how can you move without oars?"

"I keep thinking about the Archimedes screw," Chilo said. "The master devised it more than a hundred years ago to raise water. I think there must be some way to adapt it to move the boat. My thought is this . . ." He moved his hands in characteristically Greek gestures as he tried to articulate his thoughts. "As it is used, the screw is fixed in one place. When it is turned, water is forced to rise along the screw's channels until it drains from the upper end."

"That is clear enough," Marcus said. "I've seen them at work many times."

"Well, if we could fix one or more such screws onto the boat and turn them, they would exert the same force against the water. Perhaps by forcing the water backward in relation to the boat, the boat itself would be propelled forward."

"Work on it," Marcus told him.

A few days later they stood before the workshop where the young Cypriote carried out his experiments. His name was Agathocles and he had the high-strung enthusiasm Marcus had come to associate with Museum researchers, especially the younger ones. He had also noticed that it was almost invariably the young ones who came up with the most outrageous concepts, and it was they who were not afraid to question long-held beliefs.

"You see," the Cypriote said, "a mirror will reflect an image before it faithfully. Everyone knows that."

"Such is the nature of mirrors," Flaccus agreed.

"Quite so. Well, a mirror will also reflect another mirror."
At his gesture two slaves each took a plate of polished silver.
One stood before the two Romans, one behind them. They
saw their faces reflected and also the backs of their own
heads, these two images repeated endlessly until they curved
off into the distance.

"An amusing sight," Flaccus commented.

"But observe what happens when the mirrors are tilted
in opposite directions."

Their reflections slid away and they saw a distorted view
of the courtyard. It was disorienting and they looked away,
slightly dizzy.

"How do you intend to apply this principle?" Marcus
asked.

"By angling the mirrors very precisely," Agathocles said,
"I have invented a device for seeing around corners or over
walls and, I believe, to see the surface of the water from
below it."

"This I don't understand," Marcus said. "I will have to
see it demonstrated."

"Then come this way." He led them to a corner of the
courtyard where a wing of the Museum complex ended.
Here stood a framework of wood, one end of it protruding
just beyond the end of the wing. Agathocles indicated a
small mirror of silver set behind a bronze plate at eye level.
There was a slot cut into the plate. "Look through this slot.
It is important that the viewer's eyes be at optimum distance
from the reflector."

Marcus stepped up to the contraption and put his eyes to
the slot. In the mirror he could see a small fountain in the
image of a dolphin with water gushing from its mouth. He
had the disconcerting feeling that he was seeing through the
wall before him. He stepped to the corner and looked around
it. There stood the fountain. He went back to the bronze
plate and gazed once more through the slot. "Amazing," he

said. Just two angled mirrors, he thought. Like so many of
the wonderful things he had seen here, it was so simple that
it seemed somebody should have thought of it before.

Flaccus and Chilo had their turn at the slot. "Of course,
the principle works just as well vertically," Agathocles informed them. He led them to a low wall at the far end of
the courtyard. Another such device had been erected against
the wall, which was a foot or two taller than head height.
This time they could see men exercising in the palaestra on
the other side. A ladder was provided to demonstrate that
what they were seeing in the mirror was real.

"An excellent application of logic," Chilo commended.
"Adapting it to the submersible boat may prove challenging."

"The mirrors will have to be fixed into a waterproof cas-
ing," Agathocles said. "Preferably, it should be of bronze.
The upper mirror will have to be set behind a window. This
must be made of highly polished glass or purest crystal."

"Can glass be made so transparent?" Marcus said. "All the
glass I've seen distorts what you see through it."

"I have the finest glass from Babylon," Agathocles said.
"It's quite pure and can be polished so that there is very
little distortion. However, it is brittle. Crystal is more expensive and is difficult to find in large pieces, but it can be
polished until it is as transparent as air, with no distortion."

"Keep working on it," Marcus told him.

TITUS NORBANUS SAT IN A CURULE CHAIR ATOP THE
walls of Carthage. Behind him stood a line of lictors dressed
in their military uniform of red tunic belted with bronze-
studded black leather. They leaned on their fasces as they
gazed out onto the waters of the harbor. The Senate had
conferred upon him the dignity of a propraetor, despite the
fact that he had held only the offices of quaestor and aedile.

This breach of custom was part of the price the Old Families had to pay for his father's support, and it would last only for the first phase of operations, while the legions operated as part of the Carthaginian army. The legions marching into Italy were to be commanded by proconsuls and men of consular rank would command the legions in the real war to follow, the war against Carthage.

Still, Norbanus reflected, it felt good to have true imperium. And the reconquest and future wars would last a long time; plenty of time for him to return to Noricum, or Rome itself, and win election to the offices of praetor and consul. Then he could return to command the legions as proconsul. The offices would be his for the asking, as Rome's newest hero. The future was bright.

And where was Marcus Scipio? Dallying among the decadent Egyptians and, if reports were accurate, taking an almost traitorous interest in the defense of Alexandria. The fool's career was over and if he dared to return, he would be lucky to get exiled. Beheading was more likely. Not for the first time, Norbanus regretted that citizens could not be flogged and crucified, however serious their offense. It was the only blot upon his otherwise flawless happiness.

"I think we are ready to begin," Zarabel said. A ship was being rowed into the center of the harbor. She was finally going to demonstrate the burning-mirrors she had shown them on the first tour of the walls.

The rest of the Roman advance party stood along the parapet. The demonstration was for their benefit, Hamilcar wishing to impress the Romans with the invincible might of Carthage. They conversed in low voices, most of them highly skeptical of the upcoming show. The other machines were impressive, but this sounded ridiculous to them.

The ship was an old galley past its useful years. Its black-tarred hull was scarred with the marks of old battles and old storms. It had been stripped of anything useful and even its paint was long faded. It was worked into position by no more than a dozen oars, and when its anchor was dropped, the oarsmen jumped into the water and swam for shore. This did not leave the ship uninhabited, however. On the deck were chained at least a hundred men and women: felons condemned to death for varying offenses. Carthaginian law listed a great many crimes meriting death.

Zarabel signaled with her fan and the great reflectors ranged atop the wall, shining with new polish, began to swing toward the ship like the heads of malevolent gods. The Romans watched in fascination as great disks of light moved across the water like runaway suns. One by one they converged on the old galley. The wretches in chains screamed and winced and averted their eyes from the glare.

Slowly, the tarred wood began to smoke. Amid frantic screaming from the condemned and wild cheering from the Carthaginian crowd gathered on the wall, the smoke grew dense. Abruptly, the whole ship was enveloped in flame from one end to the other, as if ignited by the fiery breath of a monster from myth. The screams stopped within seconds and there was no sound louder than the crackling flames and the still-cheering mob. With amazing speed the vessel burned to the waterline and soon was nothing more than bits of blackened, smoldering wood floating upon the water. Of the condemned criminals there was no sign at all.

"It works after all," said one of the Romans.

"I don't believe it," said someone else.

"You just saw it!" Norbanus said. "Don't deny the evidence of your own eyes."

"The rowers probably set the fire before they jumped overboard," said Lentulus Niger. "The rest is just mummery to gull us."

"Do you think the Carthaginians consider us worth an elaborate charade?" Norbanus demanded. They were speaking in Latin. "The thing works, and it's just one of their weapons."

Niger made a rude and contemptuous noise. "So what? When the time comes, we'll just attack before dawn." The rest laughed.

"Or on a cloudy day!" said another.

Zarabel frowned. She did not understand their words, but their tone was clear enough. These Romans were hard to impress.

"THIS SITUATION MUST NOT BE ALLOWED TO CONtinue," said Bacchylides of Samos, the mathematician. "The Museum's reputation has been glorious for more than two centuries, since the time of Ptolemy Soter, as a seat of purest learning, of philosophy unsullied by the work of mere mechanics. This expansion of the Archimedean School will make us the laughingstock of the Greek world. Philosophers at Athens and Rhodes, at Pergamum and even Syracuse will say that the Museum has become a mere *factory!*"

"I agree," said Polycrates, chief of the academic philosophers of the Museum. "But do try to restrain your agitation. As philosophers, calm, dispassion and detachment are enjoined upon us no less than avoidance of the physical manipulation of matter."

"I apologize to you all," Bacchylides said. "It is just that I perceive this matter as an assault upon the Museum no less destructive than the Carthaginian attack soon to be borne by our beloved Alexandria."

"Quite understandable," said Doson, head of the school of physicians and priest of Asklepios. "This disruption of our accustomed serenity can cause overproduction of bile even in the system of a philosopher. But is their physical research truly so scandalous? Hippocrates had little objection to his students actually touching, even manipulating his patients."

The rest brooded. In truth, some of them secretly thought that physicians, concerned as they were with the everyday world and the problems of the body, should not be classified as true philosophers at all. At least, since the days of Plato, no physician who valued his reputation actually laid hands on a patient. He simply directed his slaves to do all the necessary manipulation.

"They may be somewhat disreputable," said Memnon, the astronomer, "but that school has devised many wonderful instruments for measuring and calculating the angles of the heavenly bodies, and for timing their movements. There is a young man at work there now who believes that an arrangement of lenses and mirrors can actually magnify the bodies of the night sky and make their details ponderable."

"A good pair of human eyes has always been enough for astronomers before now," Bacchylides sniffed.

"And as a result we have learned very little that is new in the last five hundred years," Memnon pointed out.

"The duty of a philosopher is not to discover new things," Polycrates said. "It is to ponder upon that which is known, or thought to be known. We should leave exploration to ship's captains and caravan masters."

The heads of the various schools sat at the high table of the great dining hall. It was midday and they could speak freely because the Archimedeans hardly ever came here at such an hour, preferring to work through their meal.

"Artificers," said an aged Sophist, "have their place. But is their place here, in our beloved Museum? Rather, they should be contractors like other artisans. It is absurd to class them among true philosophers just because they sprang from the School of Archimedes. That man would never have acknowledged them. He only undertook to construct his engines because his city was at war and needed the defenses.

He regarded himself as a pure mathematician. Should bloody-fingered surgeons be classed as physicians just because they follow the healer's calling?"

From one end of the table came a nasty laugh. All of them winced. Archelaus the Cynic was going to speak.

"The Archimedeans are going to keep expanding and using more of the Museum's resources and there isn't a thing you can do about it. You know why?" He didn't bother to wait for an answer. "Because they're backed by Queen Selene. She's taken a fancy to that Roman and he wants these grotesque machines. Does anybody here want to get afoul of the queen?"

There was an uncomfortable silence before Eunus the Librarian, the overseer of the Museum and Library, answered. "Queen Selene, of course, is our most generous and revered patroness. None here, I am sure, would ever speak a word of disapproval concerning her."

"By no means," said Bacchylides, all too aware that the Museum and Library existed at the sufferance of the Ptolemies. The Library was in effect a huge book factory that earned great revenues for the government, but the Museum proper, where teachers and philosophers lived at public expense and produced little of monetary value, was a luxury the court might dispense with at any time. The king's court had little interest in it and the scholars depended heavily upon the queen's beneficence, as they had in the past upon many another of her queenly ancestors.

"But might we not speak with the king?" Bacchylides said.

"You mean the king's ministers surely?" said Archelaus, reminding them all of the boy-king's incompetence, a thing no one dared voice. The Cynics were tolerated, although they were by far the most disreputable school. Their founder, Diogenes, had been a philosopher of undoubted merit, as unpleasant a man as he was. The Cynics' devotion to truth and virtue could not be denied, although their sneering way of admonishing their fellow men and their unkempt appearance made them hated. They were tolerated at the Museum in the same manner fools and freaks were tolerated at royal courts.

"Perhaps we might speak with the Prime Minister and the First Eunuch," said the Librarian. "They are not—how shall I say?—not inclined to scholarly pursuits. Yet they cannot be indifferent to the prestige of the Museum, one of the glories of Alexandria. Perhaps, once informed of this outrage, they might gently dissuade the queen from this unseemly course of action."

At these words Archelaus the Cynic laughed out loud.

ALEXANDROS THE PRIME MINISTER SAT IN COUNCIL with the First Eunuch and Parmenion, the marshal of the royal armies. These three men or rather, as Parmenion thought of them, these two and one-half men, were the de facto rulers of Egypt. The king was a boy and the queen could not lead in time of war, so power fell naturally to these three. The Prime Minister headed the government bureaucracy, the eunuch represented the court, and the marshal controlled military power. The three sat at a long table in a spacious room occupying a wing of the palace devoted to government work. Like many such rooms, this one had three walls, the fourth side being open to a broad terrace and shaded by a portico without. Its curtains were open to admit a cooling breeze from the sea.

Alexandros was a small, fine-featured man who had worked himself up from the lowly post of Grain Office scribe to chief bureaucrat through superior ability and boundless ambition. Vain and arrogant though he was, he had the self-made man's inevitable insecurity. He knew that, without noble birth and the protection of a pedigreed family, he could be cast down with far greater swiftness than he rose, and none would stir a finger to aid him.

"The armies are assembled at the Libyan border now," Parmenion said. He shoved a handful of tablets and scrolls down the table toward the other two. "Here are the latest reports, just in today by fast messenger. I will go to join them tomorrow or the day after."

Parmenion was not an Alexandrian like the other two. He was a Macedonian who had served in the royal forces since his days as a junior officer. Since the time of Alexander, young Macedonians had gone out to serve in the armies of the Successors throughout the Greek-speaking world. Like the Spartans they had gone from being a nation of conquerors to being a nation of mercenaries. He was wealthy and had estates and titles granted to him by the king and queen's father, but the years and luxury had not softened him. He was hard-featured, scarred and burned dark by the desert sun.

"You have made sufficient provision against incursions from Syria?" asked Eutychus in his piping voice.

"Two myriads under that Spartan bastard Ariston. No fat Syrian army is going to get past him. The Parthians almost have Antiochus eliminated anyway. One more push and they're in control of most of the old Persian Empire. They are going to be our big problem, and soon. We must deal with Hamilcar, and swiftly, so I can take my forces back east to face them."

"Are they really so formidable?" the eunuch wanted to know.

"They're real men," Parmenion told him. "They fight on horseback, so they move far faster than any land army. If they decide on an attack and manage to keep quiet about it, they can be on top of us before we have any warning. They use bows from horseback. It could be hard on any foot-army caught in the open. You can't come to grips with them and you just have to endure their arrows. It can break a man's spirit."

"Let them take care of Antiochus first," Alexandros said. "They will be occupied for some time gorging on the Syrian carcass. While they are doing that, we will treat with them. Primitive barbarians are always amenable to the corruptions of wealth. We will send rich presents to their leaders. The process of softening is easily begun and it spreads quickly."

"That will be the best course," Parmenion admitted. "But they might also decide that the easiest way to secure more of that gold is to come to Egypt and take it by force. I want to build a chain of new forts in the Sinai, and subsequent lines of them all the way back to the Delta: defense in depth. You can't take fortified positions with mounted, missile-armed troops. For that, you need infantry and engineers. It will blunt the force of a Parthian incursion and rob them of their most formidable weapon."

"Very sagacious," said the eunuch. "And the idea has economy. Forts cost little, and we will have at our disposal the forces already raised for the coming war with Carthage."

A secretary entered the room and told them that a delegation from the Museum awaited without.

"What do they want?" Alexandros wanted to know.

"They told me they have already spoken to the First Eunuch and he has permitted them an audience."

"I spoke with Eunus the Librarian yesterday," Eutychus informed them. "They are upset by certain activities in the Museum."

"I'll be on my way, then," Parmenion said. "I have preparations to make."

"And I as well," said Alexandros. "The Library and Museum are court business, not state."

"I believe their complaints may be of some interest to us all," the eunuch said. Something in his tone caused the others to settle back down.

Three men in the robes of philosophers came onto the terrace, passed beneath the portico and entered the room. Two were men of great dignity and fine demeanor, their clothing simple but immaculate, their hair and beards dressed with care. The third shambled barefooted like a rustic come to town. His robe and tunic were old, shabby and stained, his beard and hair a frightful tangle.

"Allow me to introduce Eunus the Librarian," said Eutychus. The eldest of the three bowed very slightly and very solemnly. "And Polycrates the academic." The other fine-looking man bowed likewise. "And this is Archelaus the Cynic." The unkempt one gave them a crooked-toothed grin and nodded insolently.

"Good day, gentlemen," said Alexandros. "How may we be of service to the distinguished scholars of our revered institution?" His tone was dry but not sarcastic.

"My lords," Eunus began. "Recently, certain developments have taken place that have upset the tranquil life of the Museum. Under the urging of an interloping Roman visitor, Marcus Cornelius Scipio, the Archimedean School has expanded its activities enormously and given our Museum the aspect of an arsenal. We find this most disconcerting."

"The visitor to whom you refer is not a Roman," Alexandros commented. "He represents the nation of Noricum."

"Of course, Excellency," Eunus said. "The modalities of diplomacy sometimes escape us. Let it suffice that he calls himself a Roman and claims to represent that extinct nation."

"I have heard something of these activities," Alexandros said. "I believe they demonstrated a boat capable of navigating under water. While I can imagine no use for such a thing, surely these dabblings in mechanical curiosities are harmless?"

"Hardly harmless, my lords," said Polycrates, all but

quivering with suppressed, unphilosophical wrath. "They ignore the basic strictures laid down by divine Plato more than two and one-half centuries ago: Philosophers are not to sully their hands by manipulation of physical matter, but are to devote themselves only to pure thought."

"I believe I remember something of this," said Alexandros, his tone growing even more arid. "He hoped that, by doing no useful work, philosophers would be classed as aristocrats. His rival, Socrates, was not ashamed to make his living as a stonecutter, I believe."

"Your Excellency is pleased to make light of the issue," said Eunus. "Yet it is—"

"The queen's behind it," Archelaus interrupted rudely.

"I beg your pardon," Alexandros said. The eunuch kept a bland expression and twiddled his fingers. Parmenion did not hide his boredom.

Eunus winced. He had wished to approach this matter obliquely. He had definitely not wanted the crude Cynic along on this mission. He had come anyway and the others had been able to find no way to stop him.

"The queen has taken a fancy to the Roman and he's got her to put her support behind the Archimedeans," Archelaus told them. "These two will take all day getting around to telling you and I think your time is more valuable than that."

"For that I thank you," said Alexandros. "And just why do you believe the queen's little hobbies, of which we have all been long aware, should be of any concern to us?"

"They devise great, outlandish new weapons of war," said Polycrates. "All day long the Museum rings with the noise of hammers and the terrible clatter as they test these machines."

The Prime Minister's eyes narrowed slightly but his tone did not change. "But Egypt is soon to be at war with Carthage. Surely this military research is patriotic in nature?"

"I've heard something of this activity," Parmenion said. "Gentlemen, one of the oldest facts of warfare is that when amateurs take a hand in it, they love to play with warlike toys. They are easily persuaded that if they just have some ridiculous machine, they can bring the war to a speedy and economical conclusion. They do not understand that only high-quality soldiers, strict discipline and superior tactics win wars. These things are not glamorous and therefore of little interest to amateurs. Military hobbyists, often of royal rank, are the bane of professional commanders."

"I quite concur," said the eunuch. "Let the queen play with her military toys and socialize with this would-be Roman. He is a man with no real standing and report has it that his countrymen are sending soldiers to take Hamilcar's pay. Perhaps we may build a facility for the Archimedeans outside the city, where they will have space and will not disturb peaceful citizens with their noise." He let out a high-pitched giggle. "Who knows? They might even produce something useful."

"We would prefer that such a facility not be associated with the Library, Exalted One."

"Gentlemen," said Alexandros, "we have heard your petition and shall give it due deliberation. If you will now give us leave, we have much to attend to."

The philosophers bowed their way from the room and the Prime Minister turned to the others.

"What is she really up to? Eutychus, I take it this is what you wanted us to hear."

"Oh, yes. Underwater boats and so forth are harmless pastimes for a royal lady, but military researches in company with a foreign soldier are quite another. It suggests to me that she has ambitions to supplant His Majesty and rule in her own right."

"How?" Parmenion said with a sour expression. "I don't care if they build a machine bigger than the 'City-Taker' of

Demetrios Poliorcetes. It's no good in a court intrigue, and that's the only way she's ever going to take power."

"Still," Alexandros said, "as long as she fancies that she represents a threat, then she does in reality, no matter how self-deluding she may be. It might be simplest to eliminate her."

"Never!" Eutychus shrilled. "She is His Majesty's only living sister and the only fit wife for an Egyptian king. We've done away with the others already. For the dynasty to be secure, he must reach an age to breed an heir on her. After that, he may do away with a troublesome sister-wife the way most of his ancestors have."

"Then get rid of the Roman," Parmenion advised.

The other two nodded silently.

Outside, the philosophers spoke as they made their way back to the Museum.

"I had hoped for a more sympathetic hearing," Eunus said. Polycrates nodded sad agreement. Archelaus favored them with a sardonic smile.

"We got the message across. Let them take it from here. You may now resume your detached, philosophical impassivity." He laughed raucously while his colleagues fumed.

CHAPTER SIXTEEN

GOVERNOR HANNO HAD FORGOTTEN WHAT EASE and relaxation were. For years, he had enjoyed the slothful life of a Carthaginian territorial governor, carrying out his undemanding duties each morning after a substantial breakfast, then lazing his way through the fine afternoons of southern Italy. In the evenings he had dined alone or with friends in the city, or had attended or given splendid banquets and at night retired with one or more of his concubines, of which he had a fine selection in all three genders and an array of ages and colors.

All that was changed now. The mainland countryside was covered with military camps. The streets were filled with barbarian soldiers, the harbor was jammed with troop transports and horse transports and supply ships of every description. There were more sailors in town than the inns, taverns and brothels could readily accommodate. Tarentum was like a city under occupation by a foreign army.

The Romans behaved well enough, he supposed, but they

had an arrogance that was disconcerting. Actually, as he thought of it, it was not so much arrogance. The soldiers acted like any other yokels seeing a great city for the first time. They gawked at the splendid temples and statuary, the luxurious appointments of one of the world's most civilized cities. They rarely brawled with the sailors, for their officers kept them under the sternest discipline. They never stole and the quaestors paid meticulously for everything required by the legions.

No, it was something else and he sought to put it into his latest letter to Princess Zarabel. *Moon of Tanit,* he began, *our allies from Noricum, or Romans, as they prefer to call themselves, do not comport themselves like our hirelings. Rather, they behave as if they were masters not only of Tarentum, but of all of Italy. I do not wish to imply that they behave insolently toward me. On the contrary, they are quite punctilious in observing the proprieties with regard to my prestige as governor. But one gets the impression that they do this because it is their custom always to accord persons of rank the proper respect due them.*

He dipped his pen, considered his next words, and put them down. *When they speak of Italy it is as if they referred to their own estates. When they speak of their sacred Seven Hills, which they do often, they seem not to be referring to the heap of ruins in central Italy once inhabited by their ancestors, but rather they speak as if it were the living capital of their nation. They have an easy assumption of lordship that is disconcerting to witness.*

He paused and thought of how best to express his next thoughts. He wished to avoid all responsibility for any looming catastrophe, but he dared not understate the state of affairs. Sighing, he resumed: *They reveal more than they know by their talk. I was given the impression that the four legions destined for Carthage constitute the bulk of Roman military power. Yet they refer to these formations as if they were only a fraction of a much larger force. And I know that they never speak lightly of military matters. I can scarcely convey to Your Majesty how serious these people are. Your Majesty has met some of them and doubtlessly has already formed this opinion. It is my fear that they act like the lords of Italy because they are that in sober fact.*

He paused, wondering whether he might be stating his case too strongly. True, he had seen no more than the forces encamped without the walls and those already upon the water, bound for Carthage. Yet intuition told him that he was seeing a small part of the real Roman military power.

Majesty, he went on, *in my unending zeal to present you with the most current and accurate information, I am sending spies northward, to inform me of all conditions pertaining to Italy north of here, most especially in the vicinity of Rome. If the would-be Romans truly intend to reoccupy the whole of Italy, and have the numbers to carry this out, I fear I do not see what may be done to thwart them anytime soon. Sicily and other Carthaginian territories near enough to be of aid have already been stripped of fighting men to carry out your brother's campaign against Egypt.*

He added: *Of course, we shall have four of their legions on our own territory, and the Noricans must be compelled to consider the future of these men in any contemplated treachery against Carthage.* He thought a bit more. *But there is always the possibility that they may consider the loss of these legions a sacrifice they are willing to make in order to win back their ancestral homeland.*

With a few more thoughts and many more compliments, he concluded this latest report and sent it off to Zarabel. Over the next few days, when he could snatch time from his duties in facilitating the transportation of the Roman legions to Carthage, he summoned various of his spies, gave them their orders and sent them north to gather information. These were of various sorts, and none was acquainted with all of the others. Some were merchant captains whose vessels called at ports all along the Italian coast. Others were small merchants who traveled incessantly on behalf of the wool, wine and oil syndicates, a breed so numerous and ubiquitous as to be all but invisible. Yet others were live-

stock buyers and slavers, men whose activities naturally
caused them to travel widely.

Even before these agents returned with their reports, he
began to receive news that alarmed him: In central Italy and
even points south of there, an unprecedented level of bandit
activity had erupted. Villages were raided; even fair-sized
towns held under siege and put to ransom. What could be
behind this? An answer suggested itself immediately: Someone very formidable was taking control of northern Italy and
the bandits were being driven south and were now desperate
enough to take such bold action. He received indirect con-
firmation when he sought to dispatch a part of his small
cavalry force north to deal with them.

"Oh, don't bother about this, sir," said the absurdly
young man in charge of the cavalry auxilia that would be
embarking after the infantry force. "We'll just take care of
them for you. It's the least we can do for our new friend,
King Hamilcar. It will be good practice for the boys." The
officer was little more than a boy himself. He was one of
two or three named Caesar. There was much repetition in
Latin names, and those of senatorial families naturally
showed up repeatedly among the officers.

As the reports of his spies came in over the next month,
Hanno grew further alarmed. Contingents of soldiery from
the north, many of them the size of cohorts or even smaller
units called maniples had entered a number of Italian towns,
especially the ones with modest ports, such as possessed naval facilities but rarely visited by Carthaginian vessels except
in vile weather. The local townsfolk, whether Ligurian or
Bruttian, Lucanian, Apulian, Etruscan or Picene, knew not
what to make of these outlandish arrivals save for one thing:
Large numbers of armed men in their streets were far more
terrifying than any number of Carthaginians across the sea.
Hanno could only concur since his was the identical situation.

Certain of his spies who were men of some military experience were able to give him the most suggestive of insights. They said that some of these alien soldiers carried and wore arms and armor that displayed all the marks of hasty manufacture but excellent quality. Most were very young men under the authority of obvious veterans of long experience.

Hanno was no soldier, but the implications were plain even to one such as himself: A mighty army had been raised up north at incredible speed. What sort of people were these Romans (for he was by now accustomed to thinking of them as such)? The usual princes of the world commonly took many months to raise even a modest army and many months more to move them in the desired direction. When emergency required the mobilization of great masses of men for war, such formations were almost always ill equipped and poorly trained and disciplined. The results were sometimes catastrophic, as witness the experiences of the kings of Persia when their immense armies encountered the small but superbly equipped and disciplined armies of Greece and Macedonia.

Then a report arrived with the news he had been dreading. A consortium of cattle buyers, among them some of his spies, had traveled in central Italy north of Campania to the Tiber, long a backwater of little consequence. They found that much had changed, and quickly. Lands once cultivated but long reverted to pasture for sheep and cattle were now being surveyed and laid out for agriculture once more. Bewildered peasants, most of them shepherds, had been barred from land where they were accustomed to grazing their stock and were told to move south. Their animals had been bought from them at a reasonable price, but they had been left in no doubt that they were no longer welcome in the territory that had once been Latium.

Even more ominous things awaited on the Tiber plain.

In open defiance of the solemn curse pronounced by Hannibal, Rome and its surrounding countryside were being reoccupied. First, traveling north along the Appian Way, they had seen old, dilapidated tombs being restored. As they neared the city, they saw men at work restoring shrines and hoisting new roof beams onto temples fallen into near-ruin. Even the painting and landscaping of the temples and their grounds were being set to rights. Oddly, soldiers, who were kept busy as ants even when they were not drilling, performed much of this work.

Most alarming of all was Rome. They were not allowed to enter the city, but even from a distance they could see that the place was all but reborn. The ancient walls were under reconstruction, river port facilities were being restored even as new roofs were placed on the temples. What looked like vast military camps covered what had once been the Field of Mars. Here gangs of slaves had been brought from somewhere to do much of the work, particularly the digging and drainage work.

Hanno put down this last report with hands that trembled. He knew the truth now: He was "governor" of a territory now under foreign occupation. And yet, the Romans blandly persisted in acting as if nothing of the sort was going on. No, their intentions were only the friendliest. Yes, they had brought along a few extra troops and left them here and there to the north, but that was only to protect their lines of supply and communication. Besides, their new friend the Shofet Hamilcar might require more soldiers for his war, and by this means they could supply the need more quickly.

Hanno did not dare admit that he had sent spies, but remarked that certain travelers recently returned from up north had spoken of a heavy military buildup and a reoccupation of Rome. No, the Romans had said, these amateurs exaggerated, as people inexperienced in military matters so often did. Naturally, the Romans had established bases and of course they had laid out adjacent fields for cultivation and had bought livestock from the local people. Roman legions were expected to be self-supporting to the greatest extent possible. That only made military sense, did the Governor not agree? As for a reoccupation of Rome itself, that was simply untrue. Doubtless some of the soldiers and attached staff went to visit their ancestral tombs and shrines, perhaps touched them up with a bit of fresh paint, but that hardly constituted a reoccupation.

Hanno nodded and smiled and acted as if he believed these outrageous falsehoods. He had little choice. Once again he wrote letters. To Hamilcar he reported that the Romans were in his territory in unnecessarily large numbers and asked for instructions, knowing that he would get none from the preoccupied Shofet. To Zarabel he wrote the un-varnished truth: Italy was back in Roman hands and there was nothing to be done about it short of a major war.

FOR HIS TEMPORARY COMMAND POST TITUS NOR-banus had chosen a spacious villa situated just without the walls of Carthage. It had belonged to a minister who had fallen afoul of the Shofet and earned the cross thereby, along with the immolation of his family in a sacrifice to Baal-Hammon. The main building was situated on a slight rise of ground on the otherwise flat coastal plain. Its terrace af-forded a fine view over a grassy field where his legions could be assembled and inspected. Its many rooms and outbuild-ings served as quarters for those of his underofficers who chose not to camp with their soldiers and the Senate rep-resentatives attached to the expedition.

On an afternoon just after inspection, ten days before the legions' scheduled departure for Libya where they would join the greater Carthaginian army, Princess Zarabel had her litter borne to the villa. After ascertaining that Norbanus could receive her in privacy, she alit and entered his staff room with stiff, angry strides, making the bells on her silver-mesh leggings tinkle.

"Titus!" Zarabel hissed. "What are you people up to?" Even visiting him in his command quarters she felt compelled to keep her voice down.

"What do you mean?" Norbanus lounged in a chair by a table stacked with documents. His rigid bronze cuirass lay on the floor beside him and he was dressed in the lightly padded arming tunic that he wore beneath the armor. It included pendant straps of decorated leather at the shoulders and a skirt of the same straps that hung from his lean hips almost to his knees. His ornate military sandals were made of red leather and came to just below his knees, their tops banded with lynx skins from which the paws and tails dangled. She thought him handsome as a Greek god but just now she was enraged at him.

"My agents report that you Romans have reoccupied all of Italy!"

"Your agents? I suppose you must refer to that fat fool Hanno. Your brother seems to have received no such report."

She seethed, having to remind herself for the hundredth time that these Romans were not fools and their minds could work as subtly as her own despite their uncouth words.

"What my brother knows is of no account. Italy is a part of the Carthaginian Empire. Your people were forbidden by Hannibal himself from ever returning. I see that you have taken this temporary military alliance to set aside that law and seize our territory."

He stood and stepped across the room to stand very close before her. "We were coming with or without this alliance, Zarabel. Our gods commanded it. Do you disobey the will of Tanit?"

"Of course not." She found his nearness overpowering and

cursed her weakness. He always knew how to turn her to his will.

"Then don't expect such impiety from us." He put a finger beneath her chin and tilted her head back. "Be honest. What is Italy to you? Have you ever visited the place? What is Italy to Carthage? A place that produces fairly cheap wool, wine and oil? Some quarries producing rather nice green and white marble? What is that to you? The slave-worked plantations don't produce one fourth what Italian peasants used to get out of the same land, so the grain business is uneconomical. All of Italy's wealth together isn't a fraction of what Hamilcar hopes to seize from Egypt. What is Italy to you?"

"Italy is nothing," she admitted. "But I resent your duplicity. If you wish to plot against my brother, that is one thing. It is another to betray me." She felt that her words were weak. She had chosen him from among the Romans for his weaknesses, but she had not understood his strengths. Most of all, she had not counted upon her own frailty nor foreseen the way her body would respond to his presence, with her mind and spirit following helplessly.

"There is no betrayal, little princess," he said, stroking her shoulder, his hand sliding down. "Your nation and mine follow courses laid down for them centuries ago. We can do nothing about that. What we can do is bend these things to our own greatest benefit. What do you want more than anything else?"

"To be Queen of Carthage," she said. "To replace my brother on the throne and raise the cult of Tanit to its rightful primacy."

"An excellent ambition. Mine is to be Dictator of Rome. Not merely Dictator for six months like those of the past, but Dictator for life. I want to humble the Old Families and set Rome on a course that will guide her for the next thousand years. Between us, we can realize both our dreams."

He slid his hands over her body, making her quiver and gasp. She was skilled in all the erotic arts, but before this man she had practiced on slaves and eunuchs. The nobles who surrounded her at court were for the most part barely men at all. The few men she had ever encountered who seemed masculine to her were too terrified of her to be interesting.

The Roman was different. He was as masculine as any stallion, he was highborn by the standards of his nation and to him she was a woman, not a semi-divine princess. The first time she had shared her body with him she had expected to control him as she always had other males. She was shocked by her own response to his brutal entry and her own ecstatic surrender. What he lacked in finesse he more than made up for in furious energy and oxlike endurance.

Her need for him had grown but she had forced restraint upon herself. She had to be discreet. Her brother would seize any excuse to imprison or kill her. It had now been the better part of a month since she and the Roman had shared a bed and she cursed herself for a weakling. The provocation had been severe, but she knew that she had seized upon it as an excuse to be with him again.

Somehow, she was not certain just how, he had lifted her, carried her back and half-reclined on his chair. There was a quick, deft movement of both their hands, and silver chains, cloth and leather straps were moved aside and she sank onto his maleness, impaling herself as the breath surged from her lungs. For a long time she had no thoughts at all, only sensations. When their coupling came to its shuddering finish, she gathered her thoughts and disengaged herself from him. He seemed disposed to affectionate afterplay but she was having none of it. She needed to retain what ascendancy she had remaining to her.

"Very well," she said. "For the moment, I will keep silent about what I know. Your seizure of Italy will be a great humiliation for my brother and of that I approve. But if you ever play me false, I will make you pray for the cross as a mercy."

"Why should I play you false?" he asked, seeming puzzled at her vehemence, as if they were two children playing a game without consequence. "You are my path to power and I am yours. Together we can rule the world."

"Only if you are completely candid with me. Otherwise, we are enemies and you know how Carthage treats enemies. Both of us tread the most perilous of roads. My brother will kill me if he suspects duplicity. Your Senate will do the same for you if they suspect your ambition. Yes, I have studied your history and I know how the Romans hate the very concept of a king."

"Indeed they do. I shall have to be very careful not to assume that title. We do, however, accept the concept of Dictator. Our custom of divided leadership has its drawbacks so in time of emergency the Senate may appoint a man of supreme, unaccountable power to guide the state until the emergency is over. I intend to win that office and perpetuate it."

"Why should your countrymen be willing to tolerate a man who is king in all but name?" She tugged her clothing back into place and walked to the silver mirror set into one wall. Her cosmetics did not seem to have been disarranged by the hurried coupling.

"It is just a matter of getting them used to the idea. My family is powerful in the Senate, they will agitate for a prolongation of my office and the people will back them." He did not add that the best way to get the Romans used to the idea of a perpetual Dictator was to keep them in a perpetual state of war. The expedition had given him a vision of conquest that stretched far beyond anything now contemplated by the Senate and people of Noricum: first Carthage, then Egypt, and with that power base secured, on to Syria and Parthia, perhaps all the way to India like Alexander. Once the Romans saw the riches to be had and the quality of his leadership, they would beg him to assume supreme power. It now amused him to think that once, like most of the New Family senators, he had thought that the destiny of Noricum lay in the dank forests of the north.

Zarabel was distracted by sounds from without. "Who is coming?"

"Probably your brother." He picked up his cuirass and swung it open on its shoulder-hinges. "He is coming to review the troops this afternoon." He put the cuirass on over his head, closed it and fastened its side-buckles, then tied the white sash of command around his bronze-girt waist, tying it in the ritual knot. From his desk he took his white-plumed helmet and put it on, tying the laces of its cheek plates beneath his chin. "Let's go say hello to him." He picked up his sheathed sword and slung it from his shoulder by its ornate leather baldric.

Zarabel took a deep breath to calm herself and assumed the hieratic demeanor she always employed among the courtiers. Satisfied that she was as chilling as always, she followed the arrogant Roman out onto the terrace.

HAMILCAR WAS BORNE FROM THE PALACE ON HIS MIL-itary litter. In deference to his current warlike stance, this conveyance was adorned with gilded shields, racks of spears and arrows, its sides painted with battle scenes, its canopy in the form of a ship's sail. At the prow-shaped front the god Patechus squatted over a warship's ram. For the sake of symbolism and good fortune, the bearers wore Egyptian dress.

The Shofet himself wore military uniform: His helmet and cuirass were of hammered gold; the greaves on his shins of hardened leather stitched all over with plaques of carved amber. His military tunic was made of scarlet silk, a marvelous new fabric only recently imported from the Far East at incredible cost. The tunic alone was worth far more than the rest of his sumptuous rig combined. Behind him such of his senior commanders as were not already with the main army rode less splendid litters, along with a number of ministers.

This was to be his final inspection before taking his army to Egypt. He was not a king, and it was the duty of a Shofet to lead the army personally, even in advanced age. At last he was to view his new Roman legions. They had appeared with commendable, indeed almost incredible, dispatch. He hoped that the Romans had not, despite their vaunting words, sent him hastily raised levies of farm boys. If that should prove to be the case, his displeasure would be terrible. He determined that rather than be seen for a fool, he would crucify all the Roman leaders, then use the troops to haul his siege engines up to the walls of Alexandria, work that was certain to get most of them killed.

But when he reached the villa assigned as the Roman headquarters, he found the legions drawn up in fine array. The bearers carried him onto the terrace and the commander Norbanus greeted him with a martial salute. Hamilcar returned it, then frowned when he saw his sister standing in the shade of a portico, dressed indecently, as usual.

He stepped down from the great litter. "Good day, Senator." Then he turned to Zarabel. "I scarcely expected to find you here, Sister."

"I wouldn't miss a spectacle such as this," she said with her maddening calm. "At last we are to see these Roman legions."

"Yes. Well, Commander, shall we begin?"

Norbanus conducted them to the front of the terrace, where sumptuous chairs had been arranged. Hamilcar took the highest, Zarabel one lower and to one side. His officers and ministers arranged themselves as protocol demanded. Norbanus and a few other Roman officers on the terrace declined to sit.

Before them, the legions and auxilia stood in lines that might have been laid out by an architect. Each legion stood formed in a rectangle, its men divided into smaller rectangles formed by cohorts, smaller rectangles yet forming each cohort's centuries. The lines were separated by a pace, the rectangles by about three paces. Before each legion stood its commander, its tribunes, its senior centurion and its standard-bearers. Four golden eagles flashed in the sunlight. Next to the eagle-bearers stood men with huge curving trumpets and others with long straight horns. By each legion its attached cavalry stood mounted, each unit with its own standard-bearers and trumpeters. The cavalry had a special trumpet: straight except for its flaring mouth, which was curved back into a U-shape. It seemed that the Romans did not march to flutes, like Greeks, or to drums, like Carthaginians.

"We will begin with the Consul's review," Norbanus said. "This is how the legions parade before the consuls at the annual muster on the Field of Mars, when they renew their oath." He signaled to the trumpeter who stood before the terrace, and the man played a tuneless series of notes upon his long, straight instrument. It was an astonishingly complex musical construction to emerge from so simple an instrument. Other horns picked up the signal and repeated it.

With incredible speed and cohesion, the soldiers began their evolutions. As the trumpets performed their complex calls, the four legions and their auxilia came together to form a single rectangle, from which forward lines detached themselves to march ahead as if to engage an enemy. When the trumpets called again, these withdrew and the next lines stepped forward and seemed to pass through by magic, for neither the advancing nor the retreating lines were disarranged by the maneuver.

"This is how we keep fresh men at the front lines," Norbanus explained. "Only a small part of the army can actually come to grips with the enemy at any one time, so it is best that the bulk of the army rest. Each line goes ahead to fight for a few minutes, then it retreats and is relieved. While the others fight, those men rest, take care of their wounded and get fresh javelins."

"Very pretty," said a scarred Carthaginian general. "But I would like to see it under battle conditions."

"You shall," Norbanus promised him, "and soon."

To a new set of signals the legions separated by cohorts into a checkerboard formation. "This is far more maneuverable than a single, rectangular mass," Norbanus explained. He showed them how lines could be detached to form a solid front, how the squares could pass through one another to give a double or triple thickness if a flank was threatened or extra depth needed, how units could be wheeled about to face a threat from the rear.

As a final demonstration, the lines tightened into close order and the rectangles seemed to shrink as shield touched shield in the front line. Then the flankers turned their shields about to cover their exposed sides and the men inside the formations raised their shields overhead until they overlapped like tiles on a roof. Then they advanced toward the terrace. The Carthaginians laughed nervously at their awkward, waddling gait, but there was concern in their laughter. There was something implacably ominous in the armor-plated army coming toward them like some great, mythical beast. Indeed, that was the most unsettling thing about these legions: They behaved like a creature with a single nervous system.

"This formation we call the 'tortoise,'" Norbanus said. "It may be used by large formations or small ones and is very useful for advancing under heavy missile fire, or against an enemy fortification. When advanced against a wall, one formation can climb on top of another until they form a stair for the men behind to mount to storm the wall." He saw their disbelieving stares and added, "Not a very high wall, of course."

When the tortoise was twenty paces in front of them it halted, each man's left foot seeming to come down at precisely the same instant. Slowly, the formation subsided as the men within went down on one knee and the shields on the flanks slanted outward.

"Might we see one of these formations climb atop another?" the Shofet said. "That might be a sight worth seeing."

"Oh, we can do better than that," Norbanus told them. At his signal, more horns sounded, these with a higher-pitched note. To the unutterable astonishment of the Carthaginian onlookers two cavalry detachments charged the tortoise from both sides. The horses leaped up the slanted shields and onto the roof, and then the men galloped about in a mock-battle, pelting one another with soft-tipped javelins amid a deafening thunder of hooves on shields.

"Why don't the horses slip?" Hamilcar wanted to know. "How do your soldiers hold so firm?" This time he did not bother to conceal his amazement.

"The men have good inducement to hold steady," Norbanus said. "A horse coming down through the roof would probably hurt."

At last the horsemen rode off and they could all hear the cheering of the citizens viewing the spectacle from atop the walls of the city. The legionaries separated into their formations and, at another set of trumpet calls, they marched past the Shofet, their centurions saluting him in passing, the men looking neither to the right nor to the left. As they did this, it finally occurred to Hamilcar that all of this had been accomplished with trumpet calls alone. He had not heard a single officer's voice raised in the usual sweating, swearing harangue. It did not seem possible, but he had seen this with his own eyes. He turned to his subordinates. "I think our money was well spent," he said.

HAMILCAR GOT A FINAL DEMONSTRATION OF ROMAN military practice two days later. It was the day for the march to Egypt. Hamilcar and his household troops, along with the Romans, would leave Carthage and march eastward, picking up the remainder of the army where it was quartered in Carthaginian territory, thence to join the bulk of his forces massed at the border.

With his principal officers, the Shofet rode from the city amid a multitude, chanting, cheering and waving holy emblems. Huge statues of the gods rolled through the streets on brazen wheels to witness and confer their blessings on the expedition. From the temple steps the priests and priestesses wailed their imprecations against the enemy and tons of incense burned to waft the prayers of Carthage heavenward.

As the procession passed the great temple of Tanit, he saw the princess Zarabel conducting the temple clergy in a hymn of praise. He did not see the cursing gestures she made toward his back, nor did he see her spit after him as she pronounced a terrible execration in a low voice.

Once outside the city, the Shofet descended from his litter and mounted a horse. With his entourage he rode to the Roman camp. It lay within an earthen rampart raised by the legionaries and he saw to his astonishment that the camp still stood: street after street of leather tents, arranged in the orderly, rectilinear fashion favored by the Romans. The men stood in the streets holding the reins of their pack animals, but not a single tent had yet been struck. He rode to the knot of officers centered upon Titus Norbanus.

"What is the meaning of this, Commander?" Hamilcar demanded. "I expected you to be ready to march!"

"It is our usual custom to be on the march before dawn, but today we waited for your arrival." He nodded to his trumpeter, who sounded a single note. The unit trumpeters repeated the note and men stooped and jerked tent pegs from the ground. There came a second note and men pulled out the supporting poles. Before Hamilcar's eyes, thousands of tents collapsed as if crushed by the blow of a single, gigantic hand.

Men swarmed over the fallen tents, folded them and loaded them on the pack beasts. With another flourish of trumpets the eagle-bearers marched from the camp gate, followed by the legionaries and auxilia in their units, then the cavalry and finally the noncombatants with the baggage animals. Where moments before there had stood a veritable city, there were now earthen ramparts with no trace of human habitation within. Breaking camp, getting into marching order and getting the whole force moving, a task that took most armies at least an hour and often far longer than that, the Romans had accomplished in perhaps five minutes.

Hamilcar knew now that he had hired some matchless soldiers and he was well pleased with the bargain. Governor Hanno had reported some troubling things about these people, but that was a trifling matter. He wanted to give an oration, to say heroic things about this momentous occasion, but somehow in the presence of these men he did not feel up to it.

Instead he said, simply: "Let's go to Egypt."

CHAPTER SEVENTEEN

FOR THE FIRST TIME IN MORE THAN A HUNDRED years, the Senate of Rome held a meeting in its ancient Curia Hostilia. The building was made of brick and even when it had been abandoned, it was far from being Rome's finest. Still, its tradition was ancient and it was sacred ground. The senators ranged along its benches could smell the new timber of its restored ceiling and roof, and the fresh paint that whitened the walls.

From without came the sound of rebuilding: hammering, sawing, the shouts of team bosses as heavy timbers and stones were raised. The scent of wood smoke and incense was heavy in the air as temples were reconsecrated and resumed their interrupted sacrifices. The augurs were in constant demand to pronounce the will of the gods on this building project or that. One obscure priesthood had even requested that a human sacrifice be performed at the rededication of the forum, as had been done at its founding. The pontifexes had rejected this with disgust. Were they barbarians, they demanded, that they resort to human sacrifice at any but the direst circumstances?

If harmony and coordinated effort seemed to be the mood of the refounded city as a whole, nothing of the sort characterized the Senate. The debates were no less raucous and bitterly divided than they had been in Noricum. Now that the great, irrevocable step had been taken, men were falling prey to second thoughts. Now that huge, warlike preparations were underway, the stakes seemed higher and the rewards or penalties all the greater. These were things worth fighting over, and the Senate fought.

"Just who is in command?" the Consul Norbanus shouted. "Our legions have sailed for Carthage and may even now be marching on Alexandria. Yet my esteemed colleague's son, Marcus Cornelius Scipio, is in the Egyptian capital, apparently acting in some military capacity, as some sort of defense expert! Whose side is he on?"

Publius Gabinius, the Princeps, stood. "Our esteemed Consul," he said, "takes far too seriously a war between mere foreign kings. Our legions did not go to Africa to defend Rome, but to support the Carthaginian Shofet. We all know what that alliance is worth. Hamilcar does not treat it as an alliance at all, but rather as a mere contract securing the services of mercenaries. Well, have we not repaid the insult by taking Italy from beneath his very nose?" This raised a general laugh and cheer.

"As for young Marcus Scipio, it was long Roman practice to attach observers to the staffs of foreign commanders, to learn the arts of war as practiced by people who might someday be our enemies."

"Not when Romans were fighting on the other side!" shouted Norbanus.

"What of that?" Gabinius said with a sneer. "Have we proclaimed Hamilcar a Friend and Ally of Rome?" There were boos and hisses at this outrageous pronouncement.

"Had that been the case, then Scipio might have to answer to charges of treason. But Hamilcar and the Egyptian boy-king are nothing to us. Personally, I look forward to receiving Scipio's report on the siege of Alexandria, along with that of Titus Norbanus. How often have we had a detailed military analysis of such an event from both sides? Surely, no one here expects a Scipio, scion of the proudest and most patriotic of families, to take up arms against fellow Romans!" There were mutterings that this was true, but Gabinius would have liked the mutters to be louder. Clearly, not everyone believed in the loyalty of Marcus Cornelius Scipio.

"Let us not waste time on this squabble," said Titus Scaeva. As last year's Consul, he had an important command in the newly built army. Although unarmed, he attended the meeting in his military belt and sagum. "One Roman, whatever his intentions, is going to accomplish little in this affair. We have much to accomplish, though.

"The distinguished Princeps Gabinius says that we have snatched Italy from Carthage, but I say that we have not. Most of the south is not under our control, and it is by way of the south that Carthage is most likely to return. We cannot ignore Liguria and the northwest, either. Remember that Hannibal surprised Rome by crossing the alps, a supposedly impossible feat."

"But that was Hannibal!" shouted an old senator. "This Hamilcar seems to be a fool!"

"Perhaps so. Perhaps not," Scaeva said. "We haven't seen him in command yet. But if he bungles this war, we know that Carthage has a short way with failures, even if they are Shofets. He may be replaced by a competent man. We must not underestimate Carthage."

Gabinius was grateful for the change of subject and for Scaeva's good sense. "Proconsul," he said, "what do you propose?"

"We have a vast army now, although much of it is un-tried. Carthage lies across the sea, and its possessions in Spain and the old Province are thinly garrisoned. But Sicily is heavily fortified and there are still Carthaginian troops there. I propose an assault on Sicily, now, while most of the Carthaginian soldiers are away in Egypt. Now we can take the island with the legions we have available to us, and take it at much smaller cost than the last time, when Hannibal's father was in command. The nearest menace will be elimi-nated and we will be in control of the nearest approach to Africa. Let me lead my legions to secure the south of Italy, then cross the Strait of Messina to Sicily!"

There was stunned silence. The audacity of the plan was astounding. Yet it was tempting, for this would be hurting Hamilcar far more than the seizure of Italy had.

The Consul Norbanus leapt to his feet. "This will mean death to our legions in Africa! Four legions! Twenty-four thousand citizens and the same number of allies and attached personnel! We can't sacrifice so many!"

Fierce old Scipio Cyclops stood. "Who is going to kill them? Carthaginians? They are Roman soldiers. They can fight their way back like the ten thousand of Xenophon! I say we place this command in the hands of Proconsul Scaeva. Let us finish securing Italy and go take Sicily! I want to tread the dust of Carthage beneath my feet before I die!" Men roared at these words. Others paled.

The argument raged on.

"THERE THEY ARE." MARCUS SCIPIO REINED HIS HORSE as they crested the ridge. The Height was not great, but it was sufficient to give them a view of the two armies facing each other a few leagues west of Alexandria. To the right lay the seashore, where the water was studded with the vessels of the Carthaginian support fleet. Even now, the Alexandrian war fleet rowed to meet it.

On the broad plain Ptolemy's land forces were arrayed along a broad front with its right flank anchored at the beach. On its left flank most of the cavalry sat mounted, and near them the corps of elephants waited patiently. The center was many lines deep and bristled with long pikes.

"Macedonians on both sides," Flaccus noted. "And they still favor those pikes."

"You'd think they'd have given those up long ago," Marcus said.

"They wouldn't do in our forests, but perhaps they're still of use in such conditions as these." Flaccus sketched the opposing battle formations on a scrap of papyrus with a charcoal stick. "Not very imaginative tactics," he remarked. "It's like they're following some old Greek textbook. Where are the legions?"

"Holding Hamilcar's right flank," Marcus answered. At such a distance it was impossible to distinguish standards and equipment, but the formation looked distinctly Roman. "He probably wants them to absorb the cavalry and elephant attacks. He should've put them in the center. The legions would make short work of those pikemen."

"I don't know," Flaccus said uneasily. "Does it occur to you that Roman armies haven't fought a large, civilized army in more than a hundred years?"

"I've considered it. But we've spent that whole time training for such a fight. They may be better organized than Germans and Gauls, but they certainly can't be any tougher."

Flaccus looked out over the water. "Look. They're already starting to fight out there." The ships rowed toward one another and fireballs began to arch from ship to ship. In the bright morning light the flames were pale and difficult to see, but the smoke trails were plain. In the clarity of the air the action was easy to follow, but at such a distance that all transpired in an eerie silence. Soon the battle lines dissolved as the fleets came together and all became a confusion of churned water and fire. Ships began to sink.

"I'm glad we're here instead of out there," Flaccus said.

"They're about to start," said Marcus. He referred to the ground armies who at last were beginning to move. They could hear the cheers and battle cries and chants, and above them the trilling of flutes and the thudding of drums. The colorful banners waved and a regiment of black Nubians on Hamilcar's right flank broke into a rhythmic, leaping dance, their plumed headdresses and waving leg bands of long, white monkey fur making a brave show as they prepared to kill for their king. With a surge, the Ptolemaic army began to advance along its whole front.

"He's taking the initiative," Marcus said, meaning Parmenion. Ptolemy was safely in Alexandria.

Flaccus pointed beyond the Egyptian army. "He's extending his line." The Carthaginian right, with the Romans at the extreme end, were stepping out in that direction, thinning the center somewhat.

"Trying for an envelopment," Marcus commented. "Hannibal's favorite tactic. It won't work, and it will leave the legions out there ready to be cut off and surrounded by the mounted troops."

"If Parmenion is clever enough to pull it off. From what I've seen so far, he's perfectly conventional. I think this calls for a drink." He unhooked a wineskin from his saddle and held it over his head, directing the stream into his mouth. He held the skin out toward Marcus but his friend shook his head. "Strange observing a battle from a distance like this, isn't it?"

"Right. I'm used to being in the thick of it. First blood now." On both sides the archers and slingers began to ply their weapons. A few heavy arrow-hurlers were brought into play, but these weapons were better suited for the siege than the battlefield. Still, where they struck the battle lines a single shaft could bring down five or six men at once.

Then the lines came together with a din that the observers could hear even at their distance. For a few seconds all was churning and flashing metal, then the dust rose and obscured most of the spectacle. They saw the Egyptian elephants charge toward the Romans while the horse cavalry made a wide circle to the left to catch them in flank and rear.

"I hope the legion commander has more brains than these people," Marcus said, striving for impassivity but without success. His tension and distress were plain as he saw the Romans under attack. There were old friends and colleagues out there, and it was largely his doing that brought them to this field. He felt that he should be over there with them, even as he chided himself for thinking so. This was not time to be thinking like a mere legion commander. He had broader horizons to consider now.

TITUS NORBANUS THRILLED WITH ANTICIPATION. THIS would be a great battle and he was in command of the legions! Back in Noricum, it would have been many years before he could have aspired to such a command, but circumstances had thrown this opportunity his way and he had seized it with both hands. Now the armies were about to join battle and his subordinate commanders awaited his orders. They hadn't been happy with Hamilcar's order to extend the line, but Norbanus assured them that it would change nothing, save to weaken the center and make the Roman role on the right flank all the more crucial. He had begun formulating his strategy during planning sessions in the Shofet's command tent. Now he knew with precision the weaknesses of Hamilcar's military thinking and he knew how to take advantage of them.

From atop his command tower he studied his dispositions. It was a lightweight but strong structure of iron-braced wood, its members fastened with iron pins, easily disassembled and moved at need. It was about twenty feet high and gave him an adequate view of the battlefield over the heads of his troops. Its platform had room for a half-dozen officers and his signalers.

The Eighth Legion anchored the right flank. It was his veteran legion, fresh from a campaign against the Germans, the logical choice to hold the crucial flank. To its left were the Twelfth and Ninth, both salted but without as many campaigns to their standards as the Eighth. In the rear of these three legions the Seventh was deployed in reserve. This was a legion made up largely of veterans recalled to the standards. Its cohorts were arranged in a long line behind the three foremost legions. It was Roman belief that a veteran, though in his forties or even fifties, was worth ten recruits on the battlefield. Should the frontline legions falter and fall back, the veterans would be there to stiffen them.

"The horses will present no problem," said Priscus, commander of the Ninth. "But the men have never faced elephants before."

"They're just big cows," Norbanus said. "Tell your boys to use the men on their backs for javelin practice. The animals will be easy to kill then." He paused a moment. "Don't kill all of them. I want some for my triumph." Behind him, the others traded significant glances. Surely, Norbanus didn't think he'd be awarded a triumph for a battle fought under the command of a foreign king.

"Now let's go over this again," Norbanus went on. "First we take care of the elephants and cavalry. By the time we've done that, Hamilcar will be in trouble because his mercenaries don't have all that much cohesion, while those professionals over there across the field look like they know their business. They'll press the center and the left hard. Once our flank is secure, the Eighth will advance. At my signal, the Twelfth goes next, then the Ninth will wheel to the left, anchored on the left-hand cohort. The Twelfth and the Eighth will wheel likewise until all three have changed front and are at right angles to the rest of the army, just like a big door swinging shut. We'll have them boxed between Hamilcar, the sea and us. When we advance, they'll have no choice except to fall back on Alexandria."

"Have you told Hamilcar that this is your plan?" Priscus asked.

Norbanus looked at him. "Tell him? Why?"

The commander of the Ninth spoke. "It seems to me that we could just keep the swinging action going until we've rolled up Ptolemy's flank and closed on his rear. We could bag the lot and let none escape."

Norbanus grinned. "Hamilcar wants us to hold the flank and that's what we'll do. We're not here to win his battle for him all by ourselves." The others nodded, understanding. Hamilcar would know who was responsible for preventing a disaster. He would value the Romans all the more. The war would continue, and their rewards would be all the greater.

"Return to your legions," Norbanus ordered. "The fun is about to start."

While his subordinates went back to their men, Norbanus savored the experience of being on his own command tower, alone except for his trumpeters and flag men. The legions glittered with steel and bronze, not as colorful as the polyglot armies of the two kings, but more purposeful. The new eagle standards sent out from Rome reared their gilded wings before the battle line. He would be the first to test this new model Roman army. History would remember him for this.

Across the field, the Ptolemaic soldiers began to advance. Norbanus observed his own reactions. He was pleased to note that he felt no trepidation, only excitement. This was what war should be—not chaotic struggles in the forest against half-savage barbarians, but a huge game of skill and nerve between civilized armies commanded by men who played for the stakes of destiny.

The cavalry and elephants came on with frightening intensity, raising a huge cloud of dust. The legions made the usual preparations for receiving cavalry. The men of the front line knelt behind their shields and braced the butts of their pila against the ground, the points slanted toward the oncoming animals. The men of the second line remained upright but slightly crouched, with their spears pointed over the heads of the first line. The men of the lines behind them prepared to throw first their light javelins, then the heavy ones.

From the Eighth Legion, he heard the call of a solitary trumpet. In response, four files on the extreme right made a right-facing movement, preparing for the customary outflanking maneuver by the cavalry. In response to calls of another horn, the right-end cohorts of the reserve legion prepared for a wheeling movement, should one be necessary, to block flanking cavalry. They would remain where they were until another call told them to move.

Norbanus realized that this was the most frustrating stage for a commander. His job was largely done in making his dispositions and briefing his subordinates. Now he would rely on their skill and adherence to his orders. The only decisions he had left to him were when to begin the wheeling movement and when, or if, to commit his reserves. He gestured to his body servant who stood below, eyes upon his master. The man came up the ladder, his satchel of implements slung behind him, along with a large jug.

The man poured wine into a cup and handed it to Norbanus. He drank, savoring the splendid Spanish vintage. The cup was of hammered gold, decorated with a relief of satyrs and nymphs. It had once been the possession of the Tyrant of Syracuse, or so Zarabel had told him. Both cup and wine were her gifts, along with all the other comforts of his command tent: the praetorium. He was quickly acquiring a taste for such fine things.

Many old-fashioned senators would be scandalized to hear that a Roman general was drinking wine from a golden cup while overseeing a battle. That meant nothing. Norbanus had less and less patience with anything old-fashioned. The new world would belong to new men. He sipped as the screams of men and horses tore through the air, then the trumpeting of the elephants, all of it seeming like a great munera put on for his benefit.

All along the Roman line the huge beasts were pressing at the legionaries even as the cavalry used them as a screen to loop around the right flank. The Romans had no cavalry as yet, but Hamilcar had supplied them with a force of Libyans: light-armed tribesmen who rode bareback, swinging their knotted locks as they snatched short javelins from quivers and hurled them at Ptolemy's horsemen from close range. Men and horses began to go down.

He returned his attention to the front lines, where the elephants were making little headway. The Roman line held and men were toppling from the backs of the giant beasts. Here and there a Roman was dragged from the line by a trunk and smashed like an insect beneath its feet. Norbanus saw a Roman impaled by an iron-tipped tusk, raised like a speared fish and hurled a score of paces through the air. Men were struck by javelins and arrows from the castles on the elephants' backs. But these losses were minor compared to those suffered by the Egyptians.

Horses and elephants were killed by the heavy Roman pila. Many more were maddened by wounds and tore back through their own lines, spreading confusion. The cavalry tried to press their outflanking maneuver, only to come against the refused wing of the Eighth, perfectly prepared to receive them on their points. The coordinated effort dissolved and fell back in confusion.

Satisfied that all was well with his own legions, Norbanus turned his attention to the center. The dust was now too thick to see much of the left flank, and he could see almost nothing at all of the great sea battle now raging beyond, but the situation of the center was exactly as he had anticipated. Hamilcar's extension had weakened it and the front lines were falling back upon the reserve. At least that band of Greek professionals was holding fast, although the front, mostly troops from the subject cities of North Africa, was getting butchered.

He wished that he could see the left better. An Egyptian breakthrough on the left would be disastrous. They could have Ptolemy's forces in their rear in no time. He knew he could keep his legions intact but the rest of the army would be annihilated and many of his ambitions with it. He would be forced to negotiate a separate peace with Ptolemy or whoever was negotiating on the boy's behalf. He would return to Rome without dishonor, and indeed with a good deal of credit, but that was not enough for Titus Norbanus. He intended to become master of Rome, Carthage and Egypt, and he would not accomplish this if Hamilcar's war with Egypt were to fail here on this field.

Abruptly, he turned and went to the rear of the platform. Below, a score of dispatch riders stood holding their reins, awaiting his orders. He pointed to one of them. "You!" He linked the face to a name: Barbannus, a young man of senatorial family. "Barbannus! Go to the left flank and find out the situation there. Return and report to me at once!"

"Yes, Proconsul!" With a look of joyous exuberance, the youth leaped onto his saddle and pounded away north. The others watched him with envy. They were all wellborn young men, most of them still in their teens, itching to get into action.

Norbanus went back to the front and held out his hand. His servant placed the golden cup, refilled, into it. He sipped and narrowed his eyes. His men were waving their weapons and cheering as the Egyptians retreated. Centurions took advantage of the lull to reorder their lines even as they wiped blood from their swords. He eyed the litter of dead and wounded men, horses and elephants before the Roman lines. They would be a hindrance when he began the wheeling movement. The men were no problem but the lines would have to split around the dead animals and re-form beyond them. Oh, well. He'd always known that a real battlefield is nothing like a parade ground.

Minutes later young Barbannus came galloping back and leaped upon the ladder directly from his horse's back. He scrambled up and stood before his commander, saluting and all but bursting with the importance of his duty.

"Report," Norbanus said.

"The left is holding. They are being attacked by some black savages, but the left is held by Spanish Gauls, tough men and well led. Some Alexandrian galleys came in close and tried to hurl missiles from their engines, but the range was too great. There is no danger on the left."

"Excellent," Norbanus said, dismissing the boy. He looked toward the center again. Things were getting desperate there. He checked his own lines. All had been reordered and the men were in the best of spirits. He spoke to his chief trumpeter and the man sounded a prearranged call. Others took up the call. The legions began to move out.

It was a beautiful thing to watch, even with the men having to negotiate the obstacles presented by the carcasses. The Eighth strode forward with great panache. And the Twelfth moved out as soon as the rear line of the Eighth

passed them. Then the Ninth wheeled left, the left-hand
man on the front line marking time in place while the whole
line to his right turned in a majestic quarter-circle until the
whole legion was facing due north. The other two legions
made their own turns and marched forward on the new front
until all were even, presenting a continuous line to the
Egyptian left flank.

Norbanus raised his hand and the trumpets brayed and
red flags waved. The legions began to move north at a slow
walk. Within moments the victorious Egyptians saw that
the situation had changed terribly. The left flank began to
fall in toward the center. Man crammed against man, body
against shield. Men fell and others tripped over the fallen.
A dismayed shout arose and panic spread. The Romans came
into contact with the enemy but they did not charge. Instead, they just pressed steadily, first hurling their javelins,
then thrusting their swords in an almost musical rhythm,
gutting their enemies, piercing their throats, cutting off a
hand here, a leg there, as calmly as workers in a slaughterhouse. Such was the jamming and confusion in the enemy
lines that Roman losses were all but nil.

Norbanus grinned as he saw a group of mounted men
detach themselves from the rear of the enemy center. They
turned north until they reached the coastal road, then they
were pelting eastward at a gallop. These, he knew, had to
be Ptolemy's commanders, heading for Alexandria as fast as
they could ride. Already, other men were leaving the Egyptian rear and retreating eastward. At first they left by units,
retreating in good order under discipline. But the forward
lines, engaged with the Carthaginians, were different. As
the pressure from their rear eased, they began falling back
hastily. When Hamilcar's soldiers pressed forward, they
turned and ran, many of them to be skewered from behind.
The rout became general.

"Signal the halt," Norbanus said. The huge, curved cornicen sounded and the legions stopped their advance. Disbelieving, the men in front of them who could still move at all joined in the rout and soon all over the field there was little to be seen except men running east in disorder. Hamilcar's light troops and cavalry harried them, cutting them down as they fled, but the troops of the center and the left were too exhausted to press a determined pursuit and exterminate the enemy. Norbanus estimated that three quarters of Ptolemy's army would make it safely to Alexandria. That suited him. He surveyed his fine lines, the quickly recovering Carthaginian forces, and the fleeing rabble, many of which had abandoned shields, weapons and honor. He saw a pair of observers sitting their horses on the crest of a ridge to the east and he wondered who they might be.

"THAT WAS WELL DONE!" MARCUS SAID, HIS JAW ALL but dropping in admiration. "Both the legionaries and their commanders behaved splendidly!"

"I concur," Flaccus said, finished with his sketches and now making notes. "Surely the commander can't be Norbanus. He's not that good. The Senate must have sent out one of the best."

Marcus watched a while longer. "No, I think it must be Norbanus. I didn't think he was that good, either, but he's devious enough to have planned this and pulled it off. I don't know any other Roman of propraetorian rank that clever."

"How do you mean?" Flaccus asked, rolling up his papyri and stowing them in a leather tube.

"He could have won the battle just now, kept up the pressure, kept his men moving and caught the whole Egyptian army in a nutcracker with no escape but the sea. But a great victory didn't suit him. It would have been a victory for Hamilcar. Instead he turned the tide of the battle and no more than that. Hamilcar will depend on him from now on. It was masterful, in its way."

"And you're more devious than I thought, to have figured it out so quickly. Speaking of the sea, how is the navy doing?"

Rapt with the land battle, Marcus had all but forgotten that men were fighting at sea. Out there, all appeared to be confusion as the two fleets were inextricably mixed together in a pall of smoke and a great litter of sinking vessels and floating oars, bodies and other debris. Gradually, he saw some ships backing away under oars, turning and heading back east. Either the sea fight was going badly, or they'd seen that the land battle was lost. One after another, they raised their masts and hoisted their sails to catch the favorable breeze. Soon, such of the Alexandrian fleet as were still seaworthy were making their way back to their home harbor. The Carthaginian fleet did not pursue.

"That's it, then," Flaccus said. "Let's go before someone down there takes an interest in us." Already, haggard, terrified men, some of them dripping from fresh wounds, were passing them in their flight. None of them had a glance to spare for the two Roman horsemen. "Now what happens," he asked as they pivoted their mounts.

"Now the siege of Alexandria begins," Marcus told him. He touched his horse's flanks with his spurs. "Now we put a few of my own ideas to the test."

THAT EVENING, HAMILCAR FEASTED HIS OFFICERS AND his allies in his great command tent. It was Carthaginian tradition to hold such a feast on the battlefield after a victory, among the enemy dead. The huge pavilion had its sides rolled up, so that the feasters could enjoy the sight of the loot and trophies and the enemy dead, and so that they could fully enjoy the disposal of the prisoners.

Before the tent were piled on one side great heaps of weapons and armor, the captured enemy banners and standards, the loot taken from the enemy camp and the tents of Ptolemy's officers. All had been abandoned in the panicked flight of the Egyptian army.

On the other side were the heads of the enemy slain arranged on poles and racks and when the Shofet's servants ran out of wood, the remaining heads were heaped in a great, pyramidal pile. All around, incense burned in braziers to alleviate the stench.

In the center, directly before the Shofet's high couch, a bronze image of Baal-Hammon stood, a fire kindled in its belly. It was not as huge as the colossi back in the city, but it stood more than twice a man's height, hauled along on its own carriage following the army like a hungry vulture. All around it, bonfires flamed like relatives of the blaze in Baal's fat belly.

Norbanus and his senior officers joined the Shofet as soon as their own men were encamped according to regulations. They were conducted to a couch next to the Shofet's own and they reclined at a long table, somewhat uncomfortably since they had retained their weapons and cuirasses. Hamilcar quirked an eyebrow in their direction.

"I assure you the nearest Egyptians are far away," Hamilcar said. "My cavalry are still in pursuit."

"It is our regulation, my Shofet," Norbanus said. "While our legions are in enemy territory, we must remain under arms." They retained their arms because assassination was not out of the question. Kings had been known to murder successful subordinates, just as a precautionary measure. Norbanus estimated that he and his officers could probably fight their way back to the Roman camp should it prove necessary. He raised his cup. Poison was also a hazard, but it would not do to show timidity here, so he drank. As always, the Shofet's wine was excellent.

The men fell to feasting, and while the courses were brought in, Hamilcar distributed rewards and praise for those who had shown especial valor. His praise for the Romans was lavish, and with his own hands he draped massive golden chains around the necks of Norbanus and his officers, and promised generous cash donatives to the common legionaries. He praised their excellent precision in the spectacular and difficult change of front that had outflanked the Egyptians with such devastating results. He did not, however, hint that this move had not been his own idea.

When the last dishes were cleared away and the cups refilled, Hamilcar ordered that the prisoners be brought in. There were several hundred of these, many of them wounded, others captured because they fell exhausted or were surrounded. Some were Alexandrian sailors that had swum ashore from sinking ships. All were tightly bound and dejected.

By this time the hollow bronze statue of Baal-Hammon glowed luridly, its head a dull blood red, its hotter belly bright orange. The priests chanted the Moloch prayer as they marched in a circle around the image, casting handfuls of frankincense onto the glowing metal. The aromatic gum flashed away in puffs of sweet smoke. When the rites were done, burly temple slaves grabbed the first prisoner beneath the arms and looked toward the Shofet.

Hamilcar stood and raised his hands with palms outward, toward the god. "O great Baal-Hammon, greatest among the Baalim, we thank you for this day's victory. In your honor we dedicate to you the flesh, blood, bones and lives of the enemy prisoners, to appease your hunger, to avert your wrath, and to plead for your further favor in battles to come. May their cries be music to your ears, and the smoke of their immolation pleasing to your nostrils. Carthage worships you, great Baal-Hammon."

At his nod, the first prisoner was cast, screaming, into the glowing belly of the god. Even before his shrieks ceased, another was cast in. This was done until the glowing image would hold no more smoking, stinking flesh. Then the other prisoners were cast into the other, surrounding fires and while this was done, Hamilcar watched his new Roman allies carefully. Norbanus seemed perfectly at his ease and the rest were at least stoic.

When the feast and sacrifice were at an end, the Romans took their leave and returned to their camp. Priscus was first to break the sullen silence.

"What barbarians! Human sacrifice! Even the Gauls and Germans at their worst were never so disgusting!"

"Peace," Norbanus said. After the day's battle, he had found the feast and the holocaust of the prisoners to be deeply satisfying. "Our allies might hear you. We don't want to hurt their feelings."

CHAPTER EIGHTEEN

"I THINK IT IS TIME TO DISPOSE OF THIS ROMAN," Eutychus said.

"Not just yet," Parmenion cautioned.

The First Eunuch studied the general with a bland expression. "I would think that you, of all men, would want to see him out of the way now."

The two watched from the highest of the western guard towers as Marcus Scipio, accompanied by Princess Selene, oversaw the defenses in preparation for the arrival of the Carthaginian army. He had been unofficial supervisor for weeks. Now that Parmenion's position hung by a thread, she had little difficulty in making the appointment official.

"I have much to do now," the general said. "Let the man have this clerk's appointment for the nonce. We will take care of him and Selene in time."

Eutychus gave Alexandros an eloquent look and the Prime Minister answered with his own raised eyebrows. Parmenion had shifted the blame for the battle to the commander of the cavalry, for failing to flank and destroy the right wing of Hamilcar's host. The unfortunate commander and his principal officers had been beheaded before the boy-king and in the presence of the rest of Ptolemy's officers, to encourage them.

The Prime Minister and First Eunuch held their own counsel. They knew all about shifting blame. They had heard reports from the battlefield that Hamilcar's right had been held by his new Roman mercenaries and that these men had fought like the old Spartans.

"Hamilcar is slow in arriving," Alexandros noted. "I expected to see his troops camped among the tombs days ago." From the western wall of Alexandria a vast necropolis stretched toward the setting sun. The Roman had urged that the tombs nearest the wall be demolished, for they would provide cover for Hamilcar's men from arrows and stones. But the Alexandrians had adopted certain native Egyptian customs and values, and to them the tombs of the dead were more important than the homes of the living.

"He is in no rush," Parmenion told them. "He won't stir from the battlefield until his siege train catches up. Hamilcar loves war engines as much as our Roman."

"He is becoming a popular man in the city," Eutychus noted, "and the princess has always been popular."

Parmenion snorted. "Popular! The mob loves him because he provides them with diverting spectacles. He plays with toys like those absurd underwater boats and the fool from the Museum who thinks he's a bird. They think there is something magical in these mechanical follies."

"Do you think any of these things could prove useful?" the First Eunuch asked.

"Maybe if the Carthaginians laugh hard enough, they'll be easier to kill," Parmenion said sourly. "Otherwise, they will prove utterly worthless."

. . .

MARCUS SCIPIO SIGHTED ALONG THE MISSILE TROUGH
of one of the improved ballistas. In testing, its doubling of
twisted cords and curved launching arms had provided an
extra fifty percent of effective range. But even this was trifling compared to the new catapults. They were still under
construction on a platform behind the wall. These had been
invented by a man named Endymion who had some theories
concerning leverage and the behavior of falling bodies. He
applied these theories to the common staff-sling and produced engines that could hurl huge weights for unprecedented heights and distances.

"Can these things really win a war?" Selene asked, doubt
heavy in her voice.

Marcus laughed. "No! But, skillfully employed, they can
give us an advantage. Nothing wins wars except superior
fighting and greater numbers and better tactics. And luck.
Let us never forget luck. But if a good tool comes to hand
and the enemy doesn't have that tool, it can be used to
advantage."

They ranged along the wall, the soldiers bowing their way
before them, and they assessed the state of the defenses. In
the harbor they saw the new warships being towed to their
docks. These were not the exotic underwater boats but they
looked as outrageous: galley-length vessels twice the breadth
of the common ships, with no trace of mast or sail. Instead,
they were covered by humped superstructures plated with
overlapping scales of bronze. They terminated in huge, saw-
toothed rams. Indeed, each ship was simply an oversized
ram, and they were not seaworthy. They were designed
strictly for harbor defense and Marcus had dubbed them
"crocodiles."

One of the full-sized underwater boats had finally been
completed and it was undergoing trials in the harbor. A

huge bronze saw protruded from its back like the spine of a dragon. A bronze housing near the bow held the mirror device for seeing above the water. It meant that the vessel could only submerge for one to two cubits and retain vision, but that would be sufficient depth to rip the bottom from a shallow-draught Carthaginian ship. Ramming without destroying the vision device was going to present some challenges, but the odd vessel's skipper thought he had devised tactics to prevent this.

Above the walls stood the burning-mirrors and the more conventional engines of war. The remnants of the beaten army were housed in the Macedonian barracks near the palace and more were arriving from the east, drawn from the garrisons of the Sinai. It would leave Egypt open to aggression from Syria, but the losses had to be made up somehow, and Hamilcar was the more immediate threat.

"It's unfortunate about the flying machine," he remarked.

Selene rolled her eyes. A man named Sostris had made several model flying machines out of reeds and parchment, and some of these had succeeded in gliding for a hundred paces or more. He was building devices large enough to carry a man, but thus far the results had been severe bruises to Sostris and broken bones to some of his slaves. He had indeed contrived to glide for modest distances on batlike wings of wood and leather, but controlling such things as altitude and direction so far eluded him. He had tried gluing on feathers, for he believed that these provided lift, but to no avail. His first designs had included flapping wings worked by the arms in the fashion of Icarus, but these had proven futile. "Men must have been stronger back then," he was heard to remark.

"Perhaps some things should remain in the world of myth," Selene said. "A man flying through the air might draw unwanted attention from the gods."

"That is very unenlightened of you," Marcus said. "Chilo

says that the gods are too great to be bothered by the ambitions of mere mortals."

"I know very well what Chilo says. But perhaps you are moving too fast into this world of the fantastic. What next? Tables like those of Hephaestos that roll about under their own power, delivering refreshments? The statues he crafted in the form of beautiful women that acted as if alive and were his servants?"

"Hardly necessary. Ordinary slaves do that sort of work just as well." He smiled at the exasperated noise she made. They had this argument often. Her original enthusiasm was cooling somewhat and he feared she was more under the influence of the Museum's Platonists than even she realized.

She turned to more serious things. "My informants tell me that my brother's controllers want you killed."

"I suppose they do," Marcus answered, unperturbed. "If I was in their position, I'd have had me killed long before now. They assumed I was a harmless crank. Now they know better."

She shook her head. "I don't understand you. I don't understand any other Roman, for that matter. You are all alone in an alien land, where the most powerful men want you dead, and you simply take charge of its defenses as if you'd been appointed Grand Marshal!"

"I have you to thank for that. You don't exactly rule in your own right, but with the king a mere boy and his ministers unpopular, you can act as if you actually had the authority to appoint me to high command. The rest is pure style."

She was bewildered. This man always bewildered her. He seemed like the most provincial, unsophisticated bumpkin imaginable, then proceeded to act like the subtlest schemer ever raised in a decadent court. "Style? What do you mean?"

He picked up a heavy ballista projectile and tested it for straightness. "It is very simple, something we learned from

the old Spartans. You know your history. Typically, a number of Greek states of some league or other would prepare
for war on some other Greeks. There might be three or four
generals at a conference, each of them bringing several thousand men to the war. Then a Spartan commander would
arrive with maybe two or three hundred men in tow. What
happened then?"

"The Spartan took charge," she answered.

"Every time. Even after the Spartans lost their reputation
for invincibility at Leuctra. Men always defer to a military
man who knows what he is doing, and shows it. In past
days, it was the Spartans. Now it is the Romans."

"And what are you Romans up to?" she asked, dead serious. "You are here helping with my defenses. Your friends
are out there with Hamilcar's army, preparing to attack. You
are playing some game, and I want to know what it is.
You've said that you will make me sole ruler of Egypt. I
want that. But not if it means being your puppet."

He drew his cloak aside and sat in an archer's crenel set
into the battlement. He patted the stone bench beside him.
"Sit here, my queen."

Frowning suspiciously, she sat, conscious as always of this
man's force and masculinity, determined as always not to let
these things cloud her judgment. She had been raised a philosopher, supposedly above such things. "So tell me."

"Those legions approaching Alexandria are not there to
help Hamilcar. They are there to make Rome great. That is
what the legions always do. I am here to save Egypt from
Hamilcar. I am also here to save Rome from Egypt."

"That makes no sense."

"Ah, but you are not thinking like a philosopher. I've
been spending a lot of time with the Archimedeans, but I've
also been attending lectures by logicians. I like the way they
analyze the nature of reality and the way we think. You see
the way Rome is acting and the way I am acting and it all

seems to make no sense. What should that tell you?"

"Don't lecture me like a child. It means that I am not in possession of all the facts, assuming that there is sense to be made. It could also mean that you are insane and your behavior irrational. Now tell me."

"All right," he said, smiling. "The fact is, Rome could take Egypt easily. Your army is weak, your court decadent, your ministers corrupt. Only Alexandria is strong. If Alexandria were to fall, the people of Egypt would not rise up to throw out the conqueror. They have been ruled by foreigners for many centuries and you Ptolemies are only the latest pack of foreigners to oppress them. They would be about as content with the Carthaginians in charge, and a great deal more so with Rome. We know how to treat subject peoples with great firmness but with fairness and always with the prospect of future citizenship and advancement."

"You think much of yourselves," she said, glowering.

"So we do, and with good reason. But I fear what Egypt will do to Rome." He paused but she said nothing. "You see, what our republic has is an extremely competitive government. Each senator wants to excel above all the others. Each senatorial family wants to have more wealth, prestige, honor and power than all the others. An incredible amount of our political energy goes into building factions and voting blocs in order to secure the highest commands.

"Right now, the Senate must be in a frenzy with a hundred senators each wanting to be commanding an army when we take Carthage. Great wealth corrupts, Selene. It is going to be bad when we sack Carthage because gold will pour into Roman coffers in incredible amounts. The lands will be divided up and the highest officers will get the best estates. It could cause us to lose our edge. I'll remind you of the Spartans again."

"What about them?"

"They were famous for their simplicity and frugality.

Even the highest nobles lived in military camps, slept on the ground, ate horrible black soup and owned no luxuries. Even their money was made of iron. But they were able to despise wealth and luxury because they were never exposed to these things. They were always easy to bribe and corrupt once they were away from Sparta, and that was why the Spartan ephors hated to send armies abroad or use them for occupation or garrison duties."

"And you think this may happen to the Romans?"

"I fear it will. Carthage must be destroyed. Our ancestors and our gods demand it. But at least the wealth of Carthage consists primarily of plunder. Once it is stripped, it is just a city on a rather nice stretch of coastline. Egypt is different. Egypt represents wealth unimaginable and everlasting. The general who takes Egypt will instantly be the wealthiest man in the world, able to set himself up as an independent king, should he so wish. He will be able to buy the loyalty of his soldiers with immense gifts that cost him little. The Senate will tear itself apart as men try to secure the important commands and prevent their rivals from doing the same. There could be civil war."

"I see. So what is your answer to this?"

"I must convince the Senate of the unwisdom of conquering Egypt, that our best course is to continue Ptolemaic rule here, to support you in power, and to stay out of Egypt ourselves."

"Do you think you can do this?"

"I think so. I have enemies in the Senate but I have friends as well. And there are a good many far-sighted men there. They will see the danger ahead and will know that the benefits of conquest must be commensurate with the risks. There will be plenty of other distractions: the Seleucids, Macedon and the Parthians.

"Since Alexander's time a sort of balance has held around the Middle Sea: The kingdoms of the Successors and Carthage have played one against the other and sometimes this nation would be ascendant and sometimes that, but there has been no real change. Now we Romans are back on the Middle Sea and everything will change."

Selene restrained a shiver. "You have great breadth of vision," she said. "I am sorry that I ever thought you ignorant and simple. Your Senate knew what it was doing in sending you to assess the possibilities for Rome."

He stood. "Come on. We haven't surveyed half the defenses yet. Let's try to stay alive for the next few days. Then we'll see about arranging the future of the world."

TITUS NORBANUS RODE AHEAD OF THE ARMY WITH his most trusted officers and a squadron of Gallic cavalry, all of them expert skirmishers and scouts. He wanted to see for himself what these vaunted defenses of Alexandria looked like. The chain of small forts west of the city were already invested and would be reduced in no great time. He suspected that their Alexandrian defenders would very sensibly negotiate an advantageous surrender, knowing already what defeat by Carthage would mean.

Before them, the walls of the city rose slowly from the flat plain. The plume of smoke from the great lighthouse was visible for hours before the structure itself came in sight. The lighthouse was visible long before they could see the upper part of the walls. But after the lighthouse, the walls were a disappointment. They had little of the stunning massiveness of the walls of Carthage. He remarked upon this to Lentulus Niger.

"So they don't use them as a stable for elephants," said the quartermaster. "And according to Brutus, the soldiers are barracked inside the city. I'd like to know more about the quality of the men manning those walls."

"We saw their quality on the battlefield," Norbanus said,

a little put out to hear the walls of Carthage so casually dismissed. He had come to take a proprietary interest in them.

"Those men did not fight too badly," said Niger. "They were poorly led, but so was Hamilcar's army. It was their bad luck to have us to contend with. And I'll wager we saw only a part of Ptolemy's army that day. He'll have more men to defend his walls, and maybe better ones."

The mounted force had ranged out in front of them and when they were within three miles of the city, the cavalry returned. Its commander, a scion of the New Family Nervius, rode up and saluted. "There's what looks like a small city outside the walls of the great one," he said, grinning. "Come have a look. We haven't spotted a single roving patrol."

They rode toward the western gate of Alexandria. "They're staking all upon a siege," Norbanus said. "There will be no fight outside the gates or the army would be there waiting."

"One more pitched battle and we could wrap this war up," said Cato, commander of the Eighth Legion. "A siege of a city this large could last for months. Years, maybe." He spat in disgust.

"What's this?" Niger said as they came upon the minor city.

"It's the necropolis Brutus and the others reported about," Norbanus said. "Did you ever imagine such a thing?"

Before them stretched a vast array of tombs, the least of them as large as a peasant's hut, many of them far larger. They stood upon a grid of rigidly straight streets, arranged in symmetrical blocks, like a smaller image of Alexandria itself. They were in the form of houses and temples, some Greek in design, some Egyptian, many of them a combination of both. Here and there stood statues of various gods, sphinxes, shrines, obelisks and freestanding pillars with lotus or papyrus capitals having no discernible function. There were even tiny parks and gardens just like the ones in the city, only smaller. They rode among the tombs, looking about in idle amazement.

"Is this wise?" Nervius asked. "This would be an excellent place to lay an ambush."

"The Alexandrians lack such initiative," Norbanus said. "They have elected to huddle behind their walls and that is where they will stay until we winkle them out."

"Speaking of the walls," Cato said, "they look larger from close up."

"Indeed they do," Norbanus said. Now they rode forward cautiously, at a slow walk. "Mucius, what would you estimate to be the range of those engines?"

Decimus Mucius Mus was a former centurion, now attached to Norbanus's staff as chief engineer. "Right about here," he said. "Best to go no closer."

"Oh, I'm not worried they'll cut loose at us," Norbanus said. "They won't waste ammunition on a few horsemen. They'll wait for the main force. I just want to know for future reference. Let's go up to extreme bowshot."

So they rode on, until they were fewer than three hundred paces from the walls. Now the battlement above the western gate was crowded by men whose plumed crests identified them as Alexandrian officers, come to see this harbinger of the Carthaginian host. The great engines atop the walls looked to Norbanus much like those defending Carthage. A few were of unfamiliar design but they all seemed to serve the same purposes: to hurl great stones, oversized javelins or incendiary missiles into the masses of an attacking army. On the harbor side they would do exactly the same to enemy ships. The only exceptions were the giant reflectors, and he saw none of those atop the western wall.

"What are those?" Norbanus said, pointing to a line of mastlike timbers that towered above the battlements. Whatever they were attached to was invisible behind the wall. From the top of each dangled a long rope and some device of chains and hooks, but distance obscured the details.

"Anyone's guess," Mucius said. "They look too long and spindly for catapult arms, but people in this part of the world seem fond of their machines. For all I know, they hold up the awnings for their circus."

"There's a familiar face," Norbanus said, almost whispering.

"Eh?" said Niger. All of them tried to see what Norbanus was looking at. Right above the gate a man leaned on the battlement, his arms spread wide. Beside him a woman gazed out at them. "You think that's him? I can't make out a face at this distance. His outfit looks Roman."

"It's Scipio," Norbanus affirmed. "I'd know that traitor from a mile away on a dark night in Donar's Wood." His voice was easy and conversational, but it carried an edge that made his companions study him. "When I triumph, I will drag him in chains along the Via Sacra and up to the Capitol and I will hurl him off the Tarpeian Rock with my own hands."

"You won't get a triumph for this war," Cato said.

"Besides," Niger added, "Rome isn't officially at war with Egypt, and Scipio's just advising Ptolemy in a war with Hamilcar. You can't charge him with treason for that." He was their superior but they were not in awe of him. Military commands were political appointments and every one of them had more experience in military command than Norbanus. Alliances could change and any of them might end up in charge.

"What we do here is just politics," Mucius said, "even if there's a bit of fighting involved."

"Nonetheless," Norbanus told them, "when I triumph, I will drag him in chains along the Via Sacra."

• • •

THE CONFERENCE WAS HELD IN HAMILCAR'S GREAT
tent. There was no banquet this time, no sacrifices other
than the ones customary for such an occasion. Beside the
Shofet sat the general Mastanabal, resplendent in a coat of
gilded scales, his plumed helmet held by a slave who stood
behind him. He looked supremely pleased and confident,
still puffed up by the victory of several days previous. He
did not accord the Romans credit for the victory any more
than did the Shofet. Near them sat the higher Carthaginian
officers and the commanders of the mercenaries.

Norbanus and his officers sat across from them. In a subtle
way the balance had shifted. Hamilcar was no longer dis-
missive of the Romans. He accorded them some deference
and the others perforce must follow. This did not go so far
as to give them credit for the victory, but it was an acknow-
ledgment all the same.

"Tomorrow," Hamilcar began when the cups were filled,
"shall be a momentous day. At first light we shall commence
the assault upon Alexandria. The gods of Carthage will smile
upon our endeavors." He looked around him and smiled.
"As, I am sure, shall the gods of our esteemed allies." If the
Romans looked astonished at the idea of Jupiter, Juno and
the rest smiling upon a Shofet of Carthage, he affected not
to notice.

"The naval forces are now in place. As we attack the western wall, the navy will attack the harbors and the island of
Pharos. Before noon tomorrow, you will see my banners flying from atop the great lighthouse." His followers applauded politely.

"A brave sight, I am sure," Norbanus commented, wondering if the Shofet really thought such a trifling gesture to
be significant.

"Your legions will have the honor of leading the first assault on the walls," Hamilcar said.

"An honor we must respectfully decline, Shofet," Norbanus said casually.

Hamilcar frowned. "Refuse? How so? Are you Romans not justly famed for martial prowess? Are you cowards that you fear to commence the assault?" Mastanabal and the other Carthaginians of high rank watched them with sardonic expressions, happy to see the arrogant foreigners put into such a position: Accept extreme peril or stand revealed as cowards.

Norbanus seemed not at all bothered by the situation. "My Shofet, generals of Carthage, we are all soldiers here. We know quite well that Alexandria will not fall to the first assault, nor to the second, nor the third. But a great many men will fall in those assaults. You do not waste such soldiers as my legionaries in this costly but necessary business. For this, you use those great mobs from your subject cities, the ones of whose loyalty you are doubtful. They accomplish the necessary work and their loss hurts only those cities you hold in subjection. My advice would be to send them in and station behind them those excellent pikemen sent to you by King Lysimachus of Macedon. Those pikes leveled at their backs should give them any encouragement they might need."

It was some time before the Shofet spoke. "I see. And I suppose you would prefer to remain in reserve?" Hamilcar glowered and his generals all but sneered.

"Oh, by no means," Norbanus said. "In fact, I envision for us a task that is both extremely demanding as well as hazardous. If I may?" He snapped his fingers and a team of Roman slaves entered the tent, carrying on their shoulders a table. They set it on the carpet-covered ground and the occupants of the tent gathered round with interest. It was knee height, perhaps eight feet by five feet, and upon it had been built a detailed scale model of the city, including the Pharos Island, the harbors and the lakeshore.

"This is marvelous," the Shofet said, intrigued in spite of himself. "Did your artisans really construct this since our arrival here?"

"Most of it," Norbanus said. "We already had drawings and surveys to work from and many of the buildings were made in idle hours while the men trained."

"And the origin of these drawings and surveys?" Hamilcar asked, reminding Norbanus that he was no fool.

"Certain Romans have visited Alexandria in recent months," Norbanus told him.

"Certain Romans have visited Carthage as well. Do you possess a model like this of my own city?"

"It is a matter of standard procedure with us," Norbanus said, knowing it was a touchy moment but understanding that protest would sound feeble.

Hamilcar smiled. "I'd have crucified you all if you had denied it." His generals laughed uproariously, as if this were the most hilarious prospect imaginable. "Now, show me your plan."

From one of the slaves Norbanus took a pointer. "The harbor and the western wall are the logical places to assault. You want to deny the Alexandrians the use of their harbor, and it is a weak spot. You could ferry a force to the east and cut them off from reinforcement from that direction, but it makes sense to leave them someplace to run. An army or a city can be demoralized, knowing that an unguarded back door is open."

"As you demonstrated at the recent battle," Hamilcar said.

Norbanus inclined his head slightly. "That leaves the lake frontage." With the pointer he indicated the narrow bench of land between the southern wall and Lake Mareotis. "The wall here is relatively low, weak, and ill-defended. Also, this is Alexandria's access to the Nile."

"It is tempting," Hamilcar said, "but the strip of land is too narrow for offensive maneuvers. It won't support enough troops, we can't get our siege towers onto it and every bit of it is under enemy missile fire. It's no wonder the Alexandrians didn't bother to build their walls high there."

"Give me that part of the operation," Norbanus said. "Let my legions work at the southern wall, and I will cut Alexandria off from the Nile and provide Ptolemy with amusement from that quarter."

Hamilcar stared at the frail strip of land on the table, then at Norbanus. "Are you mad? You will be slaughtered! There is no cover between the wall and the lake."

"We are good at this kind of fighting," Norbanus assured him.

"My Shofet," said Mastanabal, "it seems that these Romans indeed want to take the hero's role. I urge you to let them do as he asks. Why deny them the opportunity to earn so much honor?"

"Why, indeed?" Hamilcar said. "General Norbanus, I agree to your plan. At first light tomorrow, commence your operations against the southern wall of Alexandria."

The Roman party left. Norbanus was smiling and the others were pleased as well.

"That was well done, Titus," Lentulus Niger admitted. "You got us out of a stupid frontal assault and made him think that it's we that will get killed. How long will he stay hoodwinked?"

"As long as necessary," Norbanus said. "Tomorrow his attack will be repulsed, but he'll be happy because he'll see his pretty banner fluttering from the top of the lighthouse. The next few days he'll be enthralled by the sheer spectacle of it all and he won't notice that he's losing men in droves while we're taking hardly any casualties at all."

"He'll notice eventually," Cato said. "If nothing else, Mastanabal will point it out to him."

"By then he'll have accomplished little or nothing while we've cut off Alexandria from the Nile and made good headway at taking the southern wall. He can't argue with that."

"He won't argue," Cato said. "He'll send in his own men to continue the work once he sees how it's done, then he'll order us into the next assault on the western gate. What then?"

"Then," Norbanus said, "it will be time to renegotiate our agreement with our friend the Shofet Hamilcar."

CHAPTER NINETEEN

TITUS NORBANUS WAS ON HAMILCAR'S BATTLE tower when the assault began. He was not needed at the southwestern corner of the city, where his own legions were about to commence their operations. His subordinates knew their tasks to perfection and he was not needed there. A pity, really, he thought. He would have liked to lead his men personally for the sake of the honor, but this was not truly to be a battle. It was more like an engineering project. There would be nothing for him to do, while here, at least, he would be able to observe.

The tower commanded a fine view across the necropolis to the western wall of the city, as well as a good deal of the Eunostos harbor and the Pharos. It made a splendid sight as the sun began to rise from somewhere behind the city. The towers and temple roofs of the splendid polis began to gleam and the bizarre artificial hill of the Paneum took misty shape in the distance.

"A fine morning for battle, eh?" said Hamilcar, in fine

high spirits as his dreams were about to be realized. He sat on his golden throne, strewn with the skins of rare beasts, while his commanders stood around him.

"I cannot imagine a finer," Norbanus said, accepting a cup of warmed and spiced wine from a slave. It was early in the day but this occasion justified a bit of luxury.

"My Shofet," said Mastanabal, "I beg your leave. I must go and take charge of my men."

"Go, my friend, and may Baal-Hammon stand by your side this day."

The general beckoned to his officers. "Come." He donned his helmet and strode down the ramp that descended fifty feet or more to the ground below. The Shofet was left with his slaves, a small group of counselors and bodyguards, and Titus Norbanus.

"Something is different over there," Norbanus said.

"What?" the Shofet asked.

"Those mast-things. They're gone. Where are they?"

Hamilcar peered toward the city. It was now light enough to see that the towering timbers were, indeed, gone. He shrugged. "We don't even know what they were. It is no matter."

This, Norbanus thought, was most likely true. Still, it was an anomaly, and war was full enough of surprises without such worrisome matters. "Will your navy attack first, or the soldiers?" he asked.

"The same signal will start them both," Hamilcar said. "But the ships will reach their objectives first, so the first blood will be drawn on the water." He gazed proudly out to sea, where his fleet was drawn up in a vast, crescent-shaped formation, ready to swoop down upon Alexandria like a great bird of prey. The Alexandrian fleet awaited in three straight lines just without the mouth of the harbor, a mighty fleet but not so large as Hamilcar's. Behind it a great chain stretched from a fort on the northwestern corner of the city to the western end of the Pharos, blocking the harbor entrance. Taking Pharos would give Hamilcar control of that chain, as well as the other that blocked the Royal Harbor.

The sun rose gloriously above Alexandria, and Hamilcar took this as an auspicious moment to begin the battle. He raised his hand and the drums began to thunder. The soldiers below raised their shields and shook their spears and roared. At the same moment, at sea, the oars of the Carthaginian fleet rose and fell and churned the sea to foam all in unison. Men and ships surged forward. Titus Norbanus had never before seen a sight so stirring. This, he thought, was what it meant to be a king: to set such a thing in motion by raising your hand.

The army moved forward on a front a half-mile wide, but it had to divide into many files to pass through the necropolis, like a vast parade taking several roads through a city instead of only one. They were still more than two bowshots from the city wall when something strange happened: Abruptly, the mast-things appeared once more above the city walls as if swung up by the arms of giants. As they ascended, enormous slings swung from their terminals, climbing in huge, graceful arcs until an end of each was released. From each sling soared an object, small in the distance, to mount an incredible height, and then come back down with dreamlike slowness.

Only when the missiles landed among the tombs did the watchers understand how large they were. They were stone balls of at least five hundred pounds' weight and when they hit, they shattered into flesh-shredding fragments, caromed off the walls of tombs, rolled down the alleys and toppled rows of men like pieces in a game played by gods. The carnage was fearsome and the advance faltered.

"What are those things?" Hamilcar cried.

"Some sort of giant staff-sling," Norbanus said. "It must

use a new principle. Twisted ropes can't power those things. They have three times the range of ordinary catapults." He watched, saw the masts being hauled down and did some mental calculations. "You must press the assault hard. Call in the Macedonians if you have to. Those weapons are high-trajectory and they must take a long time between shots. Once the men are within bowshot of the city, they're safe from those things."

Hamilcar gave some quick orders and the drums sounded again. The faltering advance resumed. Again the giant slings hurled their missiles and again men died, but the fire was not as intense after that first volley and now the men had some idea of what to expect. They took cover behind tombs and hurried forward to get inside the range of the fearsome catapults.

With this novelty past, Norbanus and the Shofet turned their attention to the battle outside the harbor. The two fleets were nearing one another, fireballs and other missiles arching back and forth, here and there a ship already in flames. Then the fleets merged in a great confusion and the sounds of ramming and the shredding of wood and the screaming of men came faintly across the water.

The Carthaginian land force was now through the necropolis and bearing its scaling ladders toward the wall. Arrows and stones began to fall among them and men came forward with mantlets: large shields the size of doors, handled by two men. Some of these were propped up with poles and from behind them archers began to shoot at the battlements above.

The first ladders reached the wall and the bravest men began to climb. Stones killed some, and logs or stone pillars were rolled over the battlements, smashing men and ladders alike. Great kettles of hot oil were tipped over and men fell screaming.

"Why are they so slow attacking the gate?" Hamilcar said.

"I think a stone struck the ram," Norbanus told him. "It might be a good idea to take the heavy equipment through the necropolis tonight, when it can't be seen."

"I want to be in possession of Alexandria by tonight."

Norbanus shrugged. "That would be nice." He wondered if the Shofet truly believed that a fortified city like this could be taken with a day's attack. Given his overblown pride, it was possible.

"The marines are on the island!" Hamilcar said excitedly.

Norbanus looked in the direction of the pointing finger. At sea, all appeared to be mass confusion, but this was deceptive. He could see that the Alexandrian fleet was being pushed back and was almost against the harbor chain. If they didn't lower it soon, he thought, the remnants of the fleet would be crushed. Even as this thought crossed his mind, he saw the chain grow slack and ships either turned or backed water, fleeing to the safety of the harbor.

The Carthaginian ships pressed all the harder, trying to force an entrance to the harbor. Several managed to get over the chain and were among the demoralized Alexandrian remnants. One of the Carthaginian ships, on the periphery of the mingled fleets, began to swing around. It was preparing to ram a crippled Alexandrian trireme. Norbanus thought he saw a jagged log floating up to the Carthaginian, moving as if it had some purpose. The Carthaginian shuddered and, with shocking abruptness, began to sink. It went down quickly, as if it had not merely been holed but had its entire bottom ripped out.

"What happened?" Hamilcar said. "What just happened there?"

Norbanus just shook his head. It was a mystery. Then he saw something even stranger. A number of vessels rowed out from the docks to confront the intruders. More were coming through the arches in the Heptastadion. These were like nothing he had ever seen: low, scaly things like dragons floating on the quiet water of the harbor. They made for the enemy and began to ram, their weight and momentum so great that Carthaginian ships were lifted on their rams, overturned, even broken in two.

"The Alexandrians do love their military toys," Hamilcar said disgustedly. "It's no matter. They resorted to this because they could not defeat us on the water."

Norbanus shrugged. What difference did that make? The fact was, the Alexandrians were stopping the fleet in its tracks. The great reflectors atop the walls swung about, focusing the sun's rays on the enemy ships, now conveniently immobilized in the harbor. One by one, they burst into flames. This sight would once have chilled him, but he had already seen the reflectors demonstrated.

As Hamilcar had noted, the specially built troop transports had reached the island and dropped their broad gangplanks. The marines were storming ashore. These were mainly Greeks and Cilicians: men expert in amphibious warfare, which was an extension of their traditional piracy. Teams split off from the main body, some to attack the towers where the harbor chains were anchored, some to deal with the island's small garrison, others to carry the Shofet's banner to the great lighthouse. All this had been planned far in advance. Norbanus grudgingly admitted that this, at least, was an operation well planned and carried out by men who knew their work.

The sun glittered from arms and armor, from shields and helmets, and in the drifting smoke it was difficult to determine whether anyone was winning or losing. At the wall the ram had finally been repaired and it began to boom against the western gate, its bronze head in the form of a snarling demon with huge, curling horns. Drums thundered and trumpets brayed.

Altogether, Norbanus thought, it was a fine, stirring sight, one well worth traveling far to see. He settled into a folding chair and gestured for more wine. It was going to be a long day.

"THE NEW DEFENSES ARE WORKING," SELENE SAID. She and Scipio stood on a tower overlooking the harbor. It was here that the crucial fight of the morning was taking place. There would be no real danger from the western wall for some time to come, if ever. The harbor was different. The harbor was crucial, and the Carthaginians excelled at naval warfare.

"Look," Marcus said, pointing. The underwater boat, having been successful in its first attack, had chosen another target. The upper few inches of its hull was just above the water, the gleaming serrations of the bronze saw looking like nothing so much as the spine of a great reptile. In its eerily sentient fashion, it began to speed toward a Carthaginian trireme that was trying to back out of the harbor with half its oars smashed. Along the Carthaginian's side, men gibbered and pointed as the unearthly thing approached them. At a distance of a hundred paces, the hull sank from view, leaving only the jagged teeth to cut the water. Then they, too, went under and there was a momentary lull. Then the Carthaginian ship shuddered as if a gigantic, invisible hand had grasped it and shook it. There was no visible damage, but with shocking speed it filled with water and sank. A hundred paces beyond it, the underwater boat reappeared. Its hatch opened and the skipper's head appeared. Satisfied that the enemy was finished, he ducked below and closed the hatch. The strange craft began to look for another victim.

"Wonderful!" Selene cried, clapping her hands delightedly as a hundred or more enemy sailors were dragged down to their deaths. "Before long, our dragon will account for the whole enemy fleet!"

"Maybe if we had fifty more," Marcus said. "But pretty soon they'll figure out what it is. If just one of them can work up the nerve to ram, she's done. It's a fragile craft. In the long run, the plated ships may be of more use."

Out on the water, the great crocodiles were methodically ramming whatever strayed within range. They were slow, but with their great weight they crushed the enemy ships as if they were made of parchment. Time and again, they saw the stones and javelins flung from enemy catapults glance off the plating. Wads of burning pitch and tow clung to the plates and flamed furiously, but they did no damage and only contributed to the illusion that the Carthaginians were engaged with a pack of mythical dragons.

The harbor chain was cranked back into place and the enemy ships in the harbor were now cut off and without hope. One after another, the Carthaginian ships still afloat lowered their banners and sued for terms. White-robed heralds were rowed out in small boats to conduct the negotiations. Beyond the chain, the rest of the Carthaginian fleet fumed with impotence. On their side of the chain, they had won decisively. Beyond it, gods or demons seemed to have taken a hand and delivered their friends to the Alexandrians.

"How many have they landed on the island?" Selene asked.

"Enough. And if it's not enough, they will just land more. We knew from the first that Pharos couldn't be defended. They'll have it by nightfall, but it won't do them much good."

"I know," she said. "But I hate to think of our wonderful lighthouse in Carthaginian hands."

"You'll survive that. Every man they lose securing the island is one who won't be attacking the walls." He watched as a party attempted to storm the small castle at the western end of the island. It was an anchor point for the western chain. With its high walls and its small, heavily defended entrance, its tiny garrison could probably hold out for weeks even should the rest of the island be taken. That was the theory, at any rate. He knew better than to trust theories too far.

A messenger came running up to Selene. "Something strange is happening at the south wall, my queen," the man said.

She looked at Marcus. "The south wall? I thought it was invulnerable to attack."

"Nevertheless, we had better take a look," Marcus said. What now? Surely Hamilcar lacked the imagination to come up with some sort of innovation. When they reached the southwestern corner of the wall and looked over, he understood.

"It looks like some sort of shed they're building," said the captain of the corner tower. "They started erecting it just as the battle started."

On the narrow strip of soft ground between the southern wall and the lake, a long gallery of timber with a lead-sheathed roof was slowly growing, getting longer, like some strange animal. Marcus knew what it was. They had been used to encircle and reduce especially stubborn oppidiums and hill-forts. Its unique feature, one that had the defenders goggling in superstitious awe, was that the thing was built from the *inside*, as its members, already cut and notched, were passed down its length to be raised into place and fastened securely, by skilled men who did this work quickly and without exposing themselves.

"This could mean trouble," Marcus said.

"Trouble?" said Selene. "It's strange, but no stranger than our underwater boat and our bronze-clad ships. It's just a long shed, after all."

"Yes, but this is being built by Romans. When it's finished, it will control the lakefront. Alexandria will be cut off from the Nile and the interior. They'll use it as a base from which to mount attacks against the wall and the Mareotis gate."

"Can't the new catapults smash it?" she asked, alarmed that the supremely self-assured Roman was showing doubt. "They hurl missiles heavy enough to smash that shed to kindling wood."

"That would be ideal, but it's too close. Their stones would just fall in the lake. We'll have to move some of the conventional catapults over onto this wall. They'll damage it, at least." Already, arrows were coming from loops in the low wall and the lead-sheathed roof of the siege shed. Could Norbanus have come up with this idea? If so, he'd been underestimating the man. He was certain that the Roman he'd seen leading the scouting party and this morning atop Hamilcar's viewing-tower was indeed Titus Norbanus. The last word he'd received from Rome (strange, he thought, to know that it was the *real* Rome this time) had said that Norbanus, whose father was now consul, had been given provisional proconsular status to command the Roman forces in Africa.

"I thought they'd have sense enough to replace that bastard," he muttered.

"Who would have the sense to replace whom?" Selene asked.

"Just talking to myself. I'm afraid my old friend Norbanus has just handed us a surprise." Even as he watched, he had to admire both the skill of his countrymen and the excellent tactical thinking of his rival, if indeed this was Norbanus's idea. He was taking control of the southern side of the city just as he had controlled the right wing in the earlier battle and won a victory thereby. And in both instances, accomplishing his goals with an absolute minimum of casualties among the Roman forces.

Selene studied the odd structure. Just in the time they had been watching, it had grown another fifteen feet. The side facing them and the roof extended as if by magic, like some living thing. "How will they use it?" she asked.

"They can assemble men inside it and we won't know how many or where they're concentrated. It can be opened up at any point and men can pour out to attack a weak spot on the wall. And they can use it to mask mining operations. Anywhere along its length, they can sink a shaft, then bore a gallery right under the walls, undermine them or pop up inside the city some night when nobody is expecting them."

"If they try that, they'll drown," she said confidently. "Here, if you dig down just a few feet, you hit water. The walls of Alexandria are sunk all the way down to bedrock."

"I hope you're right," Marcus said, "but Roman engineers are nothing if not ingenious. They may well think of something. Cutting you off from the river and the interior may be the point anyway."

"We're not cut off," she insisted. "The whole eastern plain is wide open, not a single Carthaginian soldier watching it."

"That's a trap," he told her. "They've left it open to tempt you to run. And it's being watched, but from the sea. If it should look necessary, they'll land there in force."

"So what shall we do?" she asked.

"First, let's get some of the catapults moved over here." But he knew they would have little effect. It would be nightfall before the catapults could be in position. And at night, the Romans would emerge to heap earth against the sides of the shed. They would absorb the catapult missiles and most of the rest would merely glance off the metal-sheathed roof.

He turned to study the new catapults, the gigantic staff-slings that had already wrought such devastation among the Carthaginians. Again he was amazed at the simplicity of their design, so simple that it seemed incredible that no one had thought of it before. The heavy timber base was merely the support for a giant pin on which the sling-arm pivoted. From the short end of the arm hung a great box on another pivot. This box contained tons of rock for a weight. Oxen drew the arm back until it almost touched the ground, where it was held in place by a bronze bar connected to a trigger. A sling almost as long as the arm itself was stretched beneath it and a specially cut stone placed in its pouch. One end of the sling was attached to the upper end of the arm, the other terminated in a ring that was slipped over a shallow hook at the upper terminal of the arm. When the trigger was tripped with a sledgehammer, the box dropped just a few feet but the arm was whipped upward with unbelievable force. The sling then swung up and the ring slipped off the hook and the stone flew just like a missile from a common sling, only a thousand times as heavy.

The only problem with the wonderful device, Marcus thought sourly, was that it couldn't hit anything closer than a hundred paces. And it was dreadfully slow to reload: capable of delivering only about four missiles per hour. The speed might be improved with intensive drill, but oxen could not be speeded up. And if the siege should prove to be lengthy, the oxen would be eaten and they would have to use men for the labor.

As he mused, it struck him how strange this was: advising a foreign queen on how best to defeat his fellow Romans. Not that she or anyone else had a prayer of doing that. Even moving all those catapults to the southern wall would probably produce few if any Roman casualties. Nonetheless, it felt strange.

IN THE GALLERY, THE CHIEF ENGINEER, MUCIUS MUS, was urging his men to ever-greater speed. Legionaries, auxilia and slaves mingled indifferently, busy as ants as they passed the timbers and lead sheets and pins of wood or iron from hand to hand and the team of artisans fitted them together with wonderful skill.

"Hurry up with those timbers!" Mucius shouted. "Do you think we've all the buggering livelong day to finish this? I've seen half-tamed Gauls work harder than this and Gauls *hate* work! Do you want those buggering Alexandrians to think you're a bunch of buggering *Greeks?*" In truth he was well pleased with the men and their work, but his many long years as a centurion forbade his saying so. Customarily, soldiers only received praise from their general and then only *after* the battle was won.

Cato and Niger came down the shoreline behind the shed. Since only the north side of the shed would receive fire, the south wall was left open for the sake of light and ventilation, and to conserve material.

"When will it be finished?" Niger asked Mucius.

"If we can maintain this pace, I can have it extended all the way to the southeastern corner of the city wall by to-morrow morning," Mucius reported. "That is, if they allow us to keep up the pace. There could still be trouble. Matter of fact, if there's going to be trouble, we're going to see it soon. Look." He pointed to what was just beyond the end of the shed: Here the soft ground stopped and the pavement began. It was the city's river port. Its docks were deserted. The merchant vessels were headed for the Nile and even the fishing craft had withdrawn to the lake's southern shore.

"You see that big arch there?" Mucius went on. "That's the canal that connects the lake with the Eunostos Harbor. If I was the man in charge of defense, I'd send a warship or two out here to block us, maybe a sally of infantry to catch us while we're still at work and burn the gallery."

"If it happens, it won't be Parmenion that thought of it," Cato said. "Look up there." The others looked up through the archer's loop he indicated. They could see a man in Roman armor talking to a woman.

"Is that Scipio?" Niger said. "If it is, the woman must be Selene, the queen. Leave it to a Scipio not only to get himself appointed defender of Alexandria, but to bag himself a queen to warm his bed."

"I don't care what his job is or who he sticks it to," Mucius told them, "but if he gets just one of my men killed, I'll have him up before the Centuriate Assembly on charges of high treason."

Cato frowned. "I don't know what he's up to, but no Cornelian ever betrayed Rome."

Niger turned to Cato. "Send down a cohort of heavy infantry auxilia and another of skirmishers and all your archers. They can stand down here behind the gallery and be ready to take care of whatever comes through the arch."

Mucius scratched his chin. "That'll help. You know, to send ships out they'll have to raise the gate. If we're fast, we could get some men inside and keep it open. Get just one legion inside and we could take the city."

Niger and Cato looked at one another. "Only if Titus Norbanus orders it," Cato said. "We're not here to hand Alexandria to Hamilcar at the cost of Roman blood. And there'll be blood, never doubt it. A fight through the streets, with the enemy on the walls and the rooftops—we'd be giving away our biggest advantage by splitting up into a hundred units to take the city one street and one block at a time."

"Not to mention," Niger said, "giving Titus Norbanus eternal glory as the man who conquered Alexandria. He's not my patron that I owe him such favors. The man's never even held the office of praetor and here they've given him proconsular imperium. Let's just invest this south wall as we've been ordered and leave it at that."

"Suit yourselves," Mucius said, "but get those cohorts

down here quick." When they were gone, he returned to tongue-lashing his men. Buggering senators, he thought. Always playing their buggering politics with my boys' lives.

The cohorts arrived in short order. The heavy infantry were mostly Germans from settlements now earning their citizenship: sons of wild tribesmen defeated by Noricum and sent to colonize the Gallic territory around Lake Lemannus. They were equipped much like the legionaries except for their flat, oval shields and their handheld spears that they wielded at close quarters instead of throwing them like pila. They were ideal for this job, Mucius thought.

The skirmishers were young Gauls who wore short, sleeveless shirts of mail and skullcap helmets and bore small, round shields. They were armed with short swords and javelins.

The archers were mostly Suebi, a Germanic tribe that favored the bow. Theirs were man-height and shot arrows a yard long, tipped with small, barbed points and fletched with goose feathers. The Suebi wore no armor, and no helmets covered their long hair, which they wore on the left side of the head in an elaborate knot. Their only other weapons were knotty-headed clubs.

Early in the afternoon the trouble Mucius had predicted arrived. Even above the din of hammering and the roars of battle from the west, he could hear the clank and rattle of a massive bronze grate being raised.

"They're coming!" he shouted. "Get your men ready!"

The officer in charge of the auxilia was a young man of the Caecilian clan. This was his first command of soldiers and he was eager. "On your feet!" he shouted. "Half of the heavies to the open end of the gallery with your shields up! I don't want these Greeks to bag so much as a single slave. Skirmishers, prepare to follow me. Archers, I don't need to tell you what to do."

The heavy infantry rounded the end of the gallery and

formed a barrier six ranks deep. They held their shields high, for the moment they came around the end of the gallery, they came under a storm of arrows from atop the wall. Within seconds they formed a sort of testudo of overlapping shields to protect both themselves and the men laboring behind them. As each new yard of the gallery was added, they could take a long pace forward to make room for the next.

Amid much shouting from attackers and defenders, a pair of galleys emerged from the arch, side by side. Their decks were crowded with soldiers and these leaped ashore under cover of heavy missile fire from archers and slingers. The skirmishers, with young Caecilius leading, bounded forward to meet them. There were none of the usual slow, methodical Roman advancing tactics. With their small shields they had to get through the missile storm swiftly.

In moments, shield smashed into shield and the Gallic spears and Roman short swords began to take a toll. The Suebi picked off the archers and slingers aboard the ships while others aimed their fire at the walls to make the archers up there keep their heads down. Medical slaves came forward with litters to bring out the wounded.

The attackers fought desperately, for they had nowhere to retreat except back onto their ships. They had reinforcements coming, but these could only arrive slowly and awkwardly by filing from one ship to another, for the tunnel that gave access through the city wall to the lake had no walkway.

When the first fury of the attack was broken, Caecilius disengaged himself from the fight. "The rest of the heavies, come push them back! Archers, use fire arrows!" The skirmishers fell back and the remaining half-cohort of heavy infantry pressed forward, the weight of their arms toppling the attackers, driving them, step by step, back onto the ships. Arrows tipped with flaming tow arched over their heads and struck the wooden ships. Most were extinguished, but there were too many for the crews to fight effectively.

With a creaking of ropes, the burning galleys were towed back within the tunnel. The bronze grate came grinding down, narrowly missing the bow of one of the galleys. Fully half the sortie lay dead upon the ground and the Roman force set up a raucous, jeering cheer.

Throughout the fight, the gallery continued to grow.

TITUS NORBANUS SAW NONE OF THE FIGHTING AT the southern wall, but messengers brought him periodic reports. In the meantime, there was more than enough to see from his vantage point atop the battle tower. Assault after assault against the western wall was repelled with terrible losses. This was only to be expected. The situation was somewhat better on the Pharos.

By midday Hamilcar was looking sour. He had not gained the swift victory for which he had so unrealistically hoped. It was clear that Alexandria would not fall this day, nor for many more days to come. He was contemplating the crucifixion of a few laggard officers in order to encourage the rest, when a distant cheer drew his attention. His banner hung waving from atop the great lighthouse. Hamilcar leaped to his feet in his excitement.

"The Pharos is mine!" He turned to Norbanus. "Did you know that the Pharos lighthouse of Alexandria was named one of the Seven Wonders of the World by Antipater of Sidon? The Great Pyramids are another, and soon they shall be mine, too."

"My congratulations, Shofet," Norbanus murmured. "With two in your possession, can the other five be far behind?"

Hamilcar glanced at him sharply. Had he detected a sardonic note in the Roman's words? It was difficult to tell when the two of them were conversing in a language that was native to neither.

"This is enough for today," Hamilcar said. "I will call the main assault force back. Tonight we will bring up the heavy siege equipment under cover of night and resume in the morning."

Norbanus wondered if Hamilcar even remembered that this had been his own recommendation. "Very wise, Shofet."

"And now I want to see what wonder you have worked at the southern wall."

"I think you will find it pleasing."

Indeed, Hamilcar was more than pleased. "This is wonderful," he said, studying the ever-growing gallery. It was already well beyond the river port and on its way to the southeastern corner of the city wall. "So this was why you requisitioned all that timber and lead back at Carthage. Making use of that city model of yours, no doubt."

"It is our custom to be prepared for all contingencies," Norbanus informed him. "It goes against our sense of fitness to allow an enemy control of such a resource as this lake, when it lies within our power to seize it for ourselves."

Hamilcar nodded. "I see. Let me tell you about my own sense of fitness. Now that I have three sides of the city in my power, it offends me to leave the fourth unguarded. I shall send a landing force ashore to the east of the city and seal it off from the world."

"This is, indeed, the Shofet's decision to make," Norbanus said.

"If Alexandria refuses to fall to assault, then she can fall to starvation or pestilence. With her fleet bottled up in the harbor and her major forces reduced to throwing rocks at me from the walls, I can afford to detach a large part of my army to go southward down the Nile and secure the larger cities. They are very rich cities, Roman. Perhaps you shall have a part in this new phase of the campaign."

Norbanus bowed. "I am, of course, at the Shofet's service."

ON THE TENTH DAY OF THE SIEGE, SELENE CAME TO
Marcus's quarters. She was accompanied only by a maidservant and she left the girl in an anteroom. She found Marcus
in the courtyard, drafting one of his inevitable missives to
the Senate.

"How do you intend to get a message through?" she asked
him. "The city is surrounded."

"Not very expertly," he said. "I've cultivated a few well-
traveled and adventurous young men here, men who will
take a great risk for a great reward."

"How long is this going to last?"

"The siege? It could go on for months, but I don't think
it will."

"Why not? My brother's advisers are all but whipped.
They talk boastfully of how difficult Alexandria is to take,
meaning that they have no intention of carrying the war to
Hamilcar. They're defeated. Are you aware that the Roman
legions have left?"

"Of course. They pulled out last night, marching along
the southern shore of the lake. I suspect that they are headed
south down the river. There is nothing to stop them except
sheer distance. They can take every city down to the First
Cataract if they feel like it. Personally, I doubt they'll want
to do Hamilcar that big a favor."

As always, his calm confidence both infuriated and bewildered her. "Why do you think the siege will be over
soon? Because we will be defeated?"

"No," he said. "I think that Hamilcar will get some very
bad news soon, news that will force him to break off the
siege and the war."

"What? What news could do that?"

"Let me keep that to myself for the moment. Rest assured that it will happen. One morning soon we shall look out over the western wall and see nothing but the remains of Hamilcar's camp and nothing but a plume of dust in the air to show us where they've all gone."

She considered this, weighing many factors in her mind: matters of politics and greed and ambition. "If that is true," she said, "then we must deal with my brother and his advisers first. Otherwise, the moment Hamilcar leaves, we are both dead. If we strike now, we are safe. Parmenion and the eunuchs are in disgrace and no one will mourn their passing. We can't let them convince people that they've won some sort of victory."

Marcus smiled. "Spoken like a true Ptolemy."

"How else would I talk," she said. "I am a Ptolemy."

"The only one worthy of the name," Marcus told her. "You must hide. Go to the temple of Serapis. He's the patron deity of the city and a great mob of the citizenry are camped out on the temple grounds. The citizens love you and they will protect you there. Go now. I have to consult with Chilo. He's figured out a way to use the big new catapults against that gallery on the southern wall. Now that it's not full of Romans, I won't mind destroying it."

"Will you take your mind off fighting for one minute!" she cried, her patience ended. "We must consider the future!"

"The future?" he said, nonplussed.

"Exactly. If we live, I will be Queen of Egypt. Queen in my own right, not through marriage to my brother. I must have a consort."

"Certainly. But he will have to be someone whose birth is commensurate with your own. I am sure there are many kings and princes—"

She hissed and closed her eyes. "You've never met any of

the disgusting, degenerate creatures who call themselves kings in the eastern lands, have you?"

"I confess that I haven't. Surely there is someone suitable."

"No. I don't want some pedigreed imbecile to share my bed. He must be a man. So far, I have met only one who meets the definition. You."

For a moment words failed him. "You can't be serious. I am as well born as any Roman, but we have no royalty. I'm not even a very important Roman."

"Spare me your humility! You've manipulated Hamilcar, Ptolemy, me and the whole city of Alexandria ever since you left Noricum! Forget about breeding, you are a man who can *do* things! Do you think the first Ptolemy was born a king? He was just a soldier who was in the right place at the right time. You are a man of the moment, and I want you for my husband when this is over."

"You want me to be King of Egypt?" he said, sounding unsettled for the first time since she had known him.

She stepped close and wound her arms around his neck. "Not king exactly. Consort. It's still a very desirable position." She drew his face down to hers.

For the first time in many months something entirely personal pushed aside his discipline and devotion to duty. He wondered whether he was being utterly foolish, then he discovered that he didn't care. He swept her up in his arms. The sun would come up tomorrow no matter what the two of them did here tonight. Let tomorrow take care of itself.

CHAPTER TWENTY

HAMILCAR INSPECTED THE GALLERY, NOW MANNED by soldiers from Utica, Sicca and other subject cities of Africa. It was now much improved from the simple shed the Romans had erected. Working day and night, first the Roman soldiers and then his own slave gangs had heaped earth against the side facing Alexandria, creating a sloping ramp that protected the wooden wall against fire and the stones of catapults. Behind the shed, towers were going up. Soon they would overtop the low southern wall of the city and his archers and artillery would be able to fire down upon the defenders.

When the towers were completed, in another day or two at most, he could sweep the wall clean of defenders, allowing his sappers to attack the canal gate and give him access to the city. Who could have imagined, Hamilcar thought complacently, that the outlandish Romans would give him the key to taking Alexandria? And that the weak spot was the supposedly impregnable southern wall of the city?

"There was some sort of activity going on in the city all night," Mastanabal reported to his Shofet. "There was hammering and shouting. They're up to something." The general was looking wan these days, Hamilcar thought. Doubtless, the cross was ever in his thoughts. He had proven to be unable to take Alexandria quickly and knew all too well the fate of unsuccessful Carthaginian generals.

"Men in besieged cities often seek desperate remedies to extricate themselves from their difficulties," Hamilcar said. "They think novelties such as those absurd craft in the harbor can somehow save them."

The general was diplomatic enough not to point out that Hamilcar had made no further attempt to take the harbor. The seamen had acquired a superstitious dread of the bizarre craft that seemed more like living creatures than wooden ships driven by sails and the arms of rowers.

"I want—" the Shofet's words were cut off abruptly when they heard a whizzing noise, followed by an enormous splash in the lake behind them. "What was that?" He looked out to see the lake still agitated. A moment later water from the splash came down like a great rain.

"What just happened?" the Shofet said, unable to comprehend. Then came another splash, this one nearer to shore, casting up a huge spout of mud. A large fish landed near Hamilcar's feet and lay there flopping.

Then there came a deafening crash. Thirty paces east of the place where Hamilcar and his general stood, a huge ball of stone smashed through the lead-sheathed roof, pulping a number of soldiers and sending shudders through the whole gallery. Another crashed through the roof, then yet another.

"It's those big catapults!" Mastanabal cried, understanding now. "They've moved them across the city! They are casting stones over the rooftops to destroy this gallery! You must get to safety, my Shofet!"

Hamilcar had already figured out the last part. He could

not stay here. He whirled and began to run, certain that one of the huge stone balls would squash him like a bug. In seconds he was just one of a crowd of fleeing soldiers, shoving them out of the way with his own hands, heedless of the contamination he incurred by touching unclean flesh.

It seemed an eternity later that he was beyond the gallery and safe from the terrible missiles. He saw a man in the plumes of an officer and beckoned to him. The officer, brilliant in his gilded armor, stood trembling before his Shofet.

"Commander," Hamilcar said, "I want you to assemble all these men"——he pointed to the soldiers who had fled the gallery——"and take them to that field over there." He indicated a broad meadow at the western end of the lake, currently being used to pasture the Carthaginian livestock.

"At once, my Shofet," the man said, bowing. He strode away shouting orders.

Mastanabal came from the wreckage, picking wood splinters from his cloak and beard. "It seems the Roman project was not so good an idea, after all."

"That is not important at the moment," Hamilcar said. "You see those men assembling in the field?"

Mastanabal studied the survivors. "Yes." He estimated that three of four hundred men remained standing.

"Go get my personal guard. Disarm those men, then crucify them all."

Mastanabal understood. "Yes, my Shofet." He bowed and went in search of the guard and some carpenters. The men had done nothing to deserve punishment, but their offense was more serious than treason: They had seen their Shofet panic. They had seen him run. Mastanabal shuddered. He, too, had seen Hamilcar play the coward. Was there a cross waiting for him as well?

For the rest of the day, even as the unfortunate soldiers were nailed to their crosses and raised on display before the whole army, the huge stones continued to pound the gallery to fragments. Alexandria was once again in control of the lake and its access to the Nile and the interior. The siege would not end quickly.

"THERE GOES ANOTHER ONE!" SOMEONE SHOUTED. The crowd assembled on the grounds of the vast temple of Serapis made sounds of awe as another 500-pound ball arched high overhead, crossing the city from north to south, disappearing beyond the southern wall, so distant that the crash of its impact came only faintly to their ears. Then there was applause and cheering. People had winced and ducked at the first few missiles and found the novel sight unnerving. By mid-morning they were used to it and treated the sight as a new sort of spectacle.

Selene watched from the top of the temple steps like a priestess presiding at a ceremony. Scipio had advised her to show herself to the people as much as possible. It would help to bind them to her, he explained. This, she thought, had to be connected to his republican form of government. Egyptian monarchs expected to be worshiped. They placed no value upon popularity.

She saw a ripple go through the crowd, the way an animal's progress through a wheat field can be marked by the waving of the stalks. Someone was pushing through the crowd toward her. For a moment she went numb. This must be Ptolemy's guard coming to arrest her. It was over. Then she breathed relief when she saw the two Romans clear the crowd and climb the steps.

Selene held out her hand in greeting. "Welcome, savior of Alexandria," she said, loud enough for the crowd to hear. A great cheer went up. The Romans kissed her hands, then turned to wave at the crowd, beaming. Both were tricked out in their best uniforms: cuirasses embossed to represent Herculean muscles, red-plumed helmets beneath their arms, scarlet cloaks flaring dramatically. Even unwarlike Flaccus managed to look martial.

"Don't get too relaxed," Flaccus said in a low voice, still grinning and waving. "Your little brother's guards are right behind us, with warrants for our heads and your living body."

Selene gasped. "We must get away!"

"No," said Scipio, waving and grinning. "We stay right here, with this wonderful audience. They love you and by natural extension now they love us. They think I'm the savior—you've named me, although Chilo and the Archimedeans ought to get the credit."

"But," said Flaccus, "taking credit for other men's work is part of the politician's art. So saviors we shall be."

"I am terrified," Selene said, taking her cue from them and waving graciously to the crowd.

"They'll take it for righteous indignation," Flaccus told her. "When the guards come, be sure to be outraged. Remind everybody of our wonderful services on behalf of Carthage, and of the disgraceful performance of Ptolemy and his ministers."

"That part shouldn't be hard," she said.

"Good," Marcus said. "Leave the rest to us. This will be an exercise in the oratorical arts we've been trained for since boyhood."

"You Romans do something besides fight efficiently?" she said.

"Oh, yes," Flaccus said, "we're great talkers, too."

"Here they come," she gasped. She could see a party of armed men plowing through the crowd, causing a broad "V" pattern to ripple through it. They wore the uniform of the king's personal guard: mercenaries from a score of nations who had no connection to Alexandria and therefore were unlikely to be involved in domestic conspiracies. In theory, at any rate.

Once through the crowd, the guard, perhaps a score in number, climbed the stair. In the forefront was a young Spartan officer who held aloft a roll of parchment. "I have here," he said, "the king's warrant for the arrest of the Romans who call themselves Marcus Cornelius Scipio and Aulus Flaccus, and for the arrest of Selene, of the family of Ptolemy." The crowd stood in stunned silence.

"What?" Selene almost jumped when the word boomed out. "You dare to so address the Queen of Egypt?" Marcus stood in a most impressive pose: feet widespread, upper body half refused, head turned to glare at the officer with a majestic, eagle gaze. She had never heard a voice trained to be heard across a noisy forum or a legion encampment.

Flaccus made a broad, actor's gesture, his cloak draped gracefully from one arm. "Surely that corrupt child Ptolemy never gave you this order!" The humorous scorn in his voice was infectious. "Who was it really? That coward Parmenion, who lost the first and only field engagement of this war? Or was it that no-balls Eutychus? Or that vicious bungler Alexandros?"

The crowd began an ugly mutter. The officer looked around nervously. Then he turned to his men. "Arrest them!" he said in a half-whisper.

Hands reached for them. An ugly Syrian tried to grasp Selene's arm but Scipio's sword was already out, flashing up, then downward in a great, theatrical blow that was serious in its intent despite its flourish. The man's hand fell to the steps as he cried out and clasped the spouting stump with his remaining hand.

"Alexandrians!" Scipio shouted with a broad gesture. "They have laid profane hands on your queen! It is sacrilege! Will you allow this?"

With a roar, the crowd surged up the steps like a great wave breaking upon a beach. The guards were overwhelmed by the mass of citizenry, disarmed, cast down the steps, pummeled and trampled until the pavement was slick with blood.

"Citizens!" Selene cried. "I am your queen!" The crowd roared approval. "Ptolemy is a boy, and his corrupt advisers have brought Alexandria and Egypt near ruin. Hamilcar defeated them in the field and ever since they have cowered here, unable to take decisive action. If Alexandria has been saved, it has been only through the heroic efforts of Marcus Scipio! Will you let your city, founded by Alexander the Great, fall to the degenerate descendant of Hannibal?" A great cry of protest rose from the throng. "Then take me to the palace and I, Selene Ptolemy, will give you the leadership that Alexandria deserves!"

"Brief and to the point," said Flaccus. "Very well done, Majesty."

"But now what?" she said. "Once they know the guard failed to arrest us, they will call out the troops."

"You go to the palace," Scipio advised. "This mob will set you comfortably on the throne. I will go to the Macedonian Barracks and address the troops."

"How will you handle this?" she asked. The dice had fallen and she was resigned to following his lead.

"What you always do with soldiers such as these. I will bribe them."

"WHAT IS GOING ON IN THE CITY?" HAMILCAR ASKED. He and his officers sat before his tent in the heat of the afternoon. All day, strange cries and murmurs had been heard from within the walls. There had been much scurrying about atop the battlements and the bombardment from the catapults had ceased.

All around the Carthaginian camp, work was in progress as men built lofty siege towers high enough to assault the western wall. Others were busy with sledgehammers, demolishing tombs to make a path for the ponderous machines through the necropolis. The Shofet had finally conceded that there would be no quick victory over Alexandria and he was preparing for a long, grinding siege.

"It sounds like civil war," said an adviser.

"Excellent!" Hamilcar said. "Perhaps someone sensible has killed Ptolemy and is ready to make terms."

"What terms would my Shofet find acceptable?" the adviser asked.

"Simple ones. If the Alexandrians surrender their city at once, I will spare their lives. Other than that, they are entirely at my mercy. We will take all their treasures, Egypt will be mine to govern under the customs of Carthage, their army will be absorbed into mine and the lands are to be divided among my nobles. There is no need to make things unnecessarily complex." His council made sounds of approval.

From the western end of the camp there came a clatter of hooves, and men dodged aside as a horseman in the livery of the royal messengers pounded toward the Shofet's tent. He drew rein before the council, so sharply that his mount almost toppled. The man flung himself to the ground and all but went down on his face before the Shofet, holding a bronze tube extended in one hand. Hamilcar took it, examined the seal and twisted the cap open. He withdrew a scroll of parchment, unrolled it and read. In moments his face paled and his hand trembled.

"What is it, my Shofet?" Mastanabal asked, knowing that is was bad news from Carthage. "An earthquake? Plague?"

"The Romans!" Hamilcar choked out. "They have completely reoccupied Italy! And they have invaded Sicily!" He cast the parchment to the ground with an inarticulate cry of rage and frustration.

"But that is impossible!" Mastanabal said. "There cannot

be that many of them! We have most of their army here with us in Egypt."

"We have four of their legions," Hamilcar said. "At least ten are now quartered in Italy. Six more have invaded Sicily. Syracuse is under siege. So are Catana and Lilybaeum. Many of my garrisons have already surrendered!"

They are under strength because you stripped them for this war, Mastanabal thought. He was not entirely displeased with this development. The Shofet would need every experienced military man at his disposal now, and he could break off the siege of Alexandria without loss of honor. There would be no need to crucify a less than successful general. He considered his words carefully.

"My Shofet, we must return to Carthage at once. Egypt will still be here after this matter of the Romans is settled. Italy and Sicily have been our possessions for over a century, we cannot lose them. Most important, Sicily is less than a day's sail from Carthage. The Romans will be poised to strike in force at our sacred city!" The other counselors signified approval of these words.

"But Egypt is within my grasp!" Hamilcar cried, making clutching motions.

"And it will be again," Mastanabal said. "Already you have shown them your might. They will know that they were saved by the merest chance. They will be already half-defeated when we come back."

Hamilcar brooded for a moment. "What of Norbanus and those four legions?"

"Leave them here," Mastanabal advised. "They are alone in a hostile land, cut off from reinforcement or supply. Ptolemy's men are more than adequate to destroy them."

"I want none of them to leave here alive," Hamilcar said. "They have trained with my army and know all its details, as well as the defenses of Carthage. You saw that model of Alexandria they built. Romans study such things."

"They will die," Mastanabal assured him. "Where will they go? Egypt is hostile to them. If they march west, they enter Carthaginian territory. If they go east, they will meet the Seleucids and the Parthians. If they take to the sea, our navy owns it. Maybe they will go south down the Nile and carve another kingdom for themselves in Nubia or Ethiopia. Whatever they choose, we have seen the last of them."

Hamilcar nodded, but he remembered that once before Carthage had thought to have seen the last of the Romans.

IN THE MACEDONIAN BARRACKS, MARCUS SCIPIO AND Flaccus wrapped up negotiations with the soldiers. After protestations of loyalty for the sake of form, it had come down to money, as Marcus had been certain it would. These men were professionals and they followed a paymaster. They were not citizens of a republic, but hirelings who would serve their employer only so long as he was victorious and brought them loot. In the end, buying their loyalty was a matter of staters and drachmas on a carefully graduated scale of rank and length of service, from the generals down to the common troopers.

"Now that this is concluded," Marcus said, standing, "have your men assembled at the western gate, prepared for a sortie at my orders."

"You want a field battle against the Carthaginians?" said a hard-bitten Spartan commander. "The time for that is past. How would we get through the necropolis in any sort of order?"

"There won't be any field battle," Marcus said. "It will be more like collecting taxes. It may not be today or to-morrow, but it will be soon and I want us to be ready to attack at a moment's notice." Mystified, the commanders signified their assent. This Roman had proven himself able to deliver the goods, which certainly was not true of Parmenion or Ptolemy.

Selene met him at the palace. By her side was her brother-husband. The boy glowered at the two of them, but he said nothing. Young as he was, he knew better than that. The heads of Parmenion, Eutychus, Dion and Alexandros already sat atop pikes over the palace gate, and he had no wish to have his own join them.

"My brother agrees that all is for the best," Selene said. "His former advisers failed him wretchedly and he is ready for mature, disinterested guidance."

We can supply the maturity, at any rate, Marcus thought. He made a slight bow toward Ptolemy. "Your Majesty, I will be most happy to serve you." The boy nodded sourly in reply.

There was a banquet that evening to celebrate the occasion, for it took more than a mere siege to make Alexandrians give up banqueting. Toward the end of the proceedings, a soldier came in and spoke in Marcus Scipio's ear. He turned to Selene and Ptolemy, who had regained some of his usual placidity, knowing that he was not to be executed.

"If Your Majesties will accompany me to the western wall," Marcus said, "I will show you one of the finer sights of this war."

"Another of your new weapons?" Ptolemy said, brightening a little. He had enjoyed watching the fighting in the harbor, with the underwater boat and the bronze-clad warships.

"No, even better."

Huge litters carried them through the broad, straight streets of Alexandria. They were carried up a slanting stair to the battlements that defended the western gate of the city.

"Look," Marcus said.

At first they could not make out what was going on.

There was a confusion of running forms, men bearing torches, horses and elephants milling, unsettled at this unwonted nighttime activity. The shouts of men mixed with the neighs of horses and the trumpeting of elephants.

"They are leaving!" Selene said at last.

"Breaking camp and heading back for Carthage," Marcus told her. "Hamilcar just got the bad news I mentioned earlier."

"What was it?" He told her of the retaking of Italy and the invasion of Sicily. "So," she said, "you Romans have manipulated us: Carthaginians and Egyptians both. You have used us to your own advantage."

"Carthage and Egypt were going to war whether we were involved or not," Marcus told her. "Why should we not use the situation to our advantage?"

"Why not, indeed?" she said, mild tones covering inner turmoil. Just now, she was too delighted with seeing the Carthaginian army depart to indulge in rage. It would not do to let the Romans see her feelings in any case. But already she was making her plans. These Romans had proven to be far more than the unsophisticated soldiers they had appeared at first. Very well, if they were capable of subtle dealing, let them learn what the Ptolemies were capable of after many generations of royal intrigue. Only let them not learn beforetime.

Flaccus, always more perceptive than Marcus to the subtle nuances, read her expression. "We have been under strictest orders from the Senate to say nothing to anyone about the reconquest of Italy. The whole world will know soon. I think it is now time to establish the closest and most confidential ties of cooperation between Rome and Egypt."

"Certainly," Marcus said, understanding his gaffe somewhat too late. "Between us now we shall have Carthage in a vise. All our future efforts must be coordinated and we will take no military action without conferring with the sovereign of Egypt."

"That is for the future," she said. "What will you do now?"

"In a few hours, after the bulk of the Carthaginian forces are on the road, I shall order an attack against the camp Hamilcar is abandoning. He would need days to get it packed and moved. There may be enough loot to pay for your soldiers' loyalty."

She gazed out over the ruinous necropolis. "I will use part of the loot to restore the damaged tombs," she said. "That is what is most important to Egypt. It will help to bind the people to me."

Marcus smiled. "You know your own brand of politics. Just don't forget that your soldiers need to receive their pay regularly, with bonuses, or they won't serve you any better than they did your brother and his late advisers."

"But that is what I have you for," she said. She looked at the fast-diminishing Carthaginian camp. "Will they be back soon?"

"No," Marcus assured her. "Hamilcar's next war will be with Rome. We will destroy Carthage utterly, as we swore to our gods many generations ago. We won't make the mistake Hannibal made. We won't leave the seed of a new Carthage to come back for vengeance."

TITUS NORBANUS ACCEPTED THE SURRENDER OF THE Egyptian town seated in his proconsular curule chair, his lictors ranged behind him. This was the third such city he had taken for Carthage. There had been little fighting and no need for siege operations. It seemed that Egypt actually consisted of Alexandria and its tax farms down the river. Except in the far south, where Nubian incursions were a problem, the country was practically without soldiers. The only other garrisons of any consequence were east of the Delta, in a desert country called Sinai.

The conquered cities had yielded a rich harvest of gold and silver, jewels and other precious items. The cost of their ransom had been high. But they had not tried to bargain. These were a people accustomed to the feel of a conqueror's heel. He had avoided accepting slaves and livestock in payment. He wanted all the wealth to be as portable as possible.

When the message from Alexandria arrived, he thanked the gods that he had been so foresightful. He called his principal officers together and read it to them.

From Marcus Cornelius Scipio, envoy of Rome to the court of Alexandria to Titus Norbanus, Proconsul in command of the African Expedition, greeting.

Word has reached us that Italy is now securely within Roman hands. Norbanus paused while his officers cheered. *What is more, the conquest of Sicily has commenced.* Here the Roman officers roared approval, all but pounding one another on the back with glee. *You must now break off your campaign in Egypt. Hamilcar has fled back to Carthage and this war is over. Bring your legions back to Alexandria. We can combine them with Queen Selene's forces and be ready to march on Carthage the moment we receive word from the Senate. Long live Rome.*

AFTERWORD

HIS FACE STIFF, TITUS NORBANUS PASSED THE MESsage to his officers. He was furious but already his mind was churning. The patrician fool thought he was bested, but Norbanus was not the sort of man to regard any setback as final. There was still opportunity here.

"He takes much upon himself," said Cato.

"I thought I was the only one who noticed," Norbanus said. "He is one man, sitting beside the queen of Egypt, and he wants us to join him! I am surprised he didn't tell us to give the gold back to the cities we took it from."

"Not likely," said Lentulus Niger. "And I'm not of a mind to help Scipio make himself king of Egypt."

"My thoughts exactly," Norbanus said.

"So what is our course?" Cato asked. "We're a long way from anywhere here."

"Before I speak," Norbanus said, "I want assurances of your loyalty. In the future, men will say that I took unlawful action because my proconsular authority was terminated the moment we left Hamilcar's service."

The officers brooded on the matter. Each would have preferred to be the leader, but they were as jealous of one another as they were of Norbanus. And he seemed to have a plan, which none of them did.

"I think we have no choice," Niger said. "This army must have a leader or it will fall apart and we will all be killed. Only the Senate can appoint a new proconsul, and it will be a long time before we have any contact with Rome." A grin spread across his face. "And now it's truly Rome our orders will be coming from, eh?" Applause greeted these words. "So I say we swear our loyalty to Titus Norbanus until we hear otherwise from the Senate." One by one, the other officers all gave their assent.

"That's settled, then," Norbanus said. "North of us is Alexandria. To the west is Carthage and its territories. South is nothing but more of Egypt, then unknown land. The only direction to go is east, through the Sinai to Asia. Somewhere out there we will find a fleet to carry us to Italy. Carthage has a powerful navy, but it will be called back to defend against a Roman invasion or to carry war to Sicily. There are many fleets to the east: the island of Rhodes has a good one, so do many of the Greek cities of Asia Minor. If we encounter the Seleucids or the Parthians we will fight them and we will conquer. Maybe we'll go all the way to Greece. It's just a short sail from there to Italy."

"It's a long march you propose," Cato said.

"So it is. When have Roman legionaries ever feared a little walking? But we have arms and fighting men and gold. Between them, we will make our way back to the Seven Hills and our story will last as long as Rome herself." He looked around at them, and he was happier then he imagined he would be. He was truly on his own, in command of a powerful Roman army, and not even the Senate to answer to. Here, he knew, lay his destiny, which he had always known would be a great one. Soon he would be known as the greatest Roman who ever lived. He would crush Marcus Scipio and his whole patrician clan.

"Tomorrow," he told his officers, "we cross the river. Then we march east."